MW00639946

THE LIGHT WE LOST

THE LOST LIGHT SERIES BOOK ONE

KYLA STONE

Paper Moon Press
Publishing Company
Est. 2000

The Light We Lost

Printed in the United States of America

Cover design by Christian Bentulan

Book formatting by Vellum

First Printed in 2022

ISBN: 978-1-945410-73-4

❀ Created with Vellum

PREFACE

This story takes place in Michigan's Upper Peninsula. Real towns and cities are used in this novel. However, occasional liberties have been taken by the author for the sake of the story.

While the Munising Police Department and Alger County Sheriff's Office are real institutions, the versions within these pages are entirely fictional.

Thank you in advance for understanding an author's creative license.

"Something started in the north band of the sky ... All that part of the sky appeared burning in fiery flames; it seemed that the sky was burning. At midnight, great fiery rays arose above the castle which were dreadful and fearful. Everybody went to the countryside to see this great sign."

—actual eye-witness account from Lisbon, March 6th, 1582

“Love is the last light spoken.”

— DYLAN THOMAS

1

SHILOH EASTON

DAY ONE

Shiloh Easton woke with blood on her hands.

Heat on her face, her cheeks. Stones dug into her spine. Grass tickled her bare arms.

Blinking, Shiloh stared up at a hard blue sky. No clouds. The round disc of the sun peeked between her eyelashes, too bright to look at.

At the fringes of her vision, towering jack pines, eastern hemlocks, and cottonwoods stretched for the heavens.

But heaven was too far to reach.

Hell was right here beside her.

Wetness on her fingers. Blood, slick and technicolor red. It splattered her forearms, slippery on her palms, red lines beneath her fingernails.

Somehow, she understood it was not her blood.

The terror was like biting into a live wire. Her stomach churned. She sat up, white spots spinning in front of her eyes.

Don't look. A primal instinct echoed from the deepest part of herself. *Whatever you do, don't look.*

Shiloh forced herself to look. Her legs stretched out in front of her, worn jeans with holes in the knees, sneakers stained with mud. Past her feet lay hard-packed dirt. Glass shards and tiny bits of metal and plastic glinted in the sunlight.

The ground was torn up in the shape of footprints. Here and there, tufts of grass were matted down. A rusted forklift sat to her right next to a tiered rack of scavenged tires and rims. In front of her stood row after row of junked vehicles, cars and trucks and vans by the dozens.

Her eyes skipped past the unmoving shape lying a few yards away. The thing she didn't want to see, didn't want to know.

She couldn't remember what had happened. Why blood streaked her hands.

Unsteadily, she stood. Dizziness washed over her. Shards of glass stuck to her hair, to her jeans. She bent double, gasping, her hands on her thighs. Fear stuck in her chest like a fishhook.

Shiloh blinked, her mouth moving, silently repeating the only words that could calm her. *Montgomery, Alabama. Juneau, Alaska. Phoenix, Arizona.*

The places she so desperately yearned to see but never had. A collection in her head, lists of cities, states, and countries: places she would visit someday.

Steeling herself, she straightened. Her bloody fingers curled into fists at her sides, fingernails digging hard into her palms.

Her eyes settled on the lumpy form her brain had refused to register.

A body.

With a rush of hollow horror, she took it in. The scuffed work boots. Worn jeans, plaid shirt with the sleeves rolled up to the forearms, the familiar red handkerchief tied around the neck. His head was turned to the side, body splayed like he'd fallen backward. Or had been pushed.

She took a step closer, forced herself to circle the body. *Little Rock, Arkansas. Sacramento, California. Denver, Colorado.*

His faded John Deere cap lay a yard away in the grass. Blotches of crimson darkened the olive-green fabric. A crowbar lay beside the hat. It glistened red, tufts of hair and bits of flesh clinging to the iron.

The hard grizzled features had gone slack, silver-gray hair blackened on one side with blood and other things she didn't want to consider. Bits of bone. Brain matter. The left side of his face was caved in.

He was dead. Her grandfather was dead.

She felt dazed, shaken. Her guts twisted with grief and fear.

What had happened? She didn't know. She didn't remember. Her mind was a blank.

The blankness terrified her.

Her memory was like a movie reel fluttering to a jagged stop. There was nothing, just an emptiness. A sensation of falling, of cold fear, like plunging into a frigid lake.

Why couldn't she remember? She'd fallen through a hole in time. It had happened before. Her mind had gone blank. A chunk of minutes or hours that disappeared, a total blackout.

All this blood. The torn-up ground. Her dead grandfather.

And her brother...where was he?

Cody was supposed to be here. He helped in the salvage yard every day after school, operating the forklift, cutting up metal, organizing scraps, stacking tires.

"Cody!" She screamed his name. Her ragged voice echoed back at her. "Cody!"

There was nothing. The evening sun slanted into her eyes, painting the wrecked vehicles in shades of gold. "Where are you?"

No one answered.

Her heart felt like it was splintering inside her chest. Panic bit at her; she fought it back.

A chain-link fence topped by razor wire circled the salvage yard. A hundred yards beyond the salvage yard, a ramshackle two-story house stood atop the hill, white paint faded to gray.

The forest crept in on all sides, deep shadows spilling like oil, hiding its secrets. Her grandfather owned two hundred acres of wilderness abutting Lake Superior, the great northern lake that held its own secrets, its own ghosts.

Shiloh had been born here. She'd lived in this beautiful half-wild place her entire life, every day of the last thirteen years. This was her home.

Cody had been here when it happened. She couldn't remember, but she *knew*.

Now, he was gone.

Whoever had come here and done this to her grandfather had also done something to her brother. She felt it. She knew it.

Not dead, though. He couldn't be dead.

She should call 911. Jackson Cross would come, the undersheriff with the mournful face, who looked at her like he was seeing a ghost.

She knew what would happen. The thing the county had threatened a dozen times. The Michigan Department of Health and Human Services would come, too. The social workers. The prying questions and pitying eyes.

They would abduct her from her life, separate her from her brother, take her to strangers or a group home, which might as well be a cage. She would fade, disappear, lose herself.

This was where she belonged: wandering the woods, fishing the rivers, prowling the cliffs of Lake Superior with the wind in her hair, the sun on her face, dirt between her toes.

One thought embedded in her brain like a splinter: she needed to find her brother.

At fourteen, Cody was brooding and brilliant, a sarcastic and isolated loner. He loved to draw in his notebooks and go night fishing. His hair was a scruffy dirty blond, where hers was black as oil; his eyes blue, where hers glittered like bits of coal.

He teased her relentlessly. She loved him wholeheartedly.

They had no one but each other. Cody needed her now more than ever.

The sun sank low on the horizon, descending behind the trees. The chill in the air raised goosebumps on her bare arms.

How much time did she have before someone came to the house? Hours? A day?

Her grandfather was gone. There was nothing she could do for him now.

She couldn't stay here.

There was one place she could go. Somewhere only Cody knew about. Somewhere the authorities would never find her. From there, she could hole up and begin the search for her brother.

Shiloh moved woodenly down the rows of gutted vehicles and exited the gate, not bothering to lock the padlock, then headed up to the house. Her legs felt like lead, but she burned with a resolve that sparked brighter and brighter with every step.

Inside the shadowed house, she moved to the kitchen and washed her hands in the metal sink until they were red and raw. She scrubbed beneath her nails. She could feel the blood seeping into the cracks in her skin, staining her soul.

She yanked her long black hair into a ponytail, then dressed in hiking pants and boots, her favorite Star Wars "Do or Do Not" T-shirt layered over a long-sleeved shirt and a forest green windbreaker.

In her backpack, she packed clothes, a water bottle, purification tablets, a compass, and a topographical map of the area, along with a poncho, tarp, sleeping bag, headlamp, and fire starter from their camping supplies.

She went into Cody's room and stole his favorite black hoodie. It smelled like him, of paint and charcoal and canvas. Then she packed nuts, SpaghettiOs, Pop Tarts, and Snickers candy bars.

The only thing in her nightstand drawer was a Dangerfield PRAXIS lock-pick set Cody had gotten her. It included a short and medium hook, half diamond, and various rake picks.

Cody alone knew she was a thief. A bit of a kleptomaniac. A collector of secrets.

She shoved it in her pocket and went for the Tenpoint Turbo crossbow that hung on its hook beside her bed. She slung it over her shoulder with the limbs down, tucked under her arm, then grabbed extra bolts and added them to the quiver attached to the stock.

Her grandfather had bought her the crossbow for her eleventh birthday. A fresh pang of sorrow struck her. Grief and fear ebbed and swelled, threatening to overwhelm her.

She rubbed the back of her arm across her face and moved onto the next task, the next thing. If Cody was out there, she would find him.

Before she left the house, she stuffed her grandfather's cell phone in her pocket. She had no friends or family to call. No father who knew of her existence. No doting grandmothers or card-playing, cigar-smoking uncles.

She had a nebulous idea of an aunt out there somewhere, her mother's sister. A stranger she didn't remember.

Shiloh was entirely on her own.

As she passed the kitchen headed for the back door, she grabbed the emergency wind-up radio on the scarred kitchen table. Darkness pressed against the windows, heavy with foreboding.

Shiloh wasn't afraid of the dark.

Something snagged her eye. Her grandfather read the Marquette *Mining Journal.* She paused, one hand on the crossbow strap, the other gripping the radio, and stared.

Two articles dominated the front page. The first headline read, "Geomagnetic Storms predicted to Hit Northern Hemisphere—Auroras Expected."

Her teacher had discussed the solar storms in science class. At the time, it had fascinated her.

It was the second headline that stopped her in her tracks: "Convicted Broken Heart Killer Eli Pope to be Released on Technicality."

The newspaper was today's edition, dated May seventeenth.

Her heart thumped harder, a stuttering drum against her ribs. Cold washed over her, icing her veins. She knew who he was, what that man had taken from her.

This was not the first time she'd awoken next to a dead body.

With trembling hands, Shiloh seized the keys to the Honda Four-Trax Rubicon ATV hanging on a hook by the back door. As she reached for the door handle, the overhead light flickered out. Everything went dark. Silence descended.

Shiloh flicked the kitchen light switch. Nothing. She tried the ceiling fan. Same thing. She blinked to adjust to the shadows and pulled the cell phone out of her pocket. It was on but had no bars. That wasn't unusual this far north.

Shiloh opened the front door and stepped out onto the porch. Outside, it was night. There were no stars. No moon.

It was the aurora that transfixed her.

Above the tree line to the north, undulating ribbons of fiery blood-red draped the sky. Pulsating, brightening, softening, then growing brighter still. Transparent waves of scarlet, crimson, and burgundy, woven with threads of tangerine and flame.

The world was on fire.

Shiloh left her grandfather's house for the last time, crossbow in hand, terror and courage ablaze in her heart.

Whoever had taken her brother and murdered her grandfather would pay.

And she would start with her mother's killer.

2

ELI POPE

DAY ONE

Eli Pope prepared himself to fight to the death. Darius Sykes was coming to kill him.

Eli's gaze sharpened. His shoulders stiff, his gaze unmoving, he stood with an unnatural stillness at the back of the prison library, where he'd worked for the last three years.

It was the only place in this hellhole that brought him any sense of quiet, of peace.

Alert, he waited, his muscles coiled, hands tightened into fists.

He felt the stack of bookcases at his back. The cart of returned hardbacks two feet to his right. Twelve rows of bookcases stood in the center of the room, rectangular tables bolted to the floor on either side. Fluorescent lights buzzed overhead.

No other inmates were present. No correctional officers nearby, either. The library was the least supervised area of the prison.

Sykes knew that. He would have planned for it.

Eli sensed them like predators in the water. Three of them were slinking closer.

A thug named Angel Flud approached to Eli's left, creeping

between the bookcases. Eli recognized the sound of his dragging left leg, his halting footsteps a soft rasp on the carpet.

Fat Tommy lurked along the wall of bookcases to the right, beneath the high rectangular window. He stank of commissary-procured Axe body spray.

Eli couldn't see Sykes, but he felt him, sensed his malignant presence. Sykes wouldn't miss his last chance at Eli.

The inmates knew. They'd heard the COs talking. Hell, half of them had watched the news conference that morning.

The Michigan Court of Appeals had overturned his conviction on the basis of an illegal search and seizure. Everything—the investigation, the trial, the witness testimonies, the boxes of evidence—it was all going to be undone.

Eli Pope was about to be released from prison.

In the yard, in the chow hall, in the showers and hallways, he felt their hatred, their resentment, the shared indignation threatening to boil over.

He only needed to survive today.

Prison smelled like a mix of fear and desperation, resignation and rage. Eight years Eli had spent buried alive in Alger Correctional Facility, a high security prison located in Alger County in the Mideastern Upper Peninsula.

How he despised this place. The claustrophobia. The cramped, hot cells. The incessant stench of piss and sweat. His fellow prisoners little more than animals, their eyes flat and cunning.

Like the men who were coming for him now.

Overhead, the fluorescent lights flickered and went out. Catcalls and shouts echoed down the corridor from the main rec room. Whoops and yells. The monkeys rattled their cages.

He waited for the generator to come back on. It didn't.

Shadows darkened the prison library. A reddish, watery light streamed through the high narrow windows along the far wall. Sunset had come and gone.

Eli blinked to adjust his vision. He scanned the aisles, his spine to the bookcase, and reached for a hardback copy of *War and Peace*.

It was thick, heavy; someone's red Sharpie had scrawled an explicit insult across the worn leatherbound cover. It would work for what he needed.

His heartrate increased. Adrenaline iced his veins. He gripped the book in both hands and waited for them. Wiry muscles roped his arms, bulging as he flexed.

Scars marred his knuckles, his chest, his lower back. In prison, you never turned your back. Never let your guard down. Never truly slept. Always ready for the creak of footsteps, a sharpened shank sliding between your ribs.

There were many ways to get hurt in prison. More ways to hurt.

Eli made sure he did the hurting. His years in the military gave him a brutal edge that most inmates had learned to respect.

He knew two things: never back down, never show fear.

"No need to hide, Sykes," Eli said.

In the center aisle, an inmate stepped into view. Darius Sykes was thick as a tank, with large, muscular hands. Prison-made tattoos snaked up his ham-sized biceps. His acorn-brown hair was shorn close to his skull.

His full lips and sensuous mouth gave him an almost feminine appearance. Anyone who registered that softness as weakness soon learned to regret it—if they lived that long. The dead-fish look in his eyes revealed his true nature.

"I've been waiting for this heart-to-heart, Pope," Sykes said with a soft smile.

Sykes was a dangerous, skilled killer. He was serving three consecutive life sentences and ruled every square inch of this God-forsaken place.

As a Hell's Angels biker, he'd murdered six members of a rival gang and arranged their corpses in a macabre display along M-28 from

Wakefield to Sault Ste. Marie. He'd also slaughtered his rivals' families, including three children.

Sykes had tried to recruit Eli to join his gang of thugs. When he'd refused to kowtow, Sykes had ordered his assassination.

The would-be assassin ended up a corpse in the shower, the spray of hot water washing away the blood, the incriminating evidence. No cameras were allowed in the showers; inmates exercised their rights to privacy.

Since then, Eli had lived with a target painted on the back of his prison jumpsuit.

Sykes wanted Eli on his knees. Wanted him to suffer, to confess, to beg for mercy before the end.

Eli would die standing before he'd live a moment on his knees.

"I feel like you've been avoiding me," Sykes said.

Eli said nothing. His gaze flicked past Sykes to Angel and Fat Tommy. They stepped out from behind two stacks and flanked Sykes. Twenty feet from Eli, approximately forty-five degrees to his left and right.

Angel was a skinny Hispanic gangbanger with teardrop tattoos on his face and a gold tooth. Fat Tommy was bald as a cue ball and weighed three-hundred pounds. Immense rolls of fat strained the fabric of his prison jumpsuit.

Sykes' lips thinned. "You think you've got a miracle up your sleeve, but you ain't walking out of here, Redskin. Not crawling, neither."

Eli didn't blink. Racial slurs against his Ojibwe heritage were nothing new in this place. Nothing new outside of these walls, either.

He knew what they saw—a black-haired, sharp-faced Native American with death in his dark eyes, his strong, powerful body built for killing.

He was incredibly fit, doing hundreds of push-ups, sit-ups, and pull-ups in his cell each night and weightlifting in the prison gym. Trained in Krav Maga, he was a force to be reckoned with.

Eli checked Angel and Fat Tommy again—their hands were visible.

Angel held a plastic shank in his right hand, low at his side. Fat Tommy's hands were empty, but he could shatter bones with those hammer-like fists.

"Something happened to the power," Fat Tommy said in a thick-throated Southern drawl. "No cameras. Nobody's gonna see nothin'."

Eli didn't take his eyes off his adversaries. He didn't care why the power was out. He sensed the empty space, the lack of other bodies, of prying eyes. No one else was here, or anywhere in the vicinity.

The library was empty for a reason. The CO who normally supervised the library was likely sick in a bathroom from food poisoning, or otherwise occupied. Maybe the COs had been paid off. Or maybe they'd chosen to look the other way.

It wouldn't make the reports. Some official excuse would be made. No one would look too closely. Not the warden, not the DA, nor the governor.

The inmates and COs were united in their loathing for the Broken Heart Killer.

Everyone wanted Eli Pope dead.

3

ELI POPE

DAY ONE

Eli slowed his breathing. His pulse steadied. He readied himself.

These thugs thought they could steal what had already been stolen long ago, but he had nothing left. Nothing but the lethal ability to kill and to maim, the skill to cause grievous bodily harm.

After years of repressing his fury, he would release it. He would give these animals exactly what they wanted.

Fat Tommy cracked his knuckles. "You thought you were getting out of this joint, didn't you? The irony of it just kills me."

"It's called poetic justice." Sykes smiled, his full lips worming back from his crooked teeth. He had the face of an eel. "No one is coming. I saw to that."

Eli knew the consequences for killing one of them would be dire. It was three stone-cold killers against one. He did not have the luxury of holding back, not if he wished to survive.

He had to go in full throttle. He had to drop them as quickly as possible, so he didn't get taken to the ground. Death by stabbing wasn't how he planned to go.

Eli clenched his jaw. He tightened his grip on the book. They were coming for him, no matter what he said or did.

The eerie reddish shadows deepened. Sykes' eyes glimmered. He gave the smallest shake of his head.

Fat Tommy and Angel rushed Eli. They lunged from two different directions, coming at him from opposite sides: Angel with that vicious shank, held low and glinting; Fat Tommy up and swinging. Fat Tommy's bulk made him slow, but the power behind a single punch could knock a man out cold.

Angel reached him first. Eli's training kicked in. He stepped into Angel's attack, fast and efficient, as lethal as a cobra.

Angel darted in and stabbed with the shank. Eli pivoted toward Angel, sidestepped fast, and raised *War and Peace.* He slammed it hard across the man's face.

The thick book smashed his nose. Blood spurted from his nostrils. Angel's head snapped back, his nose broken. His forward momentum was cut short; the shank scraped harmlessly across Eli's right side.

One eye on the two other attackers, Eli adjusted his grip and slammed the book sideways into the inmate's throat. Angel threw up an arm, absorbing some of the blow. The impact still dropped him to the ground.

He sagged to the floor. He landed on his stomach, mouth opened like a fish as he gasped for oxygen. The hand holding the shank wavered.

Eli raised his leg and brought his foot down hard, hoping to crush the first vertebra. He missed, but the man's scapula gave a sickening crack. His arm was dislocated and fractured.

He wouldn't be stabbing anyone anytime soon.

As Tommy lunged from the right, Eli whipped sideways, feinting left. He absorbed the blow meant for his skull with his shoulder. Pain exploded in his muscles, tendons, ligaments.

Ignoring the pain, Eli headbutted Fat Tommy. With a crunch, the man's cheekbone fractured. Eli seized the inmate's massive shoulders with both hands and slammed his forehead into his face. He followed with a swift elbow to the side of the head.

Screaming, Fat Tommy crumpled. He clutched his broken nose and shattered cheekbones. Blood poured between his fingers.

Eli had no time to worry about consequences.

Sykes had reached him with the knife. It was not a prison shank fashioned from melted plastic but a butcher's blade from the prison kitchen, twelve inches long and brutally sharp.

With a roar, he attacked Eli, slicing in quick, powerful jabs.

Eli's adrenaline surged. He held the book in front of his vulnerable torso, protecting the internal organs in his stomach. Sykes' first knife thrust struck the cover, punching through leather and reams of paper.

Sykes yanked the knife out. *War and Peace* went flying. The book tumbled across Angel's unconscious form, thudding to the carpet.

Sykes came at Eli again, growling, slashing and stabbing.

Eli backed up swiftly, out of range of the blade.

Attempting to block or seize the knife was pointless. Trying to stop a knife was like trying to stop water from flowing. It was impossible not to get wet.

Instead, he seized an encyclopedia from the shelf and hurled it at Sykes.

It struck his right shoulder. Sykes winced but kept coming at him. He dodged between bookcases and tables bolted to the floor.

Eli turned and sprinted down the stacks to the government section. This was Eli's library. Like any proper tier one operator, he'd prepared for contingencies.

In the center of a giant economics tome, Eli found the object he needed. Inside the cut-out within the thick pages lay a shank Eli had fashioned from a section of metal bunk bed shaved to a vicious point.

As Sykes charged him from behind, Eli ripped out the shank. He spun and stepped left, slashing hard. The shank sliced across Sykes' hands.

With a shriek, Sykes dropped the butcher knife. Blood dripped to the carpet. Sykes' fleshy lips opened in a startled O.

Eli thrust the shank into the man's exposed stomach.

The homemade blade ripped through the jumpsuit, then glanced off something hard. Underneath Sykes' uniform, he wore several layers of cardboard and newspaper as makeshift armor—a common prison tactic. Sykes had prepared, too.

Sykes scrambled for the butcher knife. Eli didn't give him the chance. With his left hand, he seized the man's thick neck and shoved him back against the bookcase.

With his other hand, he drew the shank back to drive it into Sykes' throat.

"Pope!" A correctional officer burst into the library. "Stop!"

Eli didn't move a muscle, didn't remove the shank from Sykes. He was so close, he could count the broken blood vessels in the convict's bloated cheeks. The point pricked Sykes' Adam's Apple.

"Pope," the CO said, breathless. Eli recognized his voice. He glimpsed the vague shape of the man out of the corner of his eye. A young CO named Ivan Davis. "Don't do this."

"Too late," Eli growled.

"If you kill him, you're going away forever. They will put you in isolation, throw away the key, and you will never see the light of day again."

Anger burned through him. His hands shook. Eli pressed the point of the shank harder into the man's throat.

Sykes' eyes popped. Red veins streaked the yellowish sclera. His mouth opened, his purple tongue protruding.

"Pope." Davis reached for his baton with one hand, his radio with the other. A canister of pepper spray was looped to his belt. He raised the radio to his mouth. "Don't make me call it in."

With tremendous willpower, Eli stepped back and lowered the shank.

Sykes sagged. He clutched at his throat, gasping for oxygen.

Warily, Eli watched him, making sure the threat remained neutralized. His heart hammered against his ribs. Indignation burned through his veins. His fingers would not uncurl from the shank's handle.

He imagined all the ways he could kill this man, all the ways he should have.

Sykes destroyed whatever he touched. He killed women and children. Eli loathed him.

At least he was in here, locked up among other monsters. At least he would never again get out to hunt the innocent in the Upper Peninsula.

Sykes massaged his injured throat. Malice flashed in his eyes. When he spoke, his voice was hoarse. "I will come for you. When I get out, and I will, I will come to your town, your house, your bedroom. I will find everyone you love and I will hunt them down and slit their throats in front of you, one by one."

Eli stared at him, dead-eyed. "It'll be a short hunt. I love no one."

"Let's go." With a frown, the CO glanced down at Angel, unconscious on the floor. Fat Tommy had pissed himself. The sharp scent of urine stung Eli's nostrils.

Davis radioed for medical aid for the injured convicts and gestured for Eli to follow him out. "I need escorts for three injured inmates to medical. Looks like we might need an ambulance."

"I'll kill you!" Sykes screamed at Eli. "That's a promise!"

The CO turned to Sykes. "Shut the hell up." He glanced at Eli and tilted his chin toward the door. "Pope, I said let's go!"

Eli hated to take his eyes off his adversaries, even ones incapacitated, but he obediently followed the CO, his senses alert for any movement behind him. None came.

Still, he could feel Sykes' malevolent presence at his back. Even imprisoned, as long as he was alive, Sykes would be a threat.

4

ELI POPE

DAY ONE

Eli's footfalls echoed along the concrete corridor. The hoots and catcalls faded into background noise, barely discernible as they traveled from the depths of the interior to the perimeter.

Four COs rushed past them toward the library, batons drawn. They didn't glance at Eli.

"Damn reports," Davis muttered. "I'll be writing reports all damn day."

"Are you taking me to a holding cell?" They might put him in solitary. He imagined the confined space, the dank air filling up his lungs, the choking sense of hopelessness.

He despised solitary almost as much as gen pop.

Davis shook his head. "The warden wants you released immediately."

Eli rubbed his sore knuckles and flexed his fingers. Pain radiated from his shoulder. He'd nearly killed three men. This didn't make sense. "What?"

"I know it was Sykes. I know what they had planned." Davis eyed him, frowning. "The warden doesn't want a madhouse of press. Or fights or prying eyes. He just wants you gone. The governor agreed, and here we are."

Eli stared at him. "Nickerson has the library on Mondays. He was nowhere in sight. The COs were in on it."

In the library, Sykes and his friends would be strip-searched, then escorted to holding cells before being evaluated by a medical team. The officers would find the contraband weapons.

Investigative Services would be brought in. Their cells would be searched, inmates interviewed, cameras reviewed, evidence collected. The COs would be looked at, too.

It wouldn't look good for the warden or the COs involved. Even with the cameras glitchy, there would be evidence. No wonder the warden wanted him gone.

"No one is going to admit that," Davis said.

Eli didn't care who admitted to what. He just wanted out.

"Not everyone was involved. I was raised Baptist." Davis said it slow, like he was chewing the words, rolling them in his mouth. "My father always preached that no man is beyond God's grace. No matter what he's done."

"Some men are," Eli said.

Unlike the other COs, who were either disinterested or cruel, Davis was kind and patient. He treated the worst of humanity with dignity.

Eli hated him for it. The worst of humanity didn't deserve an ounce of pity or compassion. These thugs deserved the hell they'd found themselves in.

They deserved worse.

Given the chance, Eli would take great pleasure in exacting justice himself. Some crimes were unforgivable. Some criminals were monsters, not men.

Davis shrugged. "The press would usually be camped outside the gates. Lucky for you, the news cycles are covering the sun thing."

Davis paused, like he expected Eli to ask what he meant or comment about the weather. Eli did neither. Davis continued, nonplussed, "The news reporters said there might be temporary communication and power interruptions. Not like we aren't used to that up here."

"Is that what took out the power?"

Davis shrugged. "Must be."

"And the generator?"

Davis shrugged. "Dunno. I heard there was an issue, but the technicians fixed it. We're operating on emergency backup, which means no TV in the rec room."

Eli managed a grunt. His legs trembled from the adrenaline dump. All he wanted to do was lie down and sleep. He hadn't slept well in eight years.

Davis glanced at him. "You need medical to check you out? They came at you pretty good."

He sucked blood from between his teeth. "Just get me out."

"I'd feel the same way."

They strode down various hallways. At each door, Davis hit the buzzer and stated his radio call sign. The CO in the main control room verified his identity via the CCTV camera near the door and buzzed them through.

In the rec room, the inmates were rowdy, booing and hissing. A few slumped, staring at the dead screen in confusion like they expected it to spontaneously combust.

"You want to stop at your cell?"

"What for?"

"Your personal property. Journals, pictures, whatever."

"I have no personal property," Eli said.

"Anything that needs to be returned to the property room?" Davis asked. "TVs, radios, anything like that?"

Eli shook his head.

"No pictures?"

His cell was as barren as his soul. "No."

Davis nodded to himself. "Sure, sure. Okay." He turned right and led Eli down another hallway to an office. A mountain of paperwork waited for him, which he signed as a woman with colorless hair in her fifties droned, "Sign here" twenty times. He signed for an envelope with a debit card inside, giving him access to what remained of his commissary account.

At receiving, he went through another endless series of locked doors and gates, the walls shades of dull gray or vomit green. They returned his clothes, his wallet with his expired driver's license, and his dog tags.

He put his dog tags on. How he had missed the familiar feel of the chain around his neck, the tags against his chest beneath his shirt.

Five minutes later, he was outside the fence.

It was like stepping out of a cave into a different universe.

The road was deserted. The chilly air smelled of pine trees, gasoline, and dirt. It was only forty degrees, but he didn't care. The breeze on his skin felt sweet as a kiss.

No gray walls. No COs with weapons. No predators with eyes like devils and teeth like wolves.

"Would you look at that," Davis said.

Eli raised his gaze to the sky. The transparent reddish flames of the northern lights flickered overhead, dancing and undulating, almost like a living thing.

"You have someone to pick you up?" Davis asked.

"Nope."

"No one?"

"No one."

"You have a cellphone?"

Eli shook his head.

Davis hesitated. "There's a payphone at the Bear Trap Bar a mile down the road. You'll know it when you see it. You can call a cab. They know the number."

Eli said nothing. A bar at the end of the world, a desolate place for ex-convicts with nowhere to go and no one to love them. He couldn't think of anything more depressing.

Davis shook his head, sighed, and turned back for the prison gates. "Good luck, man. You can do whatever you want. You're free."

Eli didn't respond.

Eight years he'd spent in a dungeon, convicted of a crime he had not committed. He was supposed to wither and die in there. Or bleed out on the shower floor.

Now, he was out.

He'd never expected this.

Eli started walking. One foot in front of the other. Gravel beneath his boots. *His* boots, not the state's property—his own. He wore the khaki hiking pants and black T-shirt he'd worn the day they had come for him.

The day Jackson Cross had come for him.

Eli would never forget the look in his friend's eyes as he'd slapped the cuffs on Eli's wrists, the pain in his voice as he'd read him his rights. The judgment and condemnation.

What was left for him in Christmas, Michigan? In Alger County? What was left for him anywhere?

His father's house.

A bit of cash in his pocket.

His dog tags.

Eli looked up at the heavens. The ephemeral northern lights spread across the dome of the sky like the mushroom cloud of a nuclear blast.

He blinked and kept walking. Something sparked to life in his chest, hard and bright. An inexplicable desire to weep.

There was only one thing he wanted.

Davis's words rattled in his brain.

Freedom. Such a charged word. He'd fought for freedom, joined the military for freedom. Risked his life and sacrificed brothers in arms for it. He'd had it stolen from him, too.

He touched his dog tags beneath his T-shirt. To Eli Pope, freedom meant one thing. He had one goal in his ruined life.

Vengeance.

He would find the person or people who had framed him for murder, who had destroyed his life, and kill them.

Not quickly, but slowly. With great care and attention to detail. He felt no shame at the thought, no remorse, only a burning hatred.

They had taken an innocent man and turned him into a monster.

A monster was what they'd wanted. So, a monster he would become.

Hell, he already was.

5

JACKSON CROSS

DAY ONE

Jackson Cross watched the sky turn to fire.

Here in the northern reaches of the Upper Peninsula, the northern lights were not a rare occurrence. They appeared in the dead of a winter, at night, but usually in shades of green or violet.

The news had reported the eerie red aurora sightings across the United States, Canada, even into northern Mexico and as far as India, Japan, and China.

Unlike many, it gave him a disquieting feeling of dread.

"Deputy Sheriff?" Michelle Carpenter asked.

Jackson stood outside the IGA Country Store in Christmas, Michigan, which Michelle Carpenter owned and managed.

"I know what you're thinking, Jackson," Mrs. Carpenter said. "It's different this time. I know it is. I can feel it."

This wasn't the first time Jackson had been called here. Ruby Carpenter, a beautiful redhead with attitude to spare, was a troubled sixteen-year-old. She'd been arrested for shoplifting and underage drinking. Last year, she'd run away three times.

A lost cause, the sheriff claimed. Jackson Cross, however, was the patron saint of lost causes. Or so Lily Easton had told him once.

In the seven years he'd served as undersheriff for Alger County, Jackson had worked plenty of similar cases. Most had not ended well. He scratched his stubbled jaw and glanced down at his notebook. "Let me check into this and get back to you, Michelle."

Mrs. Carpenter's eyes welled with tears. "I know I haven't been the best mother, Jackson. I know my failings." She gestured vaguely with one trembling hand. "This place, it can be hard on the young ones."

Jackson knew it. He'd grown up here. This place was in his bones, had dug in beneath his breastbone like a lover—or a parasite.

Everyone complained, but few people left once they got a taste of it. The isolation and peace, the stunning but forlorn beauty. The closeness, the connection. The comfort of people you'd known your whole life.

It was different for this generation, though. Fewer jobs. Even less opportunities. The small towns and wild spaces could become claustrophobic, could strangle you.

Girls like Ruby needed out. They needed something this place couldn't give them.

Mrs. Carpenter met his gaze. "Bring my baby home."

Jackson ran a hand through his mussed, sand-colored hair. At 6'3, he was tall and broad-shouldered. Handsome enough, but he was married to the job. "We'll find her, Michelle. I promise."

Devon Harris, the new deputy, exited the patrol truck and strode across the parking lot, her expression tense as she shoved her long black braids over her shoulder. She was short but fit and muscular.

Her warm brown skin crinkled around her eyes when she smiled. She wasn't smiling now. "A call just came in, boss. We've got a dead body."

Jackson stiffened. He remembered the last time a body had been found in Christmas, Michigan. The Broken Heart Killer case.

The brutal crime that had nearly destroyed their small town, that had ripped apart friendships, families, and left them all scarred.

"Who?" Mrs. Carpenter asked, stricken. "Who is it?"

"Caucasian male in his sixties. They haven't yet officially identified the victim."

Beside him, Mrs. Carpenter let out her breath. Not her daughter. Not her problem, but definitely Jackson's.

"What else?" he asked.

"The 911 dispatcher said the witness reported signs of foul play."

He reached for his radio. "Where?"

"Off County Road 581."

Jackson froze. "Give me the address again." He prayed it would be different this time. That he'd heard wrong.

Devon rattled it off. He hadn't.

"That's Amos Easton's place," Mrs. Carpenter said.

It was still cold in May, around fifty degrees since summer didn't reach the Upper Peninsula until July. A chill passed through him that had nothing to do with the weather.

"Anyone else?" he asked Devon, his chest tight. "Any children involved?"

She shook her head. "That's all I have."

Trepidation flared through him. He needed to get to the scene. He needed to make sure. "Let's go."

"Please don't forget about my daughter," Michelle Carpenter said.

"I won't," he promised, but he was already striding toward the white and brown patrol truck emblazoned with "Alger County Sheriff" in orange on both sides. He gestured to Devon. "Get in."

Devon hurried after him. "I get to drive."

"Absolutely not."

She huffed but didn't argue.

Jackson knew the county and forest roads, the campsites, the ATV, hiking, and snowmobile trails like the back of his hand. He knew every resident of Christmas, population four hundred, and many in Munising, the closest town and home to the famed Pictured Rocks National Lakeshore.

They left Mrs. Carpenter standing forlornly in front of her store, the siding peeling, the weed-choked asphalt peppered with cracks.

Jackson drove west on M-28. Huge jack pines rose on either side of the road. They passed local stores and restaurants with holiday-inspired names—Yule Log Resort, Silent Night Campsite, Santa's Storage Facilities.

For a few minutes, Devon stared down at the phone in her lap, frowning. She was from Detroit; it showed. "Stupid Sprint. They promised cell service here."

"First thing you should know about the UP is cell service is a gamble anywhere, no matter who you have. Be prepared for that."

"Just great." Devon rolled her eyes and switched on the radio. The channels were all static. "This is eerie, this solar storm thing. I've never seen anything like it."

They turned right on County Highway 589, headed northwest. Lake Superior stretched to their right. The water shimmered tangerine. The rippling waves glittered as they reflected the aurora's colors.

He could feel the lake, that sense of vastness. The native Ojibwe people called the lake *Gichigamiing*—the "great water."

"TikTok is down," Devon said. "Maybe so many people are posting photos of the northern lights that it crashed."

He had no idea what the hell TikTok even was. Devon was young, only twenty-seven. At thirty-six, he felt ancient, weary to his bones. "Hell of a day to find a body."

"Yeah." She chewed her thumbnail. "You know who it is, don't you? The victim."

He gave a curt nod as he turned left onto County Highway 587. His fingers gripped the steering wheel as a lifetime of memories assaulted him. Every detail was seared into his mind. The silent house. The bed, the faint spatters of blood. The cold dead body of the girl. So vibrant in life, so shockingly still in death.

Lily Easton. Here and then gone. In a blink, in a frenzy of violence. The girl he'd loved from afar his entire life.

His best friend had killed her.

And Jackson, a naïve, fresh-faced deputy, had helped convict him.

Now this. A killer released on a technicality. A dead body found on the same property, separated by eight years and a lifetime of grief.

Above them, the solar storms lit up the sky in crimson waves. The aurora had a weight to it, a physical presence. He could feel it pressing down upon his soul.

As they drove up the narrow winding driveway, a disconcerting sensation gripped him, like some terrible thing was bearing down on them all.

6

JACKSON CROSS

DAY ONE

It was nearly ten p.m. by the time they reached the Easton place.

A weed-choked gravel road led them through three miles of towering red and white pines, sugar maples, and balsam fir trees. Dense underbrush scraped the sides of the patrol truck.

The aurora was so bright that Jackson exited the vehicle with his flashlight in hand but switched it off. Everything was bathed in an eerie reddish glow, like shadows cast by an immense fire.

Three county sheriff's vehicles were parked in the gravel lot. Two Munising Police Department squad cars had parked behind them.

The Munising Police and Alger County Sheriff Departments often worked together, especially on big cases. If it was an important case, the state police would be brought in.

Ahead of them, the white farmhouse was perched on the knoll of a hill. The salvage yard was located down the hill to the right, ringed by fencing lined with concertina wire.

Devon had gone silent. The sense of menace was palpable, as if Lily Easton's blood still soaked the fabric of this place.

Steeling himself, Jackson took the lead and Devon followed,

cursing as she nearly tripped on the uneven ground. Glass, bits of plastic, and debris crunched beneath their shoes. It was impossible not to step on anything.

Jackson strained his ears. Subdued voices drifted from the salvage yard. Insects trilled in the woods. A neighbor's dog barked.

Three deputies stood around a cordoned off section in the center of the salvage yard, a large area bound by fluttering crime scene tape. Gas-powered search lights cast bright white light across the crime scene.

Crime scene technicians had been called in, but communication was sporadic tonight. Even the radios were staticky. One of the deputies was hunting down the sheriff in person.

The medical examiner from Munising had just arrived; a police officer had driven out to Au Train to her home to pick her up.

Several cops and deputies processed the scene, taking photographs, dusting for prints, and cataloging evidence. The ME ducked beneath the perimeter of red tape that secured the immediate area around the victim, or "hot zone", and examined the body.

Venla Virtanen was a stout Finnish woman in her fifties with short white-blonde hair. She wore PPE over slacks and a sweater; "Medical Examiner" was stenciled onto the back of her wind breaker.

Outside the main perimeter of yellow crime scene tape, deputy Randy Hasting smoked a cigarette.

Jackson approached him. Pressure was building behind his eyes. Concern gnawed at him. "Has the house been cleared? Easton's grandkids live with him."

The rookie deputy, Phil Nash, nodded. "We did. All buildings on the property are empty."

He held his breath. "No sign of the kids? Are you sure?"

"Nobody's home," Nash said.

Jackson pulled a pair of latex gloves from his jacket pocket. "Who called it in?"

"A customer," Hasting said. "Jim Hart is interviewing him at the station."

"Okay, good." Relief flared through him, but it was fleeting. "Shiloh and Cody should be here. They're too young to drive. Besides, Easton's truck is still in the driveway."

"Maybe they're with friends," Devon said.

"Maybe," Jackson said, but he didn't believe it. Apprehension coiled in his gut. The possibility that one or both of them might be dead and hidden somewhere on the property made him physically ill.

At Lily's funeral, he'd made a promise to her casket. He would watch out for her children, but especially Shiloh.

Six-year-old Cody had been at a sleepover the night of the homicide. Five-year-old Shiloh had been there, in that house.

No one knew exactly what had occurred that night. Only that the killer—Eli Pope—had done terrible things, though he'd left the little girl alive and physically untouched.

They'd found her with smears of Lily's blood on her shirt, her cheeks, her hands. She'd been rocking in a corner, incoherent with terror. She'd mumbled a few things, but nothing they'd been able to use. Jackson suspected that she'd witnessed the horror.

He cared for both kids, but it was Shiloh who'd stolen his heart, Shiloh who reminded him so much of her mother. Black hair and blacker eyes. Small and sharp, one hundred pounds of spit and fire. She was Lily Easton's daughter, through and through.

He checked on them once or twice a month, bringing Shiloh Snickers and Twizzlers, gummy bears and gum for Cody. And books. That girl loved books, especially travel books.

As if that would make up for his inability to protect her mother from the one danger he should have seen coming.

With a deep breath, he forced himself to focus on the current crime scene. It was the best way to help them now. "What do we have on the victim?"

Hasting gestured vaguely with his cigarette. He wore a khaki trench coat. In his mid-sixties, he sported a middle-aged gut and a receding hairline. "The vic is Amos Easton. Sixty-nine years old. Caucasian."

Jackson shone the flashlight across the scene. The corpse lay face-up in a wide circle of dirt, next to a gray Kia Rio with the guts torn out of its engine. He recognized the red handkerchief, the John Deere cap, the silver hair. The caved-in skull and collapsed facial structure were harder to recognize.

"Looks like he got his head bashed in by that crowbar over there." Hasting hooked his thumb at a long thin shape lying in the dirt. Bits of bone and brain matter clung to the iron. "Blood looks dry."

Across the victim's chest, the blood spatters appeared to be smeared as if he'd been touched. There were indentations in the dirt, a couple of red streaks, like maybe someone had knelt beside the body. The perpetrator? Or one of the kids, afterward?

"Who'd have a reason to do this?" Nash couldn't grow a full beard yet. His uniform hung off his narrow shoulders like a coat hanger, but his posture was straight, his blue eyes sharp.

"Sure wasn't robbery," Hasting said. "The watch and wallet are still on the body."

"The business could have been the target," Jackson said, though he didn't believe it.

Devon made a face as she scanned the salvage yard, taking in the rows of dilapidated vehicles, the piles of scrap metal, stacks of mufflers and tires, and coils of wire and hoses. "Who could tell if something is missing? We'll have to compare everything here to the inventory. That's assuming he kept good records."

"Sounds like a job for the rookie," Hasting said dryly.

Nash frowned but didn't argue. "Who'd steal from Easton? What's even worth stealing here?"

One of the Munising police officers approached them. He tipped his gas station coffee cup in greeting without smiling. "Exactly my thoughts."

Ramon Moreno sported long black hair tied back in a ponytail, bronze skin, and a full beard. He had a sharp, sarcastic sense of humor. "That's what you're gonna find out while I go back to my soft, comfortable bed."

"You wish," Devon said.

"We all wish," Hasting said with a sigh.

Devon turned in a slow circle, appraising the property. "How much land did he own?"

"Two hundred acres," Jackson said. "A good portion of it is waterfront, to the northwest."

Devon whistled. "Wonder why he never sold it. This junkyard can't bring in that much. Hell, he probably pays more in taxes for the land than the business is worth."

Moreno slurped his coffee. "It's a losing proposition, all right."

"Lots of folks here are in the same position," Jackson said.

Poverty was endemic in much of the Upper Peninsula, which had lost the copper and ore mining and timber industries that had once thrived here, leaving behind hundreds of abandoned mines and thousands of tree stumps.

Jackson zipped his jacket against the dropping temperature. "Easton would never sell this place. It's been in his family for a hundred and fifty years, handed down from the old timber barons of the twentieth century. It's the one thing he has. Or, had."

Devon shivered. "I'd rather be in Tahiti, sunning myself and sipping martinis handmade by my personal bartender."

"Amen, sister," Moreno said.

Jackson watched the ME place small paper bags over the victim's hands to preserve trace evidence beneath the fingernails. They'd swab his hands for DNA. She annotated something in a folder and then stood, preparing to move the corpse into a black body bag, which she would transport to the morgue.

Moreno mopped his brow with a handkerchief. It was forty-five degrees, but they all felt it. The pressure building. The heat of an unseen wildfire about to overtake them.

"What can you tell us, doctor?" Jackson asked.

"From my preliminary examination, death appears to have been caused by blunt force trauma. The position of a depressed fracture on the posterior right side of the cranium is consistent with violent assault."

"From that tire iron right there?" Hasting asked.

"Could be. I still have to conduct the autopsy and tox report."

"Estimated time of death?" Moreno asked.

Dr. Virtanen pointed to various body parts as she spoke. "Algor mortis can be quite unreliable, of course. Liver mortis can take up to twelve hours. The process is still incomplete. Here and here, rigor mortis has appeared in the small muscles of the face, followed by the muscles in the upper and lower limbs. However, the abdominal muscles are still soft. Approximate time of death is between four and six this afternoon. Judging by lividity, the body does not appear to have been moved."

Jackson nodded to himself, working his jaw as he considered the angles, the odds. He turned to Devon. "What do you see?"

Her eyes narrowed. She scanned the scene again, taking her time. "Definite signs of a struggle." She walked the perimeter of the crime scene tape, careful not to disturb the ground, weaving between half-disassembled vehicles.

"We'll have to cast every footprint. Lots of fingerprints and footprints from customers." She paused, looking down, and frowned. "There's something dark over here. Looks like blood."

Jackson tagged it, and they kept moving.

She circled the crime scene like a wary creature sniffing for danger. Once, twice, three times, expanding with each circle. Her flashlight swept back and forth.

The glow from the aurora tinged everything crimson. Her shadow moved ahead of him, wavering with the sweeping flashlight beam.

Jackson followed, looking for evidence, saying nothing, his heart in his throat. He feared what they might find.

Past the perimeter of the fence line, the trees reached for the sky, trunks lined up like sentinels. The shadows deepened. The vehicles seemed to crouch as if they were living machines made of flesh and blood rather than steel, plastic, and glass.

Devon halted and pointed. "Another set of prints."

He came up beside her. Several footprints headed north. The treads were shallow, possibly a pair of sneakers.

He squinted. "Maybe a size nine. A small man. Or a teenage boy."

Devon nodded. "Could be Cody's prints. You probably wouldn't have customers coming out to the back of the fence on a regular basis. The footprints could've been left at any time."

Jackson squatted and shone the light on the ridges in the dirt. Dark red specks drew his attention. "If that's the vic's blood inside the print, then the suspect got blood on his shoe as he left. The prints are spread wide, like he or she was running."

"Fleeing the crime scene," Devon said. "Witness or perpetrator?"

"Either way, a person of interest."

"We'll get the crime scene techs on this right away." She pointed the flashlight. "They head northwest, right to the fence line—what's that?"

The flashlight highlighted a broken section of fence hidden behind a stack of rusted bumpers. They approached, skirting the footprints, careful not to damage potential evidence.

Jackson squatted, pointing at the tear in the fence that started at the ground and sliced upward approximately three feet. "This was cut with wire cutters. And not recently. You can see rust here on the ends."

"The ground is scraped clear. The section of fence was pulled back frequently."

"Someone's used this as a way to get in and out."

"Cody?"

"We're going to find out." Jackson stood heavily, his knees creaking, and headed back toward the crime scene, Devon on his heels.

He wished he was fly-fishing along the Pere Marquette River. Hell, he wished he was anywhere but here, facing down the black hole of his past.

7

JACKSON CROSS

DAY ONE

"Suspects?" Devon asked once they were back at the crime scene. "Who'd want to kill the old man?"

Moreno snorted. "Where do you want to start?"

Easton had been universally disliked. A hermit, an isolated survivalist-type, he loved his spirits and gambling. Over the years, he'd alienated neighbors and friends.

Back when he was married, law enforcement had regularly received domestic dispute calls. The wife always dropped the charges. She'd died of cancer when Jackson was ten.

Easton had been a difficult man. Most people passed him off as a degenerate drunk, but he was a cunning s.o.b. Or, he had been.

The suspect list was a long one. It'd take legwork and resources to winnow it down. Jackson had a suspect in mind. No one would like it. He hated it himself.

Jackson gave a weary sigh. "Eli Pope."

Devon shot him a confused glance. Hasting and Nash looked troubled. Moreno scowled through his beard. The veteran cops and deputies knew. No one needed to say it aloud.

Eli Pope would have a good reason for wanting Easton dead. Eight years ago, Easton had fingered Eli Pope as the suspect in his daughter's homicide, then smeared Eli's name in an infamous television interview with CBS Evening News.

In part due to Easton's public accusations, the investigation had quickly narrowed the suspect pool to one. Eli wouldn't forget something like that. He was a man who nursed his grievances. He did not forgive.

And now he was free.

"Maybe," Hasting allowed.

"The Broken Heart Killer is still in prison," Moreno said. "Maybe he'll get shivved on the toilet. A man can dream."

"They released him," Jackson said. The warden had alerted the sheriff in case Eli headed home. Jackson knew he would. Where else would he go?

Moreno let out a colorful curse. "What time?"

"We need to find out."

"We'll add him to the list," Hasting said.

No one wanted to think about Eli Pope back in the world, prowling the streets of their community, hunting for beautiful young women to steal away.

Or seeking vengeance against the town who'd turned on him.

Something dark and ugly slithered behind Jackson's breastbone. His breath quickened as a memory flashed through his mind. He shoved it down deep. This grisly homicide couldn't be related to that. The sin he'd committed all those years ago was dead and buried.

Except that it wasn't. It had just resurrected itself in the form of Eli Pope.

Across the clearing, an owl hooted. Jackson swept the flashlight back and forth. The light glinted off metal, piercing dark corners.

There were a hundred places to hide. A thousand.

Something snagged his eye. A tiny flash of color.

Skirting the crime scene, he approached the object and squatted. Approximately five yards southwest of the victim sat a crushed green

Ford Taurus. Its front windshield was busted out, the metal frame twisted and smashed.

A square of fabric was caught on a tooth of glass. He placed an evidence tag on the ground beside the Taurus and gestured for one of the deputies to take pictures. He retrieved a small manilla envelope and carefully tweezed the fragment of cotton from the jagged windshield frame.

"What did you find, boss?" Devon asked.

"This is a small enough space for a thirteen-year-old girl, if she were trying to hide. Maybe she heard the shouting. Or she knew the perp was trouble as soon as he appeared. Or Amos did, and he told her to hide. She went through the window, crouched down in the footwell. Easy enough for your shirt to snag right here while you were scrambling inside."

"That's a big jump to make," Hasting said. "I don't see it."

"This is from Shiloh's shirt."

"How do you know that?" Moreno asked.

Jackson examined the small square of fabric. It was two inches by an inch and a half, dark gray with a yellow ironed-on edge of a partial letter.

It wasn't much to go on, but it was enough.

He'd seen her wear it. He visualized the faded image of Yoda, the yellow print: *Do or Do Not. There is No Try.*

Moreno scoffed. "Even if it is hers, that fabric could've been there for weeks."

"I don't think so," Jackson said. "It rained this morning. The ground is still damp, which is why we've got good footprints to cast. This shirt is fresh. It smells like Downy fabric softener. Lavender."

"How the hell can you smell that, man?" Moreno asked, disbelieving.

He'd always had a keen sense of smell. Lily had never worn perfume, but she'd used the same fabric softener her entire life.

Easton was a habitual man. If Downy had worked for him and for his daughters, it would work for his grandkids.

Shiloh smelled like her mother.

"I'm sure the judge will love that," Moreno scoffed. "How did you know it was the killer? The scent was zestfully clean, your honor."

Devon nibbled on her thumbnail. "She might have seen it. The homicide."

Jackson suspected the same thing. "She's a material witness. So is her brother, at a minimum. We need to find them both. Sooner rather than later."

No one said anything for a moment. They studied the crime scene, listened to the night insects churring, watched the bugs swarming in the search lights. The night grew colder.

The crime scene techs would scrape the salvage yard and surrounding area with a fine-tooth comb. If there was something else out here, they would find it.

"Tomorrow, we'll gather a team to search the woods. Interview friends and family. Canvas the neighbors. We need to put out a BOLO for Shiloh and Cody."

The group nodded, their faces somber.

"And Eli Pope is our top priority."

"Good luck," Moreno muttered. "We're not doing jack squat with the power down across the UP. It's not just us. Everyone's out across the country. All because of these damn lights."

"It'll be back up tomorrow," Devon said too brightly. "Everything back to normal."

Jackson felt as far from normal as if normal no longer existed. Everything was tilted on its axis, time spinning, cause and effect turned on its side.

He was a man of order, of rules, of law. He liked things to make sense. Easton dead after all this time didn't make sense. Moreno was right. That blood-red sky didn't make sense.

It was after two a.m. by the time Jackson and Devon exited the salvage yard and made their way up the hill toward the parking lot.

The trees threw murky shadows across the oil-black grass. The aurora blotted out the stars.

"Who do we notify?" Devon asked. "The next of kin."

Jackson stilled. "There's only one person. Easton's wife died twenty-five years ago. No living parents. No aunts or uncles. No one except Lena."

A flood of memories struck him. Lena had been the older, responsible sister to Lily's reckless charm. Lena's blue eyes were serious, while Lily's brown ones had danced with mischief. Lena's hair rippled in long chestnut waves where Lily's hair had been dark and curly. They had both been beautiful.

"Lena is Easton's other daughter." He paused. "She lives in Tampa. They were estranged."

"She'll come back when she hears her father is dead."

"Things went badly the last time they saw each other." He didn't mention the trial. "She hasn't been back. Not in eight years."

"What about the kids? They'd be her niece and nephew, right?"

Jackson thought about the last time they'd spoken. Each year, he called Lena on November twenty-fifth, the anniversary of her sister's death.

They didn't share much anymore, but they would always share that. They were the two people who'd loved Lily Easton the most in the world.

Time seemed to thin, the past and present converging. He recalled how protective Lena had been when it came to Lily. How fiercely she'd defended her family and friends, who jumped in feet first to help, no matter what was needed.

That was the Lena he remembered.

"Poor kids," Devon said. "Without her, they'll go into the system."

He pulled out his phone. No service. And it was late. He'd call her tomorrow.

"She'll come," Jackson said. "She's the only family they have left. Lena will come."

8

LENA EASTON

DAY TWO

"We have a missing person."

Those were the words that drove Lena Easton, that motivated her to get out of bed before dawn every morning, to improve with each passing day.

Sweat beaded Lena's forehead and trickled down her shoulder blades. Tampa was in the middle of a heat wave. It was ninety degrees at nine a.m. She felt every sweltering degree.

Her giant Newfoundland dog sat obediently beside her, panting. "Good dog," she murmured and patted his giant furry head. "Good boy, Bear."

The Newfie was over one hundred and fifty pounds of thick chocolate-brown fur; he was pure loyalty, adoration, and mischievous affection. Bear was an intelligent, sensitive dog. He liked to work and loved a challenge.

Lena worked as a paramedic three days a week, but her volunteer work with the Canine Search and Rescue Association was her passion, her purpose. Certified in urban and wilderness rescue, Bear was her partner, both in SAR work and in life.

Lena waved at the other SAR handlers and their dogs. Base was a portable tent set up in the vacant lot next to a stucco house with Spanish tiles. Several law enforcement officials stood around, studying maps and giving orders on radios.

Once everyone had arrived, the search coordinator briefed the unit. "The subject is Stanley Mills, aged eighty-two. He suffers from advanced Alzheimer's with dementia. He lives with his son in the Arbor Green neighborhood, which abuts the Lower Hillsborough Wilderness Preserve."

Lena's stomach tightened. The state park contained five hundred acres of woods, interspersed with rivers, streams, and mangrove-covered swampy wetlands. A lot of area to get lost in. And with the heat wave...

The sun could be deadly in more ways than one.

"The son found him missing at approximately seven-thirty a.m. He checked with the neighbors and drove nearby neighborhoods before contacting law enforcement. Stanley was last seen wearing blue Crocs, a white T-shirt, and red cotton Snoopy pajama bottoms. His favorite Buccaneers cap is missing, so he likely took it with him." The coordinator clapped her hands. "Let's go find Stanley."

Lena and Bear were assigned to quadrant three, half of which was marshland and swamp. She hoped their subject hadn't wandered into the swamp. She hated snakes and alligators, but she'd go anywhere to bring the missing home.

The other handlers loaded their packs while a volunteer handed out small paper bags. Each bag contained an item of clothing worn recently by the subject. The dogs scented the items and identified their target.

"Find Stanley," Lena said to Bear. "Go find Stanley. Good boy!"

And then they were off. Lena and Bear were on the hunt, working their sector. They worked in a "Z" pattern, scenting the air until they caught the one scent they sought.

Every human being had his or her own scent. The skin gave off dead skin cells called rafts. Every person shed about forty thousand per minute.

Bear's tail stiffened, his hackles going up as he caught the scent. He barked and raced into the trees, heading toward the park.

"Good boy!" Lena scrambled after him. As they worked their way deeper into the park, Lena studied the trees, the sky, the paths the way Stanley might have seen them.

Stanley could have taken a detour, backtracked on himself, or looped away from the intended destination at any point.

Inside the park, the paths were marked by different colored diamonds on the trunks of various trees, but they were easy to miss if someone became disoriented. Or forgot what they meant.

Ahead of her, Bear sniffed the air. His tail went up, his hackles rising, and he bounded ahead and disappeared between some bushes. He'd alerted on something.

Lena followed him, struggling through the swampy undergrowth, surrounded by mangroves. They were nearing the water.

Bear stopped, turning in tight circles, tail wagging.

She saw the disturbed ground first. A patch of leaves scraped into piles along with several damp imprints. She imagined the elderly man catching a foot on a root, tumbling forward and landing on the heels of his hands and knees.

Not three feet away, a few strands of red cotton were snagged on the thorns of a briar bush.

"Good boy, Bear. Good boy." Removing a roll of blue tape from her pocket, she marked the area, then checked her compass, figured her bearings, then called it in. "Base, this is Lena. I'm a hundred yards from my east boundary, just short of the swamp. I found some red threads on a briar, possibly from the Snoopy pajama pants. It looks like he fell here but got back up again. He's headed for the swamp."

She and Bear kept going. Five minutes later, her radio crackled. "Base, this is Charlie. We just found one of his crocs. Caked with mud. Lena, Champ is alerting in your direction."

Before she could say a word, Bear barked and bounded ahead. Lena hurried to catch up.

Her boots sank into muck as she entered the marsh. Algae slicked the surface of stagnant black water. Mosquitos swarmed in dense clouds. The sweltering heat pressed down on her. Humidity curled her hair at the base of her neck.

She paused to drink bottled water from her backpack and inhaled a protein bar to keep her blood sugar levels up. She kept a collapsible water bowl for Bear and called him back to drink as well.

Ten minutes later, Bear paused and looked over his shoulder. His fluffy tail drooped. He whined. It was an alert—but not the one either of them wanted.

Lena's stomach dropped. She let out the breath she'd been holding.

Bear was trained to alert to both the living and the dead. His alert was different for each find. Trained dogs could identify the scent of death not just on corpses, but also on blood splatter, bone, and even cremated remains.

When a person died, the scent was the same, but it had the scent of decay mixed in. The smell was unique to humans and incredibly complex—a person released 478 different chemical compounds as their body decomposed.

With a heavy heart, Lena approached the spot where Bear waited, whining pitifully. Stanley Mills lay on his side in six inches of swamp. Black mud clotted his wispy white hair. Muck splattered his soaked pajama pants. In one gnarled fist, he clutched the red Buccaneers cap.

Shucking her pack, Lena knelt beside him, heedless of the water drenching her pantlegs or the six-foot alligator sunning himself on the opposite bank. "Stanley, can you hear me?"

The elderly man didn't respond. Even knowing what she would find, she still went through the motions of checking for vital signs. There was no pulse. His skin was paper white, his lips cracked. He had become severely dehydrated and had likely suffered heat stroke.

Devastated, Lena rocked back on her heels, swallowed hard, closed her eyes. Sorrow washed over her in waves, mourning for an elderly man she didn't know and had never met.

This was someone's father. A grandfather. Someone who was loved and would be sorely missed. Every loss felt like she had personally failed. She hated it.

Lena called it in on the radio, her words like stones in her throat. Then she logged in the time, date, and details in the notes on her phone. Her signal had been crappy since last night, but she didn't need cell service to take notes.

Her backpack felt like it weighed a million pounds. She signaled for Bear to return to her side, which he did immediately, head down. She gave him more water from the collapsible bowl as she checked her insulin pump.

The tiny screen read 140 mg/dl. Her numbers were good, though she felt sick to her stomach. They'd been searching for less than an hour. It had felt like an eternity.

"You did so good, boy. You did a good job. Not your fault we didn't get here in time."

Crouching, hardly noticing the water sloshing over the rims of her hiking boots, Lena buried her hands in the thick fur of his neck.

Bear snuffed mournfully and licked her face.

She tilted her forehead. Her dog lowered his snout. Their heads touched. It was one of Bear's favorite poses. Hers, too. "You did it. Good job. Thank you."

The rest of the morning was a blur. Waiting for the officers to reach her location, then the flurry of activity as they loaded the body on a stretcher and hiked back to the empty house, the grieving son.

On her return to base, she endured the excruciating debrief. It was late afternoon before they dismissed her.

On the way to her SUV, her phone vibrated in the back pocket of her jeans. She yanked out her phone, relieved. Finally, service was back. Then she noticed the identity of the caller.

She halted on the sidewalk in midstride. Bear sensed the tension and returned to her side, his tail thumping her shins. He looked up at her, panting with that goofy grin.

"It's him," she said aloud. Before she could think better of it, she answered. "Jackson."

"He's getting out."

"What?"

"It's true."

"What happened?"

"A technicality. The appeals court decided the initial search of his vehicle was illegal. They threw everything out. The blood. The thumbprint. Fruit of the poisoned tree."

She closed her eyes.

"Without the beer bottle, the DA doesn't have enough evidence to retry the case. He's getting out."

She breathed in, breathed out. Focused on her pulse, her breathing. Her sister had been dead for eight years. The man who'd been convicted of murdering her was about to be set free.

He was also the only man she'd ever truly loved.

"I thought you should know, Lena."

"When?"

"Last night. I'm sorry I couldn't get through. Service was down up here. I wanted to tell you before it was all over the news."

She'd managed to shut out the past as best she could. For years, she'd ignored the annual "anniversary" news articles, the flurry of phone calls from intrusive journalists after a salacious tidbit, jackals feeding off her pain.

"Thank you for telling me."

"Lena. There's more."

She stiffened at the strain in his voice. "What?"

"Lena. It's your father. I'm sorry to have to tell you this, but he's dead."

9

LENA EASTON

DAY TWO

Lena went still. Her body turned to stone, her legs, her arms, her chest.

Sensing her distress, Bear nuzzled her free hand. His doggy breath was hot on her skin as he licked her fingers. She patted his muzzle, ran her hands over his face, his floppy ears, the top of his giant head.

Her father. The man she both hated and loved. She hated him more. She forced the words out, calm and even, like she didn't care. Like if she pretended enough, it might be true. "What happened?"

"He..." Jackson's voice trailed off.

"Just tell me."

"Lena, he was murdered."

Lena waited for the expected wave of grief, but it didn't come. Numbness sprouted in her chest and spread slowly outward. Her veins filled with lead.

Her father had been many things, but he'd made sure she could change a tire, shoot a gun, and start a fire. Much as she resented him, she'd never resented that.

She squared her shoulders. "Tell me everything."

"The perpetrator bashed in his head with a tire iron. Last night.

Like I said, I've been trying to get ahold of you for the last twelve hours, but—"

"The solar storm."

"Yeah, the solar storm."

As if on cue, the line went dead. She called him twice before the line reconnected. Whatever was happening with these storms, she didn't like it. It made her feel unsettled.

"Are you okay?" Jackson asked. Typical Jackson, always worried about other people's feelings. "Can you hear me?"

"I'm fine." Though she wasn't, far from it. "I'll be fine."

"Can you come home?"

"That place isn't home. Not anymore."

"There will always be a place for you here, Lena. No matter what. The investigation—"

"Do you know who did it?"

"We have some leads. I promise, Lena, you'll be the first to know."

She glanced across the street at the bank, sunlight glancing off the expansive glass windows, the patrons hurrying in and out, several fanning themselves with newspapers.

There were more guests in line than usual. The banks had been shut down yesterday due to the power outages, but they appeared open. Several cars waited at the ATM.

She made a mental note to visit an ATM and take out more cash from her dwindling bank account. She always kept five hundred in twenties on hand for emergencies, but it didn't feel like enough, especially today.

"Where is Shiloh? What about Cody?"

"That's what I wanted to talk to you about."

The first frisson of fear scythed through her. "Where are they? Tell me they're okay."

"They're both missing."

With her free hand, she rubbed her sweaty temple. Bear leaned against her legs, whining plaintively. He sensed something was wrong. "What does that mean?"

"There's evidence they might have been at the scene when it happened. We're looking for them, I promise. But Lena, there's no one left to take care of them. Do you understand what I'm saying?"

Her breath came faster and faster, like she was running uphill, her lungs on fire. She couldn't feel her fingers gripping the phone.

She imagined her niece the last time she'd seen her, at five years old. That dark fringe of hair and huge black eyes. And Cody, bright-eyed but somber, an old soul trapped in a kid's body.

How fiercely she'd loved them.

Then she'd walked away.

It had felt like walking away from her own beating heart.

"Lena—" A lifetime of emotions and memories and past entwined histories in that name, the heaviness with which he spoke the syllables. In her mind's eye, she saw Jackson at eight, at twelve, at fifteen, at twenty-five.

She'd known him her entire life. It was more than knowing. They'd shared a friendship deeper than she'd ever known, a friendship that had survived tragedy, scandal, and heartbreak.

Even sixteen hundred miles apart, she could feel him out there.

"She needs you," Jackson said.

"I—I can't."

"She's thirteen years old," Jackson said, his voice soft as another round of static infiltrated their conversation. It would have been easy to pretend she hadn't heard. But she had.

"I'm not her mother."

"I didn't say that. I said you. Shiloh and Cody need you, Lena."

Lena didn't speak. She couldn't.

"You need to come back. You need to come home—"

A burst of static. Then silence.

"Jackson?"

Nothing.

She tried calling him again. No service. With shaking fingers, she slid the phone back in her pocket. A tangle of emotions churned inside her.

She'd sworn never to step foot in the UP again.

All this time, she'd told herself they didn't need her. That her presence would cause tension and drama. Her father didn't want her there. Her father had disowned her. Hell, the whole town had.

Everyone was better off without her. Those poor grieving children would forget her. Wasn't that the best thing? To forget in a way that she never could?

That's what she'd told herself every day for the last eight years.

Jackson Cross was the good one. The best of them. If he promised to find her sister's children, he would do everything in his power to do so.

It might not be good enough, a voice whispered in the back of her mind.

Lena was the searcher. The finder of the lost. She was the one who'd dedicated her life to rescuing the missing. And she was damn good at it.

Bear pushed his snout into her thigh. "You trying to tell me something?"

The dog looked up at her, tail wagging eagerly. He was ready for anything Lena had ever asked of him. He'd be ready for this, too. It was Lena who felt like the ground had been ripped out from beneath her.

She'd spent the last eight years running.

What if she'd been wrong?

10

JACKSON CROSS

DAY TWO

By noon, Jackson had gotten his third cup of coffee from Gallery Coffee Company and picked up a mocha latte for Devon, who was a sugar junkie twenty-four-seven.

He'd spent all morning knocking on the doors of the victim's neighbors before heading into the sheriff's office in Munising for the first debrief on the case.

Several officers and deputies were in the briefing room by the time Jackson arrived, including Devon, Hasting, Nash, Moreno, and two others: Jim Hart, a retired Marine and longtime cop from the Munising Police Department, and Alexis Chilton, their resident tech genius.

"About time you showed up," Moreno said. "Getting your beauty sleep?"

"He obviously didn't get enough," Devon deadpanned.

Moreno and Nash snickered.

"It's all fun and games until someone gets hurt." Jackson handed Devon her latte and started the debrief. "After a fruitless four hours of banging on doors and interviewing folks who didn't hear anything or didn't want to, I've only got this. We have a dog-walker, Dorothy McCallister, who says she walked by the victim's driveway around 4:45

p.m. She didn't see anything. No vehicles passed her during her approximately thirty-minute walk with her Cocker Spaniel, Tigger."

"That's smack in the middle of our time of death window," Hasting said.

Moreno leaned back in his chair and crossed his arms. "Dorothy's what, in her eighties now? How reliable is she? How's her hearing? Her eyesight?"

"She lives independently. The woman still shovels her own front porch," Jackson said. As Easton's closest neighbor, Mrs. McCallister had also been interviewed in the case eight years ago. Her reliability had been questioned then, too. "She's fine."

Moreno raised his hands in surrender. "Okay, okay. Didn't know you had such a thing for her, Cross." He winked. "I'll remember that in the future."

"What else do we have?" Hart asked.

"We do have the security footage," Devon said. "Easton had three cameras. One on the house, one on the parking lot and driveway, and one covering the interior of the junkyard. The junkyard camera was inoperable. I couldn't tell whether the solar flare had something to do with it or if it malfunctioned weeks or months ago. I ran the working footage this morning. It's only three days' worth, then it records over itself."

"And?" Hart asked.

"Nothing jumped out at me regarding the house footage. No visitors. Amos, Shiloh, and Cody appear, but seldom together."

She pushed an opened file across the table. "Here's the list of every vehicle that visited the Easton property over the seventy-two hours prior to the homicide. Five vehicles. Three, I could make out license plate numbers; for two, I could not. We do have the vehicle makes and models, however. I ran the plates. Any of these names stand out to you?"

Jackson read the list aloud. Every name was familiar. Gideon Crawford had been born and raised here. He had been an old boyfriend of

Lily's and now worked as a dentist. Dana Lutz ran snowmobiling tours in the winter, and Scott Smith owned the local gas station. None had recent run-ins with the law.

"Nothing sticks out." Jackson turned to Alexis. "Can you take these? Run the usual checks. See if anyone noticed anything suspicious."

Alexis nodded as she chewed on her pen. In her late twenties, her strawberry-blonde hair was shaved on the sides, the rest plopped on top of her head in a messy bun. She wore thick, oversized black-frame glasses. "Let's hope the servers are functional."

Devon clicked a few buttons on her laptop and then flipped it to face the rest of the room. The grainy footage appeared, the world rendered in indistinct black and white. "At approximately 6:30 p.m. last night, a white Jeep Wrangler pulls up. Walter Boone gets out, heads up to the house at 6:33 p.m., waits three minutes like he expects someone to be home, then turns and walks down the hill to the salvage yard."

The officers watched the grainy figure as they followed Devon's verbal description. His body language appeared normal, his shoulders slightly hunched. No warning bells went off. Just a guy in slacks and a sweater vest who needed a new fender.

They watched the empty parking lot. A minute or so later, Boone came back into view, this time moving much faster, his stride jerky and uneven, a phone pressed to his cheek.

He went straight to his car, fumbled to open it, then clambered inside and sat for about sixty seconds, still holding his phone.

"Why's he just sitting there?" Hasting asked.

"He calls 911 here. It's grainy, but it checks out. He spoke with Tammy Dale at 6:39 p.m."

Tammy was their dispatch operator, emergency operator, and administrative assistant. A no-nonsense mother of four in her late fifties with fifteen grandchildren, she kept the department running like a well-oiled machine.

They watched as Boone tossed his phone on the passenger seat.

The grainy Jeep backed up, did a U-turn, and punched the gas, roaring down the long driveway and out of sight of the camera's view.

Devon switched off the footage and closed her laptop. "Seventy-six seconds. That's how long he's in the junkyard. Long enough to walk in past all those cars to the center, see the vic, and walk straight back out. Who is this guy? Anybody know him?"

"Of course," Hasting said. "He volunteer coaches the LEGO robotics club at the high school. He coached my kid and got him a partial scholarship to MTU." He meant Michigan Technical University in Houghton.

"We interviewed him this morning," Moreno said. "His story matches with the footage. No inconsistencies."

"Did he touch the victim?" Jackson asked.

"He says no."

Jackson pointed to one of the crime scene photos spread out across the table. "You can see here and here that the blood spatter is smeared on the victim's shirt."

"Like someone was checking for a heartbeat," Hasting said.

"Possibly. But someone definitely touched him after the assault, while the blood was still wet."

Jackson and Devon exchanged a glance. It could have been the perpetrator or one of the kids. Or, the perpetrator *was* one of the kids. That was a thought he did not want to consider.

"Have the crime technicians come back with anything?" Hasting asked.

"They're still processing the scene." Jackson rubbed his temples. The caffeine hadn't been enough to stave off a headache. "We have a blood sample in a footprint, but DNA hasn't come back yet."

"Next suspect," Alexis deadpanned.

"Autopsy?" Hasting asked.

"Scheduled for tomorrow." Jackson turned to Alexis. "Where are we on financials?"

Alexis dropped her chewed pen to the table and pushed up her glasses. "I checked with the county clerk's office. Easton owed forty-nine thousand dollars in back taxes at the beginning of the year. The county was threatening to foreclose on him. He was making interest-only payments, but he was behind on those, too. Then suddenly, on April third of this year, he paid the debt in full."

Hasting clicked his tongue. "He was barely making ends meet with the junkyard business. Where the hell did he come up with that kind of money?"

"That's a good question," Jackson said. "How about his financial records?"

"We're working on the search warrant," Moreno said.

"The banks are a mess right now," Alexis said. "They're limiting how much people can withdraw of their own money. This geomagnetic storm really messed with their servers."

"My GPS was being screwy this morning," Devon said. "It said the Two Eggs and Ham Café was located on Grand Island."

"It should be," Moreno quipped. "Their omelets suck."

"It's the low earth orbit satellites, too," Alexis said. "Banking systems rely on GPS to synchronize financial transactions. If the satellites are fritzy—" She shrugged. "Bye secret Cayman account."

"You're full of it, Chilton," Moreno said.

She stared at him and wriggled her eyebrows. "Am I?"

"Okay, stay focused, everyone. Keep working on the financials," Jackson said. "If Easton is hiding a deep dark secret, that's it. Follow the money."

Alexis rolled her eyes. "Yeah, hello. That's what I'm doing."

Hasting stood and stretched. "How long is this sun thing going to be a problem?"

Moreno stared up at the buzzing fluorescent lights. "I heard on talk radio this morning that they're predicting even more of these things. Another one tomorrow. Maybe I should go to the bank and withdraw my millions before it's too late."

"Maybe you should," Alexis said. "I'd bet it's more like your last twenty bucks, though."

Moreno grinned. "Never have an ex-wife. Or three. They'll steal every hard-earned penny."

"Hard-earned? That's quite the exaggeration," Alexis shot back.

Jackson had several months of supplies socked away for a rainy day. Up here, it was prudent to be prepared for emergencies. Hell, it was prudent everywhere.

Still, he made a mental note to check the supplies in the basement. And maybe stock up a bit more. It wasn't something he talked about much; Moreno would never let it go.

"Janet Holder said the Bear Trap Inn is completely booked," Hasting said. "I heard Pictured Rocks Resorts is tapped out, and a bunch of the campgrounds, too. All the aurora-chasers want to see the best show. It's good for business."

Alexis went back to chewing the tip of her pen. "As long as all those tourists use cash rather than credit cards. They're gonna be in for a rude awakening when their plastic rectangles don't do crap."

"Good riddance." Moreno rolled his eyes. "Those aurora-chasers can kiss my fine Portuguese behind."

They finished up with a few details and then Jackson and Devon were on their feet, headed out again. Jackson wanted to visit the kids' school. Devon wanted to work the crime scene again, walk through it in daylight.

They had secured the search warrant for the property, which was effective as long as law enforcement remained at the scene. Nash had drawn the short straw and stayed the night to maintain scene security and ensure the chain of custody remained intact.

Before they could escape the building, the sheriff stomped out of his office, the glass panel shuddering in its frame as he slammed the door behind him.

Brad Underwood was a stern, imposing black man in his early

fifties with ramrod posture. Everything about him, from his clean-shaven jaw to his bald head and hard eyes screamed lifelong cop.

"How often we get a homicide around here?" Sheriff Underwood asked in a loud voice.

Across the foyer, Tammy Dale glanced at them from behind her desk, eyebrows raised. The sheriff shot her a look; she quickly bent her head and shuffled some papers.

"Not often, Sheriff," Jackson said evenly.

"Not often," Sheriff Underwood said in a mocking tone. "The last homicide caused quite the debacle."

"I know that."

"So, you're going to get this one wrapped up right quick, eh?"

"I'll do my best."

The sheriff shook his head, perpetually disappointed in Jackson. Mainly because Jackson wasn't his father, Horatio Cross, who'd served as sheriff for eighteen years before retiring ten years ago. Underwood had been the undersheriff for fifteen of those eighteen years.

He and Horatio had been drinking buddies for decades, and still were.

Jackson wasn't interested in drinking buddies. He didn't boast. He tried to keep his head down, get the job done right, and let his reputation do the talking. It didn't always work.

Men like his father and Sheriff Underwood were interested in polling numbers, percentages, glowing news coverage and cases closed. Open and shut. Everything was a popularity contest to Sheriff Underwood. If he wasn't winning, heads would roll.

He wasn't haunted by bloody crime scenes. He didn't spend sleepless nights consumed by guilt for what he had or hadn't done. He didn't seem to care about resolution for the victims, justice for the dead.

In some ways, Jackson envied him.

Sheriff Underwood tapped his foot impatiently. "Why haven't you brought in Cody Easton as a suspect?"

"We're working on bringing him in. And it's too early to determine whether he is a suspect or a witness, or if he was there at all. We're waiting on the DNA match."

The sheriff grunted dismissively. "And the girl?"

"A possible witness. We're working on finding her, too."

"What other suspects do you have?"

"We canvassed the neighborhood. You know how it goes. No one heard anything. No one wants to talk."

"You're in charge of this case, son. Don't make me regret it."

Jackson hated the man's sarcastic use of *son*. It fell just short of condescension. Sheriff Underwood never outright crossed the line into harassment, but he enjoyed coming close.

Eight years ago, Jackson had suffered the limelight for breaking the Broken Heart Killer case. He hadn't wanted it. Underwood had—badly. Maybe that's why the man disliked him so much. Or maybe there were other, grimmer reasons.

"I also have the Ruby Carpenter case—"

"Give it to someone else. Give it to Hasting or Nash. Better yet, close it. That girl is a chronic runaway. Her mother is grasping at straws and wasting this office's time, resources, and taxpayer dollars."

Jackson didn't say anything.

Sheriff Underwood leaned in close. "You hearing me, Cross?"

"I promised her mother I'd look into it."

"And now your good deed for the year is done. You have an actual job—to catch a killer so we can all sleep at night. You understand?"

"I understand." Jackson kept his gaze steady on the sheriff's, refusing to drop his gaze or flinch. He was used to intimidation tactics; he'd grown up with them.

Bradley Underwood enjoyed keeping his officers under his thumb. He was a man for whom power and authority mattered. He was a big fish in a small pond—until the state police or the FBI got involved, and then he wouldn't be.

He wanted this case locked up, and fast.

So did Jackson, but for different reasons. He wanted Shiloh and Cody protected and safe. He wanted justice—true justice—to be served.

Sheriff Underwood took a step closer and lowered his voice. He smelled of the cigarettes he'd been trying to quit for ten years. "Cross, I need to know we're on the same page in this. You and I don't want a repeat of eight years ago. With Eli Pope freed, the citizens are already up in arms. I just had Tim Brooks in my office, had to talk him out of an organized lynching on the front lawn of the Munising precinct."

He waved a hand. "Pope gets out on some asinine technicality, then we have a homicide the same day. A relative of the original victim, no less. You see where I'm going with this. How long you think before folks get crazy enough to take things into their own hands?"

"I checked with the prison this morning," Jackson said. "Eli was released several hours after Easton was killed, according to the ME."

The sheriff cursed. "They'll think he did it anyway. Damn it all to hell. And then this craziness with the sky turning red? You'd think it was a plague of biblical proportions, the way some folks are carrying on. I don't need that madness leaking into this case. I don't need that headache. Things are bad enough without people believing the world's about to end."

"Who's worried the world is going to end?"

The chief stared at him like he'd grown two heads. "Don't you see the crazy conspiracy posts on Facebook? Instagram? TikTok?"

Jackson shrugged. He didn't do social media. The outdoors was his religion; church, his solace. Fly fishing, his drug of choice. "It's not like that here."

"We got more common sense in our left nutsacks than most of those trolls south of the bridge. Doesn't mean it won't start infecting folks." The sheriff scowled. "You should watch some of those videos."

As if on cue, the fluorescent lights flickered overhead. Everyone groaned. A second later, they came back on as the generator rumbled to life. The sheriff let out a furious expletive.

"Internet's down," Tammy said from behind the counter. "This is becoming a habit."

The sheriff slapped a pile of intake forms off the counter. They fluttered to the tile floor behind him as he stalked back to his office. "For Pete's sake. Call me when the world is back to normal!"

A shiver of foreboding sparked up Jackson's spine.

"What if that's never?" Moreno asked, grinning.

11

LENA EASTON

DAY TWO

"Did you see the lights last night?" the nurse asked, smiling as she bent to rub Bear's floppy ears.

"Hard to miss," Lena said.

Bear gave a grumbly moan of pleasure, tilting his head so the nurse could hit his favorite spots. The nurses loved on him every time Lena and Bear stepped through the hospital doors. Bear adored it.

Every other weekend, Lena and Bear volunteered at the pediatric ward in Tampa General Hospital, visiting the patients and bringing a little joy where they could.

Today wasn't their usual day, but after the death of Stanley Mills, Bear had needed a pick-me-up. And Lena had needed a few moments to think, to consider her options, to make a decision that would alter the trajectory of her life.

Tampa General Hospital smelled like antiseptic and bleach. The lights were on, computers working, nurses in scrubs and doctors in white lab coats striding here and there, holding tablets or pushing young patients in wheelchairs.

Everything appeared normal.

"Oh look, they're talking about the northern lights again," one of the nurses said.

The nurse petting Bear lifted her head to watch the television affixed to the far wall in the visitor's area. Lena turned her attention to the screen, where the lights glowed above New York City's Times Square. A montage showed the aurora dancing above the Seine, flickering above the Roman Colosseum, the entire sky in flames over London and Amsterdam.

"It's magical," the nurse said.

Lena stepped closer to the TV. A few people in the waiting room were watching. Most were glued to their phones, playing games or scrolling social media.

The first newscaster was in his early forties, with a face that oozed fake sincerity. He tapped his earpiece and raised his brows, his smooth forehead wrinkle-free. "We're getting reports that another solar storm is on its way and should hit tomorrow in the late afternoon, although we probably won't see the northern lights until it gets dark."

"And what does that mean, Chase?" the second newscaster addressed her co-host, her voice chipper as she offered a conspiratorial grin to the camera.

"We can expect another fantastic light show. Get your cameras out for this one, folks. Scientists and astronomers from NASA's Solar Terrestrial Relations Observatory and the Space Weather Prediction Center are forecasting a spectacular night. I didn't even know space weather was a thing."

Samantha laughed too loudly. "Guess I'll be checking their website next time I go to the beach, Chase."

Chase's fake smile widened. "Coming up next, we have a special guest. A scientist is here to shed some light on the science behind these gorgeous auroras."

They introduced Isaac Richardson, a black gentleman in his mid-fifties, with distinguished gray hair and a tired smile. "Thank you for having me. I run the solar observatory at the University of Florida.

Think of SOHO, the Solar and Heliospheric Observatory satellite that observes the sun from space. I study the structure and dynamics of the sun's interior, mainly the causes and propagation of coronal mass ejections."

"So, this is right up your alley, Dr. Richardson," Samantha said brightly. "What's the difference between a solar flare, a coronal mass ejection, and these geomagnetic storms?"

Dr. Richardson loosened his tie. He looked nervous. "A solar flare is a tremendous explosion on the sun, which happens when energy stored in twisted magnetic fields around sunspots are abruptly released. The magnetic field lines become so warped and stretched that they snap under intense tension, much like a rubber band. The plasma explodes into space as a coronal mass ejection, or CME."

"Oh, that sounds spectacular," Samantha cooed. "Like a disaster movie."

"CMEs only affect the Earth if the eruption occurs in our direction. The superheated plasma increases electric currents and causes disturbances in the Earth's magnetosphere. When this happens, it's referred to as a geomagnetic storm."

"We've had geomagnetic storms before," Samantha said. "To be honest, I never even noticed. What makes the ones we're experiencing now special?"

"There are three major categories of solar flares. C-class and M-class flares cause little to no damage. X-class flares are the most severe, and trigger the CMEs."

"And the CMEs then trigger the geomagnetic storms," Chase said.

"Correct. The most widely used method to categorize geomagnetic storms is the NOAA's G-scale. G0 is considered harmless, while a G5 is considered extreme."

Chase raised his eyebrows. His forehead didn't move. "Are the storms we're experiencing G5 level?"

"They're much stronger. The one we experienced yesterday was a

G10, so ten times as powerful as a G1 storm. The ones heading toward us are significantly more powerful."

Lena shivered. A low buzzing filled her ears, a sense of unease slithering through her. She'd been so focused on her job that she hadn't realized the seriousness of what was happening.

Sensing Lena's anxiety, Bear climbed to his feet and pressed against the front of Lena's legs, offering comfort. His tail wagged. Lena scratched behind his ears.

The scientist continued. "For the last ten years, I've been developing predictive algorithms. In laymen's terms, I study the sun's radioactive activity and try to predict the next geomagnetic storm—when it will hit, where it will go. That sort of thing."

"Does it work?" Chase asked.

"Yes."

"And what is it predicting?"

Dr. Richardson cleared his throat. He was sweating. "The sun is like a boiling cauldron spilling over. We're looking at a half-dozen solar flares with multiple powerful geomagnetic storms hitting us in rapid succession. In 1859, a huge CME hit Earth. Known as the Carrington Event, the solar storms disrupted telegraph wires, shocked telegraph operators, and caused multiple fires."

Chase winked. "Good thing we're not using telegrams anymore."

Dr. Richardson kept going like he hadn't heard him. "In 2012, another CME as powerful as the Carrington Event narrowly avoided Earth. Studies determined that it was a superstorm, a double-CME. This happens when two CMEs are unleashed, separated by only a few minutes, which makes it significantly more powerful than a regular CME."

Dr. Richardson swallowed. "The algorithm is predicting a triple-CME, each of X50 strength or more. It will be like nothing we've seen before."

Samantha and Chase stared at the scientist, startled.

"What does that mean?" Samantha asked.

Dr. Richardson gazed into the camera with glazed eyes. "Our electric grid won't be able to withstand the barrage. The storms will fry transformers across the Northern hemisphere. The impact will be devastating. Banking systems will crash. The stock market will be erased in a day. Hundreds of millions of people will be without power or internet access or cell communication across several continents. Not to mention GPS and satellite systems disruptions."

"Like, for a few hours?" Samantha ventured, her eyes wide.

"It would take years to repair. Possibly, decades." He said it matter of fact, but there was a tremor in his voice.

Chase let out a chuckle. "That's a little dire, isn't it, Dr. Richardson?"

Lena stared at the TV in growing horror. Of course, he could be delusional. But then, so could the newscasters with their plastic smiles. Her heart rate quickened. Her mouth went dry.

Samantha shuffled several papers on her desk. She glanced down, frowned, then offered the camera an uneasy smile. "The Department of Homeland Security released a statement that the U.S. power grid is hardened against these electrical currents, and any disruptions will be temporary."

"With all due respect, a CME of this strength hasn't hit Earth in modern times. We really can't say that our grid is hardened against a force of this magnitude. I wish I was mistaken. I truly do. But I'm not."

"Thank you for coming, Dr. Richardson." Chase turned to the camera with a broad grin. "After the break, we have none other than Adele here in the studio to perform her newest single..."

Lena took a step backward. The hairs on her arms lifted. She envisioned empty grocery stores. Banks closed. Gas stations shuttered. Every cog in the supply chain upended.

People would go hungry. Mothers and fathers and children. What would they do? How would everyone feed themselves? What would come next?

If this was true, what would the world look like in a week, in a month? A sense of despair crouched at the edges of her thoughts. The regret and loss was overwhelming, almost too much to take in.

The newscasters didn't want to believe it. Maybe it was cruel to dump more doom and gloom on a planet still recovering from a years-long pandemic. Maybe that's why the media were so mindlessly cheerful, so blissfully ignorant.

No one could handle another devastating blow.

The thing was, Mother Nature didn't care a lick what you could or couldn't handle. What you were or weren't prepared for. She'd kick you in the balls anyway.

Lena did her best to be prepared on a limited budget. She had a go-bag in the back of her Honda Pilot. She had a stocked pantry and a back-deck garden.

None of that would be enough for what was coming. And she did believe that it was coming.

Soon, life as everyone knew it would be over. Her current life, the life that she'd worked so hard to build, was over. She thought of her job that she loved. Her SAR volunteer work. Getting take-out from the Chinese place around the corner. Having coffee with her neighbor.

It was like being pushed off a cliff. She felt disorientated, dizzy.

She glanced around. Half the people weren't paying attention. But some were. They were tense and worried, speaking in low voices. A couple stood and hurried from the visiting area.

She had to go. To get out of the city.

Urgency pulled at her. Soon, the highways would be clogged with millions of scared people with the same idea.

It was sixteen hundred miles from Tampa to Munising, Michigan. She would go north. She would face Eli Pope. She would find her niece and nephew and bring them home. She would give them what she'd never had—stability, security, shelter in a disintegrating world.

They would figure this out together.

Lena strode from the hospital through the glass doors into the sunlight. Tampa had offered noise and stimulation, sunshine and distraction. A constant blare of activity that kept the whispers in her head at bay.

Now though, she felt the buildings closing in, the crowded skyscrapers looming overhead, stifling her oxygen. Her stomach tightened in iron knots.

The Newfoundland fell into step beside her. He looked up at her expectantly, his tail wagging.

Lena patted Bear's head. "Time to get to work."

12

ELI POPE

DAY TWO

Eli stood in the living room of the silent house and listened. The lights were off; it was dark. Engine sounds grumbled in the distance.

Someone was coming.

They knew he was here.

He'd been home for less than six hours. It was enough time to assess the supplies his father had left behind and do some packing. He planned to leave first thing in the morning.

After his release, he'd been unable to get ahold of a car service that late in the day, so he'd hiked a mile to a dilapidated hotel and paid for a bed in cash. The next morning, he'd called a taxi to bring him home.

Home to a vacant house. His father, Gerald Pope, aged sixty-seven, of the Ojibwe tribe, had died of a heart attack three months ago.

The newspaper had reported he'd died of a broken heart, yet another casualty of the Broken Heart Killer, but Eli doubted it. They had not been close.

Before he'd passed, his father had abandoned the house and returned to the Bay Mills Indian reservation in Chippewa County, located fifteen miles southwest of Sault Ste. Marie.

He had died there. As had Eli's mother, who'd committed suicide when he was six.

The Ojibwe held a deep belief in community, in family, but Eli had never felt like he'd belonged anywhere.

His lawyer had told him that the house was stuck in probate. His father had removed him from the will, instead giving the house to a distant cousin somewhere on his father's sister's side who lived in Bay Mills. Eli barely knew him.

It didn't matter. The house was empty. It was quiet. No catcalls or whispered threats. No stench of sweat and fear. No iron bars.

He moved through the house with a flashlight he'd retrieved from the garage; the key was still under the planter by the front door. A film of dust covered everything. The bookcases, the hand-hewn furniture, the wood-paneled walls.

The house was small and simple—three bedrooms, two bathrooms, a Michigan basement—but it was clean and well-preserved.

Nothing felt familiar. Nothing felt like his.

His old bedroom had been transformed into an office years ago. Gone were the hunting and fishing gear, the dresser covered in a collection of hunting knives he'd kept sharpened to a razor's edge.

However, the H&K VP9 and holster he'd kept hidden inside a vent behind the closet door was still in place, just as he'd left it. So was the yellow manilla envelope stuffed with three hundred and seventy dollars in cash, an extra seventeen-round magazine, and a box of 9mm ammunition.

The gun safe in his father's closet was still there. The combination, his mother's birthday, had not been changed. Eli doubted the AK-47 he withdrew from it had been fired since he'd left. He'd already cleaned, stripped, and oiled it.

Eli hadn't lived in this house for years. Not since he'd signed with the military two weeks after he turned eighteen, the summer after graduation.

He'd spent the first year in the third infantry division. He got a try-out for RASP, the eight-week Ranger assessment selection program—a sadistic, brutal course he wouldn't wish on his worst enemies. After passing the course, he'd joined the 75th Ranger Regiment. Six months after that, he made it through Ranger School on the first try.

For seven years, he'd been part of a battalion that was ready to answer the call anywhere in the world within seventy-two hours. As a tier one operator, he'd seen combat in Afghanistan, Iraq, Syria, and elsewhere.

Until he'd been arrested for murder. After his conviction, he'd been dishonorably discharged. Career over. Life over. Just like that.

The engines drew closer. Eli raised his head, listening. Still barely audible, but Eli's senses were attuned to the slightest sounds, the barest ripples in the energy of the universe.

Eli thumbed the last round into the spare magazine. Flicking off the flashlight, he tucked the magazine into his back pocket and the VP9 pistol into the concealed inside the waistband holster, then grabbed the AK-47.

Carrying the rifle in the low ready position, he moved swiftly through the darkened living room into the kitchen, past the rucksack and camping gear laid out on the kitchen table, to the back door.

He exited the house, skirted the garage and circled to the right side of the front yard, keeping a screen of jack pines between himself and the driveway.

It was after nine p.m. The aurora hadn't shown itself tonight; in its place, the bowl of the sky was wide and black and sprinkled with ice-bright stars. The moon shone bright, bathing everything in a silvery glow.

A slight breeze swished through the leaves. There were no city lights, no mechanical sounds but the trilling of insects and living things moving through the underbrush.

By the time the twin beams of the headlights swung into view, washing across the front of the house, Eli was well concealed. In gathering darkness, three vehicles approached. Tires crunched gravel. Two trucks, both dark-colored, and a sedan.

He knew what they wanted, what they were here for.

Adrenaline kicked his heart into high gear. He missed his NVGs, or night vision goggles. He missed the M4 5.56x45mm carbine he'd carried in the 75th Ranger Regiment along with his optics. Not to mention his plates and tactical gear. An M203 grenade launcher wouldn't be bad right about now, either.

At least he had the AK-47. The semi-automatic rifle had heft. It was intimidating as hell. And the pistol sat snug in its holster at his back.

He reminded himself that shooting civilians like fish in a barrel would be a quick pass back to prison. Do not pass Go. Do not collect $200 dollars.

A part of him knew he should just slip away, disappear before things escalated to violence. And yet, it wasn't in him to back down.

He planned to leave at first light, but there was no way in hell he'd let them drive him to it. Or allow them to think they had.

Let them come. Let them see him. Let them understand that he was not afraid.

That when he left, it would be his choice, not theirs.

He didn't much care whether these numbskulls lived or died, but he wasn't going back to prison. For however long he continued to breathe the oxygen of this damned planet, the choice would be his. He wouldn't be caged again. He'd rather go out in a spray of bullets.

Eli waited, crouched between two trees with an excellent sight line to the driveway. Pine needles scratched his cheek, damp leaves beneath his boots, the scent of pine strong in his nostrils. The smells were overpowering after the years of want.

The vehicles pulled close to the house, revving engines, tires spitting gravel. Brights on. Aggressive and posturing. They were making a point.

Doors slammed open. A half-dozen men poured out. They gripped crowbars. A few carried hunting rifles. Burly men. Tough men. Men who lived off this hard land and survived.

Eli despised them, but he did not underestimate them.

On one knee, breath even, his heart rate steady, he watched. The men approached the front door of the house close together, swaggering in a pack. Five men. One woman.

He was outnumbered. They had weapons. He wasn't going hand-to-hand with them. You didn't bring a knife to a gun fight. If it was a gunfight they wanted, he'd give it to them.

A dark, thrumming energy filled him. Blood and violence. Misery and pain. The choice was theirs.

He rose and lifted the rifle, the stock seated against his shoulder, finger on the trigger guard. He bladed his body to remain behind the cover of the tree trunk. "Get the hell off my lawn."

13

ELI POPE

DAY TWO

Eli kept his grip on the AK-47, his gaze as cold and hard as a snake's. He did not feel fear. Not this night. Not after eight years of prison, where you were either predator or prey.

Eli Pope was a predator.

"Lower your weapons, nice and easy."

Startled, several men started to whip around.

"I wouldn't do that. I've got a rifle aimed at your backs."

They froze in place, weapons half raised. One man swore. "Damn it!"

"Wouldn't move if I were you. Not until you lose those weapons."

They cursed, furious, but they obeyed. One by one, they dropped them—a couple of tire irons, two rifles, and a revolver. One gray-haired man still clutched his pistol.

Eli shifted his aim. "You're in the open. I'm not. How do you think that's going to go?"

"Johannes," a woman said.

The man released the pistol and turned around. One by one, the others did as well.

Eli took a step out from behind the tree.

Forced to turn to face him, they squinted against the glare of the headlights. Eli saw them clearly, while he remained a shadowy silhouette.

His gaze swept across the group. Fear opened in the men's faces. That terrible flash of understanding—it was Eli who held the power of life and death; they were the powerless ones in this equation.

Eli watched them, never losing sight of their hands. As an operator, he'd patrolled environments where insurgents mixed with the civilian population. Hands hid weapons. Hands telegraphed their next move before they made it.

He wouldn't put it past any of them to be incredibly stupid and try something.

A grizzled man in his early seventies stepped forward. Whisps of white hair clung to his bald, liver-spotted pate. He wore hunting gear with a camo bandana tied around his forehead.

Johannes Heikkinen. An old-timer, the Finnish owner of a fishing charter in Munising. He lived in a fishing shack on the shores of Superior for half the year. For thirty years, he'd played poker every Thursday night with Eli's father at the Driftwood Bar.

Johannes spoke with a smoker's rasp. "The Broken Heart Killer."

The media nicknamed him the Broken Heart Killer because he had supposedly discovered Lily with another man, then killed her in a rage.

The truth was, he and Lily were not lovers in the way the media portrayed them. They'd slept together that night, after he'd seen his father and visited a few friends at a bar—the DNA evidence had proven that.

Lily was a hard person to say no to. But he hadn't loved her like that. And he hadn't cared who else she slept with.

In the hours after he'd left her house, Lily had been assaulted, beaten, then strangled in her home. A gold half-heart locket had been placed on her stomach, a lock of her own hair left inside.

Eli had not killed her. He had not left the "broken heart" locket behind as his signature. But no one was interested in the truth.

Eli smiled, flat and empty. "Leave now and I won't shoot you."

One warning for his dead father's sake. For the time Johannes Heikkinen sat him at the table when he was nine years old and taught him the game. When to fold, when to call a bluff, when to go all in.

That was a long time ago. Another life. Another universe.

Eli's gaze shifted to the rest of them. Scott Smith was in his fifties, the surly owner of the Shell gas station on Cedar Street. Eli had bought gas, ice, and bait from the man since he was six years old.

Elmer Dunn was a grizzled hunter, the owner of a handful of rustic cabins he rented to fishermen and hunters on thirty acres outside of Munising, near Alger Falls.

The fourth man was Tim Brooks, co-owner of the Northwoods Inn with his wife, Lori. Eli had spent plenty of nights drinking at the Northwoods Bar with a few buddies and talking sports with Tim, who'd often bartended while his wife ran the hotel.

Eli had spent the evening before Lily was killed at the Northwoods Bar.

"This is your warning," Tim said. "Leave and never come back. Or we will be forced to make you."

A woman said, "It'd be our sincerest pleasure."

Eli knew Dana Lutz, too. In her mid-forties, her bleached-blonde hair was pulled back in a bun, her toughened features pinched with anger, fine lines radiating from her eyes. She ran snowmobile tours in the winters.

"How the hell did they let you out?" Dana asked. It was a rhetorical question.

Eli's appellate attorney had argued that the cop who pulled Eli over that night did so without just cause and with racial prejudice.

On appeal, the search of Eli's car where the evidence had been discovered was deemed by the Michigan Court of Appeals to be an illegal search. Therefore, the evidence found was inadmissible, aka fruit of the poisonous tree.

The DA had hung his entire case on the beer bottle with Eli's thumb print and Lily Easton's blood. Without it, they couldn't win a retrial. They'd been forced to release him, free and clear.

Except for the people who still believed he was guilty as sin.

A man moved out from behind Dana. At first, Eli didn't recognize the scruffy black goatee or the heavy gut, but the broad face and faint Native features were familiar.

"Gideon Crawford," Eli said.

"Go to hell, Pope," Gideon said.

Once, they'd been friends. Played high school football. Got stoned together at beach bonfires after the prom, after losing State, and when Gideon's college girlfriend had been tragically killed in a car accident.

Pure hate blazed in Gideon's eyes. Eli didn't need daylight to see it. It emanated from the man in radioactive waves. Eight years ago, Gideon Crawford had been Lily's new boyfriend, the one who had supposedly stolen her from Eli.

Gideon Crawford would have good reason to hate him. Jealousy and grief were a potent mix. And he'd been there that night at the bar, along with James Sawyer and Cyrus Lee.

The last night before Eli's whole world went to hell.

Suspicion flitted through his mind. Was Gideon the one who'd framed him? Or maybe it had been Tim. Tim Brooks was Gideon's uncle. They could have done it together. Or hell, it could have been all of them.

"You don't belong here," Gideon said.

"This is my father's house. I have every right to be here."

"This isn't your home anymore, killer," Gideon said.

"Law says it is," Eli said evenly. It was a lie, but he guessed they didn't know the ins and outs of probate. He guessed correctly.

"Don't matter to us what the law says, we know who you are," Tim Brooks said. "What you are. What you did."

"Far as I can tell, it's still a free country."

Gideon scowled. "It's not free, not for you."

For a half a second, Eli faltered. The muzzle of the AK-47 lowered slightly. It took him aback—how easily people could turn on you; how little it took.

They all loathed him. His old friends. The townspeople who'd known him his entire life. Their hatred was a physical thing, a weight he couldn't shake off, no matter how he wished it. No matter how much he pretended he didn't care.

Something released inside him, a tightness wound like a fist. He let out a breath.

He knew better than to lower his weapon. One iota of weakness from him, and they'd be on him like a pack of wolves.

A noise registered. The low rumble of an approaching engine. A pair of headlights swung into the driveway.

The engine cut off. A car door opened. Boots hit gravel. "Stop!" The voice was loud and commanding, a rich baritone booming through the still night.

The men flinched and turned. Gideon and Tim took a few steps back, nursing their wounded pride.

A figure approached, silhouetted against the headlights of the Sheriff's office patrol truck, a shotgun pressed against his shoulder. Not aimed at anyone yet but ready and willing.

His gaze flicked to Eli, eyes narrowing at the sight of Eli Pope holding a weapon on the good citizens of Alger County.

"Arrest him," Gideon said. "He drew on us!"

"From where I'm standing, I see an awful lot of weapons on the ground. Looks like y'all came here looking for trouble. Shouldn't be a big surprise that you found it."

Eli might have laughed if the situation wasn't so serious. Vintage Jackson.

"Pope threatened us." Dana pointed a finger at Eli. "He should be arrested. He should be charged with—"

Jackson's voice remained calm, but the edge was sharp as steel. There was no give in it, no weakness. "Near as I can tell, you trespassed onto his land with the intent to attack a man in his own home. If I'm making arrests, it'll be you folks."

"Jackson," Johannes said. "He's got no rights to be here. Make him leave."

"I'm afraid I can't do that. And you can't either."

Gideon spat on the ground. "We're just doing what everyone knows is the right thing."

"I'm the law," Jackson said evenly. "And I say to stand down."

"This isn't right," Gideon said. "He can't be here. He's a murderer—"

"Everyone leave. Now."

"Come on, Jackson—"

Jackson Cross swung the barrel of his shotgun toward Gideon. "Last warning. If I have to bring you in, that's a second offense, Crawford. You've got that drunk driving charge on your record. You sure you want to do this?"

"What about our weapons?" Tim snarled. "I'm not leaving my pistol for this psycho to steal."

"Get out of my sight before I arrest the lot of you for trespassing." Jackson glanced at Eli. "Mr. Pope will allow you to retrieve your possessions and retreat."

Through the altercation, Eli stood in stony silence. He did not move, he did not back down. He watched and said nothing.

The group reluctantly dispersed. Within a minute, they had retreated to their vehicles. The trucks tore up the grass of the front lawn as they peeled out.

One by one, they roared down the empty road back toward Munising.

Eli waited for the sounds of the engines to fade to silence. Then he turned to face Jackson Cross.

14

ELI POPE

DAY TWO

Crickets chirped in the weeds. Stars shone bright overhead. The night was chilly but not freezing. It was the middle of May, but here in the north, summer was still a ways off.

Jackson dipped his chin. He dropped the shotgun to his side. "Eli."

Eli lowered his rifle. "Been a long time, *friend*."

Jackson didn't flinch. He was too strong to shrink easily, made of tougher stuff than most gave him credit for. His boyish face and quick, easy smile made others underestimate him.

Eli knew better. This man was no country-bumpkin cop, no idiot. Though he had his blind spots. Always had.

One of those blind spots had been Eli himself. Until it wasn't.

"Not your best idea to come back here," Jackson said.

"I didn't ask for your opinion."

"'Suppose you're right. Still."

Eli said nothing.

"You seem different."

"Prison changes a man."

"I suppose it would. Like war."

Jackson, of course, had never been to war. Not like Eli. Two tours in

Syria. One in Afghanistan. Time spent in hellholes no one here could possibly imagine.

In some ways, war was like prison. Or prison was like war.

Either way, it deadened you. Siphoned little bits of your soul, whatever made a person human. When you came home, if you came home, you were hurt deep down, all the way to the marrow, so that nothing could touch it—not even love.

"It's been a long time."

Eli said nothing. A dozen memories flitted through his mind. Two boys laughing. Long summer days spent fly-fishing. Snowmobiling through deep winter woods. He pushed them out.

"You have the right to file a complaint. A trespassing charge—"

"I'm not pressing charges."

Jackson rubbed his jaw nervously. A tell he hadn't been able to shake since he was seven years old, and he and Eli had faced off on the playground for the first time.

They stood in the gravel driveway, darkness surrounding them, bats flitting and diving above the tree line. Neither of them moved; they might have been circling each other, wary as wolves, each analyzing the other for weakness, for chinks in the armor, the best method of attack.

Eli flashed him a hard smile. "Why are you here?"

"To see an old friend."

"You were never good at lying."

Jackson snorted. "No, I suppose not."

"I'm busy. I have work to do."

"I can't protect you from the townspeople," Jackson said. "I can put a watch detail on your house, but we're already understaffed."

"I haven't asked for your protection."

"This is only the beginning. They'll come after you again. And they're liable to do worse next time."

Eli looked up at the oil-black sky and felt the light from stars a million years old shining down on him. Open sky. Endless space. An expanse he never thought he'd see again. "Let them come."

"Eli."

"What do you care?" The words came sharp and vicious.

To his credit, Jackson kept his head high. "My job is to protect this county and everyone in it."

"You aren't here to protect me—you're here to check on me. Make sure I haven't killed some other girl yet. Isn't that what you're afraid of?"

Jackson swallowed. Even in the half-darkness, with the headlights blurring his shape—the truth was evident in his face.

Like the others, Jackson believed in his guilt. He believed his best friend had killed his on-again, off-again lover, the woman they'd both known, but Jackson had loved.

The sharp stab between Eli's ribs surprised him. He'd thought he was numb to pain, dead to sorrow. Yet it threatened to carry him away on a red tide, to drown him like Lake Superior.

"I came to ask you a few questions," Jackson said.

"As law enforcement, or..." Eli couldn't say "as a friend." They were no longer friends. Not after the arrest, the trial, the conviction.

"In a professional capacity."

"Speak, then."

Jackson eyed him warily, like he could read his mind. Once upon a time, he probably could have. "I'm investigating a homicide."

Eli stilled.

"It's someone you know."

Eli didn't rise to the bait. He waited, watchful and wary for the trap he felt coming.

"Yesterday, Amos Easton was murdered."

His mouth went bone dry. "Lena's father."

"And *Lily's* father," Jackson said.

Eli blinked. "Of course."

Jackson was silent for a minute, his jaw clenched, eyes narrowed, as if he struggled to contain his anger. Eli didn't begrudge him for it. Jackson had pined for Lily since he was twelve years old. No one had been more devastated at her death.

Except for her older sister, Lena. A memory flashed through his mind—Eli holding Lena, her shoulders quaking as she wept in grief and horror. Her tears hot on his bare chest, her long chestnut waves in his face, the scent of vanilla and cinnamon in his nostrils.

He braced himself. "When?"

"The medical examiner puts the death between four and six p.m. on May seventeenth."

"Who did it?"

"That's what I'm investigating. Lots of folk are pointing their fingers your way."

"I was incarcerated behind concrete walls and barbed wire. Not to mention the dozens of armed correctional officers watching my every move. And the cameras. You can check." He narrowed his eyes. "You already have."

"You have a motive," Jackson said.

"But no opportunity."

"You could have hired someone."

Eli let out a harsh laugh. "After eight years? Whatever for? If I was going to send an assassin after Easton, it would've been years ago."

"Because you knew you were getting out."

"If that was my goal, I would have done it myself." The words came out before he could stop them, but it was the truth and Jackson knew it, too. He saw it in the man's eyes. Jackson knew the violence that lived beneath Eli's skin.

"Why would I waste a get-out-of-jail-free card just to kill someone?"

"Crazier things have happened. You hated Easton. You made no bones about that."

"Easton hated me first. He claimed I murdered his daughter."

Can you blame him? hung in the air, unspoken.

The irony wasn't lost on Eli that Easton could have been the one to frame him. He wouldn't put it past the grizzled old bugger to plant evidence, to lie, to intentionally destroy Eli's life. But the geezer was dead.

"You're barking up the wrong tree, deputy."

"Undersheriff." Jackson didn't drop his gaze. He took a step forward. Five feet between them. The closest they'd stood since Jackson had slapped the cuffs on him, the metal biting the skin of his wrists, fear a bitter taste in the back of his throat.

Jackson's mouth tightened. "I have a dead body. I have two missing kids."

It took a second for that to sink in. "Lily's kids are missing?"

"Cody and Shiloh."

"You think someone took them?"

Jackson turned the question back on him. "Why would someone take them?"

"To kill them off-site. To dispose of the bodies elsewhere."

"What for?"

"If they were witnesses to the crime."

Jackson didn't speak.

Eli mulled it over. He frowned. "Or one of them is the killer. Amos had a hair-trigger temper. He'd gotten physical with Lily and Lena before. Remember that black eye Lena sported junior year? She said she walked into a door. She didn't."

Jackson's expression hardened. "I'll find the truth. I will hunt down whoever did this and bring them to justice. No matter who it is."

"I hope you do."

"We'll be in touch."

"Will we?"

"Damn it, Eli." Jackson shook his head. For the first time, his implacable mask slipped. He ran a hand through his sandy hair until it stood on end. "You. Coming back here. Why? I don't understand it."

"This is my home."

"But you...after you..." Jackson's features contorted with anger and grief, with that bewildered hurt that had once skewered Eli to his soul.

It did nothing to him now.

His soul had died long ago.

Eli stepped back onto the porch. "It's time for you to leave."

Jackson turned on his heel and marched toward his patrol truck. Shadows wobbled as he made his way to the driver's side door, then half-turned to glance back at the house, at Eli, as if he wanted to say something.

Eli didn't care what Jackson had to say. Jackson was like a dog with a bone. He did not give up or give in. He would get in the way, interfere with Eli's plans. Whether it was through this investigation of Easton or another way—he was a problem.

Eli went back into the dark and silent house and shut the door behind him. He threw the deadbolt, rested the rifle against the wall, then leaned against the door.

The adrenaline dump hit him. His legs went shaky as dizziness spun through him. He felt sick.

The hatred of the townspeople didn't bother him. Not like Jackson did. The boy he'd loved like his own family. They had been brothers in everything but blood.

Eli tried to hate him but found he couldn't. Anger, yes. Betrayal, certainly. But hatred, never.

Didn't mean he wouldn't do whatever he had to do to get vengeance, no matter who tried to stop him. If it meant going head-to-head with his former best friend, then so be it.

15

JACKSON CROSS

DAY TWO

Jackson moved to his dresser. It had been an exhausting day. Upstairs, he could hear his mother and father speaking in low tones, the creak of his sister's wheelchair.

After his sister Astrid's car accident left her disabled, Jackson had moved back home to help his mother care for her. His parents were getting older; he was single. It made sense at the time.

He lived in the finished basement with a kitchenette, two bedrooms, a bathroom, and a home gym.

The cliff-side lake house offered spectacular views of the harbor and Grand Island. The lawn was manicured. Square hedgerows lined the paver driveway. The house itself was architect-designed to resemble a Lake Tahoe lodge, built of stone, cedar, and glass.

Inside, reclaimed rafter beams stretched across the twenty-foot-tall ceiling. Hunting trophies hung on the walls in the formal living room, dining room, and study: mounted deer, antelope, moose.

Once and only once, he'd brought Lily to the house. When she'd seen the giant ivory elephant tusks encased behind glass in his father's library, she'd smirked and said, "I think he's compensating for something."

It was the only time he could recall a genuine laugh at his father's expense. Mostly, he felt a mix of shame and obligation in his father's imposing presence.

His eyes avoided the mirror. The dresser was smooth and dust-free. His wallet and badge sat on one side. The other side was empty but for a 4x6 framed photo.

Four teenagers faced the camera, grinning and hamming it up. Lily and Lena in the center, Jackson on one end, Eli on the other. They wore swimsuits. The turquoise water of the swimming hole glistened behind them, their lean tan bodies glowing in the sunlight.

Jackson with that self-conscious grin, his sandy hair tousled and sun-bleached, one arm slung across Lily's shoulder, half-turned, his gaze slanted not at the camera but at her. Lily was his whole universe, his sun, moon, and stars. It was written across his smitten face.

Lena had snuggled in next to Eli's muscled torso. His arm hugged her bare ribs, tickling her just as the photo was snapped.

Those two had been inseparable through high school. Destined for each other, though Amos Easton had not approved. Folks thought they'd make it, get married and have beautiful children with Eli's soulful black eyes and Lena's beaming smile.

The photo had been taken the summer after graduation, before Eli left for boot camp and Lena escaped to U of M, while Lily remained behind, waitressing. Jackson had stayed in the UP to attend Michigan Technology University in Houghton, with plans to follow in his father's footsteps and work in law enforcement.

It was a precious, glorious, perfect summer.

Until Eli had slept with Lily.

The spark that started the wildfire that burned their entire world to the ground.

Jackson tore his gaze from the photo. The bittersweet memories flooded him each time he looked at it. A knife sliding between his ribs. He couldn't help himself.

His sister Astrid had asked why he didn't throw the photo in the trash. Or burn it.

Jackson picked up the framed photo and stared at it. He'd tried. But for some reason, he never could do it. Things had been so normal, then. Bright and good and happy.

Or perhaps Eli had never been normal, and Jackson had been willfully blind.

Eli had a dark streak. Anyone close to him knew it. He was the first to hurl an insult. The first to throw himself into a bar fight. He cut school, drank too much, drove too fast, took too many risks. A propensity for violence, the forensic psychologists said afterward.

Consequences had always seemed to mean little to Eli. His mother had died young—she'd shot herself in the head when he was six. That was the ugly rumor.

Everyone had known it, but no one knew how to handle someone like Eli. What do you say to a hurting kid whose mom blew her own skull off?

He made it easy for everyone by pushing them away first. Until he'd befriended Jackson in the third grade. They'd attended the same small school since kindergarten, but their families never socialized in the same circles.

Jackson had been a shy, timid child. He was cursed with a stutter that his father's sharp disapproval and his mother's anxious coddling couldn't cure. The other kids shunned him; the teachers looked at him with pity. Only Eli didn't care.

One day, three boys had encircled Jackson on the playground while the teacher was inside grading papers instead of monitoring her charges. They pushed him, taunting him, forcing him to say vulgar, forbidden words to bring out his fear, his nervousness, and his stutter. "Say p-p-panties, you moron."

Eli came in like a whirlwind. He'd seized handfuls of mulch and hurled it in the boys' faces. Then, without warning, he'd started punching, hitting, and kicking anybody within reach.

After that day, they had become fast friends. No one picked on Jackson, or they answered to Eli. Eli was Jackson's salvation. For Eli, Jackson was the antidote to what must have been a tremendous, unmitigated loneliness.

The Cross family had not approved. They were well bred. Their ancestors had gained their wealth in copper and iron and timber for four generations. Where that wealth had disappeared to was never mentioned. Regardless, they did not fraternize with the lesser citizens of Alger County.

According to Jackson's father, Eli had been a dirty Indian from a dirty Indian family, and like all Indians, he would never amount to anything.

Jackson glanced at the photo again. He tried to recall who had taken the picture. James Sawyer, maybe. Or possibly Astrid.

He dragged his eyes upward and met his own gaze. The face in the mirror was a stranger. He looked haggard. His eyes were shadowed.

There was another reason he kept the photo.

As a reminder. As penance.

Ever since he could remember, he'd wanted to be an officer of the law. Put away the bad guys. Be the hero. Good and bad. Black and white. There was no gray.

Until there was.

He had not been able to let go of Lily's death. There was little evidence. A witness deemed unreliable by the powers that be. The DA would never use the testimony, a judge would not grant a warrant.

Jackson knew in his heart that Eli was guilty, but there was no evidence he could use, no proof. The perpetrator was going to get away with it. That, he could not abide.

And when he'd seen the opportunity to make it right—he'd taken it.

So help him, but he had.

That choice hadn't brought him the peace that he'd craved. A thousand times, he'd prayed to God to absolve him. But God was silent.

A thousand times, he'd told himself he'd done the right thing. That he'd fixed an elemental wrong in the universe.

That one immoral deed could correct a much greater evil.

He still believed that, didn't he?

Didn't he?

16

LENA EASTON

DAY THREE

Lena lugged the last crate of supplies from the elevator of her third-story apartment and stacked it in the storage compartment of the Honda Pilot next to her go-bag. The back of the SUV and the cargo carrier were filled with supplies.

She'd nicknamed the 2002 Honda Pilot the Tan Turd, since it was old, ugly, and literally falling apart. Two weeks ago, the bumper had fallen off on her way to work. She'd rescued it and taped it into place with duct tape.

At least the Pilot was All-Wheel Drive. It had its advantages—it blended in. it didn't grab attention or stand out. That was a useful trait.

"Almost done," she huffed to the dog. "Not that you care one bit, you big oaf."

Bear napped in the Honda's backseat, tongue lolling, his big furry body taking up the entire row. A few of his toys had been tossed into the footwell, his food and water in the back. She'd left the rear passenger door open until it was time to go.

"Hey, Ms. Easton."

Lena stiffened at the sound of footsteps. She slid the crate of canned goods deeper into the back behind her duffle bag, then turned, attempting to shield her supplies with her body.

Three men strolled across the parking lot of the Westshore apartment complex. They were more boys than men, still in their early twenties, with acne and spotty facial hair.

She recognized two of them. The tallest one, Trevor Leonard, had dropped out of college during the pandemic and never went back. He lived with his parents.

"Going on a trip?" Trevor asked. His expression was petulant; he looked perpetually bored.

"Something like that."

"Where you going?" his friend asked. He was shorter, heavyset, with a wisp of a goatee and skittish eyes. He kept looking down at his phone and scowling.

Lena searched her brain for his name. Tyrell Jones. He and Trevor smoked weed in the stairwells and slouched around the grounds like a pair of mangy dogs.

Her gaze slid to the third figure, who hung back. Josh was older, in his late twenties. Close-cut brown hair, square jaw dusted with a five o'clock shadow at ten in the morning.

She'd seen him before. Lounging at a corner of the complex, watching the women. Hovering over a girl as he corralled her into a stairwell and up to his apartment.

Last year, rumors had swirled about a sexual assault charge. She recalled the police cruisers, the red and blue wash of lights across her bedroom window. The girl had dropped the charges and moved out less than a week later.

"Ah man, I still can't get service," Trevor whined in a high-pitched voice. He held his phone high in the air as if searching for a signal. "Not again. What the hell, man. This sucks, Josh."

Josh watched her. "You got service, Ms. Easton?"

"Nope."

"You didn't even check."

She stared back at him, unblinking. "I did two minutes ago."

Somewhere across the parking lot, a small dog yipped. Vehicles drove past on the road in front of the apartment complex. Staticky TVs blared from open windows. A few streets over, someone honked their horn.

Everything seemed so normal, everyone going about their regular business. It was eerie. It was easy to think you were overreacting, that things would be the same tomorrow as they'd always been.

"I'm quite busy."

Josh didn't retreat.

She was almost ready to go; these hooligans were the last thing she needed. Lena had spent last night tossing and turning. Part of her had wanted to leave immediately, to drive through the night and get that much closer to her destination by dawn.

But she knew herself, knew her limitations. Rest was a crucial aspect to health, especially for a diabetic. She'd learned that lesson the hard way.

Besides, preparation now would pay off later.

Last night, she'd been productive. Other than her go-bag that she kept in the Pilot, she wasn't prepared to leave on a moment's notice. It had never been part of the plan.

She'd packed toiletries and clothing in a duffle bag, then spent the rest of the evening organizing her supplies to load up in the morning. The water worked, so she filled ten one-gallon jugs she'd kept on hand for hurricane-related emergencies.

Her budget was small, but over the years she'd managed to collect some useful items. The mini-fridge that would keep her insulin cold on a road trip was the most critical.

This morning, she'd headed to the bank, where she withdrew her limit from the ATM and then hit the doors the second Chase opened. The teller insisted on a one-thousand-dollar limit per customer due to the ongoing system issues.

Lena took the cash and ran before they closed their doors for good.

Her next stop was the gas station, which was cash-only. She topped off the tank, filled her four jerrycans with fuel, and purchased an up-to-date Road Atlas. If satellites were damaged, GPS wouldn't work.

Finally, she visited several pharmacies. She stocked up on batteries, bleach, alcohol swabs, antibiotic ointment, Advil, and bandages. For her diabetes, she grabbed extra glucose meters and test strips, then added boxes of 100-pack syringes and glucose tablets.

There was a quantity limit of four vials of insulin at each pharmacy, so she hopped from Walgreens to CVS to Walmart. Every pharmacy she visited was running low. People crowded the aisles, more than usual.

Every three months she had to get an infusion set, reservoir, and new sensors for her pump through her prescription. She could never order more, and even with insurance, it cost several hundred dollars. Luckily, she'd refilled her prescription on Friday.

In total, she hit eight pharmacies and procured thirty-two unopened vials of insulin, both long-acting and short-acting. They expired in two years. She had twenty-four months-worth plus or minus, in addition to her current prescription for her pump.

She wrote checks where she could and used cash where they wouldn't accept checks. By the time she'd finished, her bank account was well overdrawn.

Now, nearly everything was packed and ready. She just needed to get rid of these guys.

"Where you going in such a hurry?" Josh asked again. He outweighed her by a good hundred pounds and towered over her fit five-foot, five-inch frame.

"Just a weekend getaway," she said, cautious.

"Where." It wasn't a question.

Lena raised her chin. If he was attempting to intimidate her, it wouldn't work. "Savannah," she said without missing a beat. "The Westin hotel. Meeting up with a friend from college to visit Cumberland Island and see the wild horses."

"Lots of craziness going on right now." He circled the SUV, his hands loose at his sides, examining the vehicle, taking in the crates, the jerry-cans, the jugs of water, the box of batteries, and the solar charger.

He snatched the nearest cardboard box and yanked it to the edge of the storage compartment. He lifted the flaps and started rummaging inside. The box held her medic bag, which contained trauma dressings, burn gel, splints, cervical collar, gauze, and other supplies.

Irritation scraped her nerves raw. "What are you doing?"

"Just looking. Don't get your panties in a wad."

Behind him, Trevor and Tyrell exchanged uneasy glances.

Trevor shifted awkwardly and stuffed his hands in his pockets. "Hey man, weren't we gonna check out the theater? Thought we were gonna catch a flick."

"I'm busy." He pulled out her emergency wind-up radio and solar flashlight, then tossed them back in the crate. "Looks like you're packing for the apocalypse."

She gave a careless shrug. "Not really."

Trevor and Tyrell grinned like they wished they were somewhere else, but were clueless how to extricate themselves from the uncomfortable situation they'd found themselves in.

"It's just a little power outage," Josh said in a mocking tone. "The internet has gone down before. Hackers and all that. It's totally normal. No reason to freak out."

"Yep. I'm sure you're right." Heat flushed her face, her throat. Anxiety like spiders scrabbled over her skin. Stress raised her blood sugar, sometimes to dangerous levels.

She needed to get out of here, and fast.

He gave her a derisive look. "You really think this is different? Those lights in the sky got you going coo-coo in the head?"

"At least she doesn't have a mountain of toilet paper," Tyrell said.

Trevor chortled nervously.

Josh rolled his eyes but kept his attention on her. "You one of those crazy survivalists?"

"Sure, I'm crazy," she said. "You don't want to see my crazy come out, believe me."

"You guys like, believe an EMP or something is going to destroy civilization, right? Or aliens? Funny, you don't strike me as that type."

"What type is that?" Lena said. She forced herself to remain calm, though she felt anything but.

"Crazy in the head. Tinfoil-hat-wearing freaks. The ones who emptied the stores of toilet paper and hand sanitizer last time. And they were wrong, weren't they? Turns out they were the fools."

Lena didn't rise to the bait. Anger flared through her, but she controlled herself. She didn't say that the prepared ones weren't the ones who hoarded or emptied shelves.

Also, she didn't give a flying fart what he thought.

"You do you," she said. "That's what everyone says, right?"

Josh shot an amused glance back at his two cronies. "She's got spunk."

"You have no idea."

"What's this?" Josh leaned in, pushed aside a crate of emergency pouch meals, and dragged out the 9mm ammo box. "Now this, I can use, apocalypse or not."

"That's not yours."

Josh grinned at Lena. "Fine, fine. No problem, lady. No need to get all butt hurt."

He opened the ammo box and ran his finger along the shiny rows of bullets. He whistled through his teeth. "I'm going to take this."

"No, you aren't."

"You're going to give it to me. As a goodbye gift." His eyes darkened, glittering like stones underwater as he stared at her. A hungriness in his gaze that she recognized with a cold chill. "Of course, I can think of a more...appetizing goodbye present."

Her heart clenched in her chest. "It's time for you to leave." She didn't get defensive. She didn't engage in his mental games. She just wanted him gone. "Now."

17

LENA EASTON

DAY THREE

Josh leaned in close, leering, his skunky weed-breath hot on her face. She could count the pores on his cheeks. He intended to intimidate her.

Lena didn't cower. Still, the stress was making her shaky. Her body was cold all over.

She wasn't a skilled fighter, didn't know karate, and had no superpowers. She was just a girl who'd taken self-defense classes, who went to the range to make sure she could hit what she aimed at.

And she didn't entertain fools.

"Back off."

He exhaled a sour breath into her face. "Or what?"

It was so cliché, she laughed.

Josh's eyes darkened with rage. The type of guy whose fragile ego couldn't handle female derision or rejection. His hand snaked out and seized her T-shirt. He jerked her toward him, off-balance. "If you think you're gonna—"

"Bear!" Lena yelled.

An ear-shattering bark split the morning air. Bear lurched from the backseat, landed with a scrabble of nails on asphalt, and hurtled to the rear of the SUV.

"Woah!" Tyrell took three jerky steps backward. He flung up his hands, still holding his phone. Trevor froze in place, startled.

Still holding Lena's shirt, Josh gaped at the huge dog.

Bear was no attack dog. He wanted to rescue everyone and everything, from baby ducklings to doddering old men. Every ounce of him was built to love.

But they didn't know that.

"Bear, attack!"

In the second that Josh hesitated, Lena lunged, brought her knee up and kneed him in the groin.

Josh gave a pained *oof*.

She tore free of his grip. Shaky and weak, sheer adrenaline kept her on her feet. She shoved her hand into her pocket and jerked out the Pilot's keys. Her fingers closed over the cylindrical object attached to the keyring.

Josh half-straightened, clutching his groin with one hand. He charged her.

Lena aimed, depressed the trigger, and shot pepper spray directly into his face.

With a scream, Josh fell backward, tripped, and landed hard on his butt. He dropped the box of ammo. Rounds rolled across the pavement.

His eyes squeezed shut, fiery tears leaking out as the mucous membranes of his respiratory tract swelled, causing immense pain, possibly even temporary blindness. "You stupid whore!"

"Leave now before I sic my dog on you for real."

Trevor had had enough. He spun on his heels and strode across the parking lot, shoulders hunched, shaking his head. Tyrell quickly followed.

Bear barked at Josh, a deep rumbling bass that vibrated in her chest, hurt her ears. His huge furry body made him look like a pony. With teeth.

Across the parking lot in front of Building C, a car alarm went off. A door slammed, and someone cursed. "Shut that damn dog up!"

Lena glared down at Josh. "Am I shutting up the dog? Or are we bringing in the neighbors? Or how about another squirt of tear gas? It worked so well the first time."

Josh clambered unceremoniously to his feet, one hand clutching his injured nether regions, the other clawing at his streaming eyes. He shrieked curses and insults between moans of agony.

Bear pressed against her thigh, growling. She knotted one hand in his thick fur and steadied herself, taking great satisfaction in Josh's hunched form as he slunk away.

She'd made an enemy.

If she were staying, that would be a problem.

"Good job, Bear. You did great." Her legs wobbled as she retrieved the box of ammo and the loose ammunition, then reached up and shut the lift gate. She locked the SUV. "One more load, buddy, then we're off, I promise. We can't leave without the most important thing."

Bear followed her back into the apartment. She was weak and shaky all over. Sensing her distress, he kept close, nearly bowling her over as she entered the stairwell and took the metal stairs, gripping the railing for support.

After locking the apartment door behind her, she crossed the tiny living room and leaned against the counter, gasping. She managed to slump onto the counter stool and checked her pump. Her number was 250. Way too high.

She bolused herself and waited impatiently for the shot of insulin to do its job.

Her M&P 9 Shield EZ pistol lay on the counter. Though she had her concealed carry license, she'd left the gun inside her apartment. Utterly useless when she needed it.

She wouldn't make that mistake again.

Maybe Bear would defend her. Or maybe he'd try to lick the bad guys to death. She wasn't leaving it up to chance.

Lena holstered the firearm. She liked the natural grip, the crisp trigger, and the easy to load eight-round magazine chambered in 9mm. It was simple to rack the slide, which was important when her blood sugar crashed or spiked, making her weak.

She patted Bear's head. "This baby sticks with me from here on out."

Bear whuffed his agreement.

With her blood sugar dialed in, she took a quick second to assess the apartment. The pantry and her closet, where she stored extra supplies, had been emptied out. Everything that didn't fit in the Tan Turd was stored in the roof rack cargo carrier.

Lastly, Lena opened the fridge and pulled out the precious insulin vials. It suddenly seemed so little, paltry in the face of what was coming.

Apprehension torqued through her. When you lived with a chronic illness, with a pancreas that didn't work, how prepared could you be?

For a Type 1 diabetic, it wasn't about eating healthy or counting carbs.

Without insulin, she would die.

And when it ran out? What then? She hated that she didn't know. Insulin was nearly impossible to manufacture on one's own. And it was dangerous to take once it had expired.

Who knew how difficult it would be to procure insulin in a few months? Maybe FEMA would keep pharmacies stocked with essentials, but she wouldn't bet her life on it.

Bear let out a whuff, his tail wagging. He nosed the fridge shelf like he was looking for one of his treats, which she'd already packed.

"We'll figure it out, buddy," she said. Her voice echoed in the too-quiet apartment. "We've got no choice."

18

ELI POPE

DAY THREE

Eli wiped sweat from his brow as he crested yet another hill, legs pumping as he rode the mountain bike along the weedy, overgrown bike trail. Even with the moleskin, his heels were blistered from hiking boots he hadn't worn in years.

The ground fell away and before him Lake Superior stretched wide and glassy beyond the rocky beach. The view was spectacular. The Great Lake, pristine and wave-ruffled, the hills and distant cliffs jutting from the emerald water. The towering white pines, the sun-bleached rock.

He and Jackson had spent hot summers out here in the wild, hiking, swimming, hunting, swigging stolen beer. They'd brought the girls, too, but sometimes, it was just the two of them. It was an unspoken thing. This place was for them, for brothers.

He closed his eyes and was transported back in time, twelve years old, bare skin beaded with lake water, lying propped on a sunbaked slab of rock, on his elbows next to his best friend, gulping warm beer.

Their first drink, for both of them. Jackson had stolen it from his father's liquor cabinet.

Jackson had spat his first sip out, startled at the sour bitterness, but

Eli had taken to it from the beginning and never stopped. With his culture torn away, with a childhood of trauma and despair, he had taken to addiction naturally.

It was the only thing that numbed the pain.

Eli shook the memory from his head. He dismounted the bike and wheeled it off the trail, making his way down the slope to the sparkling river that fed into the lake a half mile north.

Occasional hikers took the trail less than a half mile from here, or they hiked up the river from the wooden pedestrian bridge a mile downriver, but rarely did a human being pass through this spot.

It was a good spot, protected by the worst of the elements by the limestone bluff that rose thirty feet behind him. A flat spot between the rock face and a massive boulder the size of a car gave him further protection from the elements and prying eyes.

The river provided both fish and fresh water; he had water purification tablets, and he could boil water with the fire or his Biolite camping stove using kindling. It would also charge phones, not that he had one.

A half mile northwest, Lake Superior stretched out for three hundred and fifty miles, emerald green and clear as glass or gray and storm-tossed, depending on her temperament. A narrow rocky cove provided privacy as well as good fishing.

He had the AK-47 plus a .22 rifle he'd retrieved from his buried cache. Deer, rabbits, coyotes, and wild turkey were plentiful. He wouldn't starve.

Years ago, he had buried two caches a half mile from his father's house—just in case—but had only looted one. It was a simple five-gallon bucket sealed with a Gamma lid that made it water and air-tight, then wrapped in an industrial trash bag.

In addition to the .22, he'd stored boxes of 9mm, .22, and 7.62x39 ammo, a change of clothes, bottled water and protein bars, a tarp and rope, chem-lights, emergency space blankets, water purification tablets, and a first-aid kit.

He still fit in his clothes. The food was expired, but he ate a bar anyway. It tasted fine.

After clearing the site of twigs, pinecones, and other debris, he erected the tent in the middle of the clearing. Then, he created a second shelter parallel to the boulder, a lean-to fortification with a firing pit.

He topped the shelter with a space blanket covered with branches and leaves to disguise the shelter. He placed his bivy sack inside. This was where he'd sleep.

He stood back and examined his work. He could watch the tent in case someone attempted to sneak up on him. The lean-to shelter gave him a good killing field from cover and provided an avenue of escape if needed.

The space blanket would go far to defeat infrared. The camouflage of branches and leaves made it look like part of the woods to anyone looking through a night vision scope.

Next, he dug a Dakota fire hole with his shovel. Squatting, using his Ferro rod and a fire starter he'd fashioned from cotton balls and petroleum jelly, he started a fire, adding small bits of twigs he'd collected for kindling.

Gradually, he added thicker branches until the fire burned hot. He closed his eyes and thought of her. Not the dead girl who haunted him, but her sister. Lena Easton. The girl who visited both his dreams and his nightmares.

Where was she now? What was she doing? Did she ever think of him?

He hadn't seen her since that last night in the middle of the trial. When he realized the town was turning against her for defending him, the risk greater to her than to himself.

He'd told her to leave. To shut the door on him and never look back.

He did not regret it. And yet he missed her, every second of every day. Her absence created a hole in his chest he'd never be able to fill.

He'd made mistakes. Terrible ones. Lena Easton had never been one of them.

Hunger gnawed at his belly. He planned to heat some beans, then fish Lake Superior for lunch. A great heaviness overtook him. Exhaustion pulled at his bones, but he couldn't rest yet.

He needed to find out who had hated him enough to frame him for murder, and he wouldn't get those answers hiding out in the woods. But he knew who to talk to, who to ask.

If anyone knew something, it would be James Sawyer. He had his finger on the pulse of this town—

The distant rumble of an ATV broke the stillness. A cardinal exploded from a hemlock branch above his head, red feathers bursting into flight.

Eli stilled, listening.

In the distance, to the south, a twig cracked.

Something was out there.

Swiftly, Eli drew his VP9 and retreated behind the boulder. Half-crouched, he exited the campsite, entered the tree line, and bladed his body next to the enormous trunk of a white pine, which offered both cover and concealment. He checked his pistol; a round was chambered.

He held it low and waited, silent and listening, ears strained.

Birds trilled in the underbrush. A squirrel darted along the branch of the cottonwood above his head. Deep in the woods to his right, something large ambled along a deer path.

A fox, probably. Maybe a bobcat. Earlier, he'd seen the scat of deer and hare.

A minute later came the rustle of leaves underfoot. A step. A long hesitation. And then another.

His senses heightened, muscles tensing. It was a someone, not a something. Someone was creeping up on him. No hunter or soldier, but far quieter than most idiots stomping through the woods.

He recalled how Jackson used to try to sneak up on him and pelt him with a pebble, an acorn, or a pinecone. It never worked. Eli always heard him. Always. Eli had been the one who snuck up behind Jackson and tossed the acorn at his head.

It wasn't Jackson, though. Jackson was bigger, heavier, louder.

This creature was small and stealthy.

"I know you're there!" a young voice called out.

Eli didn't move.

"Come out like a man!" she ordered.

He laughed. The sound startled him. It was the first time he'd laughed in a great many years. "You first."

He kept his breathing steady, his limbs loose and easy, hidden behind the trunk. Ready to spring into action.

He eased to the right a few degrees, so he was still protected, but could see his adversary.

A girl stepped out of the underbrush, appearing between the thickening shadows spreading across the pine-needled earth. She held a crossbow against her shoulder, a fiberglass bolt cocked and aimed at the tree he crouched behind.

She stared straight at him. "You do anything I don't like, and I'll fire this thing."

He sucked in a breath. The effect she had on him was instant and profound. It was like being punched in the solar plexus.

She wore hiking boots and oversized overalls over a long-sleeved purple shirt, her raven-black hair in a messy braid slung over her shoulder. Suspicious black eyes like two bits of coal glared from an elfin face, her chin narrow and pointed.

Thin and wiry, she was strong judging by how she handled that crossbow. Steady as a rock, no tremble in her hands.

The girl was both Lily and not Lily. The spitting image of her dead mother, but smaller, darker, fiercer.

"I'll shoot you!" she warned.

He believed her. The crossbow's buttstock was nestled snug against her shoulder, her cheek pressed to the stock so that her dominant eye was in line with the sight. Her trigger hand held the grip, her index finger balanced on the trigger itself.

He was protected behind the tree, but this girl knew what she was doing.

"You don't want to do that."

"I'll decide what I want," she shot back. Ten yards away, she stood with her feet shoulder-width apart, back straight, shoulders square to Eli's position. "Don't frickin' move."

"How did you get here?"

"Walked."

"The ATV. That was you."

"That's none of your damn beeswax."

"How did you find this place?"

Her lip curled. "It's a free country."

The irony didn't escape him. He'd used the exact same cliched phrase last night. "This isn't exactly a public beach."

She shrugged.

"Not many people know of this place."

She stared at him, or what she could see of him.

"How'd you find it?" he repeated.

"I just did."

Jackson must have brought her here. Could have been Sawyer, but Sawyer would have no reason to bring this kid here. Possibly Lena. The thought made his chest go tight, but he swiftly dismissed the thought. Not Lena. She was long gone.

Jackson was the kind one. The thoughtful one. The one who would check in on Lily's children. Who would adopt them as a generous and benevolent uncle, taking care to show them the wild places where they'd shared so much as kids, as teens, as young adults.

Where Lily had truly been herself as nowhere else. Of course, it was Jackson.

Shiloh scowled. "I can be here, same as you. No rules against it. Nothing you can do to stop me."

"You're the one with the bolt aimed at my chest, Shiloh."

She went absolutely still. Like a wild thing caught in the crosshairs. Her eyes big as quarters. "How do you know my name?"

"Same as you know mine."

She pondered that for a moment. Her gaze never left his, her index finger still on that trigger. "You're Eli Pope. The Broken Heart Killer. You murdered my mother."

Something caught in his chest. Those words, spoken so cavalierly, so matter-of-factly, from the child whose world had been destroyed by that terrible act. "You remember me."

"Seen your picture on enough news shows."

The last time he'd seen her, she'd been a chubby, dark-haired five-year-old. A dervish of frenetic energy. The older one, the tow-headed boy—he'd been the sober, serious one.

Even at six, he'd sat calmly at the kitchen table and colored while tiny Shiloh had scaled the cabinets, opened the freezer, and consumed four chocolate popsicles while Lily and Eli had coffee on the porch.

"My little wild thing," Lily had said with a laugh.

He reached back in his memories. That had been two days before the murder. He'd come home to check on his father's deteriorating Alzheimer's for a week before departing on another undisclosed mission to Iraq.

It had been years since Lena had broken up with him and moved down to Tampa. He was lonely; he had taken comfort in Lily, as Lily had taken comfort in him. It was always casual, at least on his part.

Lily had a way of dominating every room she was in, of pulling you into her orbit whether you'd intended to enter or not. It was a rare man who could deny himself Lily Easton's tumultuous and addictive affection when she chose to give it.

Eli had never met the man who could have denied her.

He said to Shiloh, "I didn't kill your mother."

Eli didn't know why he spoke the words. He didn't owe this child anything. And yet. With her dark wary eyes on him, sharp and penetrating and fearless—he could not look away.

The girl sniffed. "Easy enough to lie. Everybody lies."

"I'm not lying."

Her eyes narrowed. "You can't prove it."

"No, I can't. That's why I spent eight years in prison. Not everyone who goes to prison is guilty."

"Most of 'em."

"Maybe."

"They had evidence. That beer bottle with your prints on it and my mom's blood."

"It was planted. Someone wanted me to go down for a crime I didn't commit. And I did."

She grunted, non-committal. He didn't blame her, not one bit. He was surprised she was still here. Astounded that she hadn't squeezed the trigger and tried to kill him.

He should disarm her. It was the smart play. Anyone who dared hold a weapon on him would've been mortally injured by this point. His fingers tightened on the grip of the pistol, but something held him back.

He did not act. Not yet.

19

ELI POPE

DAY THREE

Eli found himself fascinated by Shiloh.

She looked so much like Lily. But Lena was in her, too. In the way she tilted her head to the side while she appraised him, the frank expression in her elfin face, those sharp assessing eyes.

Once upon a time, Lena had looked at him like that, like she could see straight through him, like she already knew his thoughts before he did. His mind flooded with memories too painful to bear. The scent of her hair. Her smile. How her eyes crinkled when she laughed.

His gut knotted. His past was lost to him; his future stolen.

Shiloh took a single step into the clearing. "If I killed you, I bet I'd get away with it."

"Maybe you would."

"Maybe I should do it."

"I think you'd regret it."

"I'm not scared to kill nobody."

He had the unsettling sense that if you came at this girl with a knife, she'd come back at you with a cannon.

"Okay," he said. "I believe you."

"I'd do it if I had to. If I needed to."

"Do you need to?"

She hesitated at that. A line appeared between her brows as she wrinkled her nose. Instead of answering, she changed the subject. "My grandpa is dead."

"I heard that."

"You kill him?"

"No."

"Why should I believe you?"

"I'll tell you the same thing I told Deputy Cross. I was in a concrete cell that smells like piss and despair."

She took that in. "You talked to Jackson."

"He's looking for you."

Shiloh took another careful step forward. Her boots crunched dead leaves. She kept the crossbow in place, kept her focus. "Someone took my brother."

"Same person who killed your grandfather?"

"Yeah." She hesitated. "I think so."

"You weren't there?"

"Nope." She said it too quickly. Probably a lie, though her expression didn't change, her eyes just as fierce. "But I'm gonna find out who did it."

"Good luck to you."

"If it was you, I'll kill you."

"It wasn't me."

Shiloh said nothing for a long moment. He could see the cogs turning inside her head, thoughts flitting behind her eyes. Her finger massaged the trigger.

He considered drawing his knife and throwing it at her. He could knock that damn crossbow out of the way before she could react and squeeze the trigger. The point of the blade would pierce the soft tissue of her throat. She wouldn't have a chance.

Again, he stayed his hand. He didn't want to harm her. Or embarrass her, either.

"Maybe it was the windigo."

She blinked. Doubt moved across her face, then vanished. "I don't believe in that crap."

"But you know it."

She nodded.

In Ojibwe legend, the windigo was a malevolent flesh-eating spirit that roamed the deep woods, hunting humans to consume them, body and soul.

She had Ojibwe blood in her veins. It was in the slant of her face, her coal-black eyes, her tan skin. But more than that, it was in the way she moved, the sharpness of her gaze.

Lily had told him that Shiloh's father was a security guard at Kewadin Casino in Sault Ste. Marie, a gambling man with no interest in children. He had always suspected that it was Gideon Crawford, whose mother was Ojibwe.

But Lily had taken many lovers: a rich sailor who'd docked his sailboat in the harbor for a weekend, or a passing musician she'd visited in Ann Arbor.

"It was a flesh-and-blood monster," Shiloh said with conviction. "No make-believe thing."

"I agree."

A turmoil of emotions warred across her knife-thin face. Doubt and confusion, mistrust and uncertainty. But not fear. Whatever she was, she was not afraid, much as she should be.

She didn't speak for a moment. Her nose wrinkled, eyes narrowed as she figured out her next move. Probably deciding whether to shoot him or not before she moved on to the next item on her list.

Shiloh took another step closer, balancing at the edge of the clearing, wary as a fox. Small but dangerous, brave and fierce.

The fire in her eyes...how bright she burned.

He respected that.

She took her eyes off his concealed position behind the white pine for the first time, let her gaze drift around the campsite, taking in the

Biolite stove, the solar kettle, the flames flickering from the hole in the ground.

Her eyes darted back to him. "You're gonna live out here." It wasn't a question. She was smart. Quick on her feet. Observant.

"Yes."

"Why?"

"Because I want to."

"That's not a reason."

Because he'd been driven out of his father's home, out of his hometown. But that wasn't entirely true, was it? He'd already planned to leave. He'd always been at home in the woods.

Where most soldiers endured SERE training—Survival, Evasion, Resistance, Escape—he'd relished it. He felt a connection to the land that white people didn't feel, could never feel.

His past had branded him, scarred him. Not just prison, but his years as a spec ops soldier. The fighting, the killing, the dead.

Out here, life was simple. It was about survival, man and nature. Out here, he could forget who he was, who he'd become. All the endless, open space. The lonely hills and stoic trees. The rocky bluffs and sun-dappled green. The bottomless deep of Lake Superior.

This was the antithesis of prison. This was freedom. He couldn't explain it, how it made him feel, how his pulse beat stronger; his soul lighter. He felt it, deep in his bones. It was in his blood.

The silence brought peace. He needed this. For as long as it took, he needed it. He wouldn't let anyone take it away from him.

"Our people belonged to these lands for thousands of years. This is our home."

The girl nodded like she understood. Gradually, she drifted closer, slowly circling him. He moved with her, keeping the tree between them.

She gestured at him with her chin. "Put the gun down."

"Lower that crossbow."

She balked.

"Trust goes both ways."

"You first."

Eli hesitated. With any other adversary, he would never even consider such a thought. And yet, he obeyed. He moved out just enough that she could see him holster his pistol. He waited, tense, ready to draw it quickly if needed, ready to retreat to full cover behind the tree trunk.

His act of surrender had the desired effect. The crossbow relaxed in her hands, the bolt drifting lower. Her index finger slid off the trigger.

She took another step closer, wary and watchful, but curious. Her curiosity got the better of her. She lowered the crossbow as her gaze flicked to the fire. "How come you made the fire in a hole like that?"

"It's called a Dakota fire hole. It's designed to provide heat and a cooking source without revealing your location with too much smoke."

"How'd you make it?"

"I'll show you if you put down the crossbow."

"No way."

He shrugged. "Then I'm not coming out."

She hesitated, vacillating between curiosity and wariness.

"You can keep it right next to you. It's there if you need it. I won't come near you."

Finally, she made up her mind and placed the crossbow on the ground next to her feet. She crouched as she watched him, ready to flee or attack at a moment's notice.

Eli moved out from the trees into the campsite. He knelt and stirred the coals at the bottom of the hole. With half his attention on her hands and the crossbow, he showed her how he'd dug the fire pit with an army-style folding shovel.

He'd dug two holes in the ground, the first about a foot in diameter and a foot deep. The second was about six inches wide and dug at an angle, with a tunnel that connected the two holes that served as a chimney.

Eli had packed twigs and kindling into the bottom of the larger hole, then layered small logs on top. He showed her how he lit it with a ferro rod. The size of a pen, the fire steel didn't rely on fuel, could get wet, and could start a thousand fires before it ran out.

Eli demonstrated, striking the rod with a hard striker, moving it swiftly across the ferro rod to produce sparks that caught the tinder and swelled into flickering flames.

"The fire burns from the top down and draws a steady draft of air from the smaller chimney hole, so it achieves near complete combustion. The result is a strong, bright fire that burns efficiently, uses less firewood, produces little smoke, and conceals the flames from potential threats, especially at night. It provides warmth, and you can cook off it, too."

He pointed to a grate of green sticks that he'd woven with fishing wire and could place across the top of the hole. It would hold a pot or frying pan.

She listened, seemingly fascinated, her bottom lip protruding in focused concentration. "How do you know how to do all this stuff?"

"The army. Also, I'm Ojibwe. We learn how to live with the land instead of against it."

"You didn't live on the reservation."

"I have family who do. An aunt. My grandparents before they passed away. I spent a few summers there."

She nodded, still staring in awe at the fire. "You won't miss electricity? Cell phones and iPads? Xbox? The internet?"

"No, I don't. People would be a lot happier without some of those things."

"I like flushing toilets."

He snorted.

Something flickered across her sharp features—a hint of pleasure, of self-satisfaction—then disappeared, replaced by that hard, focused gaze, her finger on the crossbow trigger.

He watched her. How still she was, coiled and tense with an urgent energy, like she might bound away at any moment. "You want something to eat?"

She didn't answer but watched him hungrily.

"I'm just going for my pack. No sudden moves." He reached for the rucksack he'd placed at the base of the cottonwood. Opening the front zipper, he pulled out one of the protein bars he'd collected from his cache.

He held it out to her.

Shiloh stared at it like it was a snake about to bite her.

"It's wrapped. It's not poisoned."

She didn't move.

"It's chocolate."

Her eyes darkened.

He shrugged. "Suit yourself."

"I don't need no charity."

"Not charity. It's in thanks. For not skewering me like teriyaki chicken."

She thought about that.

He tossed it at her feet.

Startled, she grabbed the crossbow and retreated three steps, almost tripping on a log. The crossbow lifted for half a second; then she thought better of it and dropped it to her side.

Ducking into a crouch, she snatched the bar and slipped it into her overalls' pocket. A second later, she was on her feet again, backpedaling, the crossbow held low but ready.

Shiloh scowled. "Don't you dare follow me."

"I won't."

"I'm warning you."

"Wouldn't dream of it."

"You could if you wanted to."

Someone must've told her. Or maybe it was one of the semi-salacious factoids included in the tell-alls and news specials. They'd described him as an inscrutable Native American murderer. Dealer in spirits, rain dances and powwows, a supernatural tracker with bird feathers in his hair and war paint on his bronze-skinned face. She could've heard it from anywhere.

"Don't give me a reason to."

She pursed her lips, considering, then nodded. Spinning on her heels, she turned abruptly and darted across the clearing, headed for the dark space between two spruce trees.

The girl retreated into the woods on light feet. Even in hiking boots, she hardly made a sound. A crushed leaf here, a broken twig there. She was a natural. A little training, and she'd move almost invisibly, like he did.

As he tended the fire and cooked his dinner, he couldn't get her out of his thoughts.

This half-feral creature that appeared out of the forest. This girl with the haunted eyes. Hungry as a stray dog, fierce as a wolverine.

That terrible night, she'd lost more than he had. Maybe that was it. She reminded him so much of them—of Lily and Lena—the only women he'd ever cared about.

Shiloh should have hated him, but she didn't. She should've tried to kill him; she hadn't.

He couldn't explain it, this strange, light feeling in his chest. Like he could breathe deeply for the first time.

Eli wanted her to come back.

He hoped that she would.

20

JACKSON CROSS

DAY THREE

That morning, Jackson and Devon met the medical examiner at the Munising hospital morgue, which they used to store bodies under a contract with the county. The room was cold and sterile.

When they arrived, Dr. Virtanen was bent over the corpse, which lay on a gurney in the center of the room, a tray of medical instruments beside her. She straightened and looked them over without smiling. She wore gloves, sleeves, booties, and an apron. Goggles were perched on her head.

She walked them through the autopsy she'd conducted so far. Amos Easton was sixty-nine-years old and weighed one hundred and ninety pounds. "Positive identification was established matching premortem dental records. The manner of death was homicide. The cause of death is exsanguination due to external hemorrhage."

The tire iron was indeed the murder weapon. The lab had matched Easton's DNA.

Dr. Virtanen pointed to the cranial area. The skull was so deformed that Jackson had difficulty imagining a human face had ever existed. "See these fractures here? The blows fractured the maxilla, the upper jawbone, here and here, as well as a left orbital rim fracture."

The perp had swung at the victim's head five times. The first two blows came from an upward slanting angle that suggested the assailant was shorter than Easton's six-three frame, and right-handed.

Bile churned in his stomach, but he couldn't look away. The sterile smell of antiseptic stung his nostrils. Because the corpse was found and refrigerated within twenty-four hours, at least the decomposition stench was minimal.

"How much force would be required to land blows like this?" Jackson asked.

"A lot."

"A grown man? A teenage boy?"

Dr. Virtanen nodded, thoughtful. "Could be a teenage boy."

"How about a teenage girl?" Devon asked.

Jackson shot her a look.

Devon shrugged. "No reason to be sexist."

"It's within the realm of possibility," the ME said. "But unlikely."

"Takes a lot of hatred to smash in someone's head until they're hardly recognizable as human," Devon said dryly.

Dr. Virtanen pointed to an evidence envelope on the counter. "I've collected fingernail scrapings, clippings, and removed debris from the victim's hair."

"Thank you." Jackson took the envelope, checked that it was sealed, then signed the Chain of Custody log on the back.

"Was the victim under the influence when he died?" Devon asked.

"Don't expect the toxicology report anytime soon," Dr. Virtanen said. "As you know, it takes months when things are normal. With these strange power outages, who knows? The system's been down since Monday night. I won't be able to release the final autopsy until I have the tox report in hand."

Dr. Virtanen gestured at the stryker saw sitting on the counter next to the sink. A pair of pruning loppers for cutting ribs lay next to it. "I'm about to open up the cranial cap. Time to put on safety goggles and full PPE gear."

The rest of the autopsy took three hours. The medical examiner used a foot pedal to control the start and stop of her audio recorder. As she worked her way through the autopsy, she spoke aloud, mentioning everything she did, including specific measurements of internal organs.

Devon took photos so they didn't have to wait for them from the ME, but they didn't learn anything new that was relevant to the case.

After the autopsy, they drove to the sheriff's office, logged in the evidence, then headed to the Dogpatch restaurant across the street from the Munising precinct.

They ordered the UP's famous pasties, beef and root veggies folded into a pastry shell and baked until juicy and tender. The pasty was pronounced with a soft "a" like "pass," and had been invented as portable meals for Cornish miners in the mid-nineteenth century.

Devon looked down at her food for a moment, as if debating whether she still had an appetite, then she shrugged, picked up her pasty and shoved a huge bite in her mouth.

She chewed loudly. "Mmmmm."

Jackson didn't touch his plate. Much as he loved pasties, his stomach churned. He couldn't get Easton's mashed-in face out of his head. He'd known the man for his entire life. Disliked him for that long, but no one deserved to die like that.

"You're a sensitive soul, aren't you?" Devon asked as she swallowed another mouthful.

"I knew him. I know everyone here."

Devon shot him a sympathetic glance. He hated that look. Nothing much worse than pity.

She cleared her throat. "When I was a beat cop in Detroit, I got the domestic calls. The battered women, beaten halfway to Sunday, screaming for help, but you know what? They always went back the next day, like a dog to its vomit."

A memory from long ago flitted into his mind. He pushed it away. "It's usually more complicated than that."

"You get immune to it after a while. You don't have a choice." She took another bite, looked out the window at the marina, the placid bay. Her voice dropped. "The kids, though."

He saw it then, a shadow flickering behind her eyes. That haunted look. Things had been hard for her. He hadn't asked why she'd left Detroit and come all the way up here to the middle of nowhere.

There was something closed in her expression. She was tough, and she needed him to believe that she was tough. Vulnerability could be seen as weakness, especially for a female officer. She'd tell him when she was good and ready.

"I know what you mean," he said. "About the kids."

He'd long suspected that Easton had occasionally smacked his girls around when he was drunk. They had never admitted it, but there had been bruises, that darkness in their eyes.

He'd wondered about Cody and Shiloh, too, but he'd never made the call. Maybe he should have.

Jackson pushed around his potatoes. They'd canvassed neighborhoods, checked with the local businesses, and put out BOLOs.

There was no sign of her or Cody.

He'd barely slept last night, tossing and turning, imagining her somewhere out in the Hiawatha National Forest, cold and alone and scared.

"What's next?" Devon asked after swallowing an enormous bite of the handheld meat pie. She licked her lips. "I could have another one right now. These are so, so good. The best part of the UP."

"The school," he said. "We need to track down Cody's whereabouts. Who his friends are. Where he might hole up if he got himself into trouble. We can ask about Shiloh, too, but be careful. We don't want to let any potential suspects know that she's a witness. The perp might not have seen her."

"Sounds like you don't think they're together."

"I don't think anything yet. I go where the evidence takes me."

Devon smirked. "Said every TV detective hack ever."

"Mock me, but it's true." He pushed back his plate. Even the sight of food made him sick.

Devon looked at her phone with a forlorn expression. The last three days of rolling power outages had made her grumpy. She flashed him the latest feed on her Instagram. "Look, service again. The world is restored."

She scrolled through photo after photo of the auroras. Jackson glanced at a few of the comments: *#Nature's Fourth of July #I'd rather have a hot shower.*

"Look at this one." It was a striking photo of Lake Superior, probably taken from Grand Island. The undulating waves of the aurora reflected off the water in a near perfect double-image. The hashtag read: *#the world ends not with a bang but with a beautiful whimper.*

The blood drained from his face. He read the words, reread them, felt them echo somewhere deep in his soul.

It seemed like half the news agencies were reporting on the blackouts, long lines at gas stations, and the potential damage to low earth satellites. The other half made jokes about telegrams catching on fire.

He hadn't had time to check his supplies in the basement or even visit a grocery store. He wanted to make a trip to Marquette, just to be safe. The largest town in the UP, Marquette boasted a Target and Walmart and a couple of camping stores.

There was too much to do. A homicide to solve and missing kids to find. He had a habit of putting aside his own needs, working himself to the bone to solve a case.

But the cases never ended. There was always someone who needed saving.

He pushed his chair back and stood, waving down the waitress for the check, which he and Devon split. Devon followed his lead. "Back to work we go."

They walked a block in the cool May sunshine to where they'd parked the patrol truck across from the marina.

Jackson looked across the bay toward Grand Island, the lush green island and recreational area located a half mile north of the harbor. The harbor itself was smooth, the water a rich emerald green.

The sky was a rich blue, with no hint of the aurora that would be back in force again tonight.

Devon opened the driver's side door. "Shall I drive?"

"Until you've earned your stripes, I drive."

She smirked at him but moved out of the way. "After you, boss."

21

JACKSON CROSS

DAY THREE

The Munising Middle-High School shared a campus and was conveniently located right on the bay off M-28.

There were few cars in the parking lot—a couple of sedans, a rusted red Toyota Tacoma, a metallic blue F150, and a dirt-crusted white Jeep Wrangler in clear need of a wash.

"I bet they got the day off of school," Devon said enviously. "Jerks."

Jackson's lip twitched as he pulled into the familiar parking lot. So many memories here. Some good. Some awful. An image of his older brother Garrett flitted through his mind.

Garrett had been a quarterback and golden boy, but he'd spiraled into drugs and addiction, bad choices, and then worse ones. After an arrest for dealing his sophomore year of college at MSU, he'd been kicked off the football team, expelled from school, and returned home in shame.

A week after a particularly vicious fight with their father, Garrett had left one summer day and never returned. Two months later, he'd sent a post card from Mackinac Island. Then a month later, from Saginaw Bay on Lake Huron, a fisherman's paradise.

He'd gotten a job. He was happy. Leave him alone.

And then, nothing. Not a birthday phone call. Not a visit. Not a Christmas card.

Deep down, Jackson couldn't blame him. They hadn't been close. And families could be difficult, especially his.

While Garrett had been the black sheep, Jackson had felt pulled toward the other extreme. He'd played the peacemaker, as if one wrong move might send his family spiraling into disaster.

He followed the rules, believed in the rules. The rules held everything together, even if by only the thinnest filament.

"You planning to sit in there all day?" Devon asked. She was already out of the truck.

"Old memories. Sorry."

"You went here, didn't you? Not many people live in the same place from cradle to the grave, you know."

"I'm not dead yet. There's still time."

She rolled her eyes. "Right."

Jackson climbed out of the truck, shut the door, and pocketed the keys. He felt heavy. The bitter memories weighed him down. They weren't the worst ones.

He thought of Lily, how her effervescent laugh had made him smile, no matter what happened at home. Or how Eli's wry grin reminded him that his friends had his back.

He missed that simplicity. How black and white things had been. Good and bad, right and wrong.

Before the betrayals. Before the hurt and the jealousies, before it all fell apart around them.

"Jackson Cross, it's good to see you." A tall, broad-shouldered man approached them before they reached the front doors. He was dressed in pressed khaki slacks and a black button-up dress shirt. Fit and trim, he was in his late forties, with salt and pepper hair, a kind face and firm handshake.

David Kepford had been the principal for ten years. He was a fixture in the community. A downstater from Grand Rapids, he wasn't a true Yooper. Some people cared about that sort of thing here.

"How's the fly fishing?" he asked.

Jackson smiled grimly. "Never enough time. The job has a tendency to come first, second, and last."

"Don't I know it."

"We'd like to talk to you about the Easton kids," Devon said.

David's expression turned sympathetic. In a small town, news traveled quickly. "It's a tragedy, what those kids have been through. I understand that they're missing."

"Any information you can give us in this regard would be greatly appreciated," Devon said.

"As you can imagine, we had to cancel school for the week. No power. And we don't have a generator." David gave a rueful shrug. "Budget cuts. Anyway, most of the teachers are at home, but I'm happy to answer any questions you have. It's a beautiful day. Why don't we walk and talk?"

Jackson and Devon fell into step on either side of the principal. David Kepford carried himself like a soldier, back straight, shoulders square, his stride long and confident. Jackson recalled something about a military stint in Afghanistan years ago.

Devon took out her notebook and flipped it open. "How was Cody's behavior in the last few days? Anything unusual leading up to the homicide?"

"Cody wasn't at school on Monday. But that's not unusual for him. I do recall seeing Shiloh standing alone by the bike racks after school."

"What can you tell us about him?" Devon asked.

"Cody is smart, but he doesn't apply himself. He's quiet. Serious. He's always sketching in a notebook. Truancy is a real problem. I checked; he missed twenty-six days over the last school year."

"He ever talk about what things are like at home?" Jackson asked.

"Not that I can recall."

"How about things you or other teachers observed?" Jac "Cuts or bruises. Unusual behavior."

"Those kids always have bruises. Shiloh climbs trees, falls off boulders, running around those two hundred acres like she owns it. Cody, not really. He's pale. Doesn't get enough sun. But there's never been anything obvious. Nothing actionable."

Jackson nodded. Even hammered, Easton had still been smart. If he had hurt his grandchildren, he wouldn't leave obvious bruises.

"It's more a feeling, that haunted look they both have. But then, they've experienced trauma from the brutal loss of their mother. Maybe it's that."

"Maybe," Jackson echoed.

"Any friends we can talk to?" Devon asked.

"Cody is a loner. Sits by himself. Eats by himself. Never participates in sports or after-school programs, except LEGO Robotics. He did get into that this year. I don't think anyone really knows him, other than Shiloh."

They reached the field behind the school. David halted before a fresh white line. Across the field, a figure bent over the grass with a can of spray paint. Two soccer goals stood on either end. The grass was too high, like it needed a haircut.

The man straightened and waved at them. He wore oversized denim overalls and scuffed brown work boots. White paint splattered his hairy forearms.

"Who's that?" Devon asked.

"Calvin Fitch, the janitor. He does whatever odd jobs we need done around here."

"We'd like to talk to him," Devon asked.

The principal waved the janitor over. Jackson and Devon waited. The sun shone bright overhead. A raft of white clouds drifted above the trees. The temperature was a pleasant sixty-five degrees, no wind, but rain was in the forecast. And another solar storm.

When Fitch reached them, they politely excused themselves to speak to him privately. Whenever possible, they interviewed potential witnesses alone.

"What can I do ya for?" Fitch still carried the can of spray paint. He was overweight, with slouching shoulders and lanky, dun-colored hair.

"We'd like to ask you about Cody and Shiloh Easton," Jackson said.

"Who?" Fitch's eyes clouded, then cleared. "Oh. Yeah. I know them. Don't talk to the girl much. I've seen the boy around after school sometimes."

"Where exactly?" Devon asked.

He stared at them, his eyes squinty in a wide, plain face. "Out near the field. Meeting with other kids."

"Meeting them? Like for what?" Devon asked.

Fitch gave an exaggerated shrug. "Just telling you what I see. They talk like I'm not around, like they don't see me. But I hear things."

"Can you give us specifics?" Jackson asked.

"If they want something, for a party. You know, they say to talk to Cody."

"Something like what?" Devon prodded.

"You know. Pills. Uppers. Downers. That sort of thing."

"Drugs," Jackson said flatly. He pushed down a wave of anger. Kids dealing drugs in middle school? What the hell. Drugs in Munising usually traced back to one place—James Sawyer.

Fitch shrugged again. His expression was dull, his words slow. "I dunno. I do my work. Keep my head down. But that's what I heard."

Devon asked him a few more questions, but Calvin Fitch didn't have anything further to add. Jackson thanked him, and he shuffled back to the field, shaking the can of spray paint.

They walked back to the principal, who was waiting for them. They didn't say anything about the drugs, for now.

"Has Cody ever been violent?" Devon asked. "Got into fights?"

The principal ran a hand through his hair. "Yeah, there was an incident. It happened after school a few months ago, during the Robotics club. Walter Boone is here, in the coach's office. He was there."

Jackson and Devon exchanged a glance but didn't say anything. Boone had discovered the body.

"Let's talk to him," Jackson said.

The principal led them inside the building, through darkened hallways lined with lockers to a small office off the gymnasium. He remained in the gym.

Boone sat behind a metal desk, typing on a laptop. Behind him, an opened window let in light and fresh air. Bookcases were decorated with photos of LEGO projects and beaming students. A few third-place ribbons were tacked to the wall. A pair of binoculars hung on a hook by the door.

"You must be here about the murder," he said in a mild voice.

"We are." Devon glanced down at her notebook. "We understand you found the victim."

"Not something you ever expect to see, especially not up here. It's a terrible thing, a horrible thing. Truthfully, I've had nightmares. Have you arrested anyone yet?"

"We're investigating several angles," Jackson said.

He shut the laptop and folded his hands on the desk. In his early forties, he had a bland, amiable face. "I'm here to help in any way I can. How are the kids? I've been thinking about Cody. That poor kid."

"What can you tell us about him?" Devon asked. "We understand he had a fight with another student?"

Boone leaned forward. "Cody has a temper, it's true. It doesn't come out often, but when he's pushed, it's rather frightening how angry he gets, and how quickly."

"Can you tell us what happened?" Jackson asked.

"Chad Wellington was picking on Cody. Stealing his notebook, ripping up his drawings, calling him a pussy, that sort of thing. I know we're supposed to reserve judgment, but that kid is a real prick."

Devon jotted down notes.

"Last month, this kid starts going after his sister as well. Saying she smelled. That her clothes were dirty, her hair. That she was dirty. Wolf Girl, I think Chad called her."

"I bet Shiloh took the term Wolf Girl as a compliment," Jackson said.

"I don't really know her."

"Did it bother Cody?" Devon prompted.

"It made him mad as hell," Boone said. "They had a few verbal altercations. Chad pushed him once. Then one day, after school, I had the students in the gym working on one of the robotics challenges for an upcoming competition. Chad excused himself to go to the bathroom. Cody followed him. He had a piece of metal in his backpack, probably from the salvage yard. He took it to Chad's knee. Chad played soccer. Not anymore. He might always walk with a limp."

Jackson nodded, remembering. "That was Moreno's case. Cody was a suspect, but there was no definitive I.D. No evidence. And the victim wouldn't talk."

"Chad refused to name Cody," he said. "He wouldn't even tell his parents who did it. But I know it was him."

Devon wrote in her notebook, her braids spilling over her shoulder. "Did he ever say anything about his grandfather? Did they get along? Any fights?"

"He doesn't like his grandfather, I can tell. He doesn't like to be home very much. He hates working in the salvage yard. I think that's why he joined the robotics club. Not because he likes being here, but he hates being there more." Boone shrugged. "He goes out on his boat on school nights, so he comes to the club tired a lot."

"What boat?" Jackson asked. "Cody didn't have a boat."

"He calls it the *Little Neptune*. That's all I know." The man pursed his lips. "I don't think he did this, if that's what you're hinting at."

Devon kept her expression neutral. "We're just asking questions."

"No one wants to pin this on a fourteen-year-old kid," Jackson said. "Least of all, us."

"I sure hope not. No one in this community wants to think there's a killer among us. I hope you solve this case quickly." Boone rose and stuck out his hand. His palm was soft when Jackson shook it. "Anything else I can do to help, just let me know. Enjoy the northern lights tonight. I hear they're going to be quite spectacular."

Devon thanked the principal. Two minutes later, they were out in the sunshine, headed for the patrol truck.

Devon chewed on her thumbnail and gave Jackson a sidelong glance.

"Spit it out," Jackson said. "I know you have something to say."

"I know you don't want it to be Cody," Devon said, her voice soft. "But the evidence is pointing in his direction. He's strong enough to wield that crowbar. He has a history of violence. He didn't get along with his grandfather. And if he was dealing drugs for James Sawyer..."

Jackson sighed, a tightness in his chest like a clenched fist. He didn't want it to be Cody. He truly didn't.

Devon said, "We have to follow the evidence. No matter where it takes us. Some TV detective hack told me that not so long ago."

Jackson said, "I know."

22

SHILOH EASTON

DAY FOUR

There were strangers at Shiloh's house.

Shiloh had forgotten cash. The SpaghettiOs and strawberry Pop Tarts she'd packed wouldn't last forever. And she was down to her last jerrycan of gasoline for the four-wheeler.

That was a problem.

Her grandfather kept a stash of silver junk coins and a stack of cash in a shoebox underneath a loose floorboard in front of his dresser. He hadn't known that she'd seen him, creeping down the hallway to watch him count his coins, the way they glinted in the light of the Coleman lantern.

She just needed a way to get it.

She had holed up in a cave between Christmas and Munising, a couple miles from the shores of Superior and three miles as the crow flew from Eli's campsite.

It was a cave she'd discovered years ago with Cody. They'd set up a fort when they were kids. The walls gave her a sense of security and protection; plus, it kept the rain out.

The lack of a water source was a major pain, but an ATV trail ran a quarter of a mile behind the cave and connected to all the major arteries that would take her where she needed to go. It was easy to get in and out. A good place to hide.

The aurora had returned last night, even stronger than before. It felt like living on an alien planet. It was so bright at night that she didn't need a flashlight even in the dark, everything bathed in eerie shades of rust orange and blood red.

Where the northern lights usually appeared for a few minutes to a few hours, these had lasted all night. They were beautiful and terrible at the same time.

Shiloh stood on the ridge of the western edge of her grandfather's property. The white farmhouse perched on the hill a hundred yards to her right. Two hundred yards down the slope to the east lay the salvage yard.

Just in case, she'd approached via the ATV trail her grandfather had blazed two decades ago rather than the main driveway. She'd parked it a hundred yards back, off the trail behind a screen of jack pines. It was a good thing, too.

She watched the cops, deputies, and technicians in papery uniforms walk around, snapping pictures, dusting for prints, and collecting evidence in little envelopes. Yellow crime scene tape circled a section of the salvage yard.

An uneasy feeling seeped into the pit of her stomach. No way would she get inside the house now. Not tonight, maybe not tomorrow either.

As she watched, a figure broke away from the group. The figure ducked outside the crime scene tape and shaded his eyes as he scanned the property.

He turned in a slow circle, studying the house on the hill, the woods, the slope, and the crest of the ridge line where Shiloh stood.

Head up, shoulders hunched against the wind, he headed toward her.

Shiloh shrank back. She took cover behind two beech trees. It didn't matter. Somehow, he'd already seen her.

The figure drew closer. He crossed the weedy parking lot and jogged between the law enforcement vehicles. She knew that confident gait, the windswept hair, the five-o'clock beard scuffing the square jaw.

A part of her wanted to run, but she didn't. Not yet. She braced herself, every muscle taut, ready to bolt like a fawn.

Jackson Cross halted at the bottom of the steep incline. Thorny underbrush tangled with wild raspberry and thimbleberry brambles climbed the side of the hill.

She was forty feet above him. If he came after her, she could run.

As if he could sense her thoughts, he called out, "Don't run."

Her feet flexed in her sneakers. Her crossbow was lashed to the four-wheeler, but she had her knife at her hip. She wasn't scared.

"Shiloh, please. I need to talk to you."

Jackson raised both hands in the air, palms out, like a sign of surrender. "I won't chase you. I know I can't catch you."

She snorted. At least he knew it.

He paused, as if thinking through his angles, his options. "Are you hungry? I've got a Snickers bar in the truck."

Her mouth watered. Her stomach growled. She wasn't stupid. She knew exactly what he was doing. Snickers were her favorite.

Since she could remember, Jackson had been a fixture in her life. He'd show up at home or school, always with candy. He'd ask her questions about school, about her grandfather's drinking. Whether she was studying hard and doing her chores.

On Christmas and birthdays, he brought her books. *Anne of Green Gables* and *To Kill a Mockingbird* and other ones, travel books on Indonesia, Portugal, and Crete. The topographical map of Munising.

Shiloh raised her middle finger and flicked him off.

Jackson shielded his eyes and smiled.

He was like that. Didn't matter what she said or did, how rude she was. He kept coming back.

She had no idea why he cared. He did stuff for Cody, too, buying him fishing gear, taking them both fly fishing, but it was Shiloh he worried about.

Once, when her grandfather was drunk, he'd told her that Jackson had been in love with her mother. And that he hadn't known how to fall out of love, all these years later.

Her memories were snippets. Dappled sunshine and a laughing voice. Being carried through a storm, rain on her face. A soft song and warm hands cradling her as she drifted off to sleep. Running through the woods, chasing a fluttering dress and dark streaming hair.

She'd just turned five when her mother had been murdered in the next room, when Eli Pope was convicted and sentenced to life in prison.

She didn't remember much from that day. She'd fallen into another hole in time, like with her grandfather.

She remembered a limp body. Dark hair spread across the pillow. Blood on her mother's face that she'd tried to wipe away. Sometimes, a shadowy shape at the corners of her vision.

Maybe she'd remembered once, but she didn't anymore.

"Shiloh," Jackson said again, louder.

She blinked, returning to the present.

"Let's sit down and have a conversation. With Twizzlers, hot chocolate. Chocolate sprinkle donuts from Miner's Pasties and Ice Cream."

Damn him. He knew she had a wicked sweet tooth.

Her gaze flicked to the officers down at the junkyard. They weren't paying attention to Jackson or to her. Shiloh folded her arms over her chest and shook her head. She had a mission. And she didn't trust Jackson as far as she could throw him.

"You're going to send me to social services."

"I won't."

"I don't believe you."

Jackson half-turned and glanced behind him. He ran a hand through his hair, then scrubbed his jaw. He turned back around. "There's a lot going on right now. Maybe you don't know about the power outages. The cell towers are down again. It's got people antsy, worked up."

"I know about the aurora."

"We don't know what's going to happen. It could get worse."

"I'm fine."

He stared up at her, squinting. His jaw worked, like he was trying to spit something out, but it kept getting stuck in his teeth. "There's also a convict that was released from prison. He's—"

"I know about Eli Pope."

Jackson pursed his lips. "He's dangerous and violent, Shiloh. Especially to you. Stay far, far away from him."

She glared at him. "If you're trying to scare me, it's not working."

She wasn't sure what to make of Eli Pope. Sure, he was dangerous. She sensed that right off. He intrigued her. He knew stuff that she wanted to know. Survival stuff. And things about her mother, her grandfather, her own past.

"Stay far away from him, Shiloh. I mean it."

"You don't get to tell me what to do."

"Look, I don't like the thought of you out here. Not like this, not now. It's not safe."

"Not my problem."

Jackson sighed. His shoulders bowed like he carried an incredible burden. "I have to do my job. I'm sorry, but I do. You're a minor. You're alone out here with no parents, no guardian."

"I can take care of myself."

"I've never doubted that. But that doesn't change the law. I have to bring you in, Shiloh. You and Cody both."

Shiloh knew plenty about social services. How they dragged certain kids away, never to be seen again. Or maybe they did return, but they were completely different people.

"No thanks. No way."

"Shiloh, please." He was begging now. He looked scared, desperate.

Fear started to creep in. Adults weren't supposed to look scared.

They weren't supposed to be desperate. Apprehension flared through her, every nerve on edge.

"I know what happened with your grandfather. I know he was killed, and that you were there."

The numb darkness descended. She was back there, crouched in the passenger footwell of the half-crushed car, springs from the torn seat poking her spine, shards of glass in her hair, snagged in her shirt, stuck to her skin.

And then, nothing.

Her memories were blank. Wiped clean. Only the thudding fear, the terror in the back of her throat, twisting her guts to water. *Algiers, Algeria. Luanda, Angola. Porto Nova, Benin.*

Trembling, she mouthed the comforting words, the familiar litany the only thing that could bring her back from the edge, that could force the panic to recede like a red tide.

"Cody is missing," Jackson said.

She willed herself to focus on the lists in her head until her breathing steadied and the panic receded. She needed to focus on Cody, finding Cody.

"He ran away like you did," Jackson said. "Is he with you? Do you know where he is?"

Cody had not run away. Her brother was lost, taken, stolen. Buried down deep in a hole and calling for her.

"We can find him, Shiloh. We can help him."

The cops could do more than she could. Find important stuff on computers. Bash in doors and arrest people. Rescue her brother from the monster who'd spirited him away.

The temptation needled her. How easy it would be. To give in, to give up. To let someone else do this monumental, impossible, terrifying thing.

"Cody might be in trouble."

She saw it again in her mind's eye—Cody buried alive, drowning in dirt.

Her breath caught in her throat. Jackson was one of the good guys; she'd never feared him a single moment of her life. What if she could trust him? What if he could help her and Cody?

"I can't do any of that if you don't come down here and talk to me. If you don't tell me where he is."

Indecision clutched her. Doubt and mistrust warred with hope and faith.

"There are people looking for him." Jackson waved his arm to take in the suits behind him, as if he weren't one of them. "They're searching for him right now. They have the resources to find him, Shiloh. It's better if he comes to us willingly."

Shiloh stiffened. "You think he did this."

"If you know he didn't, you need to tell us, Shiloh. We have to go on the evidence. You're a witness. You can tell us what happened. If that clears your brother, then that's how you can help him."

Her tongue stuck to the roof of her mouth. It was difficult to swallow. "He didn't do anything."

"Shiloh—"

"No!" She shook her head, emphatic. Anger bubbled up fast and furious. "Don't tell me what to do, Jackson Cross. You aren't my father. You've got no claim on me."

He looked pained. "I'm trying to help you. You and Cody both."

"We don't need your help. Leave Cody alone!"

"It'll be okay," Jackson said as if he were trying to convince himself as much as her. "It's going to be okay."

Another lie. Her heart juddered against her ribs. She'd known he would betray her. He was an adult like all the rest. An imposter. He pretended to care but none of them did.

"Come down, Shiloh. Please. I know you're cold and hungry. I'll make sure you're safe. I promise."

Bitterness sprouted deep in her belly. Wetness stung her eyes. She blinked it back fiercely. They weren't trying to help Cody. They were going to lock him up. They'd lock her up, too, if she gave them the chance.

"You're a liar."

"Shiloh, no. Let me explain—"

Shiloh took a step back. She pushed through scraggly brambles until she stood on the trail, frustrated, discouraged, and angry.

Jackson started up the side of the hill. He was coming after her.

"Go to hell, Jackson Cross."

And she turned and was gone.

23

LENA EASTON

DAY FOUR

Lena tapped the brakes. Cars, trucks, and semis crowded the highway ahead of her. Chewing her bottom lip, she glanced at the gas gauge. Still half a tank.

In the back seat, Bear raised his head and whined.

She sighed. "You have to pee, don't you?"

Apprehension flickered through her. She wanted to drive without stopping. Every stop carried risk and increased danger. Every hour, every day that passed brought them closer to anarchy.

On the radio, newscasters discussed damaged cell towers and overloaded networks. Sprint, Verizon, and T-Mobile carriers put out statements that technicians had been dispatched across the country to repair the damage. They did not mention how long the repairs would take.

This afternoon, her GPS had stopped working altogether. Good thing she had the road atlas.

Taking the highways was a calculated risk. In a crisis, the best bet was to avoid other people, but using backroads meant more miles, more time, more stops, more gas.

She absolutely could not afford to run out of fuel.

They'd taken I-75 through Ocala and Gainesville, then across the border into Georgia. In two days, they'd gone almost five hundred miles, from Tampa to just outside of Atlanta.

Traffic had slowed them down. Today, there were far more vehicles on the road than yesterday. Many vehicles towed trailers. Plenty of RVs were on the road. Most cars were stuffed with boxes, crates, and suitcases, much like her own.

A lot of people were paying attention, packing up and heading out of the cities into rural areas.

Last night, she'd driven the last hundred miles with the sky like a red ocean, the aurora undulating waves. The way the lights swayed across the velvet-black heavens reminded her of jellyfish drifting in the deep.

She'd never seen anything like it. Even Bear had awakened for the show, leaning his head out the opened window, tongue lolling, grinning like a hairy brown fiend.

"It's pretty but it's dangerous, buddy."

Bear chuffed in response.

"How dangerous? It's going to be bad, that's all I know."

She'd contemplated utilizing some of her cash to spring for a hotel room, but she couldn't justify spending two to three hundred bucks simply to sleep.

No way was she leaving Bear alone in the Tan Turd. Or leaving her supplies unattended.

Instead, she'd found a truck stop outside of Marietta and parked between two semis. The place was packed. She'd checked three different truck stops before she found an open spot.

She'd slept with her M&P pistol on the center console beside her, fully loaded with a round in the chamber. If something happened in the middle of the night, she'd be damned if she wasn't ready to defend herself with lethal force.

Bear was protective, but he wasn't the optimal guard dog—he wanted to lick and love on almost everyone—but he was a good warning system. He'd bark if anyone got anywhere near the SUV, whether it be human or squirrel.

As she passed billboards for carpet stores in Dalton, green hills rose all around them. She listened to the radio as scientists discussed the stunning auroras at tropical latitudes—over Cuba, Hawaii, Jamaica, the Bahamas, as far south as Portugal.

Millions of people in dozens of countries had canceled work and school to throw lavish midnight parties, dancing in the streets, setting up tents and lawn chairs to watch the sky.

She rolled her eyes and switched channels. How could so many people not realize what was coming? The information was out there, if they were willing to listen.

"...The FAA has grounded all planes, leaving millions of travelers stranded leading up to Memorial Day weekend. The FAA released a statement that it was necessary to cancel flights due to damage to low earth satellites. Stay tuned for further updates..."

She switched the station again. "...The primary threat of a CME and the resulting geomagnetic storms is to electrical power transmission grids, oil and gas pipelines, undersea cables, telephone networks, railways, satellites, et cetera. Small-scale electronics won't be affected, but we won't be able to access any of the systems we depend on. For example, almost every system from communications to banking to aviation is dependent upon GPS data..."

As they approached the Tennessee border, traffic increased again. Bear woofed unhappily, tail thumping the window, the back of her seat, the back of her head.

"Oof." She reached back with one hand and swatted his fluffy butt. "I know, I know. Bathroom break. Just give me a second."

A wave of dizziness washed over her. One eye on the road, she checked the screen on her pump. Her blood sugar was getting low at 80.

Time to eat. With one hand, she rummaged in her bag, pulled out an apple juice box and granola bar, tore off the wrapper with her teeth, and ate while driving.

A blue rest stop sign appeared ahead of them. Bear thumped the back of her seat with his tail. He stuck his head between the seats and panted in her ear, hot doggy breath on her face.

He needed a break. So did she. Her thighs burned, her butt was sore, her head pounded. They still had a thousand miles to go. "I know. We're stopping, I promise."

Her muscles tensed as she pulled off the highway and navigated the parking lot. The place was packed. Every parking slot was taken. Several dozen vehicles had driven over the curb and parked in the grass.

Lena followed suit, snagging the last spot beside a picnic table.

She holstered her pistol before exiting and opening the door for Bear. He bounded out with a relieved woof and promptly began peeing on the rear wheel.

Lena stepped back and scanned the parking lot. She could feel eyes on her. Families were crammed at picnic tables and spread out on the grass. Several children were crying. People looked frazzled and stressed.

She got food and water for Bear, then checked the mini-fridge. Still good and cold.

The alarm beeped on her phone. Lena needed to calibrate her pump and sensor every twelve hours. That meant pricking her finger, using a test strip, and inserting it into her glucometer to read her blood sugar, then loading that number into the pump.

Every seven days she needed to change her infusion set and sensor, but she hoped to get to the UP by then.

Quickly, Lena calibrated the pump while keeping one eye on the parking lot, her ears straining for unusual sounds.

Tension drummed through her. She needed to use the restroom, but she was loathe to leave her supplies. The refrigerated vials inside that ugly SUV were her life, her salvation. "Stand guard, Bear."

Embarrassing as it was, weird as she felt, she squatted right there in the parking lot next to the Tan Turd and did her business.

Bear rounded the side of the SUV and stared at her, head cocked, ears pricked.

She glared at him. "Really? You're supposed to be keeping an eye out."

He plopped on his haunches and gave her a goofy grin.

"That's it. You're fired."

After using wet wipes to clean up, she tried calling Jackson again. Was he paying attention to the warnings? She knew how he was. When he was on a case, it consumed him.

He would believe her—she knew he would.

Sometimes the phone rang, sometimes it didn't. Texts didn't go through. She'd managed to connect once for twenty seconds, enough time to tell him she was coming but not to tell him to get ready.

With a sigh, she pocketed her phone and scanned the horizon. No sign of the aurora, though dark clouds bristled on the horizon to the south. Electrons sizzled in the air, the wind picking up, whipping strands of chestnut hair into her face.

A storm was coming. It was headed straight toward them.

24

JACKSON CROSS

DAY FOUR

"What do you have?" Jackson asked.

"Dumb phones aren't working." Devon set the phone on the table and squeezed into the booth. "Again."

"Everything's scrambled because of the solar storms," Jackson said.

Devon chewed on her thumbnail. "I thought that'd be done by now. Every day, they're like, 'Surprise! We've got another one. Gotcha!' It's not funny anymore."

"The universe has an ironic sense of humor."

"Or a perverse sense of punishment. I feel like the ant under the magnifying glass being tortured by the gods. I just want to check my Insta ten million times a day. Is that too much to ask?"

They were grabbing lunch at the Falling Rock Cafe on Munising Avenue before heading back out. Devon had ordered another beef and potato pasty; she couldn't get enough of them.

Jackson dug into his broiled whitefish, the best tasting freshwater fish, reeled in from the deep waters of Lake Superior. Though the town didn't have power, the restaurant was running on a generator.

Devon had spent the morning with the crime scene techs while

Jackson had hooked up with the park service to search for Cody Easton's missing boat.

They'd found nothing. Neither had the Coast Guard. If the fishing boat had become unmoored—or intentionally released—it could be in any of a hundred coves or inlets along the coast.

After lunch, they planned to head back to the crime scene and hike to the coast from Easton's property. Outside, the sky was turning an ugly shade of gray; they needed to hurry.

The case file was opened on the table between them. Devon pointed to a crime scene photo of the print with blood transfer that they'd found near the back fence. "The DNA came back. It's the victim's blood. We found a shoe box for a pair of size nine Nike Air Force 1 sneakers in Cody's closet. Morena tracked down another pair at a shoe store in Grand Marais. The treads match the plaster cast of the footprint."

"That's a popular shoe. Could have been someone else."

"It's most likely Cody, boss. You know that."

"It still doesn't mean he's the perpetrator. Keep going."

"Most of the prints were a size eleven in mens. Cody is a size nine. Amos has sneakers that are a size eleven, boots that are eleven and a half. The smaller prints, size four in womens, match the shoes in Shiloh's closet. A couple of prints match Walter Boone, but he discovered the victim, so that's to be expected. We have dozens of partials we haven't been able to match. Customers came into the salvage yard all the time."

Jackson leaned forward and rubbed the stubble on his jaw. "And the murder weapon?"

"Easton's prints are on it. Cody's prints aren't in the system, but the techs lifted a print off his chromebook's fingerprint reader. Cody is also a match."

Jackson shook his head. It was far from a smoking gun. "Cody worked in the salvage yard with Amos. He could have picked it up a dozen times for a legitimate purpose."

Devon looked dubious.

"What else?"

"There is a partial print on the tire iron that doesn't match any hits in the system. Hasting is tracking down the list of customers over the last thirty days, focusing on the five folks who visited within seventy-two hours of the crime. We'll see if we get lucky."

"We need more than luck."

Devon finished her pasty and used a crust of bread to sop up the last of the juices. A line appeared between her brows. She was focused, considering the options, the angles.

Jackson knew what she was thinking. "Say it."

"Here's what I have." She ticked off the evidence on her fingers. "No signs of a suspect entering or exiting the property. Cody's fingerprint on the murder weapon. Cody's likely footprint with blood transfer that places him at the scene, near the victim. Cody's established propensity for violence. He has the means and opportunity. And the motive.

"Say he's had enough of his grandfather's drinking and snaps. Or maybe Easton goes after Shiloh and Cody defends her, like he defended her from that bully at school. Cody kills his grandfather, then panics and flees. Shiloh witnesses the horrific cycle of family violence repeat itself, gets scared, and runs away."

It was the obvious answer.

It felt like the air had been sucked out of the room. "It doesn't feel right."

"Maybe you're too close to it."

It was possible. Maybe more than possible. Still, he didn't want to believe it. Jackson clenched his jaw. "Don't count your chickens before they're hatched. There's a lot of directions this case could go yet."

"Occam's Razor seems relevant here, boss."

"When you hear hoofbeats, think horses, not zebras."

"Exactly." She paused. "Underwood seems like he's under a lot of pressure to close this case fast."

"I know that."

He felt the pressure like a thousand bricks slowly crushing his chest. There was never enough time. He'd hardly been home in four days. He had yet to investigate Ruby Carpenter's missing person's case. Her mother had stopped in at the sheriff's office this morning, begging for an update.

Though Sheriff Underwood had told him to drop it, he wouldn't. He'd have to investigate on his own time. He'd called her friends and discovered nothing. He'd also talked with Shiloh and Cody's classmates and come up empty.

Devon shook her head. "How hard can it be to find one teenage kid?"

"Two teenage kids," he said. "Don't forget Shiloh."

She was still in the wind. He'd tried to follow her yesterday, but she was too fast. She knew the woods far better than he did; there were a million places to hide.

Hiawatha National Forest alone accounted for 879,000 acres of rolling hills, dense forests, and wetlands. It contained hundreds of miles of ATV, snowmobiling, and hiking trails.

When the waitress came by, Devon ordered a mocha latte to go, extra chocolate syrup. Jackson asked for black.

"We're about out of syrup, hon," the waitress said. "We're running low on a lot of things. Tomorrow, we'll be operating on a reduced menu. No more coffee."

Devon stared at her. "What do you mean, no more coffee?"

The waitress shrugged. "We haven't received a delivery since this thing started."

Jackson's phone rang as the waitress took their cash payment. It was Hasting. Local calls went through occasionally; long distance calls were the issue.

Still, it failed twice before he finally got ahold of Hasting. The connection was staticky.

Jackson gripped the phone. "Spit it out before we lose service."

"The warrant came through. Sprint delivered the goods. We still haven't found Easton's phone, which means it's either been destroyed or the battery died. Last time it pinged a cell tower, it was in Alger County. Sprint was able to bring up the call log. Normally, we'd get the text messages, too, but they're having server issues and don't have it yet. Big surprise."

"And?"

A buzzing silence. Then static.

"Hello?"

"I'm here, I'm here." Hasting's voice came through tinny, half-fading, but clear enough for Jackson to make out his words. "You're never gonna guess who's on that log. And no less than five times in the last ten days alone."

"Hasting, for the love of all that's holy, spit it out."

Hasting paused for dramatic effect. "James Sawyer."

25

JACKSON CROSS

DAY FOUR

Devon lowered her binoculars and pointed. "What's that?"

Jackson joined her along the lip of the bluff. In the distance, storm clouds gathered. Lake Superior whipped herself into a frenzy, the waves crashing against the cliffs.

A dense fog had rolled in as they'd hiked the two-mile trail from Easton's salvage yard to the edge of his property along the coast.

He had no idea why Sawyer had called Easton, but they were going to find out. Hasting and Nash were looking for Sawyer, but Jackson knew he wouldn't speak to them. He was slippery as an eel. Everywhere at once, his fingers in every pie.

Jackson would have to do it himself. It was a task he dreaded.

Devon grabbed the sleeve of his jacket and pointed. "There!"

Jackson followed her gaze. Great boulders littered the base of the cliffs. To the left was a sheltered cove with a narrow sliver of sandy beach.

A dock jutted into the water. A weathered shed stood anchored to flat rock near the cliffs, likely used to store ropes, fuel, tackle, and other boating paraphernalia.

"There's no record of a dock here," Devon said. "No permit ever pulled. I checked the county records this morning."

"Amos probably built it himself and ignored regulations and permits. No surprise, there."

Devon edged closer to the drop-off, trying to get a better look at the dock, but she was too close.

"Be careful," Jackson called.

Small pebbles gave way beneath her feet and tumbled over the edge of the cliff. Devon took a rapid step back from the ledge. Her brown skin went ashen. "It's steep here."

"That's why you stay away from the edge."

"Yeah, yeah. I got it." She raised the binoculars again, then pointed. "I think there's a path down to the beach over there."

They gave the edge a wide berth as they headed east until the narrow path revealed itself. It was a rocky, steep descent. It took a good five minutes to pick their way down to the dock itself.

"It's in good shape," Jackson said. "Used recently, too." He studied the smooth straight boards, the lack of algae build-up on the wood or the rope pilings.

"I see something. Down at the water line, among the rocks."

Jackson looked where Devon pointed. Past the dock fifty yards, a litter of boulders crowded the base of a jagged cliff. One of the boulders was smoother, brighter than the others.

He stared harder, squinting. The boulder moved, bobbing with the waves.

"It's a fishing boat," Jackson said. "Flipped upside down."

The storm drew closer, the sky darkening, the heavens about to open up and drench them.

Cautiously, they picked their way along the sandy beach, climbing over water-slick boulders, mindful of the swirling eddies and deeper pools between the rocks. The wind threatened to pull them off the rocks into the wild surf.

As they approached, Jackson recognized the name painted onto the side. *Little Neptune.*

They'd found Cody Easton's boat.

Jackson's phone rang. They'd hiked back to the salvage yard in pouring rain. He pulled it out of his pocket, relieved. Every time cell service went out, he wondered if it would return.

Six new messages blinked back at him. Four from his mother, one from his sister. A voice mail from Hasting, but it was just static.

And four missed calls from Lena.

Anxiety hummed through him. He'd been worried for days. Sixteen hundred miles was a long journey; still, she should be here by now.

He gestured for Devon to go on ahead to the patrol truck. He ducked into the corrugated metal shed, which smelled like gasoline and cut grass.

Rain dripped down his face. His hair was plastered to his scalp. He pressed the call button.

She picked up on the fourth ring. "Jackson."

"Lena. You okay?"

"Shiloh..." Lena's voice came through tinny and distant. She sounded stressed. "Is she safe? And Cody?"

"We're still looking. We could use your help."

"I've had some...troubles. Bear and I are okay. I should be there tomorrow but...need to tell you..."

The phone spat static.

"Lena? Can you hear me? Lena?"

"...Jackson. Have you seen the news...about the sun? The solar storms?"

"Yes. I have some supplies. We're set for a while."

"That's not good enough. It's going to get worse...a lot worse."

His gut clenched. Lena was smart. He'd always trusted her judgment. He'd been so consumed by this case, he hadn't paid attention like he should have.

"There was a scientist on TV... I believe him, Jackson. A big one is coming...bigger than this planet has ever seen...he said it's going to change everything. It's coming. In a day. Maybe two. We need to get ready."

Rain drummed the metal roof. Outside, leaves swirled in gusts between the rows of desiccated vehicles. The crime scene tape flapped wildly, bright yellow against gray sky and mud-brown earth.

The aurora had returned, flickering faintest red behind the clouds. Beautiful yet ominous.

His stomach filled with razor blades. "Get here as soon as you can, Lena."

"Jackson...It's the beginning of the end."

The phone went dead.

26

ELI POPE

DAY FOUR

It was a rough afternoon on Lake Superior. The wind buffeted Eli. Electrons sizzled the air. A wall of angry dark clouds roiled across the western horizon, headed their way.

Two men met Eli at the dock. One wore a heavy woolen shirt and a close-fitting fisherman's cap, the other was tall and rake-thin, with scarred knuckles and a lazy eye. Hard men. Criminals.

"I'm looking for Sawyer," Eli said.

"Sawyer's busy."

"Tell him it's Eli. Eli Pope."

The shorter, fatter man glared at him, unmoved. His tiny eyes were piggish in his fleshy, windburned face. His nose was crooked; he looked like the type of man who started bar brawls and finished them.

"Tell him," the one with the lazy eye said. "Go."

The short one huffed but obeyed, stomping down the deck toward several boats in their slips. He gesticulated at another man busy unloading crates from a nearby speedboat.

Eli waited on the dock. The fat man kept an eye on him like he might steal a crate of fishing tackle out from beneath his nose. The tattoo scrawled up the side of his thick neck was a Russian symbol he recognized but couldn't quite place.

Among several other business ventures, clean and otherwise, James Sawyer owned Sportfishing Charters, which hugged the west side of the bay, sandwiched between an outfit offering glass-bottomed boat shipwreck tours and Pictured Rocks kayaking tours.

A sleek white yacht bobbed at the far end of the dock. *Risky Business* was scrawled in gold script on the rear. A black and white skull and crossbones flag hung from the gaff. Sawyer was nothing if not ironic.

A man disembarked the yacht, leapt over the side, and landed easily on his feet. He strode down the dock, the wind whipping unruly dirty blond hair into his eyes. His gaze settled on Eli. For a long moment, they stared at each other. Then his weathered face broke into a smile. "Well, if it isn't Eli freaking Pope."

Eli dipped his chin. "Sawyer."

James Sawyer was tall and lean and muscular, with a three-day beard, high sharp cheekbones, and crafty eyes set wide, like a shark's.

Depending on the light, they were blue or gray, but there was no depth behind them, no emotion. Just a flat watchfulness. An alertness, like a wild animal always looking for the trap—or his next meal.

"The prodigal son returns," Sawyer said.

"Something like that."

"You've got balls of steel. I'll give you that."

Eli's lips twitched. "That ever in question?"

"Not for a second." Sawyer gestured at the sleek yacht behind him. "Come take a ride with me."

"In this weather?"

Sawyer met his gaze and did not look away. His eyes were neither friendly or unfriendly, just watchful. "You scared?"

"Never."

"Didn't think so." Sawyer glanced behind Eli as a third man approached.

Eli felt incredibly uncomfortable. Four of Sawyer's protection team surrounded him. They were armed and looked tough. Professionals. Former military.

Sawyer glanced at one of his lieutenants. "All clear?"

The man nodded.

Sawyer gave Eli an apologetic smile. "I have two counter-surveillance teams at each end of the dock, watching the area. If you came here wearing a wire, the cops would be nearby. He just told me no one is covering you or surveilling us. You came here alone."

"I could have told you that."

Sawyer grinned. "I'm sure you would have." He pointed at an antenna array and dish on his yacht. "I even have a drone detection system. The DEA can be, shall we say…intrusive."

"Like I said, I'm alone."

"They'll just need to search you. You understand."

Eli bristled but allowed Sawyer's mercenaries to frisk him. The one with the fisherman's cap passed an RF meter—radio frequency detector—over Eli's body.

"Boss," Lazy-Eye pointed at Eli's pistol, his knife.

"We'll take good care of them," Sawyer said. "Trust me."

Eli didn't trust Sawyer as far as he could throw him, but they'd always had an understanding, a certain rapport. And Eli wanted answers.

After Eli had removed his weapons and handed them over to one of the mercenaries, Sawyer motioned for Eli to climb aboard. Without a word, two armed men who'd been aboard disembarked, leaving Sawyer and Eli alone on the yacht.

With expert precision, Sawyer maneuvered the boat from its slip and out into the choppy bay. Eli glanced back at the dock, where six burly men stood watching. He observed the tell-tale bulge of weapons beneath their jackets.

They did not appear pleased that Sawyer was leaving them behind.

"A few of my men are former Russian GRU special forces. You can never be too careful these days."

"I can tell."

"Isn't she a beauty?" Sawyer returned his attention to his boat. "Fifty feet of pure power. State of the art. Hydraulic progressive Trac thrusters. Warping winches so I can easily muscle in a spring line against wind and currents. Teak floor and solid wood cockpit."

"Sure," Eli said, though he didn't care.

At the cockpit, Sawyer looked like a king surveying his domain. He was lanky and loose-jointed, his movements seeming lazy and unhurried, but there was intent behind everything he did.

Of that, Eli had no doubt. Some things never changed.

"Anyone else, I'd tell 'em to go fly a kite. I'm incredibly busy. These solar storms have opened a host of exciting business possibilities. Not you, though, Eli. I always have time for old friends."

The words held hidden meanings, secret barbs. Though Sawyer had hung out with them from middle school through high school and beyond, often joining up for kayaking, cliff jumping, drunken bonfires on the beach—he had never belonged to their inner group.

That intimacy, the specialness they'd shared had been reserved for the four of them—Eli and Jackson, Lily and Lena. Eli suspected that Sawyer had resented his outsider status.

Still, Sawyer had brought the crazy to the party. The booze. The weed. The harder stuff. Sawyer always had access and shared liberally—for a price. By his sophomore year of high school, he was the prime dealer of anything illicit for the under twenty-five crowd.

Whatever you needed, if Sawyer didn't have it, he could get it.

Their senior year of high school, Sawyer's father had been arrested for narcotics trafficking. He had been the link between two criminal organizations, a gang out of Detroit and an organized crime baron in Quebec.

For more than a decade, Sawyer senior had trafficked illicit substances between Sault Ste. Marie, Canada, and Sault Ste. Marie,

Michigan, using mules to cross the bridge into Canada multiple times a week.

Sawyer's father was still imprisoned in the Alger Correctional Facility prison, serving the remainder of a twenty-five years to life term. Rumor had it that Sawyer had taken over his father's business, with the goal of transforming himself into a kingpin of the Upper Peninsula's criminal underworld.

Eli had heard that Sawyer ran a syndicate of criminals from Mackinac Island up to Whitefish Bay, and west at least as far as Copper Harbor, the northernmost point in Michigan.

Sawyer was smart. No law enforcement agency had ever been able to pin a thing on him, not even a traffic ticket. Eli admired him for that, if little else.

They motored out of the cove into open water. Six-foot waves slapped the hull. The sky and lake blended together—gray as slate and just as unforgiving.

"How was your stint in the slammer? I heard it was rough for you."

"I survived. Luckier than some. Unluckier than others."

"Luck had nothing to do with it. I did what I could to help you in there."

Eli had run across a few of Sawyer's foot soldiers in prison. Sawyer Senior still had sway. His son held more. They had reached out to him, he'd rebuffed them. He wasn't a joiner. After that, they hadn't bothered him.

Still, he didn't doubt Sawyer's word. If one of his people had gotten wind of an assassination attempt, they could've put a lid on it before anyone laid a hand on Eli.

Not even Sawyer could touch Darius Sykes, though. Sykes was a monster of a different breed.

"Never let it be said that James Sawyer isn't loyal to his friends."

Eli snorted. "You have a misguided sense of loyalty."

"Kept you alive, didn't I?"

Memories threatened to choke him. Shadows moving along

concrete walls. The glint of a razor blade. The gleam of teeth before they bit. Hard men who enjoyed hurting.

He thought of Sykes. The monster's promise to hunt him down and slaughter anyone Eli had ever loved.

"I kept myself alive."

"What are you doing here, Eli?"

"Seeing an old friend."

Sawyer gave a hard smile. "We both know that's B.S. Sounds like something Jackson would say, not you. I didn't take you for a blowhard. But people change, I suppose."

"I'm here for information."

"Information I have." He shot a sideways glance at Eli, dispassionate, assessing.

Eli had the sense that Sawyer didn't care whether he'd killed Lily or not. Whether he was the Broken Heart Killer or innocent. It was a disconcerting feeling. He'd been judged and found wanting by everyone else. Sawyer didn't have a conscience.

Sawyer raised his voice over the thrashing wind. "You interested in a job? I could use a man with your particular skill sets."

Eli didn't answer. He waited for Sawyer to elaborate.

After a beat, Sawyer said, "I'm speaking of your tactical abilities. Of course."

"Of course," Eli said stiffly. "I'm not looking for a career change."

"A man needs money. No matter who he is."

"I'm fine." He wasn't, but he wasn't about to become indebted to someone like Sawyer.

Eli waited. This was feeling more and more like a mistake. His lungs constricted. There were no walls here, no manacles, no locks, but he felt trapped.

There was no escape on Lake Superior. No land within sight, only the gray bucking waves.

Sawyer smiled at him as if he knew exactly what he was thinking—and enjoyed it. It was a shark's smile, cold and calculating.

A second later, Sawyer's shoulders relaxed and he slapped Eli on the back. "I heard you were camped out in the woods."

"I like the woods."

"Well, damn, so do I, but I don't care to sleep out in the cold with spiders crawling all over me and mosquitoes eating me alive. Not unless it's for a good reason." Sawyer side-eyed him and flashed him a vacant grin. "Of course, you are Ojibwe. You have that wildness in your veins, I guess."

Eli stiffened. The boat rocked beneath him, but he kept his balance, muscles tensed, senses alert for the slightest movement from Sawyer. Sawyer's men had stripped him of weapons, but he didn't need a gun to do damage.

An elbow to the throat, a fist to the kidneys to incapacitate him, a swift kick behind the knees and a push to send him over the side of *Risky Business*, tumbling into the depths of a lake so deep and cold, it might as well be the ocean.

"It's a shame, is all I'm saying. Man of your talents being wasted."

When Eli didn't say anything, Sawyer continued. "Opportunity exists in chaos. You know this better than anyone, I'd bet. It's like a fight. The man who throws the first punch wins."

"Usually."

"Yes, usually."

Sawyer didn't speak for a minute. He seemed to be listening to the roar of the wind with his entire body. He had likely memorized the shape of every bluff, every cove and bay and shoal.

He was a man of the Great Lake, born to live on the water, as thirsty for the waves as Eli was for the woods and streams and dirt beneath his fingernails.

Eli admired that about him. Always had.

"There's a short window of opportunity here. I'm going to seize it, Eli. I have plans. You say the word, and you're welcome on board. My right-hand man. You and me, together. We could do something big. Real big. Larger than you can even imagine."

Eli said nothing. He wasn't interested. Never would be.

"Storm's coming," Sawyer said absently. "Lesser men would get off the water, seek safe harbor. I say, drive into the storm. Face it, conquer it, become it."

"If it doesn't kill you first."

"Nothing can kill me. I'm the cockroach that survives the apocalypse. If you're smart, you can be, too."

Eli shook his head.

"It's coming, you know. The apocalypse. It's real this time. With a little advice, you could set yourself up well."

"I'm not here for your advice, Sawyer."

Sawyer shot him a look. His expression still placid, the slightest annoyance flaring in his eyes. "Then, pray tell, why are you here?"

Sawyer maintained eyes and ears everywhere. He would know almost everything that went on in the town he called home, illegal or otherwise. He was the type of man you wanted on your side. He was plenty dangerous otherwise.

An asset when he was with you, as long as he could be controlled. As long as he obeyed orders. Eli had known plenty of men like him in the army. The rogues. The cowboys. The criminals. They tended to get weeded out quickly.

Sawyer, however, was a survivor.

Eli said, "I want to know who framed me."

27

ELI POPE

DAY FOUR

A thick wall of fog rolled in. The shoreline had disappeared. It felt like the entire world had disappeared with it.

That the land they would return to, if they returned, would be far different than the one they'd left.

Sawyer didn't give any indication that he was surprised or taken aback. His expression didn't change. He said nothing for several minutes.

Eli recalled him as a teenager, perpetually scheming and manipulating, that disheveled hair and disarming smile entrancing a bevy of adoring girls and duping the authorities.

Sawyer wore emotions like masks he could put on and discard at will. It was seldom that he revealed a true feeling. Even when he did, it was for a reason. To lure in an ally, to lower an enemy's defenses.

Everything was a calculation with him. Always had been.

The yacht sailed into the wind. Huge waves broke against the hull again and again. Cold spray hit Eli's face, his torso and limbs. He blinked the water from his eyes but didn't look away. To do so would be seen as a weakness, he was certain.

"I'll throw you a freebie. This once, for old times' sake."

Eli wasn't sure if he was supposed to grovel, to wax eloquent with gratitude. He didn't play games. He said nothing.

"I don't normally do pro bono. It's poor business, you understand."

"I know the drill."

For several minutes, the roar of the wind and waves were the only sounds. Thin lines of foam whipped the water white and frothing. Sawyer expertly maneuvered the boat around a finger of rock thrust above the surface of the water. He was controlled, alert, exact.

There was something shrewd and cunning in Sawyer's windswept face. Whatever Sawyer claimed, this wouldn't be free. The price would be steep.

Eli had known that going in. When the time came, he'd pay it—or eliminate the debt another way. There were always options for a man like Eli.

He hardly felt the cold burn of the wind. Impatience snarled in his chest. Anticipation mingled with trepidation. He was both desperate to know and dreaded the truth.

What it would mean. The implications. The fallout.

"I need to know who planted the beer bottle. I need to know who framed me."

"You sure you want to know? There's no going back from that. Once you've leapt from the cliff, the only direction is down."

Eli didn't hesitate. "Yes."

Sawyer nodded to himself. "Who were you with that night?"

"I went to the Northwoods Bar. Had a couple of beers with Gideon Crawford. Tim was bartending." He closed his eyes, remembering. "Cyrus Lee sat at the bar with some buddies. Sheriff Underwood was there, moaning about the Lions' loss."

"What did you do after the bar?"

"Went to see Lily." It had been a short visit. There and gone by eleven p.m. A single mother with two young children, Lily had still lived at home. Amos was usually out of the house, gambling and drinking. That night, he hadn't returned until dawn.

Eli had slept with Lily but didn't love her. There was too much darkness inside him. He had loved Lena, but he had never been able to keep her. She was too pure, too good, especially for him. He'd ruined the best thing he would ever have.

Beneath Lily's beauty, there was a sliver of darkness that matched his own. They had both been damaged. Lily had wanted him, despite —or maybe because of—her sister. And he had not turned her away.

They had deserved each other.

Eli had plenty to be ashamed of. Guilt was an intimate friend. Mistakes and bad decisions littered his past. But he had not killed her. Of that, he was innocent.

"And before the bar?" Sawyer asked.

"I went to Jackson's. We watched the game."

He'd thought it through a thousand times in his cell. Every time, he'd come up empty. Tim Brooks and Gideon Crawford would have had access to his used beer bottles. Cyrus Lee, too. But what reason would they have to frame him?

Sheriff Underwood had always despised him. Good old-fashioned racism. Or maybe he'd just wanted to close the case fast and Eli was the simplest target.

Then there was Amos Easton, who had hated Eli since the day fifteen years ago when Eli had seen the bruise on Lena's face. Eli had confronted Amos, threatened to kill him if he laid a hand on Lena or Lily ever again.

"Jackson's, huh?"

"It wasn't him."

"Are you sure?" Again, no reaction in Sawyer's expression. Just that shark's smile that played around his lips. "Who got the press? The praise? The promotion to undersheriff?"

"Jackson. He never wanted that stuff."

Sawyer shot him a pitying glance.

Nausea churned deep in his belly. It wasn't sea sickness. "He never wanted that stuff. He didn't care about the press."

"You're certain?"

"Yes."

"There were...anomalies in your case. There were rumors of an unreliable witness. The judge wouldn't give them a warrant." He gave a careless shrug, then hunched his shoulders against the biting wind. The dark clouds opened up and rain poured down, heavy droplets pelting the yacht.

"They'd decided early on that it was you. Once you were in their crosshairs—" Sawyer raised a hand to the side of his head, made a gun of his finger, and mimed pressing the trigger. "They were going to nail you, no matter what they had to do."

"That doesn't mean it was him."

"It was, Eli. It was Jackson."

"How do you know? How can you know for certain?"

"Because I've had a particular officer of the law on my payroll for five years. He gets regular payments, which he needs to feed his healthy addiction to eight balls of blow—and hookers. Both of which I supply him. I have the film. He'd go to prison. I own him. One night, I got him particularly hammered. He told me everything."

The blood drained from Eli's head. A great rushing filled his ears that was not the wind. His legs went weak. "No."

"The officer that stopped Eli did so on Jackson's instructions. He 'found' the evidence Jackson had planted for him to find."

His tongue was thick in his mouth. He couldn't get enough oxygen. "What cop?"

Sawyer gave a sharp bark of laughter. "My informants are my own."

Eli stared across the lake, unblinking. The haunting landscape of mist and dark water. Never had he been so starkly reminded of his own mortality. How brutal and fickle Mother Nature could be.

"The aurora will be back again tonight," Sawyer said, nonchalant. "She'll do her worst with a Mona Lisa smile, just like this girl does." He gestured at the lake with his own enigmatic smile.

Eli couldn't focus on the maze of his words. He was reeling from

Sawyer's revelation. Rolling the words in his mind like agate stones polished by the rushing surf.

He could not find defects in the logic. Neither could he make an argument against the sickening twist in his gut that confirmed the truth of Sawyer's words.

Maybe Sawyer was lying, but he didn't think so.

Sawyer watched him with dark eyes. "The question now is, what will you do with that information?"

Eli didn't respond. He couldn't.

"I wonder," Sawyer said slyly. "I wonder what you will do."

"Take me back to shore."

"What chaos will you wreak, Eli Pope?"

Eli met his sharp gaze with his own. "I said take me back."

Sawyer threw back his head and laughed. Eli could barely hear it over the wind.

Mist glued Sawyer's dirty blond hair to his forehead in sculpted curls. He looked like a creature of the sea, a captain bravely manning the *SS Edmund Fitzgerald* freighter before it sank in the storm-tossed waters in 1975, a modern-day Ulysses determined to avoid the siren's song.

"Sawyer!" Eli said.

"No need to worry," Sawyer said. "I will always get you back, safe and sound. Haven't I just offered you a massive favor?"

"There's a price." He barely heard his own words over the rushing inside his skull. "There's always a price with you."

Sawyer's smile reached his eyes for the first time. Sunlight playing on dark water. Obscuring the monster of the deep sliding beneath the placid surface. "There's a price for everything, my old friend. Most people just don't realize that they're paying it until it's too late. All of life is a transaction. When you know that going in, you're going to come out with the better end of the deal."

"I make no deals."

Sawyer said, "Sometimes, you don't have a choice."

He worked the throttle and turned the yacht in a slow arc. Waves sloshed the hull. The rain slapped down as they motored back toward shore. The fog obscured everything. Eli could see no land, no safe harbor.

The brutal cold of Lake Superior would drown a man within sight of shore as mercilessly as it would out in the middle of open water. Submerged logs, dangerous rocks below the surface, sudden gales that drove hapless ships into unforgiving outcroppings.

Over three hundred and fifty shipwrecks littered the cold dark bottom of the lake. At least half remained undiscovered to this day. A thousand generations had lived and died on this lake.

How many more? How many lives would sink, simply vanishing, never to be seen again, never to be found? How many had been thrown overboard, bodies intentionally dumped? Possibly by the man standing next to him.

"They say over ten thousand people have lost their lives to this lake," Sawyer said as if he'd read Eli's mind. "Eerie to think about, isn't it? Some of those bodies still down there. Right beneath us."

"Lake Superior never gives up her dead."

"No," Sawyer said. "She doesn't. She keeps her secrets."

Finally, the rugged shoreline appeared out of the dense fog. Mere outlines in the murkiness. The bright beam of a lighthouse shone like a tiny star in a universe of gray. The beacon leading them to safety.

"So do I," Eli said, so quietly that the storm took his words and whipped them away. "So do I."

28

JACKSON CROSS

DAY FIVE

Saturday morning dawned bright and sunny. The northern lights had lit up the sky the night before, putting on a spectacular show. Inside, the lights had flickered, power surging before it went out and did not come back on.

Jackson's family was sitting at the dining room table when he came home from running errands around ten a.m.

His father, Horatio, fiddled with a radio set on the table next to a platter of bacon, eggs, and pancakes. Jackson's mother, Dolores, bustled around the massive kitchen in heels, serving everyone but herself.

Once, they'd had a maid and an in-home chef. Those days were gone, though his parents both cared about keeping up appearances.

The table was set with a meal fit for a king. Mounded platters of sizzling bacon, scrambled eggs, and fluffy pancakes. Large glasses of orange juice. Homemade cinnamon rolls no one was even eating.

Jackson felt sick. "I thought we talked about this. We should ration our food. The power is going to be out for a long time."

His sister Astrid snorted. "The power company has their people working on it now. They're saying a couple of days, as soon as the damn auroras end."

"They're wrong."

"It's just a power outage," Astrid drawled. Her eyes were half-lidded, like she'd already taken more than her share of Valium. She was on a multitude of prescriptions. "We've weathered them fine before."

Astrid was almost six feet tall when she stood. She was broad-shouldered, sturdy, and beautiful. Their family's Scandinavian descent was apparent in her ice blue eyes and silky blonde hair that framed striking Nordic features.

Astrid had never been able to maintain a regular job. With their family's considerable wealth, she hadn't needed to. She was not confined to a wheelchair but used one due to the chronic pain in her legs from the drunk driving accident that had shattered them fifteen years before.

Dolores bent over backward to see that her every need and want was met. They all did.

"There's food at the grocery store," Dolores said. "I don't understand, honey. We're fine. Everything's fine."

"When is the last time you went to the grocery store, Mother?" Jackson asked with a calmness he didn't feel.

"On Monday."

"Before the auroras started."

"What's your point, Jackson?" Astrid asked.

"The local grocery stores are empty. I checked this morning."

Dolores paused over the frying pan and blinked at him. She had no answer. She'd never considered the possibility. In her late fifties, she was slender as a whippet and wore a white pantsuit, her silver-streaked hair swept back in a French twist.

Astrid gave him a patronizing smile. "I'm sure things will be restocked by tomorrow."

"Not this time." After his phone call with Lena, he'd listened to several radio station broadcasts. While some still downplayed the disaster, a few were taking it seriously.

Lena was right. If the geomagnetic storms worsened, the power might not come back on for a decade. Society as they knew it would collapse.

Horatio sighed. "Not this prepping stuff again."

"If not now, when?" he snapped. "When we're all starving with nothing to eat?"

His mother shrank back, a look of consternation on her face.

"Jackson," Horatio said sharply.

"I apologize, Mother. But the fact remains. And why are all the lights on? We should save the generator only to run the essentials—"

Astrid waved her hand to encompass the expansive dining room, the massive house. "These are the essentials."

Flustered, Dolores touched the pearls at her throat. She wore them without fail, even on days she didn't leave the house. Her face went pale. "Surely you're joking, Jackson."

"I'm not."

"I can't live like that. We can't live like that."

Lena's words echoed in his mind. "We need to get ready."

Astrid guffawed. "Get ready for what? Armageddon? Please."

"You're not listening—"

"That's enough!" Horatio barked. "You're scaring your mother, Jackson." His father spoke with a booming finality. He took a sip of coffee and set the mug next to his half-eaten plate of eggs and bacon. "Enough."

Jackson was at a loss for words. She didn't get it. They didn't get it. No, they refused to understand because they didn't want to.

An engine rumbled outside. Astrid's boyfriend pulled into the driveway in his red Ford Mustang. Cyrus Lee entered the house without knocking, as if he belonged there.

Dolores greeted him with a kiss to the cheek. She scurried around the oversized kitchen, getting him a plate he was perfectly capable of getting himself.

"Thank you, ma'am," he said with exaggerated graciousness. He sat next to Astrid's wheelchair and shot Jackson an appraising glance.

Cyrus was an unwelcome fixture in the Cross household, at least to Jackson. Where Astrid was an intimidating presence, even in her wheelchair, Cyrus was thin, wiry, and bristled with dark energy. He had a narrow, ferrety face.

He came from money and good breeding. His great-grandfather had been the owner of a prosperous copper mine in Keweenaw County. For work, he did some sort of Wall Street day-trading from his couch.

Cyrus had dated Astrid for years. They'd never married. In all that time, Jackson had never grown to like him. He was entitled, arrogant, and damn creepy.

Jackson figured his parents were simply grateful that someone wanted their disabled daughter. They only cared that his pedigree was respectable.

Dolores retrieved a second cup of coffee for Astrid. "Sit down, Jackson. Eat with us."

He'd lost his appetite. Guilt and resentment needled him. This was his family. For better or worse.

Jaw clenched, he moved around the house, flicking off light switches. His family watched him like he was an alien creature they didn't understand.

Morning light streamed through the oversized bay windows. Outside, past the double-level deck, the lake reflected the pristine blue of the sky, clouds like billowy cotton.

He strode through the gleaming kitchen and made for the basement stairs.

"Where are you going?" Astrid asked.

"To check our stores. Make some notes. See where the holes are, and shore them up while we still can."

"Good luck with that." There was a false syrupy sweetness in her voice that grated on his nerves. He ignored her.

He had a list in his head. It was growing by the second. More propane for the generator. Batteries. Anything solar powered. More ammo. Additional first aid supplies.

Would they need to grow their own food? He was terrible at that sort of thing, but Dolores loved gardening. Instead of roses and lilies, they needed heirloom seeds and materials to build a green house.

Jackson's parents assumed money and influence could buy their way out of any problem. Not this problem. And not this time.

He doubted they knew how to deny themselves anything. They continued to consume everything around them like they'd done their whole lives, as their ancestors had done for generations.

Their baron grandparents and great-grandparents had exploited the land and water, stripping the earth of precious metals, cutting the great timber without a thought to conservation, to what might be left after they'd ravaged it.

They had never stopped to consider the sources of their consumption. Or that the resources they squandered could be used up.

As he descended the stairs, he took the flashlight from his belt and flicked it on. He lived in the finished basement. A storage room was located to the right of the downstairs bathroom, inside the home gym.

The last time he'd checked their stores a few weeks ago, he'd built up six months of food, toiletries, and first aid for the four of them. He didn't consider himself a prepper, but when you lived in a hostile land like the UP, you needed to be ready for anything.

Inside the storage room, it was windowless and dark. He swept the flashlight beam over the wooden shelves he'd built several summers ago—and froze.

He blinked, looked again.

Every shelf was completely barren. The five-gallon buckets of beans and rice were gone. The plastic containers of MRE were gone. The boxes of canned goods, of vegetables and fruits and tuna. It was all gone.

29

JACKSON CROSS

DAY FIVE

Jackson's hands shook. The flashlight wavered. He stared, stricken.

What the hell had happened? The months of buying extras, the time spent organizing the supplies by date, rotating food in and out. All wasted. Disbelief, frustration, and anger warred within him.

All this time, he'd felt okay, confident he had this stash. He'd had time to figure things out. Except now he didn't.

They had no backup. No reserves. No safety net.

Jackson backed out of the storage room without bothering to close the door. Numbly, he moved to the stairs. Frenetic thoughts ricocheted inside his head. He couldn't focus, couldn't think.

A growing sense of alarm built inside him. He was balanced upon the lip of a cliff, far too close to the edge, vertigo about to push him over.

Astrid rolled her wheelchair to the top of the stairs. "Something wrong, brother?"

Jackson stood at the base of the stairs and stared up at her. "What the hell did you do?"

Astrid loomed above him. Cyrus stood behind her, a silent hovering shadow. In the shadowy light, his eyes were bottomless.

Jackson's hands balled into fists at his sides. Anger roiled through him, sharp and bitter. He struggled to control it, to control himself. "What did you do?"

"Whatever do you mean?" she asked.

He hated it when she spoke like that. Derogatory, insulting, but with a cloying, saccharine sweetness. Smiling at him, her hands caressed the wheels of her chair, as if simultaneously taunting him and reminding him of her helplessness.

That was the problem. No one could get offended. No one could get upset. Astrid was forever the maimed crippled girl, a permanent victim. No matter what she did, how she treated people, her small cruelties.

"Where the hell is everything?" he demanded.

Her pretty smile widened. "You know I have a heart for charity. I donated all those boxes to people who really needed it. The Harbor was so grateful to receive all the supplies. It will do some real good."

"How?" he choked out. "When?"

"On Monday, actually. They brought a truck. Cyrus helped lug everything upstairs. He was so helpful. You work all the time, anyway. I knew you wouldn't notice, and you didn't."

He vibrated with restrained rage. How could she? How could she invade his private spaces, steal what didn't belong to her?

But he knew how. And he knew she'd enjoyed every second of it.

Her blue eyes glinted. "You don't need to be so selfish. You're the one always talking about helping others. And all along, you had this stash you were hoarding, all to yourself."

"That was for us. For all of us. To hold us over in case of a disaster, or..."

"Or what, Jackson? Nothing. Nothing is happening. We're fine."

"We're not fine. That's what you don't get."

"Then you'll figure it out, won't you? You always do."

He climbed the stairs with legs like cement. The anger drained out of him, replaced with a dull emptiness. He felt like a stranger in his own house.

He reached the top step. "Move."

His sister gave him an even, appraising stare. A tiny sneer appeared at the corners of her mouth. "Mind your manners."

"Please."

Very slowly, she wheeled her chair back, allowing him passage. Her eyes dared him to challenge her. To fight. To yell. To lose his cool.

Cyrus said nothing; he didn't need to. He stood behind Astrid and smirked. Jackson resisted the temptation to punch him in his smug face. He would deserve it, too.

Jackson knew this familiar song and dance. His parents would rush to her defense. His mother would cry. His father would yell. They would do their best to make him feel small, to put him back in the comfortable box where they kept him. It's what they did.

"Jackson will take care of us," Dolores said. She sat at the table and with a full plate, but she hadn't taken a bite. "Won't you, Jackson?"

"I'll fix it," he said heavily. "I'll figure it out."

Dolores rose and circled the long dining table. She approached him and placed her dry, thin hands on his face. She drew him close and kissed his cheek. Her breath smelled of vodka.

Love tugged at him—love and obligation. He had never known one without the other.

Once, he'd dreamed of leaving and never coming back. Escaping the way that Lena had, the way his brother had. With his brother's abdication, then his sister's accident, he was the only sibling left to care for this crumbling dynasty.

He touched his mother's silvery hair. She leaned into him, her bones thin and fragile as a bird. "What would we do without you?" she murmured into his chest.

He knew he would keep doing what he always had. He would

swallow his anger and find a way to take care of them, to keep them safe, whether they deserved it or not.

It was his responsibility.

Jackson kissed the top of his mother's head and gently extricated himself from her grasp.

"Where are you going?" Cyrus asked as Jackson headed for the front door. It was the first time he'd spoken to Jackson that morning.

Jackson took his keys off the hook and pocketed them. "I'm going to Marquette for supplies. I have to replace our stores that Astrid gave away, if it's not too late already."

Astrid crossed her arms over her chest. "No nuts."

"I am aware."

"They'll kill me. I'm deathly allergic."

"I know," he said with a patience he did not feel. "Nuts are an excellent survival food for the rest of the family. I'll be careful and keep them separate from anything you would eat."

She looked at him like he was the crazy one. He felt the strain of their expectations, their needs. It was a burden he'd carried his entire life.

Cyrus slouched into a chair at the end of the table and pulled out his phone but didn't look at it. He watched Jackson with an intensity that was disconcerting.

Jackson met his gaze until he looked way. Furious with all of them, he clenched his jaw and fought it down. He was the peacemaker. As frustrating as they were, they needed him.

And, much as he hated it, he needed Astrid's help. He'd been putting off the Ruby Carpenter case for far too long. "I have a case. You might be able to help."

Astrid beamed at him. "Of course I'll help you, big brother. I love helping other people. It's what I do."

"Ruby Carpenter. Her mom says she usually stays at the Harbor."

The Harbor was a youth homeless shelter located just outside of

Christmas. The facility provided a clean, safe bed for the night, drop in laundry and shower services, and free counseling.

In her great benevolence, Astrid volunteered two nights a week—when she wasn't out doing who-knew-what with Cyrus.

"Yes, I know her. She's been in and out since she was twelve years old."

With a pang, he thought of Shiloh. Out there somewhere, lost like Ruby. He thought of Cody, how he'd been trapped in that rambling house with Amos Easton, potentially driven to kill.

They weren't the only ones who'd slipped through the cracks. The UP had seen its share of lost girls. Lost boys, too. Mostly runaways. Victims of overdoses, domestic violence, tragic accidents.

They didn't have the resources to find them. He felt like he'd failed them all.

"She's not at the shelter," Astrid said. "I check the logs. She hasn't been there in at least a month."

"Do you have any idea where she might have gone?"

Astrid shrugged. For someone who worked with troubled teens, she could be incredibly indifferent to the plight of others. "She's had boyfriends in Marquette. There's a shelter over there she's talked about before. Don't remember the name. Sorry."

He was headed to Marquette anyway. He could kill two birds with one stone. "I'll check it out."

She squinted at him. "Why are you wasting your time with her? She's nothing but white trash."

"Your sister is right," Horatio said in derision. "That girl is a chronic runaway. Her older sister was, too. That whole family is trouble. Besides, you have far more important things to focus on."

"Funny, the sheriff said the same thing."

"Sheriff Underwood isn't the sharpest tool in the toolbox, but he's right." Horatio Cross leaned back in his dining chair and studied Jackson. "You want a prayer of being sheriff yourself, you need to reorder your priorities, son. Solve the important cases, and stay in the sheriff's good graces. The city manager and the governor, too. Sheriff is a political position."

As the prior sheriff of Alger County, his father's priorities were and always had been political alliances. Power, influence, and authority.

Jackson cared for none of those things.

While his father valued power, Jackson coveted a life of order. Right and wrong. Black and white. He sought order, rules, his faith—they were his solid ground.

Nothing more and nothing less.

"Her mother deserves to know where she is." His stomach twisted in knots. It was difficult to focus. He couldn't stop thinking of the empty storeroom, what that meant for their future.

He had to escape this house. He couldn't breathe enough oxygen. Without another word, Jackson opened the door and left his feckless family behind.

30

SHILOH EASTON

DAY FIVE

Shiloh spent an hour listening to the wind-up emergency radio she'd borrowed from her grandfather's shed. She'd rather listen to music, Billie Eilish or Glass Animals, but there were only staticky messages about the power outages and satellites not working.

There was still no power in town. At night, she drove the ATV down the long country roads. Even in what passed for town, it was dark and quiet. Those who had generators were careful in conserving what fuel they had.

Using her lockpick set, she'd broken into Sheldon Murphy's shed behind his farmhouse and stolen the jerrycan of gasoline he kept for his riding lawnmower.

She felt bad about it, but not enough to stop.

And then last night, she'd gone to Lindsey Mae Sutherland's out on Dancing Fern Lane because she baked chocolate mousse pies on Fridays to serve for potluck at church.

Shiloh knew this because she and Cody had been dragged to church whenever their grandfather felt too guilty for slapping them around and decided God could save him. God never did.

Shiloh had been devastated to find zero pies in the rank refrigerator. Instead, she'd rummaged in the cupboards and borrowed an unopened jar of peanut butter, a bag of Doritos, and five Oriental Ramen Noodle packages. Jackpot.

She never stole anything crucial. She took bags of M&Ms and Snickers, frosting-coated Pop Tarts and Lays potato chips. Occasionally a book she liked. *Call of the Wild* and *The Man in the Iron Mask* had been bootlegged from lakefront vacation homes.

She'd discovered something else in Mrs. Sutherland's house. On the kitchen counter sat several flyers. The flyers featured a photocopied image of a girl with red hair, black eyeliner, and a hard, unsmiling mouth. "Missing: Ruby Carpenter" was scrawled in big block letters above the picture.

Shiloh knew this girl. Ruby had gone to the high school but had dropped out. Shiloh had seen her talking with Cody several times out by the bike racks after school. Cody would give her something, and she'd hand him cash, their movements sneaky and furtive.

The hairs on the back of her neck had stood on end. But what did it mean? That's what she didn't know.

Before she'd left, she'd stuffed one of the flyers in her pocket. Now, it was somewhere in her backpack, a wrinkled mess.

Her stomach rumbled. She put thoughts of the flyer out of her mind and set about making dinner. She'd brought some food but not enough. Camping by yourself was harder than it looked: gathering firewood, starting a fire, boiling water, catching food, and then cooking it.

You had to be incredibly patient. And you couldn't make mistakes. She'd burned the first hare she'd caught in a snare to a black crisp. Hungry as she was, it was inedible.

Shiloh had managed to recreate the Dakota fire pit the way Eli had shown her. She crouched next to the pit outside the mouth of the cave entrance and heated up a can of SpaghettiOs in a cast iron pan.

She was tired and dirty, hungry and alone. Her scalp itched. Ants had invaded her sleeping bag, probably because she'd curled up there and eaten half the Doritos bag last night. She'd never missed a shower so much.

Eli made it look easy.

She kept thinking about him. How he wasn't what she'd expected. How he smelled of woodsmoke and kerosene. Not what a murderer should smell like.

She'd gone back to his campsite three times in the mornings since she needed to refill her water bladder. She would hang back, staying within the woods, where the shadows crouched, shielding her.

Shiloh felt drawn to him, fascinated by this strange man who chose to live in the woods. She should hate him. All her life, she'd heard horrific stories about him, the terrible things he'd done. The boogie man of her childhood. A monster. The cannibalistic windigo.

But she didn't see a monster or a windigo. She saw a man who hadn't hurt her. Who'd talked to her like she mattered. Who didn't belittle or scorn or send her away.

She no longer believed that he'd killed her mother. He was dangerous, certainly, but a different kind of dangerous.

Besides, she had the crossbow. If she felt threatened, she could always shoot him.

When she visited the camp site, he never looked at her directly, but she had the feeling he'd known she was there the whole time. He tended the fire, gathered firewood, fished the stream, washed his clothes, and sterilized water in a weird gadget that looked like a small rocket.

She watched him pull off his shirt and drape it over the handlebars of the mountain bike he'd leaned against a nearby jack pine. He was strong, his chest and arms padded with ropy muscles.

Her gaze was drawn to the long, thin scars on his stomach. On his lower left side was a dime-sized pucker of shiny flesh, as if from a bullet. A minute later, he'd pulled out another shirt from his pack and tugged it on, hiding the brutal landscape of his flesh. He adjusted the pistol he carried tucked inside his jeans.

Then he bent, removed a protein bar, and set it on a rock in the middle of his campsite, then went about his business. She knew what he was doing. He was coaxing her out into the open. It worked.

She'd crept out of the trees like a fox—wary and anxious, but eager, too. And so hungry. The crossbow was in her hands, nudged up against her shoulder, a bolt loaded.

"Hey," he said.

She didn't respond.

Eli sniffed. "You smell. Had a bath recently?"

"None of your damn beeswax."

He angled his chin at her crossbow. "You can put that down. I'm not going to hurt you."

"That's exactly what someone who's gonna hurt you says."

He sat on a log he'd dragged near the fire and studied her. "Keep carrying it. Bet your arms are getting tired. Good luck eating that chocolate protein bar with your hands full."

He made a good point. She edged closer. The crossbow did weigh a ton. Her mouth watered traitorously.

Shiloh lowered the crossbow and set it on a large flat rock, still loaded. Withdrawing her knife, she held it low at her side and snatched up the candy bar, then retreated several steps.

"Better?"

"If you touch me, I'll peel your face like a potato."

The corners of his mouth twitched. "Understood."

Keeping one eye on Eli, she ripped open the wrapper with her teeth and took an enormous bite. Flavor exploded in her mouth. Delicious chocolate and caramel and nuts.

She wanted to close her eyes to relish the exquisite joy of chocolate, but she couldn't take her attention off the wolf.

A tame wolf was still a wolf. And nothing about Eli Pope pointed to tame.

Shiloh pointed to the rocket-shaped thing next to him. "What's that?"

"It's a solar kettle. You fill it with water, then open the sides like this. The reflective sides conduct heat and boil the water, sterilizing it. You never want to drink water from the lake or the river without filtering it first. You can use the hot water to make coffee, tea, oatmeal, whatever."

"Why don't you just boil water over the fire?"

"It takes a lot of effort and uses a lot of firewood. More than most people think."

"Yeah, it sucks hairy coconuts." She chewed on her candy bar. Her gaze settled on a rumpled shape draped across the log beside him. "And that?"

"That is called a ghillie suit."

He showed her how he'd taken a surplus camo hunting jacket and sewed on strips of burlap from a coffee sack over brown netting, using fishing line, 550 paracord, a sewing needle, and some glue. He'd used braided jute twine and demonstrated how he separated the twine into separate fibers. He tied them into the netting all over the jacket and then added twigs and leaves.

"It's the art and science of camouflage. It breaks up the human outline and helps you blend into your surroundings. This is how you disappear in plain sight."

"To sneak up on people before you kill them?"

He shot her a sharp glance. "Something like that."

"Like a lion hiding in the grass while it creeps up on the antelope," she said in awe, impressed. She wanted one.

The river gurgled, the water running clear over mossy rocks and submerged branches. It was sandy near the river, the ground pebbled with stones. Black flies swarmed over the water's surface.

While Eli worked on his ghillie suit, Shiloh dug one hand into the front pocket of the hoodie she wore—Cody's hoodie—and pulled out the small baggie she'd discovered in the pocket a few days ago.

Through the plastic, she rubbed her fingers over one of the little blue pills.

Shiloh knew what her brother did, that he gave certain kids Adderall pills in exchange for money that he was saving for art school. This was what he'd given Ruby Carpenter.

She thought of the missing person flyer with Ruby Carpenter's photocopied face.

Cody and Ruby had known each other. They were both missing. What did that mean? What was the connection? Was there a connection?

And if there was, how would she find it?

She wasn't acting like a hunter. What had she done so far? She'd broken into some houses and wandered around Christmas and Munising, avoiding cops, jumping at her own shadow.

Downstream, a great blue heron stalked its prey. It stepped stiff-legged in the shallows. A moment later, it plunged its beak below the surface, then plucked a wriggling fish from the water. She watched the heron swallow it whole.

Though it wasn't cold, she shivered.

It was time to hunt.

31

JACKSON CROSS

DAY FIVE

As Jackson drove fifty miles west to Marquette, he considered the case, the many threads that had seemed so disconnected, but might not be.

Cody was a prime suspect in his grandfather's homicide. He had motive, means, and opportunity. He had a history of violence. His bloody footprint put him at the scene.

And then there was Sawyer, always lurking in the background. Why had Sawyer called Easton so many times? Was there a connection between Sawyer using Cody as a drug dealer and the murder? Or the fact that Cody had borrowed a boat registered in Sawyer's name?

There were too many coincidences. Jackson did not believe in coincidence.

What if Sawyer had ordered Cody to kill his grandfather for some reason? But why? There were too many unanswered questions.

He needed to talk to Sawyer himself. Even if Sawyer wouldn't talk to anyone else, Jackson might be able to get something out of him. Though far from friends, they had decades of history between them.

Needing a distraction, he turned on the radio and listened to the news. Norway, Switzerland, Belgium, Germany, and dozens of countries across the Northern Hemisphere reported complete blackouts. The stock market had closed, along with all financial institutions.

China's public transportation system was down. Hundreds of cargo ships were stranded off the ports of Singapore, Shanghai, Los Angeles, and Houston. Massive global shortages were being reported across the food, medical, and transportation supply chains.

The authorities made no mention that the cascading effects might be permanent.

Apprehension shivered through him. Things were getting worse. The old adage about panic was a thin excuse. People deserved the time to prepare. They deserved the truth.

He entered the city and drove through the streets of Marquette. He passed long lines at a food bank. The gas station lines snaked around the corner. Grocery stores and hardware stores were packed.

The afternoon's bright blue sky felt insidious. Like Mother Nature was mocking them, playing with them like the Greek gods played with human fates.

At the first homeless shelter, Room at the Inn, they recognized his photo of Ruby Carpenter, her red hair and defiant pout. Astrid was correct; Ruby had stayed here, but not for over a year. No one had seen or heard a word from Ruby Carpenter.

He gave them the standard missing person information. They promised to keep a lookout.

He felt his hope dwindling. She was out there, somewhere. He wanted to bring her home, especially now with the looming disaster. He'd made a promise. And Jackson hated to break a promise.

The second shelter was located on the outskirts of Marquette. It was a small home run for indigenous girls and women, called simply *Nindaanis* House. *Nindaanis* meant "my daughter" in Ojibwe. It was unlikely that Ruby had stayed here, but he would check anyway.

At the front counter, Jackson showed his badge and pulled out the slightly wrinkled flyer. "Have you seen this girl?"

The woman behind the counter was in her seventies. Wrinkles

scoured her face, her silver-white hair pulled back in a braid. She was Native American, likely Ojibwe.

She sat behind a plexiglass window, two ancient computers set atop the countertop, the screens blank. The cracked yellowish linoleum floor had seen better days. Two vanilla-scented candles set on the counter flickered, deepening the crevices beneath her eyes.

The woman frowned as she took the flyer through a slot in the glass. "She is far from home if she is here. But I have not seen her. I am here every day; if she walked through these doors, I would know."

Disappointment constricted his throat. He turned to go.

"Wait." The woman's chair squeaked as she wheeled across the room, opened a filing cabinet, and riffled through it. She yanked out a photo and squeaked back to the plexiglass window.

She shoved it through the slot at Jackson. "You come here searching for your pretty white girls, but how about this one? You never come looking for them."

Jackson held the 5x7 photo of a girl of about sixteen. Long glossy black hair. Lovely dark eyes. High cheekbones. She wore ripped jeans and a tight white T-shirt, her arms crossed defiantly over her chest. Dark marks speckled her forearms. She was Ojibwe.

"She came from the Keweenaw Bay Indian rez, but she talked about a half-brother in Bay Mills. She stayed with us three months at the start of the year. She was addicted to heroin, but we got her into a sponsored treatment program with methadone. Many girls don't make it, but she was cleaning herself up. She had dreams, things she wanted to do. One of the ones who might make it."

She grimaced like it pained her to speak the words. "Her half-brother offered her work in Munising, leading kayaking tours to Pictured Rocks for the tourists. I do not remember his name. She left in March and promised to call when she arrived. No one has seen or heard from her since then. My cousin in Bay Mills says that she never arrived."

Jackson couldn't tear his gaze away from the girl's haunted eyes.

There was something about her. Something both tough and soft, tragic and strong. "What is her name?"

"*Niibin* is her real name. It means 'summer' in our language. Summer Tabasaw, in yours."

"I'll ask around. See if I can find her."

Her gaze hardened. "Will you?"

"I will."

From the other side of the plexiglass, she jabbed a thin finger at him. "Do you see those marks on her arms?"

He looked at the photo again. He saw them. He knew what they were. "Cigarette burns."

"She didn't do that to herself. It was her mother. They say a mother would never do things like that. They can. They do."

He swallowed. He'd seen those burns on child abuse victims. On addicts. Domestic violence cases. And on Lily.

Wild and haunted, a bright girl running from a darkness inside herself that he'd never understood in his youth, and still didn't understand now.

"No one cares about these girls. They die. They go missing. They leave with bad men and do not return. No one looks for them. Not downstate, and certainly not here."

"I care," Jackson said.

"Do you believe the electricity will return?" the old woman asked abruptly.

He hesitated. No one had asked him that outright. "No," he said finally. "I think that things are going to get bad. Very bad. It may be a long time before it gets better."

She nodded, seemingly satisfied with his honesty. "If this happens, there will be more to fear than hunger."

"What do you mean?"

"The monsters of society, they hide. But when there are disasters, when bad things happen, the monsters gain strength. They feed on pain and fear."

"I know."

"They won't need to hide anymore. They will hunt in plain sight. Who will stop them?"

He couldn't take his eyes off the woman, her beetle-black eyes. A tightness in his chest, his throat dry as old bones. "I will," he said. "I will stop them."

She leaned back in her chair, scorn and disbelief in her wizened face. "Do you believe that?"

"Yes, I do." He tapped the photograph. "May I have a photocopy of this picture?"

"No electricity. The things done before can no longer be done the same way." She studied him for another minute, her bloodless lips pursed, wrinkles spanning the skin around her black eyes. "Take it. You said you'll look for her. So look. Do what you have said you will do."

He didn't know this woman from Adam, yet he felt her words like an accusation, like a pronouncement of guilt.

"Ma'am," he said, his words measured as he slipped the girl's picture into the pocket of his windbreaker. "I will try."

32

JACKSON CROSS

DAY FIVE

At Lake Superior Outfitters, the shelves were sparse. In another day or two, they'd be barren. The aisles were crowded, people hurrying with their heads down. A sense of quiet urgency permeated the store.

No music played over the speakers. The fluorescent lights were off. Daylight streamed through the front windows and glass double doors. The deeper into the store he headed, the darker it was. Near the back, people used their phone's flashlights to scan the shelves.

Jackson pushed the old woman's words out of his head and focused on the task at hand. He would worry about what she'd said later.

He procured a couple of solar chargers and extra solar panels, a second camping stove, several wind-up flashlights, an emergency wind-up radio, battery and solar LED lanterns, and extra propane canisters for the grill and portable heaters he had in the garage.

He stocked up on ammo for his Remington shotgun and Glock 17, then picked up the last solar dehydrator. With a dehydrator, he could keep meat preserved, along with fruits and veggies.

When he checked the generator aisle, they were all gone. A smaller secondary generator would be helpful to augment their whole-house generator, which hooked up to their propane tank.

The checkout lines were long. Fifteen to twenty people in each lane. The store accepted cash only; the handwritten sign was taped to the front door.

The next person in line could only purchase half of her cart's contents. She swore at the cashier and stormed off with the half she'd paid for.

The couple in front of him tried to pay with a credit card. They had a solar generator in their cart, along with sleeping bags, a rocket stove, and a portable water purification system.

The cashier explained in a flat voice that the machines were down. He looked bored. Not even an impending apocalypse could get a rise out of him.

The couple argued, cajoled, begged. The woman had choppy blonde hair and wore an oversized hoodie with sweatpants. Her partner was a heavyset guy in a green Packers jersey. He smelled of cigarettes.

"We have a checkbook," the woman said. "Come on. Just let us pay and get out of here."

The cashier shrugged. "Like the sign says, cash only. If you don't have cash, I can't help you. If you don't step aside, I'm gonna have to call security."

The woman cursed and flicked him off. The man's hands formed fists, legs splayed like he was prepared to fight. His face reddened with embarrassment and anger.

Jackson tensed, ready to intervene. He wore plain clothes, but he carried his service pistol, concealed by his windbreaker, and he had his badge. This wasn't his jurisdiction, but he'd get involved if things got dicey.

The cashier stared them down. "Step aside, please."

"Move along!" someone behind Jackson shouted.

Grumbling, the couple left their cart where it was and stalked out of line.

Jackson pointed to their cart. "I'll take that generator."

"If you got cash, you can have it. That's the last one."

He always kept cash on-hand for emergencies. "I do."

"Lucky dog," muttered the guy behind him, a middle-aged man in a plaid shirt and trucker hat that stated, "Truckers do it Best."

The cashier strolled around the counter and dragged the couple's cart out of the way. A pile of carts loaded with unpaid-for camping supplies crowded the front of the check-out aisle.

The remaining folks in line grew quiet. The tension was tangible. A few lowered their heads, bills clutched in their hands, silently counting through clenched jaws. They eyed the abandoned carts greedily.

Jackson peeled off a large number of twenty-dollar bills. Movement snagged the corner of his eye. A cop's intuition made him look up.

The couple hadn't left the store. They lurked near the front doors. The woman kept her back to the check-out as she pretended to peruse a rack of sunglasses.

The guy in the Packers jersey telegraphed his intent with furtive movements. He crept closer, his expression nonchalant.

As the cashier counted out Jackson's change, Packers snuck up behind him and seized the cart with the solar generator.

Jackson took three swift steps past the check-out counter and reached the perp. The man didn't have a chance to move. Beneath his windbreaker, Jackson nudged him with the muzzle of his service pistol.

Packers flinched, startled. "What the—"

"Law enforcement," he said in a low voice so only the man could hear. "You don't want to do this, trust me. It's not the way to go."

The man froze. His face contorted in fear and anger.

"Release the cart. Go to your wife and leave the store. Don't come back. Do as I've instructed immediately, and I won't arrest you."

Fear won out. Packers released the cart and lifted both hands just high enough to keep them in Jackson's sight without drawing attention. "I'm going, man. I'm going." He hesitated. "I'm sorry. It's just—my wife..."

The woman turned around, one hand on her swelling belly. She had to be eight months pregnant. Jackson hadn't seen that from behind.

"We've got another little one at home." Packers' voice was strained. "She's five, and she's asthmatic. We need electricity to run the nebulizer when she has an attack. We know the power might not come back on for a long time. I've never stolen in my life—I would never—we need that generator. I'm sorry."

Pity welled in Jackson's chest. He felt himself softening. He had the money. At the same time, cash was king. He knew he would want it later. And yet, it wasn't in him to turn his back on a young family, not when it was within his power to help.

The cashier stared at them, as did the people in line behind him.

"Everything all right there?" the trucker asked.

"Everything's good. Just chatting with a friend." Jackson lowered his voice. "Take the generator."

Stunned, Packers stared at him, open-mouthed. He'd expected to be arrested. Or at the least, forced to leave empty-handed.

"It's yours. As long as you take a word of advice," Jackson said. "Burn that jersey. Get yourself a Lions one instead."

The man blinked. Then a slow smile spread across his face. "Hell no, sir. But I appreciate the thought."

Packers took the cart and returned to his wife. Their heads bent as he whispered something to her. The woman tossed a grateful look over her shoulder at Jackson.

Together, they hurried from the store as if they feared someone would steal their treasure before they got it home. Give it a week or two, and they might not be that far off.

Jackson waited for them to leave before he returned to the counter and accepted the change from the cashier. He loaded the back of the truck and headed for the nearest superstore.

Near empty shelves greeted him. He imagined the only reason they weren't completely bare was the cash-only rule. With banks closed for days, folks couldn't access their own money. Few people had enough cash reserves on hand.

Families hurried from aisle to aisle, dumping products into their carts as if in a trance. People looked tense, worried, and anxious. No one made eye contact.

The toilet paper was gone, as was sun block and bottled water, but he managed to snag a few quarts of bleach for water purification. Their house was on well water. He was glad he'd installed the solar well pump a few years ago.

Astrid had mocked him, but after the propane for the generator ran out, the solar pump would provide water to the sinks and showers and flush the toilets.

He filled two carts with the leftover canned goods like tuna, ravioli, green beans, and beets. Next was peanut butter, beef jerky, powdered milk, sugar, salt, and baking soda.

Then he grabbed the last of the large bags of dry beans, pasta, and rice. He added five-gallon buckets, some mylar bags, and oxygen absorbers for long-term dried goods storage.

By the time he finished, his cash reserves had dwindled to less than a hundred bucks. It was dark when he hit M-28 and headed east toward home. Above him, shades of crimson, tangerine, and hints of green striped the sky in undulating curtains.

He'd gotten no closer to finding Ruby Carpenter. Or Shiloh and Cody. He'd just added another missing girl to his list.

His truck overflowed with supplies, but it seemed meager compared to what lay ahead of him. What lay ahead of them all.

33

LENA EASTON

DAY FIVE

The Tan Turd rumbled along I-75, headed toward Toledo. The green rolling hills had flattened out as Lena passed corn and soybean fields. Heavy traffic had slowed them down.

They'd had to refuel outside of Columbus, Ohio. Without generators, many gas stations were closed. The ones still operating were rationing. Ten-gallon limits, cash only.

She'd stopped at five stations at different exits to fill the tank and the jerrycans, wasting three hours. There were long lines. Vehicles were backed up along the roads, horns honking, people losing their tempers.

Everyone was edgy and agitated. No fights had broken out, but a few had come close.

Now, though, every gas station she passed was closed. They had no electricity to run the pumps, or they had run out of fuel.

With her jerrycan reserves, she should have just enough to get to Munising.

She scanned radio stations, chewing a glucose tablet and sipping an apple juice to raise her blood sugar.

One station discussed rumors that the president, the vice president, the National Security Council, Congress, and the Supreme court were being moved to undisclosed locations.

Photos had been released of two white 747s leaving Andrews Air Force Base. They were the "Night Watch" E-4Bs that provided an airborne command post for the president and could direct large-scale military operations or respond to major disasters. They were also hardened against EMPs and CMEs.

Both Pacific and Atlantic submarine fleets had been spotted leaving ports. Large numbers of military aircraft were rumored to be headed to undisclosed locations. State guard units were being ordered to report to their staging areas.

She shivered. She didn't know what it all meant, only that it wasn't good.

How long until the country descended into pure chaos? When people's pantries ran dry in a day or two? She'd read that many families only kept three days' worth of food on hand.

Paying attention to the early warnings could be the difference between making it and not, between reaching sanctuary and being stranded a thousand miles from safety with no vehicle, no gas, and millions of scared and desperate people standing between you and your destination.

She glanced in the rearview mirror. Bear sat happily in the back, head stuck out the window, floppy ears streaming against his skull, mouth open, jowls flapping in the wind.

Lena couldn't help but smile. No matter how bad things might get, as long as she had Bear, she could endure it.

Bear barked.

"I know, I see it."

Something was up ahead. Lena slowed, but she had no intention of stopping. They approached a caravan of three vehicles on the side of the road—a minivan, an SUV, and a Prius.

A kid of twelve or thirteen stood on the shoulder, thumb out to hitch a ride. Beside him sat three little kids in varying states of disarray, two of them crying. A little girl stared at Lena with wide and frightened eyes.

Next to the Prius, four adults stood in a huddled circle, heads down, gesticulating wildly, as if deep in a serious conversation. They must have run out of gas.

The little girl waved.

Bear barked in greeting.

Pity tugged at her, but what could she do? There were too many of them to hitch a ride. She couldn't afford to give them a drop of fuel, or she wouldn't make it, either.

Bear gave a plaintive whine, his huge head stuck out one window, his fluffy tail banging the glass of the opposite window. He was tired of being cooped up. He wanted to play. Mostly, he wanted hugs and kisses from adoring little people.

"Sorry, buddy. I'm really sorry, but we can't stop."

It hurt her heart. Everything in her wanted to help. She had the sinking sensation that everyone would need help soon, and there would be no one to give it.

The task was too overwhelming, too enormous.

What would these highways look like a week from now? A month? She thrust the what-ifs out of her mind and focused on the here and now.

The end of the journey was within sight. She just had to make it there.

34

SHILOH EASTON

DAY FIVE

After dark, Shiloh took highway 58 out of Munising and drove the four miles northeast to Sand Point Beach.

She parked the ATV next to a gray hatchback. She recognized several vehicles that belonged to Munising High School students.

Shiloh wore Cody's black hoodie beneath her jacket. It was still cold at night. Since the beach was tucked behind Grand Island, it was sheltered from the worst of the wind.

There were lovely views of the bay, Grand Island, and the old wooden East Channel Lighthouse. She wasn't here for the views.

A massive bonfire had been constructed on the beach. Camping chairs and blankets were strewn across the sand. Dozens of teenagers ringed the fire, their faces highlighted in flickering lights from the fire and the aurora ribboning the night sky above their heads.

Tense voices drifted across the beach. Someone had brought a battery-operated radio and set it on a piece of driftwood. A BTS song played at full volume, but no one was listening.

Girls whispered to each other, their expressions tense and upset. The guys huddled in groups or threw stones into the lake. Couples sat in camping chairs, holding hands and staring at the sky.

For once, no one had their phones out. Probably because their batteries were all drained.

She'd heard rumors of the bonfires at school on Monday, before she'd lost time, before she'd awakened to a nightmare.

Some of the seniors had planned a party every night to celebrate the Northern Lights. With school canceled for the week and the internet fried, there was little else to do.

Shiloh approached a couple of girls and asked them about Cody, and then Ruby. She showed them the flyer. They brushed her off. She was just a kid. No one wanted to pay attention. No one cared.

She moved among the crowd, searching for someone who could help her. She heard snippets of conversations: complaints about the lack of social media, dead batteries, missed TV shows.

Most of them were talking about the power outages. How long it would last, how the supply chain would be affected, what it might mean for graduation, for college and jobs, the future. Several people looked like they'd been crying.

Across the bonfire, a Hispanic girl with long curly hair sat on the sand, her head bent as she strummed a guitar. Shiloh recognized her. Gabriella Velazquez was a junior at the high school. She was one of Cody's customers. And she was friends with Ruby.

Shiloh strode across the expanse of beach, circling the bonfire. The heat licked her cheeks. A drunk guy danced around the bonfire, arms held high, beer sloshing from his red SOLO cup.

He almost spilled his beer on her. "Hey, sorry!" he called after her, his words slurred.

Shiloh barely noticed. She halted in front of Gabriella. "You know Cody."

Gabriella stopped strumming and squinted up at her. Her skin was ashen, her features pinched like she was upset. "Do I know you?"

"You know my brother. Cody Easton."

"I don't know him."

"Like hell you don't. He's missing."

She made a face. "That's none of my concern. I'm busy."

"I'm trying to find him."

Gabriella bent her head again, her hair a curtain across her face. "Well, I can't help you."

Frustration surged through her. Shiloh considered stabbing the girl but resisted. It was one way to get exactly what she needed, but perhaps not the wisest method. You got more flies with honey than vinegar, or something like that.

Instead, she said, "You get your pills from him."

Gabriella's head snapped up. Her bloodshot eyes narrowed. "How do you know?"

"Tell me what I want to know, and I won't tell the cops."

"Go away. I'm not scared of you."

"You should be." Shiloh stuck her hand into the front pocket of the hoodie. Her fingers closed around the baggie of pills. She didn't like that Cody had been dealing, but if it would help her get what she wanted, she'd do anything. "I have some."

Gabriella's eyes gleamed, her pupils large in the reddish glow radiating from the sky. "What do you want?"

"I'll give them to you if you can help me."

Abruptly, her hostility vanished. "Okay, fine. Fine. I'll talk to you. I don't know anything about your brother, I swear. I'm sorry he's missing. I heard about what happened to your grandfather."

"Yeah, well. Sorry doesn't fix anything."

"I guess not."

Shiloh sucked in a breath. "What about Ruby? You know her."

"Yeah, sure. We're friends."

"She's missing, too."

"She'll come back in a few days with some wild story to tell about a new boyfriend or some cool thing she did. Her mom's freaked, but Ruby can take care of herself. She's not missing. This is what she does."

Shiloh pulled out the baggie and dangled it in front of her. "Tell me everything you know anyway. Anything weird. Anything out of the ordinary."

Gabriella didn't take her eyes off the pills. "She did say one thing. About this truck she kept seeing over and over. On her street and outside the café where she works and stuff. Ruby's dramatic, though. She's always trying to make things more important than they are."

"What did the truck look like?"

"It was blue, that's all I remember. I think she said it was the janitor's truck. Of the school. It freaked her out."

"He was following her?"

"I dunno, I don't remember. He's weird, though. He's been there like forever, and barely talks, but like, looks funny, right? You get it." She shrugged. "I don't think it's anything. The only reason Ruby hasn't called is because the phones are dead. I don't know why you're trying to find her."

"That's my business."

"You gonna give me those or not? I could really use them. This whole solar flare situation has been really stressful for me. I can't stop crying. I don't know what's going to happen."

"It's the end of the world."

"Yeah, maybe." Gabriella reached greedily for the pills.

Shiloh tossed the baggie into her outstretched hand. "If you tell anybody I gave you these, I'll yank out your tongue and feed it to you."

Gabriella blinked.

"Have a great night."

She left Gabriella gaping after her as she spun and headed back across the beach toward the parking lot.

35

SHILOH EASTON

DAY FIVE

The lock *click, click, clicked*, the sound loud in the silence. Crickets churred in the night. The aurora danced bright enough in the sky that she didn't even need a flashlight.

Shiloh wrinkled her nose, her lower lip protruding as she concentrated on picking the lock of the trailer's back door. The front door had a new fancy lock, but the side door that entered through the laundry room was basic, a simple pin tumbler lock.

Ripe for the picking. She smiled grimly at the joke. Cody would have appreciated it. Cody *would* appreciate it—when she found him.

Carefully, she picked back and forth, moving the pins up and down inside the lock until she sensed the gap between the key pin and the driver pin lining up with the shear.

The door unlocked.

The information that Gabriella had given her seemed flimsy, insubstantial. But she had nothing else to go on. No clues, no evidence, nothing.

It didn't seem promising, but this was the only lead that she had.

Calvin Fitch lived at the end of a dead-end dirt road. Rusty cars cluttered the narrow street. Glass glinted along the shoulder of the road in the grass. Broken beer bottles tossed into the ditch.

Most of the houses were in disrepair, sagging singlewides set on concrete blocks. Shin-high weeds clutched at the faded siding. A propane tank was hooked to the side of the trailer. No vehicles were parked in the grass driveway.

Two lawn chairs sat on a flat patch of dirt beside a creek that ran through the back of several properties. Black flies and mosquitos swarmed above the black water.

Fifty yards to her right, a second battered trailer sat on blocks under a great weeping willow. A rusted beater truck was parked at the front door. There was no driveway; only wilted, weedy grass.

She glanced behind her. The curtains twitched. She waited, frozen, until they fell back into place and went still.

Once inside, she closed the door behind her and stood for a moment, letting her eyes adjust to the darkness. The air smelled musty. The trash can in the kitchen was empty but for a couple of Stouffer's frozen dinners. The dishes were done and dried on the counter.

Shiloh searched the trailer, ducking beneath windows and using a small penlight, the beam pointed down to avoid detection. She'd parked the four-wheeler at the top of the street, off the road behind a cluster of cottonwoods. You could never be too careful.

Cautiously but quickly, she moved, her heart thumping against her ribs, her breath caught in her throat, her senses on alert for the rumble of a car engine or sweep of headlights.

She flipped couch cushions and checked beneath furniture, careful to put everything back as she'd found it, no embroidered pillow out of place.

In the first bedroom, she found an unopened box of condoms in the bedside drawer, *Sports Illustrated* and *Car and Driver* on the night-stand. A striped bedspread, the bed made. She upended the mattress, discovered nothing but dust bunnies.

On the nightstand stood a framed photo of a years-younger Calvin Fitch, arm-in-arm with a bearded man who looked familiar. They were squinting against the sun, surrounded by old-growth trees, a derelict cabin behind them—weeds, rotting wood, a rusty birdbath encrusted with vines off to the righthand side.

She'd seen that face before, but she couldn't place it. It was benign, forgettable. A boring adult in a sea of adults. Balding hair, bland chubby cheeks, weak chin.

Making a mental note of the man's face, she returned to the search. On her hands and knees, she checked beneath the bed: a shoebox of old photos, plastic storage bins, a cardboard box labeled "cat toys."

Her frustration grew. She rifled through drawers and closets, and even unscrewed the grates from the vents. So far, the man was impossibly dull. And normal.

She rummaged through coat pockets—Chapstick, a few quarters, lint, and a receipt for a boat rental from the marina. She switched on the laptop sitting on the desk. Nothing happened. It was dead.

She checked the drawers, the filing cabinet, a side table against the wall with framed posters of various football players hung above it. Bills. Boring stuff. A bookcase with boring books on birding. *Birds of Michigan: A Field Guide*, and *Wild about Michigan Birds*.

Chagrined, she slumped in the black pleather office chair. The wheels squeaked beneath her weight. Hot defeated tears stung her eyes. She'd checked everywhere. Nothing suspicious or out of the ordinary.

Another dead end. It felt like running full tilt into a wall. She had no other leads, no strings to pull, no resources.

Tilting her head back, she closed her eyes. The fake leather stuck to the backs of her bare thighs. She needed to leave. It was past time to go, and yet, she couldn't quite give up. There had to be something.

The doublewide was so quiet. No ticking clock. No refrigerator hum. No rumble of a generator or the pings from various electronics.

Absolute silence but for her own breathing, the sound of her pulse in her ears.

Shiloh stood. The chair pushed back, wheels squeaking in protest. She shoved it back into place, slightly angled away from the desk as she'd found it.

Leaving the second bedroom slash office, she padded down the carpeted hallway into the kitchen. Scanned it again. Cupboards, sink, countertops, fridge and stove and trash can.

No food and water bowl in the kitchen.

She sniffed the air. A bit musty and stale.

No kitty litter smell.

Swiftly, she jogged back through the living room down the narrow hallway to the bedroom. Kneeling, she bent until her cheek pressed against the vinyl floor as she swept the penlight beneath the ruffled duster.

The penlight highlighted the plastic bins labeled summer and winter clothing. The Christmas box. The box labeled "cat toys."

Maybe his cat had died. It was possible. The box forgotten beneath the bed.

Shiloh flattened herself onto her stomach and reached for the box. It wasn't dusty. No moth balls or dust bunnies, no grit on her fingertips. The floor beneath the bed, too, had been swept clean. As if it were accessed frequently.

Pulling it out, she sat up, legs crossed, and set it in her lap. An oversized shoebox. No lock. No secret code or key required. It was nothing.

Still, her hands trembled as she set down the penlight. The aurora pulsed red through the curtains. Shiloh removed the lid.

Polaroids. Hundreds of photos filled the box. The second thing that registered in her brain—the photos were of girls. Most of them were older than her, but still teenagers. The poses. All that skin.

Her heart went cold inside her chest. Her hands turned clammy. An ill feeling expanded within her belly. She nearly vomited.

Everything in her wanted to hurl the photos away. To scour the sight from her brain, to burn her fingertips where they'd touched the pictures. Instead, she forced herself to riffle through them, gently, carefully, touching only the edges.

There were no pictures of Cody. No boys at all. It didn't make her feel better.

Gingerly, she picked up a Polaroid from the stack. A pretty girl with black hair and no smile. The girls in the photos were strangers. Somewhere, someone knew them, loved them. They had mothers and fathers. Sisters and brothers who missed them.

Nausea churned in her stomach. Disgust roiled through her. She felt violated. Rage crackled through her like a forest fire.

This man was sick. The worst kind of windigo. He should be locked up or shot.

Shiloh voted for shot. She'd volunteer her crossbow.

And yet, at some deeply selfish gut level, she was disappointed. She'd come for Cody. What did this monster have to do with Cody's disappearance? What if it was nothing at all?

She had thought that Ruby's disappearance must be connected. Two kids from the same town—gone. It had to be more than a coincidence. But maybe it was. She was grasping at straws, and she knew it.

A distant sound registered deep in her consciousness. She blinked, startled. The rumble of a truck sounded somewhere outside.

Her heart leapt into her throat. It might not be him. It could be a neighbor. Nothing to worry about, no reason to panic—

The rumble grew louder.

The truck was on this road.

Frantic, she placed the lid back in place, slid the box back beneath the bed. Was it exactly where she'd found it? To the inch, to the exact degree? Would he know? Would he sense her presence, her touch? With shaking fingers, she smoothed the ruffled duster.

Springing to her feet, she shoved the Polaroid she held into her pocket, seized the penlight, and switched it off. The guest bedroom was located at the rear of the doublewide. The aurora outside was bright, distracting. No reason he would've seen it.

She sprinted for the doorway, reached the hallway, and slid into the kitchen as the twin beams of headlights washed across the living room. Shadows wavered across the walls.

Would he glimpse a shadow among shadows? Wouldn't he be night-blinded by his own headlights? He hadn't seen her. She'd get away by the skin of her teeth.

Half crouching, she lunged across the expanse of the kitchen floor and reached the laundry room, slipped inside, nearly tripped over the broom leaning against the wall.

And then she glanced down. Shoes in a neat row in front of the washing machine—a pair of tennis shoes, a pair of khaki-colored sandals, and a pair of work boots. Black. With white stitching up the sides. Red laces.

A cold darkness enveloped Shiloh, like she'd somehow fallen backward into her own shadow. She knew those boots. Remembered the salvage yard, a crowbar dripping blood.

No time to consider what it meant. Time to go. To get out.

She fumbled for the door handle. Her hands clumsy as two blocks of wood. The knob turned. She wrenched it open.

Her pulse thudded so loud she couldn't hear a thing. He could be right behind her, reaching out to seize her braid and yank her back into Hades itself.

Shiloh ran. Her feet pounded, arms pumping, breath ragged, torn from her throat. She sprinted across patchy grass, trampled through a garden at the rear of the yard, terrified.

She sprinted through several backyards. Brambles caught at her legs. Thorns scratched her skin. The glow of the aurora tinged the forest red. She could see. If they were looking, someone could see her.

Twigs slapped her face. A tree root tripped her. She flung out her hands, caught herself on the trunk of an oak tree. Then she ran again, gasping, lungs on fire.

At the end of the road, the Honda FourTrax waited behind the cottonwoods. Relief flooded her veins. Her legs turned to water. She yanked the key fob from her front pocket and straddled the four-wheeler, then jabbed the key at the ignition.

She missed. Her hands shook so badly, she tried twice before the key finally went in.

Behind her, an engine roared. Not her own. Down the street. The truck. A menacing growl like a living creature. A predator on the hunt.

She cursed under her breath. Panic threatened to strangle her. But she turned the key and the engine roared to life. She switched the gear control into drive while releasing the brake, both hands gripping the handlebars, and accelerated like a bat out of hell.

36

SHILOH EASTON

DAY FIVE

The ATV bounced through a narrow break in the trees and burst onto the old logging road.

Shiloh jerked the handlebars, turned hard, and headed east toward the town of Christmas. Her headlights caught the rutted road ahead of her. Great spruce, pine, birch, and hemlocks towered on either side, forming a gnarled black tunnel into the red-washed dark.

Behind her, a second pair of headlights bounced onto the road. Shiloh glanced in her rearview mirror, her pulse a roar in her ears.

Harsh lights bore down on her, catching her in the spotlight. The dark shape of a truck loomed behind the glare, ominous and indistinct.

She'd driven every logging road within twenty miles of Christmas and knew the twists and turns like the back of her hand. Problem was, this guy might, too.

Her mind raced; she visualized what lay ahead. The weed-choked gravel road curved in an undulating S, skirting Christmas before snaking toward Munising.

The logging road stretched on for a good ten miles before it hit another road. Few vehicles traversed the roads this time of night; he would overtake her long before then.

Shiloh rounded a bend, breaking slightly and leaning into the turn, then pushed the throttle and sped up to forty, forty-five, then fifty. Far slower than the powerful truck chasing her.

She felt small and helpless. Overpowered and outmanned.

He would catch her. He could run her over.

The ATV rounded another curve. She crouched, rising up from the seat to lean and keep from tipping. The truck's headlights kept her pinned, swallowed her up. Caught her like a fly in a web.

To her left, the dense forest bristled, thick tree trunks grew close together, standing tall and silent and unbending. No passage to slip through, no pathway to outmaneuver the monster at her back.

To her right, the ground fell away, descending into a steep ravine littered with rocks and scraggly underbrush.

He had her.

The truck gunned its engine, loud and aggressive. Taunting. It roared behind her—thirty feet, then twenty.

Adrenaline shot through her veins. She held on tight, her arms rigid, muscles taut and straining. Sweat beaded her forehead, gathered beneath her armpits. Tendrils of her hair stuck slick to her skin.

If she lost control for a second, the ATV could skid out from beneath her, pitch her over the ravine, or send her careening into a wall of trees at fifty miles an hour.

The truck jammed in close. The driver honked the horn.

She flinched, clenched the handlebars tight and gritted her teeth. There had to be a way out of this. Had to be. She just had to find it.

The truck dropped back. Thirty feet. Then fifty. Then a hundred. The headlights receded. Was he gonna let her go? No. He wouldn't.

If he knew what she'd seen? If he even suspected?

Shiloh held his freedom in her hands; they both knew it. Girl and driver. Predator and prey. No way to walk away from this.

He could not let her go, just like she could not ignore what she'd found.

She'd go to Jackson—if she lived long enough.

The FourTrax took another bend, this time too fast. She skidded up on two wheels, overcorrected and slid across the road. Gravel spit beneath her tires. Her heart thumped. A block of ice in her belly.

Behind her, the truck reappeared. The vehicle came barreling around the curve, tires growling over gravel, headlights stark and glaring.

It came up fast, so fast. The headlights grew impossibly large in her rearview mirrors. The glare was blinding. She couldn't see. Couldn't think.

Then the truck shifted left and pulled up alongside her. It was painted a dark color, maybe blue. Big shiny grill. Large, thick tires. The driver was a shadowy smudge at the edge of her vision.

She dared not take her gaze from the road for even a second.

She tried slowing. He slowed with her.

She sped up, he shoved in tighter. His huge wheels spat gravel mere inches from the four-wheeler.

Her exhausted muscles strained, clammy fingers cramped on the handlebars. How long could she last? The road was endless, her fear bottomless.

Past the cone of the headlights, the logging road fell into red-tinged darkness. Twenty yards ahead, a sharp curve to the right appeared.

Shiloh turned too fast, barely maintaining control.

He turned with her. Tires squealed. He swerved in and clipped her rear.

The FourTrax lurched and fishtailed. It plowed sharply right, toward the ravine. No control. She was utterly helpless, a scream locked behind her teeth.

The ATV plowed across the weedy shoulder, teetered on a narrow ridge of earth. For a second, the four-wheeler hung suspended on a filament of air.

Then she pitched over the edge.

The world spun. The FourTrax flipped end over end. Trees cartwheeled. Ground and sky tumbled like a washing machine on spin cycle.

Her fingers were ripped from the handlebars. Separated from the ATV, her body was loose and flailing. She was flying, spinning into darkness, toward a bottom she could not see.

Her body bounced down the ragged slope like a ragdoll. Her shoulder struck a rock. Her right shin hit something—tree trunk, branch, boulder.

Her heart slammed. Terror in her throat. Falling, sliding, scrambling for purchase and finding none. Dead leaves crumbled beneath her fingernails. Damp leaves slid beneath her. Bushes scratched her arms, her face, yanked hair from her scalp. Twigs jabbed her palms.

Whether by miracle or instinct, she managed to throw her weight sideways. Her right shoulder glanced off a thick poplar trunk and spun her onto her back.

She slid a few yards. Her spine hit something relatively soft—a thicket of bushes.

Finally, she rolled to a halt. Half-twisted on her side, legs bunched up. Pain radiated from her ribs, her right shoulder. Her left ankle throbbed.

A thunderous din came from above her. The four-wheeler was coming down. The machine slammed against boulders and bent saplings as it crashed down the hillside.

No time to move. To escape. To do anything but scream.

Shiloh shrank into a fetal position, threw her hands in front of her face, and braced for impact.

With a screech of wrenching metal, the ATV smashed into the trunk of the poplar tree, not five feet up the slope from where she huddled. The great tree shuddered. Leaves rained down on her head and torso.

The FourTrax sputtered. Smoke billowed from the twisted wreck.

The engine ticked in the abrupt stillness. The headlights flickered and then died.

Shiloh heaved in great rasping breaths. Her lungs burned. Her pulse roared. Everything hurt. The world was still spinning.

She was alive.

But the threat was not over.

37

SHILOH EASTON

DAY FIVE

Shiloh's head swam. Her pulse thudded in her throat. She pressed one hand to her chest to make sure her jackrabbit heart hadn't thumped its way out of her chest.

She strained her ears. In the aftermath of violence, the forest had gone quiet. No night sounds. No owls hooted or coyotes howled, no creatures scrabbled through the underbrush. Even the wind had died.

The headlights blared from the ridge line, probing the woods like spotlights. The white glow filtered through the leaves. Shadow and light made strange shapes in the night.

The crimson aurora undulated through the black sky, like a bloodstain you tried to scrub clean, but couldn't erase.

She lay on her back, staring up at the headlights. She dared them to move, begged them to move. They didn't. The truck had stopped fifty feet above her.

Maybe he'd exited the truck and was peering down into the void. Deciding whether to go after her, weighing the odds.

Shiloh didn't dare breathe. If she moved, he'd hear her. He'd smell her terror like a wolf and sniff her out.

Her breath came in shallow, panicked gasps. The air smelled of dirt and sap. *Vienna, Austria. Minsk, Belarus. Brussels, Belgium.* She had to calm down, to think.

Up on the ridge, a sound reached her. A muffled curse. The crunch of leaves and twigs underfoot as a large figure stomped through underbrush.

A narrow beam swept across the trees, playing across her hiding spot. He had a flashlight. He was coming for her.

He made so much noise that she had the opportunity to move. Gingerly, she sat up, feeling for broken bones. Everything hurt, but she could move her legs, her arms.

Using the poplar trunk, she pulled herself to her feet. Pain shot up her ankle. She'd twisted it. No way could she run now.

In a race, she could beat any boy her age. She was fiercer, faster, stronger. But with her injured ankle, this man would win.

She longed for her crossbow. Stupidly, she'd left it back at the cave, choosing speed over weaponry. She still had her knife, her fingernails, her teeth. And her cunning.

Frantically, she scanned her surroundings. It was hard to see anything in the murky shadows. If she used her penlight, she'd give herself away.

Steep walls of rock and earth rose on either side of her. Everywhere she looked were more woods, more trees. Snarled branches and dense underbrush blocked her way. There were few places to hide.

The forest that she loved took on a sense of malice. Hints of eyes, yellow in the red-tinged darkness, peered out of the gloom. Gnarled roots writhed underfoot, threatening to trip her, to trap her, to drag her under the damp earth and swallow her up.

A grunt echoed from above her. Curses and insults from a muffled masculine voice. Twigs crackled underfoot. The flashlight beam swept back and forth. He was higher up the ravine, searching the wrong places. But not for long.

Any moment, the flashlight beam might pin her, revealing her location.

Her gaze settled on the poplar tree and the smoking wreck at its base. Branches forked from the large trunk at regular intervals, starting at chest level. The lowest branches were as thick as her waist.

Her pursuer would expect her to run. Any sane person would run. If she couldn't find a hole to squirrel into, she would climb. Up, out of sight. Out of reach.

If he had a gun, she was screwed. Otherwise, it was her only chance.

Shiloh jerked her penlight out of her pocket, switched it on, and threw it deeper into the ravine. Then, she climbed. Gritting her teeth against the pain, she reached for the branch above her, pulling herself upward with the strength of her arms and her good leg, then levered herself to the next branch. Her ankle throbbed.

In the semi-darkness, she worked by touch, checking the branch first to ensure it would hold her weight. Shadows chased her up the trunk. Ten feet, twenty, then thirty.

She was a strong climber. Long summers spent outdoors made her agile and swift. As she climbed, she worked her way around the tree so that the trunk blocked her from the road.

Below her, the sweeping flashlight beam settled on the wrecked four-wheeler.

Shiloh froze. She clung to the branches, her stomach pressed to the trunk, the bark rough against her cheek. An ant crawled up her arm. One foot was stabilized. Her injured ankle hung unsupported, but she didn't dare move.

Thirty feet below her, a man approached the wreckage. He slid down the embankment, cursing. As he thrashed through thorny underbrush, the beam of the flashlight never wavered from the crash site.

Her breath lodged in her throat. She waited for him to look up. Waited for those predator eyes to zero in on her. Would they glow in the dark like a bobcat's? Or a wolf's? Or maybe he was the evil windigo spirit made flesh.

Did he have a gun? What would he do if he found her?

Her mind began to disconnect, unconsciousness threatening to draw her away. That blankness coming for her. She felt it happening and fought to stay present. *Prague, Czechia. Copenhagen, Denmark.*

Shiloh bit down on her tongue until she drew blood. The taste of copper filled the back of her throat. She swallowed and pressed her cheek harder against the bark. Holding her breath, she forced herself to look down.

He stood beneath the poplar tree, breathing hard. She couldn't make out details. He was too far below her, too many branches and leaves obscuring her view. He was merely a dark shape behind the beam of the flashlight, a menacing unknown presence.

"Where are you?" he said aloud. "Come out, come out, wherever you are."

One fact did not elude her, however. She could tell by the shape of him, how he walked, the tenor of his voice.

The man who hunted her was not the school janitor.

He was not Calvin Finch.

The man studied the wreckage, head down. Then he squatted, pulled out his phone and snapped a picture of the bumper stickers she'd plastered on the back—I Heart Paris, the Statue of Liberty, Machu Picchu. He took a photo of the registration.

The man stood, turned in a slow half circle and swept the flashlight across the ground. His shadow was black as ink on the ground.

Don't look up.

Don't. Look. Up.

He caught sight of the penlight's glow and moved away from the tree, headed further into the ravine. He paused, then walked several yards west. Stopped again in front of a mulberry bush and picked up the penlight, then stood there for a long silent minute, as if bewildered.

Or thinking it out. Considering the options. Where a small girl might disappear to.

Panic seized her. He was going to figure it out. Any minute, he was going to—

Above them, a second set of headlights appeared on the logging road. The man went rigid. He flicked off the flashlight.

The headlights drew closer. The noise of a car engine invaded the unnatural stillness. Shiloh clung to the tree, willing it to come closer, for the driver to see the man's truck, to stop.

Folks were courteous in the Upper Peninsula. They watched out for their neighbors.

The headlights slowed and came to a halt behind the truck. Doors slammed as two figures exited the vehicle. Low murmurs of concern drifted across the ravine.

"Hello?" a female voice called. "Anybody need help down there?"

"I see shattered glass on the road," a male voice said. "Looks like an accident."

The man cursed. The nearness of it startled her, set her heart thumping. She could barely make out the shape of him as he turned back and started up the steep side of the ravine, climbing up to the road.

Shiloh waited, her body taut as piano wire. Her fingers felt like claws, her muscles cramped. The ant crawled across her cheek. A larger bug worked its way into her pantleg and wandered up her left shin.

The man called out to the couple in a friendly voice. Disarming. Non-threatening. There was an exchange of mingled voices, their words too indistinct to discern.

More doors slammed. A pair of headlights flickered from high beam to low beam, then the truck's engine growled as it pulled off the shoulder and back onto the road. It drove north. A moment later, the second vehicle followed behind it. Gradually, the noises faded to silence.

Minutes passed. Maybe hours. An owl hooted from somewhere.

Only when she'd stopped shaking did she dare to move, to make the laborious descent, limb by limb, branch by branch.

When she reached the bottom, her ankle gave out and she crumpled to the leaf-littered ground. She curled into a ball, her knees tight to her chest, arms wrapped around her legs. Leaves stuck to her clothes. Pine needles snarled in her hair.

Shiloh was a thirteen-year-old girl in the woods at night. Not brave, not fierce. But scared and hurt and terribly, utterly alone.

38

ELI POPE

DAY SIX

A soft crackle.

Eli's eyes opened.

He'd been dozing, dreaming of blood and war, of prison and broken bodies. He never slept soundly, half his senses constantly alert to danger, to the slightest sound or sensation.

The sound came again.

It was three a.m. Something was wrong.

Instantly, his hand moved for his weapons. His VP9 and AK-47 lay beside him within easy reach. AK-47 in hand, he rose to his knees and peered from the firing port he'd built into the lean-to.

At his twelve o'clock, thirty feet ahead, the tent sat in the middle of the clearing. The aurora bathed the site in a soft red glow. He'd placed a chem-light in the tent and used heated rocks from the campfire in the general shape of a man—head, body, legs. Luckily, the tent was floorless.

If enemies tried to sneak up on him, even on IR, it would appear like Eli was sleeping oblivious inside the tent. Even if they didn't have infrared, they'd see a light source inside the tent, giving Eli the precious seconds he'd need to engage or flee.

He strained his ears. The burble of the river. The buzz of night insects. The rustle of the trees.

A twig bent and snapped. The swish of footsteps through leaves.

The sounds came from the southwest—maybe thirty, forty yards. Outside the perimeter warning he'd set but headed his direction.

Something—or someone—was out there.

Over his clothes, he slipped on the ghillie suit jacket he'd made to blur his shape against the forest. Within two seconds, he'd exited via the rear of the lean-to, pistol holstered and rifle in hand.

A cold, calm alertness descended. His breathing slowed. His heartrate steadied.

Half-crouched, he circled behind his shelter to the left, shifting from the cover of the boulder to the cover of an enormous white pine, the trunk as thick as a tire.

His barefoot footsteps were quiet; he moved as one with the shadows. Silent and invisible and lethal.

A rattle of rocks against tin: his perimeter alarm system had been tripped. The alarm consisted of a length of fishing wire attached to metal cans filled with pebbles. It was simple yet incredibly effective.

Eli took a knee, braced himself, and raised the AK-47 to his shoulder. His finger rested on the trigger guard. He peered through his ACOG scope and waited for his prey.

Whoever hunted him would receive a rude awakening.

The moon hid behind a raft of clouds. It didn't matter. The aurora was bright, red flames undulating overhead, outlining familiar shapes in crimson. The trees. The Dakota fire pit. The fallen log he used for seating. The makeshift clothesline. The tent, the boulder hunched behind it. The lean-to.

The river gurgled over rocks and logs. Small creatures slunk through the underbrush. His mind emptied of all thought but the task at hand. Eliminate the threat. Shoot to kill.

Another sound. A cry like a wounded animal.

The hairs on the back of his neck rose.

Twenty yards to the east, juniper leaves trembled, agitated by whatever creature—animal or human—disturbed it. Through a thicket of elderberry bushes, past the cluster of jack pines, beneath the canopy of a maple.

Silent, Eli rose to his feet. Remaining crouched, light on his feet, he placed each step with care, heel to toe.

Every movement slow and deliberate, he began to circle the outskirts of the clearing, shifting from tree to tree, from cover to cover as he closed in on his target. Muscles tensed, weapon up, ready to fire.

Five minutes later, he rounded a cluster of boulders and his target appeared. Eli stared down at it for several heartbeats. Not an it—her.

Shiloh Easton curled in a fetal position on the ground. Her right leg had tangled in his tripwire. Her crossbow lay a few feet away, like she'd dropped it as she fell.

This girl had dragged herself from somewhere. Her camp at the cave was about three miles via the ATV trails—or somewhere even further. Limping, bleeding, in pain. He couldn't imagine how difficult it had been. At least she'd been able to take the trail.

In her right hand, she clutched her small knife. Like she was ready to fight demons and monsters, even to the point of collapse.

A groan escaped her lips.

In the half-darkness, he could see she was hurt.

Alert for danger, he scanned the woods and listened hard. He studied the ground, the trees, the rocks and rise of the hill leading to the bluffs beyond them. There were no shadows that did not belong.

Satisfied that they were alone, he slung the rifle over his shoulder and crouched beside her. He wasn't a medic, but he knew first aid and kept an IFAK—individual first aid kit—in his rucksack.

He felt her pulse. It was strong and steady, though fast. He checked her breathing, then skimmed her body with his hands, searching for wounds, for broken bones, for blood.

She whimpered when he touched her shoulder, and again when he felt her right ankle. It was already swollen. Twisted, possibly sprained.

Pausing, he again listened to the forest sounds. Nothing out of place. No signs of danger. Untangling her foot from his tripwire, he reset it, feeling the lumpy ground for the stones and replacing them inside the can.

"Don't leave me," Shiloh said.

"Did anyone follow you?"

She shook her head.

"This is going to hurt."

"I'm not scared."

He grunted, bent, and gathered her into his arms. For so fierce a soul, she was light as a feather. How young she was. Young and vulnerable and alone.

He cradled her as a shepherd cradled a lamb and hurried back to his campsite.

"My crossbow—"

"I'll get it. Don't talk. That makes it hurt more."

She turned her head and buried her face into his chest. A mewling sound escaped her lips, like a wounded kitten. Fury flared through him, hot and sharp, at whoever would harm this child.

Eli knelt and half-crawled into his shelter, then lowered her atop his bivy sack. Shucking the rifle but keeping it close by, he reached for his rucksack and withdrew his flashlight and IFAK.

"I need to check you for injuries," he said gruffly. "That okay?"

Shiloh stared up at him with eyes wide and unblinking, black as beetle shells. She did not flinch or cry out. Her teeth gritted against the pain.

Bruises bloomed across her left shoulder and upper chest. Cuts and scrapes marred her bare arms. A nasty bruise was turning a deep blueish black on her left shin.

He checked her visually—her skin tone was pink. Her breathing and chest movements appeared normal. She was alert and could speak in complete sentences. She could move her arms and legs, though her right ankle was swollen and tender to the touch.

Luckily, her ribs had escaped the brunt of it. Without an x-ray machine, he had no way to know whether they were cracked or broken. He'd treat them the same either way, as long as there was no flailed chest injury, where three or more adjacent ribs were fractured in two or more places—a grave wound.

Using a battery-operated lantern for light, he rinsed the cuts with sterile water from his water bottle and dressed them with antibiotic ointment, then used liquid band-aid to seal the lacerations. He reinforced her ankle with a splint he kept in his rucksack.

His fingers were too rough. Awkward and fumbling. He didn't remember how to be gentle, how to treat fragile things with such care. His hands were built for violence. He wasn't any good at this.

He growled in frustration. "I should take you to a hospital."

"No," she said.

"You should see a doctor."

"They'll get the police."

"That's a good thing."

"No."

"You need—"

"No!"

"A hospital—"

She raised her knife and pointed it at his chest.

He stilled, kneeling beside her. In one hand, he held gauze, in the other, ointment. "Put it away."

"Promise. No hospital."

"Put the knife down, damn it!"

She sucked in a pained breath. The point of the knife settled at his breastbone. He crouched over her, unmoving. He knew ten ways to disarm her, but he didn't want to do it like that.

She didn't take her eyes from his. They burned fierce and

undimmed. "The police will get social services. They'll take me away. I'll never come home. I'll never find Cody. They think he did it. I know he didn't. No police. No hospital."

He shook his head. This was a bad idea. A terrible idea.

Maybe Jackson was right. He was going about this all wrong. The professionals should handle this, handle her. This was a mistake.

And yet.

At the same time, she was not wrong. He knew what it was like to be the one sucked into the massive, indifferent machine of the justice system, how swiftly the jaws of the law could consume you. It didn't matter if you were innocent.

He couldn't bring himself to betray her. She had come here, hurt and scared. She'd come to him when she had no one else. Didn't matter how many times he told himself he didn't care. That she was none of his business.

"No hospital," he said. "No police."

The knife lowered. She let out a relieved sound that was half sigh, half groan.

He took the blade from her limp fingers and set it beside his rifle. "What happened?"

"The four-wheeler went off the road. Into the ravine."

Shiloh must have been thrown free of it, or her injuries would've been much worse. "An accident?"

She stared up at him. Shook her head.

"Someone did this to you."

She didn't have to answer. Her burning eyes revealed the truth.

"Who?"

"I don't know yet."

"You didn't see him?"

"Too dark."

"Any details? Any information you can give me?"

She shook her head in mute fear.

He leaned back on his heels and appraised her. She was battered, but not broken. Not on the outside. The most dangerous scars were on the inside, where they did their damage unseen.

She gave him a beseeching look. "Hungry."

Despite himself, a smile tugged at his lips. He dug around in his rucksack and retrieved two Snickers' bars. "I'm out of the protein ones."

"Even better."

He peeled back the wrapper and handed one to her, taking the other for himself. He propped her head up with a pillow so she could eat without choking. "How's your jaw? Okay?"

She chewed cautiously, then nodded.

They sat in silence while they ate. She pointed for his water bottle, and he handed it to her. She finished the candy bar in a few bites and then drank half the bottle without coming up for air.

The girl's eyelids slid closed. Exhaustion slackened her features. She'd held on as long as she could. Now she was here with him, safe, where she could let go.

He put away the IFAK and stuffed the bloodied gauze into a plastic trash bag. He checked outside and walked the perimeter. He retrieved the crossbow, then checked the decoy tent. He examined the hushed landscape for several minutes before slipping inside the shelter.

He checked on Shiloh again. "Sleep, girl."

"Don't leave," she said without opening her eyes.

He said, "I won't."

As she drifted into sleep, an alien emotion plucked at his chest. So foreign he didn't recognize it. His hardened, scarred heart was numb. Deadened from war, from prison. Nothing left of him but rage, bitterness, and vengeance.

As a convict, he'd been reduced to an animal. He'd lost everything but that instinct to kill.

Maybe, just maybe, he hadn't.

Eli would not sleep more tonight. He'd sit and keep watch all night. This night and the next and the next, for as long as she needed.

He looked down at her and whispered, "Whoever did this, whoever made you so afraid. I'll find him, and I'll end him."

39

ELI POPE

DAY SIX

Eli felt eyes boring into him the second he opened the door to the IGA Country Store in the town of Christmas. The bell above the door jangled in welcome.

He wasn't welcome here. He knew that. But he needed a few supplies, for himself and for Shiloh, who was sleeping soundly in his lean-to shelter. And so, here he was.

He'd biked back to his father's house and drove the silver 1998 Pontiac Bonneville into town. Surprisingly, it still had gas in the tank and ran fine.

He moved down the narrow aisles. The lights weren't working; watery daylight streamed through the dusty windows. The generator hummed as it provided power to the refrigerated section in the back.

He'd planned to get something halfway healthy for Shiloh to eat, but the shelves were barren. Most items were out completely. Two of the freezers were empty, the refrigerator carried the few beers that remained.

He recognized the woman behind the counter, Michelle Carpenter. Her father had run the place when Eli was a kid. Later, she had taken over the store after her parents died, while Eli was overseas fighting classified wars that the average American knew nothing about.

Every time he'd returned home on leave, he'd visit the store for his favorite beer, Molson Canadian. Mrs. Carpenter had kept it stocked for him, traveling across the border once a month to source it.

Now, the woman watched his every move, her back straight, one hand on the counter, the other clutching her cell phone. Her face formed a rictus of revulsion and hatred.

His skin grew hot, his hands clammy. He felt himself shrink inward, growing smaller and despised himself for it. He should be used to this by now, his black heart inured to rejection.

Why had he thought this was a good idea?

Eli stood still in the center of the beer aisle. Frozen in place. He didn't know why he'd bothered to check. She didn't stock it anymore. Why would she? And even if she did, it was already gone.

The Molson Canadian beer he'd loved had convicted him in the end. A fingerprint on a bottle, a spot of blood. The tainted bottle left in his car for the cops to find.

The doorbell jangled, and two people entered. Tim Brooks and Gideon Crawford. They were former friends—and they'd been part of the mob that had accosted him on his doorstep.

Eli tensed. His VP9 was holstered at the small of his back beneath his black T-shirt, a round chambered. The AK-47 he'd stowed in the backseat of the Bonneville beneath a blanket. He had no intention of using either weapon, but he wouldn't back down if it came to it.

The men were arguing about the best fishing spots in Alger County and didn't notice him at first. Instinctively, he checked them visually for weapons; they appeared unarmed.

He thought of the night they'd spent drinking eight years ago. How one of them might have taken a used beer bottle from the bar and framed him. But no, Sawyer had told him who had betrayed him.

He still didn't want to believe it.

Gideon caught sight of him, elbowed Tim, and they headed straight for him.

On wooden legs, he exited the beer aisle and took his meager supplies to the counter—bleach to purify water, a handful of Snickers bars to bring back for Shiloh, a bottle of soy sauce. The soy sauce wasn't a necessity, he just wanted some damn flavor with his dinner.

He felt the presence of the two men behind him. They'd gone dead quiet.

Eli dug in his pockets and set two wrinkled twenties on the counter.

"Your money is no good here," Michelle said.

"I have the right to shop." His voice was too quiet. The resolute indifference that had served him in prison had deserted him. He knew this woman, this place, these people.

"I don't serve killers."

He couldn't meet her eyes. Humiliation permeated his insides, his tongue thick in his mouth. A sickening sense of claustrophobia overwhelmed him. The empty shelves crowded in, the shadows heavy and thick.

In that moment, it didn't matter that he wasn't guilty. Suffocating shame threatened to choke him.

"I called the police," Mrs. Carpenter lied.

He knew she hadn't—there was no service—but he didn't correct her.

Her body shook with anger, accusation in her eyes. "I used to babysit Lily. I have a daughter. If you lay a hand on her, I will fillet you and hang your entrails around your neck and drown you in the lake, and that would not be the death that you deserve."

"You need help, Michelle?" Tim Brooks asked.

"Looks like we need to take out the trash," Gideon snarled.

They sounded like bad TV actors. It didn't matter. Eli felt like he'd been sucker punched in the gut. Mortified, he wanted nothing more than to escape to his campsite in peace.

"Keep the change." He scooped up his items, leaving the cash, and backed away.

Mrs. Carpenter said nothing. Her red-rimmed eyes glistened like she was on the verge of weeping. Her hands pressed flat on the counter, palms down, fingers splayed, as if they were holding her up, like her willpower was the only thing keeping her upright.

Eli spun on his heels. The men stood behind him, blocking his way. A surge of anger broke through his chagrin. He made a lunging motion at them. "Move, or you'll regret it."

The men scrambled backward. Fear and loathing warred across their features. Fear and self-preservation won out. Gideon's shoulder struck the rack of touristy magnets, and several clattered to the tile floor. Tim bumped into a shelf holding the last bags of Doritos.

Eli marched between them, unmolested.

"Don't come back!" Gideon spat at his back.

The bell over the door jangled before Eli reached it. Jackson Cross strode in, dressed in his deputy's uniform. His sandy hair mussed, a five o'clock shadow rimmed his jaw, bruises beneath his eyes like he hadn't slept in days.

Tired or not, those clear hazel eyes swept the store and took in the situation in an instant. He nodded his head at Michelle. "Mrs. Carpenter." He turned to the men. "Keep shopping. Have a good day."

Jackson opened the door wide and motioned for Eli to follow him out.

Eli obeyed without argument.

Once they were a good ten yards past the front door, Jackson wheeled on him, his expression livid. "What the living hell, Eli."

"A man has to shop."

"Then drive to the Soo. Or Marquette. Or anywhere but here. Can't you see these people can't handle it? You're liable to get yourself shot."

He couldn't help himself. "I think you have that the other way around."

Jackson threw up his hands. "I'm trying to keep the peace, here. I'm doing my best to keep a volatile situation from exploding."

"Sounds like you're doing a bang-up job of it."

"What the hell does that mean?"

They stood a few feet apart. Lines bracketed his old friend's mouth, framed his tired eyes. He looked like he'd aged a decade since the last time Eli had seen him.

"You find Easton's killer yet?"

"Maybe I'm looking at him."

The sick feeling was fading fast, replaced by a familiar anger that Eli wore like a favorite pair of jeans. The anger fed him, soothed him, drove him. "Screw you, Cross."

"No. You do not get to do this. You do not get to turn this around like you're the injured party here. You cannot torment these townspeople. They've grieved for eight years. Let them live with their ghosts. Leave them alone. Live out there like a survivalist hermit in the National Forest, I don't care. But do not interfere with my county. Do not cause trouble. I am warning you, Eli."

Eli went still. He had never responded well to threats. His lip curled in derision. "Or what?"

Jackson stood taller, his eyes flashing. "I'm not the naïve little kid who once followed you around like a puppy, worshiping your every move. You can't manipulate me. You can't lie to me. That kid that believed in you? That person is dead. Dead and gone. He died with Lily."

"I don't doubt it," Eli said, quieter. A dark current hummed through him, but he held it in check. He remembered Sawyer's accusation, the insinuation. And he wondered.

"What do you think you can do to me, Jackson?" He paused a beat. "Or maybe the real question is, what have you already done?"

40

ELI POPE

DAY SIX

A rusted pick-up rumbled past the IGA's parking lot. The passenger's side window rolled down. He recognized Dana Lutz. She spat out the window and gave him the finger.

Eli gave her the finger in return. He tensed, anticipating another altercation, but the truck kept going.

"You have no idea, Eli," Jackson said. "No clue. You're out there in the boonies, rubbing two sticks together while things are falling apart here in the real world."

Eli made an exaggerated show of looking around. "I don't see anything falling apart."

"Just because it's happening slowly doesn't mean it isn't happening. The frog sits in boiling water, doesn't he? He doesn't realize it until he's cooked through. People are going to need a lot of help real soon. I'm trying to figure out how to give it. How to prepare for what's coming."

"What's coming, Jackson?"

Jackson gave a helpless shrug. "You know the power is out across the country, right? The entire Northern Hemisphere has gone dark. Banks are closed. The internet is down. Planes are grounded. Michelle's usual delivery is three days late with no restock in sight.

They're reporting rioting in some of the big cities. People are already running out of food."

"I'm good. I can live without civilization just fine."

Jackson snorted. "No one's worried about you. Civilization *wants* to live without you. It's the rest of them I'm worried about."

Eli looked at him steadily. When you cared so little about your own life, it was difficult to muster up sympathy for nearly eight billion faceless souls. He didn't like the people he knew, let alone the masses he didn't. "People will adapt. Or they won't."

Jackson threw up his hands. "You only see things from your own distorted perspective. That's nothing new. I'm wasting my time. I have work to do."

Anger flared through Eli; he tamped it down. "You're doing such a great job with Shiloh."

Jackson's gaze sharpened. "How do you know anything about Shiloh?"

Eli didn't answer. He turned on his heel and started for the Bonneville. He still held the bleach and candy bars; he'd stuck the soy sauce in his front pocket.

Jackson followed him. "Wait."

Eli stopped short. A word had been spray-painted in dripping red across the rear window of the car: KILLER.

How long had he been in the store? Ten minutes? Fifteen? Who had seen him drive in? The two idiots in the store were gone; they had peeled out a minute ago.

His father had driven the big silver Bonneville for twenty years. Everyone knew whose it was. They would know who drove it now.

Jackson saw it but gave no indication that he cared. Fine. Eli would ignore it, too. What was one more humiliation? One more act of hatred to throw on the pile.

"Why did you say her name? Eli! Answer me."

He moved to the passenger door and deposited the bleach, candy bars, and soy sauce in the front seat. He paused, considering. There was no way he would give up her location to Jackson. At the same time, Jackson could do his damn job if he had more information. "She was there. She saw it happen. Easton's murder."

"How do you know that?" Jackson demanded.

Eli turned back around to face him. "Maybe you should do a better job protecting your witnesses."

"You've seen her? You've talked to her? What the hell? Stay away from her, Eli. So help me, if you hurt her—"

"I resent the insinuation against my character."

Jackson sputtered, a muscle jumping in his jaw. Tendons stood out like cords against his neck. It took him a moment to regain the control to speak again. "Where is she?"

Eli stared at him, impassive.

"She's a little girl alone in the woods. She needs help!"

"Maybe," Eli allowed.

"Tell me where she is, or bring her to the station. That's an order, Eli. I can arrest you. I can throw you in jail for any charge I wish. Don't tempt me."

"She doesn't want to come in. Until she does, I'm not telling you a damn thing."

Jackson took two rapid steps and jabbed his finger in Eli's face. "You don't get to do this!"

Instinct and rage took over. Eli seized Jackson's right hand, twisted it hard, and flipped it nearly backward, bending Jackson's arm at the elbow at an unnatural angle. Jackson's bones ground in protest beneath his grip.

He could've broken the man's wrist; he stopped short.

Hurt and surprise flashed across Jackson's face. He hadn't expected it. He should have.

Jackson wasn't a weakling. He was strong and fit; he knew how to shoot, how to throw a punch when he had to, but he was a poet at heart, a philosopher. No elite soldier. He hadn't fought and bled and survived inside a cage filled with the worst kind of animals.

Grunting in pain, Jackson shoved Eli in the chest with his free hand. He did not reach for his sidearm. "Let. Me. Go."

Eli glanced across the parking lot. Through the dusty windows, Michelle Carpenter stared at him. The blood drained from her face, repugnance in her eyes.

Jackson shoved him again. "So help me, Eli."

Eli released Jackson's wrist. He stepped back.

"T-t-that's assault of an officer." Eli hadn't heard Jackson's stutter in fifteen years, maybe more. It came out in moments of great distress. Jackson was angry. He was also afraid, but not of Eli.

"If you arrest me, I'll never tell you where Shiloh is," Eli said flatly. "I will never help you."

"Like you would ever help anyone but yourself."

"You don't know me."

Jackson rubbed his wrist, breathing hard. He looked at Eli. "No, I don't. I never did, did I?"

"Is that what you tell yourself so that you can sleep at night?"

Jackson blinked.

Memories flashed through Eli's mind: the blur of the trial, the accusations, the expert testimony on strangulation, on fingerprints, and domestic violence. The faces in the courtroom, the hostility of those who had once known him, even loved him.

Sawyer's damning words echoed in his ears.

"What did you do, Jackson?" Eli asked.

"I don't know what you're talking about."

"I was framed. I told you that. Someone framed me. I didn't drink that Molson Canadian at Lily's house that night. I didn't leave it in my car. I did drink one three hours earlier at your house. I left it in *your* trash can."

A shadow shifted behind Jackson's eyes, a thing Eli recognized only because he knew it so intimately himself—shame.

Sawyer had been telling the truth. Jackson *had* done something.

He'd colluded in tampering with the evidence. Had he planted the beer bottle himself?

Whatever he had done, he must have believed wholeheartedly in Eli's guilt. He believed it still. Eli could see it written across his face.

Eli felt stripped bare. His breath like glass in his throat, his skin flayed from his bones. Jackson Cross. His brother, his best friend.

It hurt. Even now, even after all this time.

"What did you do, Jackson?" Eli whispered.

For a second, the shame was there in Jackson's eyes. It swam black and oily beneath the surface. And then it vanished. Jackson's face closed, his expression hardened with resolve.

With a grimace, he shook his head. Whatever secrets he carried, he would keep them close to his chest. Until Eli forced them out into the light. Until he enacted his own justice.

"I did my job." Jackson kept his eyes straight ahead. His skin had gone pale. He was pale all the way down to his soul. "I put a murderer behind bars."

Eli took a deep breath. The old pain burrowed inside him, a hollowness in his chest. Abandonment. Betrayal. And the anger that had served him for eight years, for his entire life.

A bitter smile carved his face. "So help me, Jackson. If you were the one who did this to me, I will kill you."

His words were a wound between them. A wound that would never heal.

Eli left Jackson standing alone on the cracked, weedy asphalt, staring after him.

He returned to the Bonneville. He opened the door, sat in the driver's seat, and inserted the key in the ignition. The engine started, and he pulled out of the IGA parking lot.

The word KILLER still painted across the rear window—and seared into his soul.

41

JACKSON CROSS

DAY SIX

Jackson stood at the bow of the *Risky Business* as Sawyer expertly handled the yacht, motoring them through the bay out into the lake. The black and white skull flag rippled in the wind.

Grand Island rose before them, a dim shape in the fog. Mist swirled at its base, drifting across the placid surface of Superior.

Few boats were out; the boating season hadn't started yet. With the local businesses shuttering due to lack of electricity, most of the tourists had headed home, even the aurora-watchers.

"You, me, the boat, and open water," Sawyer said. "It's the only way to talk."

Sawyer's protection team had frisked Jackson before allowing him anywhere near Sawyer. No weapons. No wires. There were six mercenaries that he could see, several more that he couldn't. Sawyer's mercenaries were tough, stern men, well-armed and not averse to violence.

They went over him again with an RF meter, then took his wallet, cell phone, keys, sunglasses, everything—anything that could have a recording device implanted or tracking device to put on the boat.

Jackson knew Sawyer's rules. It was why he'd left Devon behind. You came alone, or you didn't come at all.

It was a risk. It was dangerous. Jackson knew that. No law enforcement officer in his right mind would board a boat unarmed with a known criminal.

Jackson needed answers. And if getting them quickly meant he didn't go through normal channels, then so be it.

He also knew that Sawyer played by his own sort of rules. They'd known each other their whole lives. They had history. And that history would protect them both.

It was a risk for Sawyer, too, to speak with Jackson without a high-priced attorney present. But Sawyer had always appreciated an element of risk.

"To what do I owe this pleasurable visit? It's been a while." Sawyer's dirty blond hair was windblown. He wore pleated khaki shorts and a pale blue polo shirt. He looked the part of a scruffy sailor married to the sea, but they both knew he was much more than that.

"You're a hard man to pin down, Sawyer."

Sawyer gave a nonchalant shrug. "I'm busy. It so happened that today's fishing charter trip was canceled. The CEO of First Northern Bank quit his job and is bugging out to his cabin in the Porcupine Mountains."

"I'm investigating the Easton homicide."

Sawyer turned his gaze on Jackson, his expression unreadable. Jackson had always found Sawyer's flat eyes disquieting.

Even as kids, Sawyer had been different. He could turn his charm on and off like a light switch, become your best friend or your worst enemy at the drop of a hat.

"May I ask you some questions?"

"You're free to ask, Jackson. Whether I answer is up to me."

"Of course. What is your connection to Easton?"

"Business associates."

"How so?"

"That's private."

"Where were you on May seventeenth between the hours of three and six p.m.?"

"Out here, on my boat."

"Can anyone confirm that?"

"You're asking questions like I'm a suspect here, Cross." His gray eyes narrowed. He'd never looked more shark-like—or dangerous. "Be very careful in what you say next."

Jackson was extremely aware of his lack of a sidearm. He felt naked, exposed. His hands hung loose at his sides, ready to curl into fists. His wrist was still sore from his altercation with Eli.

Jackson knew how to defend himself. And he would fight if necessary. He didn't think it would come to that. "You wouldn't try anything, Sawyer. You know better. So, let's not pretend that you would."

His smile faltered the tiniest fraction.

"Killing a law enforcement officer? That would be dirty, even for you. Not that you could accomplish it if you tried."

Sawyer studied him for a long moment, his smile pasted like a sticker onto his face. He moved back a step and raised a hand, palm out in a gesture of surrender. "Touché, old friend."

"I am not your friend."

"So people keep telling me. I'm starting to feel rejected, Cross. It's not a feeling I appreciate."

"I don't care about your feelings."

"You hate me, don't you?"

Jackson started. It wasn't a statement he'd been expecting. "That has nothing to do with it."

"Sure, it does." Sawyer kept his gaze on the bluffs. "You were always jealous. Of me with Lily."

Jackson stiffened. He tamped down the surge of embarrassment mixed with anger. He hated hearing Lily's name out of Sawyer's mouth. That it was also the truth was a bitter pill to swallow.

Lily's eye had always wandered to the bad boys. Eli and Sawyer. And occasionally, Gideon Crawford. She'd bobbed between them throughout their high school years, into college, and beyond.

Lily had loved Eli, but Eli's affections were...complicated. When he rejected her, she went to Sawyer or Gideon for comfort and distraction.

Most people believed that Lily's children were Sawyer's, or at least that Cody was. But Sawyer hadn't claimed either of them. Not when they were born, not after Lily's homicide, and not now.

Jackson had despised him for it. It felt like a weakness, this resentment he'd harbored for years. As much as he despised himself for it, he couldn't help it.

"I'm here to talk about Easton's homicide, not the past."

Sawyer grunted. "It's always about the past. The past never dies. When you finally figure that out, maybe you'll become a decent cop."

"Undersheriff."

Sawyer only smiled.

Jackson smiled back. He was used to criminals trying to get a rise out of him. Hell, his whole family did it for sport.

"We have the phone calls. We have the logs and the texts." They didn't have the texts, but Sawyer didn't need to know that. "Before the system went down, we traced the money. You created several shell accounts, but it came from you. The money Easton used to pay off his property taxes. He was going to lose the land. All of it. Then boom, in one fell swoop, he's got the money to pay off three years of back taxes? It was you. And I want to know why."

Sawyer gave a noncommittal grunt.

"You paid him for something. Payback. Revenge. There are a hundred reasons why criminals get into bed with each other. Maybe he didn't do what you'd paid him for. Maybe things went badly. Or he was blackmailing you for something."

Sawyer didn't blink. "I thought you wanted Cody Easton for it."

Frustrated, Jackson gritted his teeth. Somehow, Sawyer often knew things he shouldn't know. Jackson suspected Sawyer had a paid informant on the Munising Police Department payroll or in the Sheriff's office, but he'd never been able to prove it.

"Cody is a person of interest. That's all."

"And I'm the Queen of England."

Jackson sighed. "I'm keeping my options open. You're looking extremely good right now. You've got the motive. The means. How about opportunity? I'll ask you again, where were you the afternoon of May seventeenth?"

"On my boat, like I said. Fishing."

"By yourself, I presume."

Sawyer laughed, a flat, empty sound that grated against Jackson's ears. "Of course not. I was with Cyrus Lee and a few others. They'll swear by it."

"I'm sure they will." Jackson rolled his eyes. Sawyer's minions would do anything for him. "We're going to be looking hard at you, Sawyer. Your business, your boats, your financials, your comings and goings. I imagine a man like you wouldn't appreciate such scrutiny."

"No, I suppose not."

"So, it's in your best interest to clear your name. If you're clean, tell me so that I can move on and hunt down the real killer. That's all I want, Sawyer. I don't care about whatever else you're up to."

To the right rose the rocky cliffs of the Pictured Rocks coastline. The fog was lifting, the coastline hazy and indistinct but still spectacular.

His breath caught in his chest. Seagulls wheeled and soared above the cliffs, white specks against the iron-gray sky.

Thousands of years of wind and water had molded the shoreline into a fifteen-mile expanse of dramatic cliffs. Dozens of waterfalls splashed down the cliffs, the water mingling with minerals in the sandstone to create giant abstract works of art. Shades of browns and reds from iron, black from manganese, greens and blues from copper, like God Himself had painted the rocks in brilliant color.

"All right, Jackson," Sawyer said finally. "You want the truth? I'll throw you a bone, but only because I'm in a giving spirit. You want to talk? Let's talk."

42

JACKSON CROSS

DAY SIX

Sawyer watched the mist-shrouded cliffs. "I assume you know the DEA has a hard-on for me. They've been trying to nail me for years, just like you have. Surveilling my reputable businesses. I'm not supposed to know." Sawyer winked at him. "But I know. They're watching the docks twenty-four-seven now. I appreciate my privacy, if you know what I mean."

Jackson waited him out. He knew about the multi-jurisdictional task force that included the Michigan State Police and the DEA. They were under orders to stay out of it. But this was bigger than that.

"I had protection. Line certain pockets, and they'll throw you a bone when you need it. When Samuel Anderson died in that pandemic surge last year, I was left with a...hole in my resources. I'm nothing if not resourceful, Jackson. I'm sure you know that by now."

Jackson knew.

"This is all hypothetical, of course."

"Of course."

"Let's say our hypothetical businessman is moving considerable product. He's the main source for the entire UP and has gained traction downstate as well. Branching into new services, reaching new clients. Business is booming. But now he needs a secondary location for certain...exchanges. Away from prying eyes."

He shrugged. "What is it realtors always say? Location, location, location. Let's say that Easton's private dock afforded us the advantages that we needed. Two businessmen worked out a deal. That's it, Jackson. No more, no less."

"Then why would you kill him?"

"Why indeed. And that why is critically important, Jackson. Hypothetically, that certain individual is devastated that Easton is dead. Things were working out just fine before he got himself axed."

Jackson let Sawyer's words sink in. Considered them, turned them over like stones in his mind, looking for the cracks, the weaknesses, the defects. He found none.

"I had no reason to eliminate him, Cross. You're looking in all the wrong places."

Jackson had the same unsettled feeling. "And Cody Easton?"

"What about him?"

"Cody Easton was using a small aluminum fishing boat called the *Little Neptune*. It's registered in your name."

"I lent it to him."

"Why?"

"Because he asked. He likes to go night fishing. A boy needs a pastime, a real one. Not that drawing and poetry crap. He was going to buy it. I hired him to work it off."

"What did Cody do for you?"

"Odds and ends."

"Can you be more specific?"

"Am I talking to a cop or a concerned citizen? My answers depend on you."

"I want the truth."

Sawyer looked across the water. "Cody isn't a bad kid. Too soft. Moody. He needs to be toughened up. He wanted out of this town, so I told him he needed money to do that. Real money, from a real job, not serving ice cream to drunk tourists three months a year for minimum wage."

Jackson felt sick. "It's true, then. You had him dealing at the middle school, you pig."

"Name calling will get you nowhere," Sawyer said wryly.

"What the hell is wrong with you?"

"It's business, Cross. That's all it is. Good business. Seeding the next generation. They're going to do it anyway; I might as well be the one who gets rich off it."

"You're disgusting."

"That kid will go to college now. He can paint toilets for art galleries or write poetry or whatever the hell he thinks he wants. But it's going to get him out. He won't be trapped here like..." Sawyer's voice trailed off. He looked away, out across the bluffs, and shook his head. "I'm giving him a future. Which is more than you or anyone else can say."

Anger filled him. Everything he did to keep this county together, to make it a safe place for kids to grow up. Men like Sawyer came behind him and knocked it all down.

Crystal meth was an epidemic in the Upper Peninsula, as it was elsewhere. In wide rural swaths of the state, where treatment was scarce and the drug was anything but, meth had eclipsed the opioid epidemic.

"You're a monster and you don't even see it, do you?"

"Settle down, Jackson. You're always so uptight. I don't give the babies the hard stuff, okay? They get Adderall, Ritalin, and Vyvanse. The usual suspects. I have a soul."

Jackson doubted it. "You're destroying lives, not saving them."

"You say 'tomato', I say 'to-mah-to'."

"Did Cody use?"

"Nah. My people don't use. They're not stupid."

It didn't make him feel better. "You have no conscience."

Sawyer gave a dark laugh. "Conscience? What's a conscience but religious and social structures designed to keep the individual small and docile and under their thumb?"

"There's right and wrong."

"There's no such thing. There never was."

Jackson shook his head. There was no use arguing with him.

Sawyer was a different sort of monster, but not the kind that Jackson was searching for today. He'd have to verify Sawyer's alibi, not that Sawyer's friends were reliable, but he did believe him. As long as everything he'd said checked out. Sawyer would have no reason to kill Easton.

Much as Jackson hated it, that left Cody.

Sawyer steered them closer to the rocks. Massive boulders slipped by beneath the surface of the water. It appeared that the yacht would strike them, but somehow, they skimmed over the surface. The boulders were deeper than they appeared.

"This county is balanced on a precipice, Cross."

"I know."

"You aren't stupid. That's one thing you never were. Naïve, yes. Blind, certainly. And pathetic. But not stupid."

"Is there supposed to be a compliment in there?"

Sawyer responded with a question. "You know what's happening, don't you?"

Jackson turned his attention from the rocks and faced Sawyer. The afternoon sun had burned off the last of the fog. The surface of the water barely ruffled, smooth as glass, the whole world reflected upside down. "You tell me what you think is happening."

Sawyer grinned. The light hit his eyes for the first time, and he looked happy as a kid at Christmas. "So glad you asked. You think the power is coming back?"

Jackson hesitated. There was no reason not to say it. "No, I don't."

Sawyer nodded, like he was confirming something to himself. "So many people are still too slow to get it. They've had what, a week now of these freak light shows? They've watched the news until they lost power and their TVs went dark. They can't use their phones, can't sign onto the internet, can't get cash from the banks, can't get gas from gas stations. They can't use their credit cards. And still, how many people think everything will go back to normal? At least half."

"Agreed."

"It's an opportunity."

"It's a disaster."

Sawyer sighed. "You have no imagination. Anyone ever tell you that?"

"No."

The sun burned bright overhead. Shaking his head as if disappointed, Sawyer swung the yacht around and headed back to the harbor.

"There are finite resources, Jackson. Always have been, but now it's for real. For keeps. Someone is going to be king of the mountain, and it's not who you think."

"Whatever you're thinking, don't try it. You won't win."

"We'll see, won't we?"

Seagulls arced overhead, squawking to each other. Their cries echoed as the *Risky Business* sailed past a massive cavern hewn out of the rock face. A pile of huge, car-sized boulders had buried a narrow band of shoreline.

"Remember that I helped you, Jackson. When the time comes."

"Remember that I didn't arrest you, when the time comes."

Sawyer grinned. "Touché."

A few summers ago, a two-hundred-foot shelf of bluff had collapsed without warning. That was the way of things out here; you never knew when solid ground might crumble beneath your feet.

Sawyer's grin broadened. "Pay attention, Jackson. Things are about to get very interesting."

43

JACKSON CROSS

DAY SIX

Jackson stood on the dock, watching a few boats entering and exiting the harbor. The big tourist tours had been canceled. Hand-written signs on most of the shop doors stated, "Closed until further notice."

He'd been on Sawyer's boat for less than two hours; it had felt like an eternity. The temperature was in the low sixties, but he was sweating, damp wet circles beneath his armpits.

The view was stunning. The white boats against the pristine green of the lake. Birds wheeled in the eggshell blue of the sky. A dog barked somewhere.

Still, he felt the darkness pressing against him, insidious, invisible. How could you fight what you couldn't see? How could you stop a train thundering down the tracks?

He could feel the vibrations beneath his feet, this terrible thing that was coming.

Sawyer was right in some ways. They could imagine, they could predict; they could prepare and warn and try to ready themselves. Thing was, no one knew how bad it would really get.

Even here in paradise, in a place this isolated, there were shadows. Enemies both seen and unseen, lying in wait, ready to rise up.

Did he have what it would take to fight the encroaching darkness?

Did any of them?

Jackson's radio crackled. It was Devon.

He hadn't had his radio with him on Sawyer's boat. He brought the radio to his mouth. "What is it?"

"I've been trying to raise you all morning," Devon said, breathless and alarmed. "Couldn't get a signal."

He tensed. "What happened?"

"Tourists reported an accident outside of Au Train, off an old forest road near County Road 552, near Candle Creek. A crashed ATV at the bottom of a ravine."

Jackson stopped breathing. "Are there bumper stickers on the back? One says 'I Heart Paris.' The other one is New York City, I think."

"Yeah," Devon said. "That's the one."

His heart contracted in his chest. "That's Shiloh's. Is she hurt? Is she okay?"

"We're doing a sweep of the woods. No sign of her yet. I sent Nash to check the hospital. But the ATV—looks like a hit and run. Someone ran her off the road, boss."

"I'm on my way." He strode down the dock toward the patrol truck parked in the empty parking lot. "I'll be there in ten minutes."

Alarm flared through him. This was what he'd feared. A little girl, out in the world alone, where anything could happen.

Jackson sped through town. There was far more traffic than usual. The cabins, hotels, and RV resorts were filling up, and not with aurora-chasers. Almost every vehicle he saw was an RV or a Jeep or truck loaded with supplies.

People were headed north, bugging out of the cities, planning to hole up and wait this thing out.

His only thought was finding Shiloh. If something had happened to her...if she was dead...he'd never forgive himself.

Ruts marred the dirt road. Overgrown weeds choked the shoulder. Tall jack pines, towering oaks, and slender beech trees crowded both sides of the road. The thick canopy cloaked the sun.

A minute later, he pulled up behind Devon's car, leapt out, and approached the scene, careful to preserve potential evidence.

To his left, the ravine dropped a good forty to fifty feet. Birds twittered. The air cooled considerably this deep in the woods. Mosquitos whirled in thickening clouds.

Small flags marked a deep set of tracks along the shoulder. Judging by the size, the distance, the depth of the treads, they were from a pickup truck. The treads looked aggressive, like they were specialty offroad tires. Hopefully, the tech guys could match them with a manufacturer, brand, and model.

The tracks deepened and swerved where the truck had slammed its brakes to keep from hurtling over the precipice. A pair of narrow tracks were smeared beneath the larger tracks of the pursuing vehicle.

His heart in his throat, he gazed down at the path of shattered underbrush that led into the ravine.

"Over here, boss!" Devon called from below him. Her voice filtered through the dense trees. "Come down slow. Watch your step. I fell twice."

Bushes snagged at his windbreaker, thorns clawed his pantlegs. Damp leaves slid beneath his boots, threatening to send him sprawling. He used vines and branches to steady himself as he descended into the ravine.

Two-thirds down, he caught sight of the ATV.

The mangled wreck of the four-wheeler lay crumpled at the base of a poplar tree with low spreading branches. He stared at it, his eyes blurring, imagining Shiloh crushed beneath it, battered and lifeless.

He told himself not to care, not to become emotionally invested. It was impossible, especially with this case. It was that care that drove him, compelled him. Forced him to work harder and longer, to refuse to give up.

It also blinded him. Haunted him. Stalked his dreams and nightmares.

"She was thrown free," Devon said. "She must've been." She stood ten yards away at the bottom of the ravine. She pointed. "Got a few droplets of blood over here."

Jackson stayed well clear of the scene, circling it cautiously, studying the ground, the matted tracks. Two pairs of prints. One smaller, one much larger. He didn't know if the larger prints matched the unknown prints found at the salvage yard. They needed to make plaster casts.

Devon set an evidence marker next to the tree. She pulled an envelope from her pocket with gloved hands, swabbed a dark droplet on a section of bark about chest-high, then placed the swab into the envelope and marked it.

She circled the scene and approached the ATV again. "Boot prints here and here."

Jackson saw the same thing she did. Dismay knotted in his gut. "He followed her down."

"He did."

"Not an accident."

"No." Devon squatted near the ATV's crumpled rear fender. The I Heart Paris bumper sticker was nearly unrecognizable. "We've got paint transfer."

She pointed to a faint blue streak, then pulled out her phone and photographed it. He'd given her one of the extra solar chargers he'd purchased in Marquette.

She glanced up at him, frowning. "We'll get our tech guys on it. They'll get a paint match. Together with the tires and prints, we'll find the perp who did this."

Jackson felt impotent. They were the long arm of the law, but their hands were cuffed. "The records are online. And online is offline."

A blue jay perched on a branch twenty feet above their heads. He chattered angrily at them for invading the peace of his woods, his sanctuary.

"We'll have to do things the old-fashioned way."

Devon swatted at a mosquito. "Gotta start somewhere."

"Have you called it in?"

"Can't reach dispatch. I had to drive back into town just to get within range to radio you."

Their radios worked on a repeater system, essentially radio towers that required electrical power. With the repeater network down, their portable radios and in-car radios would only transmit and receive within a short range.

Frustration surged through him. "Damn it!"

"I'll go in person. Looks like we're doing everything in person. What a colossal waste of time and resources."

They climbed the ridge, feet sliding in the muddy leaves, breathing hard with exertion by the time they crested the ridge. Jackson walked back, studying the tire tracks along the shoulder.

Devon watched him, her useless phone in one hand like an extra appendage, her other hand fisted on her hip. "What is it, boss?"

A dark understanding slithered through him, a cold tingle at the back of his skull. "Someone found her. Hunted her down."

"She was a witness. Like we thought."

"A fourteen-year-old boy couldn't do this."

Devon studied the ground, the story it told. "No."

"Cody Easton didn't kill his grandfather. Someone else did," Jackson said. "And that someone came after Shiloh."

"Could be a coincidence."

"Someone running a girl off the road less than a week after her grandfather is murdered? It's not."

Devon nodded slowly. "They were both witnesses."

"And now they're both in danger." Jackson rubbed his temples and groaned. "Why couldn't she just come to me like a normal kid? What the hell does she think she's doing? I can't protect her if I don't know where she is!"

Devon approached him and placed a hand on his arm, compassion in her eyes. "I know you care about this kid. About both of them. We'll find them, okay? She's still out there."

He couldn't breathe. "She's hurt and scared and alone."

Devon didn't blink. "Yeah, she is. But we've got a lead. That's more than we had an hour ago. The perp doesn't know it, but he just gave us the clue we need to nail him."

He forced himself to focus, to think. "We find the truck, we find him."

The early evidence had pointed at Cody. Clearly, it wasn't him. And then Sawyer, but it wasn't him, either. Eli Pope had still been in prison at the time of the homicide.

So who, then?

The puzzle pieces didn't fit. He felt like he'd been reading the scene wrong, the whole thing. Going at it backward. He needed to figure it out, and fast. Shiloh and Cody's lives depended on it.

Jackson shook off his sense of impending dread and steeled himself. "Fred Combs owns the autobody shop off Adams Trail, near the Bear Trap Inn. The man is old as sin. If anyone keeps a filing cabinet around, it's him. Bet he knows every vehicle and every driver in the county."

Devon's lips flattened into a thin line. He rarely saw her without a twinkle in her eyes, but there was no twinkle now, only grim determination. "Let's go."

"We'll take the patrol truck. We'll come back for your car later. We need to conserve gas. Get in the truck."

"Yes, boss." The merest flash in her eyes. "But I'm driving."

44

LENA EASTON

DAY SIX

The fire in the sky flared brighter than Lena had ever seen it.

Great swaths of burning crimson writhed like translucent snakes eating each other's tails. The Aurora had never seemed more alive, heavenly wraiths pulsing with both beauty and menace.

It took incredible focus to keep her eyes on the road rather than stare gaping through the windshield. It was surreal, ethereal. Almost supernatural.

The Tan Turd's radio spat static. Garbled nonsense erupted from every station. AM or FM, it didn't matter.

From the backseat, Bear rose to his haunches and whined. He didn't like the noise. Lena didn't, either. She switched it off.

"It's getting stronger, right? I'm not seeing things?"

Bear woofed.

"That's what I thought." She rubbed her weary eyes. It wasn't even dark yet, but the northern lights shimmered bright in the sky.

Her stomach growled. Sweat broke out on her forehead. She felt a little shaky, too. Damn it. She'd forgotten to eat, so focused on driving that she'd missed her last meal break.

She had to be careful; she couldn't afford to let her health slide.

She checked her pump, then reached for an apple juice box and a package of crackers and cheese.

"Dinner of champions." She glanced at Bear in the rear-view mirror. "Don't judge."

Even though she'd skirted the city, huge traffic jams outside of Detroit had slowed her down. She'd inched her way through Ann Arbor, where she'd attended the University of Michigan.

Most of the exits were backed up. It appeared that everyone was attempting to leave at once. She couldn't imagine the state of things within the city itself.

She'd passed dozens of vehicles marooned on the side of the road, out of fuel. Hotel parking lots were overflowing as stranded people found themselves desperate for shelter.

On I-75, she drove through Flint and then Saginaw forty miles later. The further north she went, the more the traffic thinned.

A forest-green station wagon drove ahead of her. She'd kept their taillights in her sights for the last hundred miles.

Gradually, cities and towns faded away. The trees grew taller and closer together as the familiar woodsy scent of Northern Michigan hit her senses. It smelled like home.

Who was she kidding? She had no home anymore. She'd abdicated the places of her childhood and fled, intending never to return.

Yet here she was, ten miles from Mackinaw City. The nearly five-mile Mackinac Bridge separated the lower and upper peninsula, a stretch of steel that bridged two distinct worlds.

A twenty-three-hour, sixteen-hundred-mile drive had turned into four days. How much faster could she have traveled if she hadn't been alone, if she hadn't needed to stop frequently to tend to her blood sugar and care for Bear, if more gas stations had been functional...

There were too many 'if's', too many unknowns.

She'd done the best she could.

Trepidation snarled in her gut, her fingers taut on the steering wheel, her mouth dry. Once she crossed the bridge, she was one hundred and thirty miles from her destination.

She checked the fuel gauge; as long as she didn't hit another traffic jam, she'd make it.

Bear gave an anxious whine. He stood in the back seat and nosed the window. She knew the Newfie like the back of her hand, knew his barks, woofs, head shakes, whimpers, and whines.

He was nervous. Concerned about something he could sense but she couldn't.

She slowed. "What's wrong, boy?"

Before he could respond, a loud boom echoed. Then another and another.

Ahead of her to the right, a power line exploded. Sparks flew. Smoke billowed, tinged red with fire. A second one. Then a third.

All down the line, flames and smoke and sizzling sparks exploded into the night.

Lena gaped in astonishment.

The station wagon slammed its brakes. It veered left, tires squealing as it skidded sideways and came to an abrupt halt in the center of the highway.

Lena hit the brakes. The Tan Turd squealed in protest. Her seatbelt jerked against her chest as her body was thrown forward. Bear growled, nails scrabbling. His big body smacked the back of her seat.

The SUV jerked to a jarring stop. Less than five feet of asphalt between the two vehicles. The Tan Turd was untouched.

Relief flooded her. For a second, she sat, stunned.

As far as she could see, power lines sizzled and buzzed, pulsing with powerful surge after powerful surge. It lasted fifteen, maybe twenty seconds. It seemed to go on forever.

Someone screamed.

It was coming from the station wagon. A woman sat behind the steering wheel, staring straight ahead. Two kids were in the back seat.

One pounded on the glass with tiny fists, mouth opened. The aurora bathed their terrified faces in the red glow.

Adrenaline icing her veins, Lena made a quick visual check of the road for downed power lines to ensure it was safe, then bolted into action. She leapt from the SUV, grabbed her medic bag from the back, and dashed to the driver's side of the Volvo.

Several cars whizzed past, driving onto the shoulder to avoid them. No one stopped. Most cars were full of suitcases and boxes. More and more people were getting the hell out of Dodge.

She pounded on the window. The woman turned her head, blinking and dazed. She was in her early thirties, with short brown curly hair and scared eyes.

When she noticed Lena, she unlocked the door. Lena opened it and peered inside. "You okay, ma'am?"

"I—I think so."

Lena looked her over, checking for injuries or signs of shock, asking her a series of questions. She was alert, oriented, and unhurt, just startled. Normally, Lena would call 911 and get them to a hospital just in case. That wasn't happening now.

After checking with the woman, Lena offered the kids some fruit snacks, then gestured for her to step out of the vehicle.

"What—what just happened?" the woman asked.

"The geomagnetic storm overloaded the transformers. It probably happened across the country. Do you have somewhere safe to go?"

"We're on our way to my brother's house in St. Ignace."

"Get there as quickly as you can."

The woman stared at her. Then she looked at the sizzling transformers and back to Lena. "It's real, isn't it? It's really happening."

"It's real."

"I've been listening to the news every day. It's hard to know what to believe. But I thought it was better to be safe than sorry, so we left Atlanta."

"Good thinking. Buy whatever supplies you can. Whatever's left."

Lena held her gaze. “Get ready for all hell to break loose. Protect your kids.”

“Okay,” the woman said, steeling herself. She straightened her shoulders, mopped her face, and glanced back at her children. “Okay. I will.”

Lena got back in the Tan Turd. She watched the mother return to her vehicle and comfort her scared kids. They looked at her with total trust.

Lena hoped they would be okay.

There was no coming back from this. What came next would be pure chaos.

Bear chuffed in her ear as she started the engine.

“Strap in,” she told Bear. “From here on out, it’s gonna be a bumpy ride.”

45

JACKSON CROSS

DAY SIX

The smell of motor oil and cigarette smoke wafted through the empty front office of Fred Comb's Automotive Body Shop.

Jackson scanned the waiting room—scratched linoleum, a couple of metal chairs, car magazines scattered across a coffee table. No secretary sat behind the yellowed counter.

Behind the counter, a door dented from decades of use led to the shop. It was unlocked. Jackson and Devon let themselves in, Devon trailing behind Jackson.

They maneuvered past bays with various vehicles on hydraulic lifts, stacks of tires, work benches laden with tools, and a couple of rolling creepers shoved against the wall.

The mechanic was leaning over a rusty Jeep, the hood up, a wrench in one hand. A battery-operated lantern provided light. He turned as they approached.

"Nice to see you, Fred," Jackson said.

"What'da want?" Fred Combs was an old goat in his mid-seventies, with grease beneath his fingernails and liver-spotted hands. A halo of stiff white hair billowed around his head like Einstein.

Devon showed him the wrecked ATV pictures on her phone and explained the situation. "We were hoping that you could help us."

He barely glanced at the phone. He spoke with a heavy Yooper accent. "Yeah, I got customers. They got cars and trucks in all sorts of colors. What's it to you, eh?"

"We need a name and address of anyone who owns a vehicle in this particular color. That's all."

He grabbed a grease-stained towel from the rolling table beside the Jeep, scattered with wrenches, screwdrivers, a socket set, and a drill. "My customers appreciate their privacy, don't ya know. I don't go 'round giving personal information like that. I might lose customers if word got out that I was doin' that sort of thing."

Jackson gritted his teeth. "You want a murderer loose in the community? That affects everyone, even you."

Combs scowled. "We already got one. You ain't done jack squat to solve that problem, now have you?"

"Eli Pope has been contained. He's not going to be an issue."

Combs gave a disbelieving grunt. "I'll believe that when I see it. Damn Redskins, always up to no good."

Jackson stiffened. "What did you say?"

"Nothin', just like I got nothin' to say to cops." Hostility radiated from the old man's every pore. Wrinkles radiated like spiders' webs across his hard leathery face.

Jackson appreciated the benefits of life in a rural, isolated, half-wild place. Its insular nature, its privacy, that close familiarity. The safety of neighbors who would look out for one another.

There were also folks who disliked authority. Fiercely independent, used to doing their own thing, they wanted the government to stay the hell out of their business. Law enforcement were outsiders, even if they were their own sons and daughters.

"This perp ran a little girl off the road." Jackson got up in his face. Combs flinched, tried to back away, but the Jeep prevented him. He had nowhere to go. "He's still out there."

Combs turned his head and spat tobacco on the oil-stained concrete floor. "Just like your daddy. Coming in here like you're owed, you're entitled. You and your family believing you're above the law, that you make the law. You don't got everyone in this county in your pocket, Cross."

He felt the ticking clock in his blood. He couldn't see the timer, didn't know where the bomb was, but he knew it existed.

It was counting down. He was running out of time.

They needed a break. Just one little break.

Helpless frustration flared through him. Investigating a case was difficult enough when the world worked as it should. With the DMV down, they had no way to search registered vehicles.

It should be a simple matter to narrow it down. Instead, they were no further than before.

This ornery knucklehead had the information they needed tucked inside his liver-spotted, frizzy-haloed skull. And he wouldn't give it to them.

His hands clenched into fists, tendons standing out on his neck. "I know you know who owns that truck."

Combs patted the breast pocket of his grease-stained overalls like he was searching for a pack of cigarettes. "I don't owe you a damn thing. Get the hell out."

Jackson's frustration seethed into anger; it flashed hard and bright. He took a lunging step and jabbed his finger in the old man's chest. "You know, damn it! You can help us, and you're refusing! You know this truck!"

There were answers here. The answer they so desperately needed. In that moment, he was willing to do anything to get what he needed. What Shiloh needed.

"Tell me!" he shouted into Combs' face. Spittle struck the man's whiskered cheeks. "Who owns the damn truck?"

Combs' breath came in uneven wheezes. His weathered face reddened with anger. "Yeah, sure, I know who owns that truck. I've got what you need, and you're never gonna get my help. How you like them apples, eh?"

Jackson stepped back, breathing hard. His anger had startled him. How fast it had surged. He lifted his hands, showed his palms to the old man, the best apology that he could muster.

Combs gave him the finger. "Get the hell out of my shop before I report you."

It was an empty threat. He was old school; a man who took care of his own business and didn't want the aid of law enforcement. He wouldn't go crying to Sheriff Underwood. And he had no reason to—Jackson had controlled himself, if barely.

"Thank you for your time," Devon said sweetly.

"Don't come back!" Combs snarled.

Jackson stalked from the shop into the waiting area and shoved through the front doors into the cool late evening air. Devon followed him.

His stomach grumbled, but he was too upset to eat. Besides, most of the restaurants were closed. There was no power. Generators were running out. No supplies had been delivered for days, either.

They stopped on the sidewalk, halfway to the patrol truck. Sweat beaded his brow, beneath his armpits. Dusk was falling; the aurora already danced in the sky, brighter than he'd ever seen it. Long blood-red shadows stretched across the grass.

He felt shaky. He needed the calm and quiet of a river and a fly-fishing rod, some peace and time to think. But there was no peace to be had.

Devon watched him. "You okay, boss?"

"I'm fine." His hands were trembling. He shoved them in his pockets.

"You got him angry enough to get us what we needed."

Jackson shrugged, reluctant to admit how angry he'd been, too. He felt himself losing it. Losing himself.

The law was logical. It was cerebral. It was about following the rules. It offered control.

But he did not feel in control.

"We have enough for a warrant," Devon said. "You did good."

Jackson nodded. "We have probable cause. We know what he has and where it's located. He has material evidence in a felony assault investigation and is refusing to turn it over."

"Then let's go find a judge." Devon strode past him. "I assume you have someone in mind."

Jackson hurried to keep up. "I do."

46

LENA EASTON

DAY SIX

Lena drove up the winding driveway leading to Jackson's house. She'd barely made it.

The gas gauge ticked at empty, the Tan Turd struggling with every mile as she passed the places of her childhood. The familiar roads. The forests that stretched for hundreds of miles.

At last, the big stone house appeared at the top of the ridge. Behind it lay Lake Superior, glittering crimson as it reflected the northern lights. The aurora was so bright, it might have been sunset rather than ten p.m.

Jackson stood on the porch of his parents' house as if he'd sensed her arrival. He wore civilian clothes, faded jeans, and an Alice in Chains T-shirt, still with that boyish smile, that rumpled sandy hair.

He looked older though, and sadder, like life had dealt him a nasty blow that he'd never recovered from. Her chest squeezed with long-dormant affection.

He lifted a hand and waved.

Bear leapt from the backseat and trotted beside her as she made her way up the driveway. His tail wagged, excited to meet a new person, to make friends. Lena felt the same urgency.

With every step, she felt herself returning to the past. Rewinding time, the months and years and days flashing past. Four best friends laughing together, weeping together, arms entwined, a thousand memories of hot and sparkling summers, cold winters spent sledding, cross-country skiing, and snowmobiling, huddled close before a warm fire, unspooling stories and songs and half-drunk dreams.

They'd been her escape, as they'd been Lily's. Each of them had found solace in the others for their own reasons, a solace none of them could find at home.

It was the reason she'd come here first instead of the rambling white farmhouse she'd grown up in. It would be empty and silent, her father dead and the kids missing.

Lena paused at the top of the driveway, her feet rooted in place.

"Hey you," she said.

Jackson said, "Hey you, back."

With a grin, he bounded down the porch steps, his strong arms opened wide. He drew her into a bear hug. At first, she stiffened. Slowly, she allowed herself to melt into his arms.

In his familiar embrace, the stress of the journey leaked out of her. He held on tighter. Warm and strong and comforting, like a fuzzy blanket on a cold night.

He had been her confidante, her best friend. They'd understood each other. Where things with Eli had been hot or cold, a rollercoaster of love and heartbreak, Jackson had been calm, even, dependable. A lighthouse in the storm.

Years of loneliness washed over her. How could she have forgotten? How she'd missed this. Missed him. She loved this man like a brother. "Jackson."

"Lena." His chest vibrated against her cheek as he spoke. "It's been a while."

She choked out a half-laugh, half-sob.

For the first time in nearly a decade, she felt it, that pull. That connection to her soul she thought she'd lost. Maybe it had just been misplaced.

She was the prodigal daughter returned.

"I'm so glad you came, Lena. I really am."

She pulled back and gazed up into his face. "You look so old."

He managed a tight smile. "And you look the same as the day you left."

"How are things here?"

"Better than out there, but not by much."

"Tell me you have Shiloh and Cody."

His face fell. "Not yet. We're getting close. We have a lead. The grid down is making everything harder, but this is my job." He squeezed her shoulders. "I promise you. I will find them."

"I can help you. Bear and I, that's what we do. We find the missing."

He smiled wearily. "Get some rest, first. You look exhausted. Stay here with my parents for the night. Tomorrow will bring enough troubles."

"I know."

Jackson released her and took a moment to greet her dog. He bent on one knee and reached out a hand for the Newfie to sniff. "This must be Bear."

Bear perked up. Tail wagging, he slurped the side of Jackson's face with his pink tongue.

"Well, hello to you, too. I think he likes me."

"Don't get cocky. He likes everyone."

Jackson patted Bear's fuzzy head, rubbed behind his ears, then rose to his feet. He frowned, looking her over. "Your skin is pale. You feeling dizzy? Do you need to eat? We've got an unopened can of frosting inside. And apple juice. Still your favorite?"

Lena couldn't repress a smile. More than anyone, Jackson had been attentive to her illness, checking in on her, always with a juice box in his backpack if she needed it.

She had forgotten how wonderful it felt to be known so well. "Still my favorite. Thank you."

They were just-in-case people, natural caretakers. The ones who ran toward danger head-on and never blinked. Jackson wanted justice, to catch the bad guy, while Lena wanted to save everyone, even the unsavable.

"We have so much to catch up on," Jackson said.

"I want to know everything," Lena said.

Neither of them mentioned Eli Pope. The wound was still raw and tender to the touch. That would come later.

On the porch, the front door opened.

Jackson went rigid as his mother wheeled his sister onto the porch. "Well, hello dear," Dolores said with a smile that appeared genuine. "It's been so long. Come in, come in. I was just making dinner."

Astrid eyed her. She was as pretty as Lena remembered, with her long, silky blond hair and bright green eyes. "Another mouth to feed. I thought we were rationing our food, Jackson."

"I can leave," Lena said quickly.

"She's staying." Jackson didn't turn around, didn't bother to look at his family. "She's come a long way."

Astrid pursed her lips and smoothed her shiny blonde hair. Then she smiled brightly. "I guess you'll just make yourself at home, Lena. You always did."

Astrid had never been anything but polite, and yet Lena had always felt that Jackson's little sister disliked her. She had the same slippery sensation now, but she forced a smile in return. "Thank you for your hospitality. It'll only be tonight."

Lena turned to Jackson. "Do you have electricity? I've been powering the mini-fridge with the car adaptor, but the fuel tank is on empty."

"We have the generator. Bring your insulin inside." Jackson squeezed her arm like he could read her mind, could sense her anxiety ratcheting up. "I promise. We'll figure it out."

The tension released inside her, like a closed fist opening. The stress and pressure and heartache. The trials and struggles to get here.

The rest of the world fell away. For the first time in four days, she felt at peace.

Lena Easton was finally home.

47

JACKSON CROSS

DAY SEVEN

"We got him," Devon said.

"Who is it?" Jackson asked.

After work yesterday, Jackson had stayed up far too late reminiscing with Lena. He was thankful she was back home and safe. Now, it was time to get to work.

It was time to catch a killer.

Devon smiled and shoved her braids behind her shoulder. "He's right here, sitting in an interrogation room."

Jackson didn't breathe. "Tell me."

"You're never gonna believe it."

The county courthouse had closed yesterday. It had taken hours to physically track down a judge at a bar in Grand Marias, at the far corner of Alger County.

The courts were a mess. Everything was a mess.

The president had finally declared a national emergency. All systems were down across the country—internet, cell service, GPS. FEMA had been deployed to dozens of large cities to provide food and water to a populace that was fast running out of basic needs.

Despite the chaos, they'd caught a break. Once the warrant had been served, Fred Combs gave up the information they needed.

The specific shade of blue paint color was Velocity Blue. It belonged to Ford Motor Company, starting with model year 2018.

Fred Combs had three customers who owned a Ford F150 in Velocity Blue built between 2018 and the current year model: Darryl Harlow, a mailman in Shingleton; Susan Ashton-Hutch, a married accountant in Chatham; and Calvin Fitch.

Fitch was the proud owner of a Velocity Blue 2019 Ford F150 Lariat outfitted with a bull bar. According to Combs' handwritten records, Fitch brought the truck in for regular oil changes and tire rotations. He'd purchased new Maxxis off-road tires two months ago.

Combs had scribbled in an appointment for this afternoon at 3 p.m.: fender damage and paint match repair. Calvin Fitch would not make that appointment.

Thirty minutes ago, Moreno and Hasting had picked him up from the middle school campus. Now, Fitch sat in an interrogation room, like a fish caught on the line.

A fish that could easily slip off the hook if they weren't careful.

Sheriff Underwood stood next to Jackson, his hands behind his back, his features tense. "What do we have on him?"

Alexis Chilton pushed her black-framed glasses up the bridge of her nose and stared at her blank laptop screen like she wanted to beat it with a hammer. "I can't access the state or federal databases, but Fitch is a janitor at an educational facility. He would've been fingerprinted and background checked for employment. A criminal history would've flagged him."

"What else?" Jackson asked.

"Our internal server is still functional, for however long it lasts. A couple of speeding tickets in the last five years. He was picked up for loitering outside the Horseshoe Falls Gift Shop in 2019. The owner, Lydia Duncan, felt that he was watching her. It made her uncomfortable. She thought he was shoplifting, but the officers didn't find anything on him."

"That's not much," Hasting said.

"Any connection to the victim?" the sheriff asked.

"None known for Easton, but he works at the kids' school," Jackson said.

"You find his truck yet?"

Devon shook her head. "It's not at his listed address. Patrol visited the other two owners. Hastings laid eyes on both vehicles. No damage or scrapes. No sign of an accident."

"It could belong to a tourist," Moreno said.

"Unlikely," Jackson said. "We've got Fred Combs' records. The Maxxis Trepador off-road tires on Fitch's truck are special order. The casts at the scene look extremely close to a match."

It would take more legwork to confirm with the manufacturer, which would take days, if not longer. It was enough for now.

Fitch was good for it. This was it. He could feel it.

"What the hell is the motive?" Sheriff Underwood asked, glowering at Jackson.

"We suspect he killed the victim but didn't know that Shiloh was present. Somehow, he found out that she was a witness and tracked her down. He ran her off the road in an attempt to cover his tracks. The truck will connect him to the hit-and-run, but we've got nothing that connects him to Easton. Yet."

"You think this is him?" Moreno asked.

"It's the best lead we have," Jackson said.

"It's weak," Sheriff Underwood said dismissively. The man looked like he hadn't slept in a week. They were all haggard, exhausted, and stressed. "You're grasping at straws."

"He lawyered up yet?" Jackson asked.

"He didn't ask," Moreno said. "We said we needed his help, good citizen style."

"Good. Let's keep it that way."

Jackson glanced at Devon. "You ready to take a crack at him?"

She nodded. "Let's do this."

"Don't screw this up, son," Sheriff Underwood said darkly. "We need a win."

Jackson bit back a sharp retort. Even now, the sheriff was as condescending as ever. "I'm well aware, sir."

He ignored Sheriff Underwood's glare and straightened his shoulders. Anxious energy buzzed in his veins. His heart thudded, his mind a whir of questions and answers as he prepared himself for a game of mental chess.

The stakes were high. A murderer on the loose. Two missing kids. The country balanced on the brink of disaster. Much as he resented it, Sheriff Underwood was right. They needed this win.

Jackson and Devon removed their gun belts. Jackson entered the room first. Devon came in behind him, carrying the scant case file folder.

The room was small, with white walls, a metal table bolted to the floor, and plastic folding chairs. There were no two-way mirrors, but microphones and cameras were embedded in the wall.

The air smelled stale, like old coffee and body odor. The generator hummed. The fluorescent lights buzzed and flickered overhead.

Fitch looked up with squinty eyes, fidgety and restless. Like the last time they'd seen him, he wore denim overalls with scuffed brown boots. His lanky, dun-colored hair looked unkempt; he hadn't shaved in days.

Jackson scraped back the chair and took a seat. He leaned back, legs crossed, confident and calm, and faced Calvin Fitch.

48

JACKSON CROSS

DAY SEVEN

Devon took a seat beside Jackson. She set the file on the table and offered Fitch a disarming smile. "Good morning."

Fitch stared at her with suspicion and didn't respond.

Devon spoke in a polite, soothing voice. "If you work with us, clear up a few questions we have, we can get you out of here even faster."

Fitch glanced at her, unsmiling. "I didn't do anything wrong."

"We'd really appreciate your help." Jackson waved a hand absently. "I apologize if you're uncomfortable. We're conserving our fuel, so the air conditioner isn't running."

He shrugged. "It's fine."

They needed to Mirandize him. It often caused suspects to shut down, but if there were questions about culpability, they needed to have their ducks in a row for the DA. There was nothing worse than getting a confession they couldn't use to nail the perpetrator in court.

"Calvin, we've got some questions we'd really like to know. Given the circumstances, I just need to read you your Miranda rights since we don't know what you're going to tell us."

"Am I a suspect?"

"Right now, we don't have any suspects." Devon gave an apologetic shrug. "Unfortunately, that means we have to treat everyone as a suspect."

"Do I need a lawyer?"

This was tricky. Jackson kept his voice light, his expression neutral. "You can talk to an attorney if you would like to, but it'll take a while for a public defender to get here. With phones down and everything that's going on, it could take hours."

His expression darkened. "Principal Kepford wants me to disinfect the classrooms while the students are home because of the power outages. It's a lot of work."

"We'll get you out of here as soon as possible, I promise." Jackson pulled a card from his pocket and read the required paragraph, though he had it memorized. "Okay, Calvin. Do you understand the rights as I've read them to you?"

Fitch picked at his nails. He looked nervous. "Yeah. Yeah, I understand."

To begin, they asked him some easy softball questions. They wanted him to feel comfortable, to build a rapport with him.

More importantly, Jackson was learning his style: how he reacted when he was calm and comfortable versus how he responded when he was under duress or being deceptive.

Devon asked the questions while Jackson paid attention to how the suspect spoke, his body language, his facial expressions and posture.

"You're still going to work, even though school is canceled?" Devon asked. "I'm impressed."

"Always stuff to do. Those kids, they leave everything a mess. No one knows how to clean up after themselves no more." He nodded to himself, stiff like his neck was attached to marionette strings.

"Did you see all those transformers fry last night?" Devon asked.

"Yeah."

"Crazy, right?"

If there had been any doubt before, there was none now. It would take months, likely years to repair thousands of transformers across the U.S. Not to mention the damage to the satellites and communication systems.

"Yeah, crazy," Fitch mumbled. His wary gaze ping-ponged between Jackson and Devon. He shifted uncomfortably. The chair legs scraped the floor.

"I'm sure you've heard about the Easton homicide," Jackson said.

Fitch folded his arms across his chest. He stared down at the table, frowning. "Of course. Everyone has. That convicted felon, the soldier. He done it, I heard."

Devon offered an encouraging smile. "We've heard things, too. But we can't arrest people based on hearsay. We've got to dot our I's and cross our T's, you know?"

Fitch stared at her. As when they'd interviewed him at the school about Cody, he seemed slow. He took his time to answer questions. That dullness in his eyes—was it a ploy? Plenty of calculated killers hid in plain sight.

"Maybe," Jackson allowed. "We're eliminating suspects. It's arduous but it's a necessary part of the process."

"Can you tell us what kind of vehicle you own?" Devon asked.

He didn't answer.

"A Velocity Blue Ford F150 truck is registered in your name," she said. "Model year 2019."

"That's a nice truck," Jackson said, acting impressed.

Fitch hesitated. He uncrossed his arms, drummed his fingers on the table. "What's it to you? Don't see how that's any of your business, anyway."

Jackson kept his expression nonchalant, fighting his impatience. "We're just asking a few questions. That's all."

"And then you can be on your way, back to work," Devon said. "We're truly sorry for the inconvenience."

The apology did the trick. He'd expected an interrogation, not contrite deputies with rueful smiles. He blinked. "Okay. Yeah, sure. I have a truck like that. But I didn't do nothing with it."

"I'm sure you didn't. But can you tell us where it is?" Jackson asked.

"I don't want no trouble."

"No one said that you're in trouble," Jackson said. He wanted to keep him talking. The last thing they wanted was a demand for legal representation. If he asked for a lawyer, the interview was over.

Fitch glanced at the clock enmeshed in wire on the far wall. It was frozen at 6:06 p.m.

"There was an accident," Devon said.

"I don't know anything about an accident."

"A hit and run. An ATV was run off the road near County Road 552."

"I didn't do that."

"We have to ask questions to help us figure out who did," Devon said. "A little girl was riding that ATV. She got hurt."

Fitch tensed. "I don't know nothing about that. You're mistaken. It wasn't my truck."

"We know that it's your truck," Jackson said softly. "We checked the mechanic's records to the tire treads at the scene. We confirmed it's a match." There were rules about deceiving suspects; a ruse was permissible as long as they didn't fabricate false evidence.

Fitch paled. "I don't know nothing about that."

"Why don't you start by telling us what happened," Jackson said.

Fitch inhaled shallow breaths. He rubbed his hands together, blinking hard.

"Maybe you didn't even see her," Jackson said. "That road is dark. Or maybe a deer ran out in front of you. It's understandable. Accidents happen."

Fitch shook his head, faster and faster. "No. It wasn't me. I didn't do anything."

"Do you know where your truck is, Fitch?" Devon asked.

"Maybe it was stolen."

"Look, we want to help you," Devon said. "But you've got to be straight with us. We'll be honest with you if you can be honest with us."

He licked his lips, eyes darting everywhere but at Devon and Jackson. "I don't know. I don't know where it is."

"We need your help to eliminate you, okay?" Jackson leaned back in his chair and crossed his arms. "Can you tell us where you were on Thursday night?"

"I don't know."

"You can't remember? Think about it."

He wrung his hands. His eyes were glazed, dull and scared like a cornered animal. He was afraid, and he hated them for his fear.

"Let's figure this out together," Devon said. "I'm sure it's a misunderstanding."

"I was at the Northwoods Bar, okay? All night. I had four or five Jack Daniels. Maybe six. Played some pool with Cyrus Lee and Jay Addison. Tim Brooks was the bartender. You can ask him. He'll remember me."

Neither Jackson nor Devon made a move. Outside the room, an officer would be leaving right now, headed for the bar to verify Fitch's story.

"Were you intoxicated when you drove home?" Devon asked.

He nodded, jaw clenched, angry at them for dragging it out of him. "I'll lose my license for a year if I get another ticket, okay?"

"How did you get to the bar?" Jackson asked.

"I drove."

"You drove your truck?" Devon asked.

He hesitated. His right eye ticked. "Yeah, of course."

Jackson said, "Are you sure?"

Fitch looked guilty, like the kid caught with his hand in the cookie jar. "I took the Jeep. Wasn't supposed to, but I should get to go where I want, too."

"What Jeep?" Devon opened the file, perused the scant paperwork. "You don't have another vehicle registered in your name."

Jackson closed his eyes. He recalled the Jeep Wrangler parked in the school parking lot. A blue F150 had been parked next to it, too. He'd just reviewed the in-car footage from his patrol truck last night. His heart began to pound.

"Why were you driving a Jeep instead of your truck?" Devon asked.

"I wasn't driving the truck that night. I didn't do nothin'."

Fitch stared at them, belligerent. He was about to clam up. He was about to demand a lawyer, and they would lose him right when they were so close.

The pieces were falling together, a terrible picture taking shape.

Jackson leaned in, hiding the urgency crackling through him. "I believe you, Calvin. We believe you. You lent it to someone. You were being a good friend. You didn't know what would happen."

"Yeah, a friend. Okay? A friend had it."

Devon's eyes narrowed. "Then who? Who had it?"

Sweat beaded Fitch's broad forehead. "I'll get in trouble."

Devon offered him a sympathetic, doe-eyed look that could have melted the hardest of hearts. "We're trying to get you out of trouble."

Dismay curdled in Jackson's stomach. Alarm bells went off in his brain. He knew. He knew what Fitch was hiding; he just needed him to say it aloud. "We need a name."

Fitch shook his head. One nail was bleeding. He sucked at his thumb, eyes wide with fear. "Nah, I can't."

"A name, Calvin." Jackson stood, scraped back his chair, and went to the door. Fitch's eyes followed his every move. Jackson opened the door and gestured, as if Fitch could stand up and walk through it, easy as pie. "It's that simple. You can go home. Right now. Today."

Fitch's posture collapsed. Whatever internal battle he'd had with himself, it was over. He lowered his head, the wings of his shoulder blades hunched inward. He mumbled something indecipherable.

Devon frowned. "Say it again."

"My cousin," Fitch said in a defeated voice. "Walter Boone."

49

SHILOH EASTON

DAY SEVEN

Shiloh's ankle hurt like hell as she rode into town on Eli's bike. Luckily, it wasn't sprained. Eli had tended the worst of her wounds. She'd slept the whole next day and the next night.

Then, that morning, she'd stolen his mountain bike. Technically, she'd borrowed it. She planned to give it back. Eli had been awake when she'd left anyway; the man never slept.

She'd almost told him about the man in the black boots, almost showed him the photo of the girl she'd stolen from underneath Calvin Fitch's bed. Almost but not quite.

A lifetime of mistrust was a hard thing to overcome. Her whole life, she'd been alone, except for Cody.

Still, Shiloh recognized when she was in over her head. The time she'd spent recovering at Eli's campsite had clarified things in her mind. She had clues that law enforcement needed.

The plan was to drop off the envelope at the Sheriff's office or the police station. Maybe leave it with the front desk and tell them to give it to Jackson Cross.

On second thought, they could have wanted posters out for her. As soon as she showed her face, they'd grab her. Not a good idea. She'd drop it off, then run.

She turned onto Main Street in Munising. The bike was too big for her, but she could handle it. Her crossbow, she'd left back at the cave, though she hated to do it. It was incognito time.

It was sixty degrees at ten a.m., perfect weather for her navy-blue hoodie, the hood drawn over her face, her black hair in a ponytail. With her features in shadow, along with the baggy sweatshirt and loose jeans, she could pass for a boy.

There were tons of cars in town. Lots of folks packed the Dollar Tree and Dollar General parking lots, the grocery store, and the hardware store.

The Munising public library was still open. The parking lot was empty. Shiloh biked into the lot, parked the bike near the entrance, and limped in. Her ankle throbbed when she put weight on it. Other than the librarian, Shiloh was the only person there.

Guilt pricked her for mutilating the magazines, hiding behind a carrel as she cut out the letters and words she needed and glued them onto a plain piece of paper, items she'd borrowed from the librarian.

No one needed *Cosmo* or *Good Housekeeping*. Not when things were normal, and certainly not now.

Using the magazines, she'd written what she knew: the photos under the bed, the blue truck, the black boots. Then she placed the photo of the girl in an envelope. On TV, detectives could figure out your handwriting.

She was careful. She wouldn't get caught.

"You're the first person I've seen in three days," the librarian said as Shiloh stacked a few reference books on the counter.

The librarian checked out the books with paper and pencil, using a Coleman lantern for extra light. Mrs. Grady was a trim, attractive woman in her late-forties who wore flowy, colorful skirts and billowy peasant blouses, her long silver-streaked hair in braids.

Mrs. Grady peered at the books. *A Dummy's Guide to Homesteading* and *Edible Plants*.

"You're gonna start a garden, eh?"

"Everyone should."

"I have a feeling you might be right."

"Why don't you close like everybody else?"

The librarian gave her a probing look. "People still need books. For entertainment, but for learning, too. With everything going on, they've forgotten, but they'll remember again. When their phones die. When they can't stand the blank screen of their TVs and laptops any longer." She gave a grim smile. "They'll be back, and I'll be here."

Mrs. Grady knew who Shiloh was, but she didn't seem the type to listen to police scanners—or turn in recalcitrant runaways against their will.

Shiloh and Cody had spent more than their fair share of time here after school, sometimes even during school hours when they felt like cutting. Or when their grandfather had been drinking too much.

Mrs. Grady never turned them in. Never said boo about it to anyone. One time, he'd come in searching for them, drunk and ranting. Shiloh had been sitting cross-legged in the fantasy section; Cody on the computers in the carrels, researching drawing contests.

Mrs. Grady had threatened to call the cops, real loud and in front of everyone. Then, after he'd stormed out empty-handed, Mrs. Grady had brought them Twix candy bars and bottled waters. Shiloh had loved her ever since.

Shiloh slipped the books into her backpack and shoved the straps over her shoulders. She'd forgotten her library card; Mrs. Grady hadn't even cared. "Thanks, Mrs. Grady. I'll return them next week."

Mrs. Grady peered at her over the counter. "You okay, honey?"

Self-conscious, Shiloh touched her swollen lip. She smiled, though it hurt. "You should see the other guy."

Mrs. Grady looked pensive. Her hair was messier than usual. Her eyes were red like she'd been crying. For a second, it seemed like she was going to say something, maybe *I'm sorry for your loss*, blah blah blah. She didn't. "You're taking care of yourself?"

Shiloh drew herself to her full height. "Damn straight."

"You can always come here, honey. I hope you know that. I'll keep this place open as long as I can. As long as I'm still breathing."

A surge of emotion warmed her chest. Her cheeks went hot. Shiloh blinked rapidly, spun on her heel, and limped from the library. No use trying to speak with her throat tight and this damn wetness in her eyes.

She hopped awkwardly on Eli's bike, turned right from Munising Avenue onto Lynn Street and headed toward the Sheriff's office. The bay shimmered in the sunlight between the buildings. The sky was a perfect blue, not a cloud in sight.

She parked a block down, wound the bike chain around a lamppost, and locked it. The rest of the storefronts were closed.

Maggie's Boutique had a sign that read, *Open No Matter What! Cash Only,* though no one stood behind the counter. The touristy knickknacks, hats, magnets, keychains, and racks of sunglasses looked untouched.

Shiloh kept close to the building overhangs, in the shadows. The hairs on the back of her neck stood on end. It felt like everyone was watching her.

What if he was out here? In a car. On the street. In one of the shops, peering at her through a darkened window.

He could be anywhere. Could be anyone. Following her right now. She didn't know him—didn't know his face. Terror scythed through her. The invisible monsters were the worst kind.

She wanted to see evil, to fight it face to face.

Footsteps echoed behind her. Her heart leapt into her throat. She flinched, whipped around.

Behind her, a couple hurried up the sidewalk. The woman wore hiking gear with a pink gaiter around her neck. The man had a beard, his blond hair tied back in a ponytail. They both wore heavy-duty hiking backpacks.

"What are we going to do?" the woman said. "I can't get stuck here. I've got to get home. I've got kids—"

"I know, okay? Everyone knows. We'll figure something out."

They passed Shiloh and hurried toward the corner gas station, where a dozen vehicles crammed into every available inch of asphalt. A red minivan blocked the road in front of the gas station like they'd run out of fuel before reaching the promised land. Cars honked at each other.

Her stomach growled. While she waited to cross the street, she tugged a Snickers bar out of her pocket, ripped off the wrapper with her teeth, and ate it. Chocolate stuck to her fingers, and she licked it off.

Another car idled past. A white Jeep with muddy tires, splatters of muck gunked to its undercarriage and fenders. It coasted to a stop and pulled to the curb not twenty feet ahead of her. The license plate was covered in mud, too.

The Jeep driver switched off the engine. The driver stepped out, pocketed his keys, shoulders hunched as he headed for the hardware store. Several people hurried out the double front doors, clutching wood two-by-fours, rolls of plastic, tarps, and various tools.

Shiloh froze midbite. She forgot how to breathe. Her eyes were glued to his feet. Black work boots. White stitching. Red laces. A dull roar filled her ears.

He wasn't driving the blue truck, but it didn't matter.

It was him.

50

SHILOH EASTON

DAY SEVEN

Outside the hardware store, the man stopped, still turned away from Shiloh.

Panic clawed at her throat. A loud roaring sound filled her ears. *New South Wales, Queensland, South Australia, Tasmania, Victoria, Western Australia.*

She forced herself to calm down, to breathe. Gradually, sound returned. Keeping to the shadows, she looked down the street. The man in the boots still held the front door open, chatting with another customer. Their words were muffled and indistinct, but the tone was friendly. They knew each other.

The customer wore a blue police officer's uniform. He was tall, with dark hair. His hands rested on his belt. She recognized him. He'd been at her house with all that crime scene tape.

The cop laughed. The man in the boots slapped his shoulder and chuckled, then entered the hardware store. The door swung shut behind him.

The terrible truth sank in. This monster was friends with cops. Hell, maybe he was a cop himself.

She wasn't safe with the police or the sheriff's office. She never had been. Jackson couldn't help her; she couldn't trust him or any of them.

Walking into that police station was tantamount to surrender. And Shiloh Easton did not give up or back down, not ever. It wasn't in her blood.

On wooden legs, Shiloh retrieved her bike and found a hiding spot around the corner of the alley between the bakery and the flower shop. There she waited, breathless and tense.

Anxiety torqued through her. This was too big; she should find Eli.

She didn't trust any adults except for Eli...but he was too far away. The Jeep was here now. The license plate was covered in mud. She had to follow it, or he would get away.

She would follow him all the way down the rabbit hole.

Twenty minutes later, the man in the boots exited the hardware store, carrying a shovel and a folded brown tarp beneath one arm. Shiloh crouched, peering around the corner.

He glanced down the street at the closed gas station, gave a sharp shake of his head, and got into his vehicle. She listened to the engine rumble to life.

Shiloh mounted the bike, hands gripping the handlebars, one foot on the pedal, ready to go as soon as the white Jeep rolled past.

A moment later, it did.

Dread scrabbled up the knobs of her spine. Every cell in her body screamed at her to do the opposite of what she intended.

Follow the monster to his lair.

It was the only way.

For a few blocks, she kept it within sight. The Jeep drew further and further away. It swung a left off M-28.

Bicycling as fast as she could, she reached the intersection and jerked the handlebars left.

The bike skidded, tires biting asphalt. She nearly lost control but righted herself. Her ankle throbbed, her muscles aching in protest.

A dot of movement far ahead, a glint of sunlight on the metal roof, the engine already fading. She rode as hard as she ever had, teeth clenched, jaw grinding, furious with herself, with the bike, with her own mortal helplessness.

It wasn't enough.

No way could she bike as fast as he could drive.

By the time she reached the next intersection at Jasper Avenue, the Jeep had completely disappeared.

She craned her neck and looked left, then right, then left again.

It was gone.

She'd lost it.

Angry, defeated tears stung her eyes. Coasting to a stop, she screamed at the sky, "You stupid maggot-riddled piece of dog—!"

A lawn mower growled down the street. Crows chattered from the branches of a maple tree growing next to the stop sign to her right. No other sounds but the steady whirr of insects and her own ragged gasps.

Dismay filled her. She could feel her brother slipping away. His smile, his touch, even the memory of him was fading. Like she didn't deserve to remember him. All those times he'd rescued her, saved her, stood between her and her grandfather's fists.

This one time, this once when he needed her, she was failing him.

She closed her eyes, breathing deeply. *Anchorage, Alaska. Nassau, Bahamas.* She pictured her maps in her head. All the paths converging to lead to her brother, if only she could suss out the correct one.

If only she were smart enough, clever enough. Brave enough.

Balanced on the bike in the middle of the road, she forced herself to breathe, to think. She thought of the clues. The pictures hidden beneath the bed. The blue truck. The boots. The empty trailer.

In her mind, she walked through the trailer again, cataloging everything: the birding books, the photo of Calvin Fitch with his arm slung around that man with the familiar bearded face she still couldn't quite place.

The one that had snagged her attention before she'd remembered the cat box beneath the bed. Calvin Fitch arm in arm with that familiar man—the man who'd driven the white Jeep.

They'd been squinting, sun in their faces. An old clapboard cabin behind them. Rotting and warped wood. Weeds everywhere. Vines climbing up one side. An old hunting cabin.

Her breath caught in her throat. Steadying the bike, she unslung her backpack and unzipped it, rifling through her stuff until she pulled out her topographical map and the DNR state forest roads map of the area.

Studying it, her brow creased, head tilted. The Hiawatha National Forest boasted over two thousand miles of state forest roads for recreational riding. She traced a line with her finger from the cross-section she stood at along Jasper Avenue all the way north to a network of forest roads.

There were several derelict cabins scattered along that route. She and Cody had found most of them on their explorations. There was access from the Elderberry Trail, an isolated snowmobiling trail that passed behind her grandfather's property.

She and Cody rode their ATVs on that trail sometimes. She knew it well, and she knew how to get there. She knew these woods, the hills and trails, the forest roads and wild miles of shoreline.

She shielded her hand over her face and looked west.

It was possible. Maybe more than possible.

He might be at one of those cabins. He might not.

She set her jaw. She'd return to her cave and gather what she needed. And then she'd check every nook and cranny, unearth every rock and climb every mountain, descend into every hole in the whole damn world if that was what it took.

If that was the price fate demanded of her, she would pay it.

51

JACKSON CROSS

DAY SEVEN

Jackson and Devon stood in Walter Boone's empty house. Sunlight streamed through the windows. The house was too quiet, an eerie silence Jackson was getting used to.

No HVAC unit switched on and off. No low hum of the refrigerator. No ticking clock in the kitchen. Without electricity, the world was fast transforming into a place of quiet desperation.

Boone's address was listed as a small yellow cottage in Au Train off Woodland Road, fifteen minutes west of Munising. Moreno and Hasting had gotten a warrant and were searching Fitch's trailer.

No one had known that Fitch and Boone were cousins on their mother's side. Jackson had seldom seen them together, though they both worked at the Munising Middle School. Technically, Fitch did; Boone was a volunteer.

Boone's tiny house looked pretty as a picture. Neat and clean, the bed made. Towels hung on the rack in the bathroom. Knickknacks on the end tables, a glass coffee table stacked with books—*A Birder's Guide to Michigan* and *The American Birder's Association Field Guide.*

Jackson recalled the binoculars hanging on the hook in Boone's office at the middle school. There were no pictures anywhere. No other personal artifacts. No signs of life.

"Boone found the body," Devon said. "He must have returned to the crime scene to give a valid reason for the presence of his prints."

"It looks like it. But why? What's his motive to kill Easton? And where the hell is he?"

They only had parts of the puzzle. It was maddeningly unclear.

Jackson riffled through the kitchen cabinets, the usual plates, bowls, glasses, silverware, and pots and pans in the drawers. The pantry was empty but for some spices and a can of kidney beans. "Does it feel like no one actually lives here?"

"I'm getting that vibe." Devon stood in front of the fridge. "Ready? Brace yourself."

She opened the fridge. No foul odor from three-day-old rotting food assaulted them. "Bottled water and some mustard." She sounded disappointed. The freezer was equally barren.

"Maybe he cleaned it out once the power went out."

"Maybe." Devon sounded dubious. "He's lived here for fifteen years. It's so..."

"Sterile," Jackson finished.

"Right."

"If he's not here, then where is he?"

They stared at each other, the unanswered question immense in the unnatural silence.

Jackson rubbed his jaw in frustration, turning in a circle. He had that feeling again, a cold tingle at the back of his skull. They were close, so close. "What the hell are we missing?"

Just then, Moreno pulled in, driving fast. His tires kicked up dust. He exited the patrol truck and hoofed it up the porch into the house, panting. "We found something at Fitch's trailer."

"Spit it out, man," Jackson said.

His eyes darkened with anger. "Polaroid photos. Of teenage girls. Fitch admitted that Boone kept them at his trailer. Boone moved in with him, pitched in with the rent, but kept his official address here."

"How do we know the pictures aren't Fitch's?" Devon asked.

"We'll test for fingerprints, but for now, we know this much. Boone is in some of them."

The truth struck Jackson like a jackhammer to the chest.

All along, they'd focused on Easton as the primary victim. Amos had been contentious, unlikeable, a belligerent drunk. It had been an easy assumption to make.

But Amos hadn't been the target. He was the collateral damage.

The kids had been the targets from the beginning. Either Shiloh or Cody—or both.

He had been wrong about everything.

"It's him. He's the one."

"He knows we're onto him," Devon said.

"Wherever he is, he's got hours on us," Moreno said. "The owner of the hardware store, Danny Ellison, says Boone stopped in around eleven a.m. That's the last time anyone has seen him."

"Not long after we picked up Fitch," Devon said.

A chill raced up Jackson's spine. "He set his cousin up to be his canary in the coal mine. He knew we'd suspect Fitch first. We'd sniff Boone out eventually, but he'd get the warning when we got to Fitch."

Devon cursed.

"There's more," Moreno said. "Nash talked to the librarian, Mrs. Grady. Once he relayed the seriousness of the situation, she admitted that she'd seen Shiloh Easton. This morning, in town, just before eleven."

Jackson stopped breathing. "Boone could have seen her."

"It's possible."

"We need boots on the ground. Now. Everyone we can get. We need badges checking every vacation rental, every hotel, every campground."

"Damn it!" Devon said in frustration. "No phones."

"You'll have to track them down, one by one. Go to Chief Erickson's house if he's not at the precinct. Find Sheriff Underwood. Get who you can on the radio. See if Hasting can drive to the Soo and get Steve Rickshaw, the Chippewa County Sheriff."

Devon nodded, shoulders tense, expression grim.

Moreno shook his head. "Everyone is tied up with the crisis at the Locks. They called in everyone. The state police. The Coast Guard. A riot broke out this morning. People are trying to get at the supplies in the containers stuck in transport."

"I need to find Shiloh," Jackson said. "This maniac ran her off the road. If he thinks she can ID him, and that we're on to him, he'll be hunting for her."

Devon shot him a look. "If you've got any aces up your sleeve, now is the time to play them, boss."

Devon was right. His nerves were frayed. Fear pushed him to the edge. "Eli Pope knows where Shiloh is. I know he does. Enough with the games. I'm getting answers or so help me, I will shoot him myself."

Devon's eyes widened. "You sure about this?"

He'd never been less sure in his life. He knew only that a little girl was in grave danger. Shiloh and Cody were counting on him.

If that meant he'd have to climb into bed with the devil to save her, then so be it.

"Do you know where he is?"

Jackson headed for the door. "I know him. I know where he'd go. I can find him."

Devon reached out and grabbed his arm. Concern flashed in her eyes. "Jackson. I'll do everything I can—I swear it."

Everything might not be enough. He didn't say the words aloud. It would be challenging fate, an admission to the universe that he doubted. That in the end, his faith might fail him.

He gave her a grim nod. "Take me back."

Devon dropped him off at the Sheriff's office. She took the patrol truck and he switched to his Chevrolet Silverado 1500, but not before collecting supplies he might need in his search—more ammo, his Remington shotgun and county-issued AR-15, some flashbang grenades, and a pair of NVG binoculars.

He drove thirty miles over the speed limit, reckless, taking corners too fast, running stop signs. The passing seconds and wasted minutes felt like grains of sand passing through the hourglass.

Only so many grains of sand, only so much luck.

Jackson was fast running out of both.

52

JACKSON CROSS

DAY SEVEN

It took an hour to reach Eli's campsite from the nearest trailhead. Jackson had suspected where he might go; he knew he'd been right when he discovered the trip wire—if he hadn't been looking, he would've stumbled right over it.

This place had once been Jackson's favorite spot, too. Before Eli had gone and ruined everything.

So many memories had been made here: Eli and Jackson fly fishing, wiling away the summers at the swimming hole with the girls. The beach upstream where they'd built the firepit and watched the stars, while they drank to ward off the despair crouched at the edges of their lives.

He heard Lily's effervescent laugh, saw a bare-chested Eli plunge through the river, grab her around the waist, and pull her under. How Lily had looked at Eli with naked adoration, ardent desire. How Eli had looked back.

Jackson had watched them, sitting on the flat rock beside Lena, who had been sunbathing, eyes closed, a backward baseball cap over her face.

Jealousy had curled in his stomach like a snake eating its own tail. Lena hadn't seen a thing.

He remembered Eli holding Lily beneath the water. The bubbles streaming, the water disturbed as she thrashed.

"Eli," Jackson had said. "What are you doing?"

Eli looked up, his eyes dark, face unreadable.

Jackson half rose. "Eli! Let her go!"

Eli released her and swam a stroke backward. Lily came up, sputtering. Her arms pinwheeled as she gasped. Water streamed down her face, tendrils of chestnut hair stuck to her cheeks, her forehead.

"You jerk!" she screamed.

Eli's expression darkened. He'd stalked from the river, hands clenched at his sides, water streaming from his shoulders, his chest.

"Eli!" Lily had called after him, still in the lake. She smiled, pushed her wet hair back from her face. In only an instant, she'd gone from angry to charming, tantalizing. Everything always a big joke. "Don't be mad. Come back!"

"She wanted to see how long she could go," Eli had muttered as he'd strode past Jackson. "She told me to."

Lena sat up, groggy. "What's going on?"

But it was already over. It had only been a moment. Jackson had felt it, though. A frisson of doubt and fear; at what Eli might do, what he was capable of.

He'd hated himself for it at the time. Later, that memory had haunted him.

Jackson blinked and shoved the painful memories down deep. It was one of many when it came to Eli, to Lily, to those sun-drenched moments that hinted of the shadows to come.

The campsite was empty.

"I know you're here," Jackson said loudly.

With one hand on his sidearm, he surveyed the scene. The Dakota fire pit. The log for seating. The tent in the center of the clearing. The ground swept clean of footprints. To his left, a couple of damp shirts hung over a fishing line stretched between two trees.

Blue jays twittered in the trees. Thirty feet to his right, the river burbled over moss-strewn boulders. The clear water sparkled in the dappled sunlight. A heron strutted in the shallows. It watched him, wary, ready to take flight if he made a sudden move.

"Enough with the games," he said. "Come on out."

Something struck him in the back of the head.

He spun around. An acorn lay on the ground behind him.

He felt Eli's presence though he couldn't see him. Like a cool touch on the back of his neck, a ghost walking across your grave. The hairs on his arms stood on end.

"Got you," Eli said.

It was a game they'd played a million years ago. Jackson would try to sneak up on Eli and nail him with an acorn or a pebble. He'd never managed to hit him. Eli had known every time.

Jackson couldn't see Eli. He was hidden somewhere within the cover of the tree line, blended into his surroundings. Anxiety ate at him, but it was too late to back down. He was pot committed.

He kept his hand on the butt of his service pistol. His pulse thudded in his ears, but he didn't reveal his nervousness, his desperation. Like any predator, Eli could sniff out weakness.

"Come out, Eli."

Ten yards away, a shadow moved among denser shadows. Eli appeared from between two cottonwoods. He wore a homemade ghillie suit—twigs and leaves woven into netting over his back, shoulders, and head. Black mud streaked his skin beneath his eyes.

His feet were spread shoulder-width apart, the butt of an AK-47 pressed to his shoulder, the barrel aimed at Jackson's chest. He looked every inch the skilled killer that he was.

Jackson had expected the hostile reception. Didn't mean he cared for a weapon pointed at him. "Put the gun down, Eli."

"I would, but how do I know you won't shoot me? I seem to recall a promise to that effect."

"You're going to have to trust me."

Eli guffawed.

Startled, the heron took flight in a flurry of wings. Across the river, a squirrel scolded them from the branch of a jack pine.

"I'm here to ask for your help."

"There's a bald-faced lie if I ever heard one. You're going to have to do better than that, *friend*."

"It's not a lie. It's not a trick."

"Heard that before."

Jackson stared down the barrel of the AK-47, his heart pumping. He was painfully aware that Eli knew a hundred ways to kill a person, none of them using a bullet. "Please put that away."

"Forgive me for not taking you at your word."

"Damn it, Eli! Stop playing games."

"The only one playing games is you."

"Shiloh is in danger."

A brief silence. Eli's expression didn't change. His Ojibwe features were sharp as a blade, black eyes glittering like obsidian.

"Did you hear me?"

"You're barking up the wrong tree. As usual." He paused. "Unless you're here to plant more evidence."

Jackson didn't flinch. He knew he had it coming. "I'm here for Shiloh."

"I don't know where she is or what she's doing. I don't care."

"You're lying on both counts."

"Good thing I don't care what you think."

"She came to you."

Eli didn't answer for a moment, as if deciding whether to continue the deception or start playing straight. Jackson needed him to play straight.

"I care for Shiloh, Eli. I care what happens to her. That's why I'm here. That's why I'm asking for your help. I have nowhere else to turn."

"What makes you think I would help you?"

Jackson licked his dry lips. "Somewhere down deep in that black soul of yours, you have a soft spot for Lily's daughter. I don't know why. I despise the thought of her anywhere near you. My back is against the wall. I don't have a choice."

Eli didn't lower his weapon. Something crossed his features—a hint of concern.

"You helped her after the accident."

Eli didn't deny it.

"Is she hurt?"

"Banged up. No broken bones."

Anger thrummed through him. "And you didn't take her to the hospital?"

"I patched her up. The hospital would have notified social services. She was terrified." Eli's mouth hardened. "Her injuries were superficial."

Jackson looked around the campsite. "Where is she now?"

"She stayed with me for two nights, then she did her thing and disappeared. She's flighty. Has trust issues. Remind you of anyone?"

Jackson ground his teeth in frustration. "Eli!"

"She's fine."

"Except that she isn't." Jackson had to push past Eli's defenses. Get him to see how high the stakes were, that they mattered to Eli, too. "I know you didn't kill Easton. Neither did Sawyer. Or Cody. Someone else did."

Eli studied him.

"We had it wrong. I had it wrong. It's Walter Boone. I still don't know why he was after Cody, but he was. We think Cody was the target, not Amos. Shiloh witnessed it."

"I'm listening."

"He knows about her. He tried to run her off the road and clipped her four-wheeler. We found it a mangled wreck off that old forest road near County Road 552, near Candle Creek."

Eli's eyes darkened.

Jackson caught it—a flicker of anger, a shadow there, then gone.

"We can't find Boone."

Eli stilled. "What do you mean, you can't find him?"

"He's not at his house. Looks like he hasn't been there for a while. We can't get access to his financial records, credit cards, or phone logs because every system is down. He's in the wind."

"You think he knows you're on to him."

"Yes."

"And that he's going after Shiloh."

Fear churned in his belly. "Yes."

"He doesn't know where she is. No one does."

"You do. And we don't know that, not for certain. He could have followed her. He could've picked her up in town. On the trail. Anywhere."

Eli's face remained impassive. Jackson couldn't tell what he was thinking—he seldom could, even when they were best friends.

"This man is dangerous. We think he already got to Cody. Whether that boy is dead or he's being kept somewhere, I don't know. If Shiloh thinks Walter Boone has her brother, what do you think she's going to do?"

It didn't need to be said aloud. They were both thinking it. That feral, half-wild child would set out on her own. She would not ask for help. She had courage, but she was also reckless and would get herself killed trying to be brave.

Eli's eyes flicked to the campsite. He scanned their surroundings, hardly moving. His gaze roamed constantly, his muscles bunched and tense beneath his ghillie suit.

"Where are your fellow officers?" he asked. "Shouldn't they be searching every square inch of this place? Turning over rocks to see what's squirming underneath? Arresting innocent people?"

"They're otherwise occupied. Phones are down. Communications screwed to hell. Servers disrupted all over the country, half the planet. There's a riot at the Locks."

The Soo Locks in Sault Ste. Marie was the world's busiest lock system; over 85 million tons of cargo passed through the 21-foot drop between Superior and Huron on freighters. There were goods on those cargo ships that people wanted—badly.

"So?" Eli said.

"There are more riots downstate in Detroit and Grand Rapids, Kalamazoo. People getting scared, starting to panic, realizing the government won't be able to save us all."

"The world is going to hell."

"Yeah, looks like maybe it is. But I still have a job to do. And that job is to apprehend Boone for the homicide of Amos Easton. I intend to do that. But Shiloh is my priority."

Jackson cleared his throat. "I promised her mother. On her grave. Not that you would understand that." He took a breath, struggling to tamp down his anger, his frustration, his desperation. He could feel slender threads of hope slipping through his fingers. "Shiloh is more important than either of us."

"That, we can agree on."

"If you care about her, then you have to help me find her. She's a little girl, and she trusted you. Do not let her down."

A tense minute passed. Eli didn't move. He might have been a statue, no emotion on his face, no twitch in those rock-steady hands holding the AK-47.

Jackson knew his mind was whirring, examining the angles, looking for traps. He had the unsettling sensation that Eli wasn't looking for a trap as much as setting one of his own—one for Jackson.

The two of them, alone in the woods. No cell service. He was the undersheriff of Alger County. He was about to head into the remote wilderness with a former elite tier one soldier, a convicted killer. A killer who had every reason to hate him. To want him dead.

Jackson was capable with a gun; Eli was an expert. Jackson could fight; Eli had been made for it.

Jackson's heart kicked into high gear. Adrenaline shot through him. He had to be smarter. Had to be faster. And when the time came, if it did—he needed to be ready.

As if reading his thoughts, Eli smiled for the first time. It was a wolf's smile, the smile of a predator on the hunt.

Eli lowered the rifle. "Then let's find her."

53

SHILOH EASTON

DAY SEVEN

The cabin stood in the center of a small clearing. Tall trees rose around it. Junk in the overgrown yard, weeds as high as her knees. She'd checked three other cabins on her route before finding this one.

The ramshackle building looked cheap, slapped together. The dusty windows stared at her like blank eyes. Faded green paint peeled from the front door. Three concrete blocks served as steps. The roof sagged, the shingles carpeted in moss.

It was the rusty birdbath in front of the cabin that had drawn her attention. The same one from the picture. She'd forgotten it until now.

This was it. This was the one.

A sense of palpable wrongness sifted into her pores, her skin, her bones. Nausea slicked her insides. The closer she got to the cabin, the sicker she felt. Her gut knotted, her palms clammy.

Her first instinct was to rush to the battered front door and use her lockpick to break in. The truth lay in wait for her inside those shabby walls. She knew it. Felt it. Cody was in there.

Shiloh dropped to her hands and knees. The crossbow slid off her shoulder, but she jerked it back and crept forward, leaves in her face, twigs snagging her hair, her kneecaps muddy.

A spider crawled over her right hand. The leaves of a fern tickled her cheek; a twig poked into her ear. She ignored it all, focused on the cabin, drawing closer through the tangle of underbrush.

The grass driveway consisted of twin ruts to the right of the cabin. A lopsided shed stood behind the cabin, along with an outhouse. A pile of firewood next to it, a rusted wheelbarrow covered in leaves. Three rain barrels were stacked along the left side of the cabin.

It didn't look derelict, but neither did it look lived in. It existed in an in-between state, like the witch's candy house in the Hansel and Gretel stories. Or a secret abode in the stories of fairies and fae, demons and goblins—mysterious, compelling, dangerous.

The air was still. Crickets and insects buzzed in the underbrush. No vehicle was parked out front. But maybe he parked somewhere else and hiked in. Didn't mean no one was there.

Time passed. Seconds, minutes. Hunger rumbled in her belly. With one hand, she dug into her sweatshirt pocket and tugged out a Snickers bar. Tearing the wrapper open with her teeth, she took a few bites, caramel and nuts sticking in her teeth, chocolate coating her tongue.

It was her second candy bar of the afternoon; she was still hungry. Leaves rasped beneath her sleeve as she stuffed the trash in her pocket and returned her focus to the cabin.

Impatience gnawed at her. The cabin was deserted. No one was here. It was silly to be afraid. Besides, who knew how much time she had before someone *did* come? She was wasting precious seconds, her chance to find Cody before it was too late—

The cabin door swung open.

Shiloh stilled. Every muscle went rigid.

A man stepped onto the porch. He wore the same green sweater vest from earlier. His sleeves were rolled up. A pair of binoculars hung on a strap around his neck. He had a bland face and thinning blond hair.

Dizziness washed through her. She knew him. In the photo, he'd been much younger, with a beard. At night, it had been too dark. In town, he'd faced away from her. But now she knew exactly who he was.

Walter Boone looked like he'd stepped from Munising Middle School onto a foreign planet. He looked so normal, so average. The indulgent uncle. The quiet next-door neighbor. The polite guy you never gave a second glance.

He didn't belong here. Nothing about this felt right.

Instinctively, she lowered herself belly-first to the ground and peered through the leaves. Her gaze lowered to his feet. Black leather. White stitching. Red laces. Mud crusted the soles.

It was him. No mistake. The man she was certain had taken Cody.

Boone stepped down to the overgrown grass. Weeds scraped his shins as he moved across the clearing toward the rutted path that traced the right boundary of the property.

A minute later, the distant sound of an engine roared to life. It rumbled for a few minutes before fading into silence. Boone must have hidden his vehicle somewhere with another exit point.

Shiloh waited five minutes. Answers were inside that cabin. Not just answers, but her flesh and blood brother, alive and breathing, eyes bright as he shot her his lopsided grin. *What the hell took you so long?*

She could give up. Turn back. Get help. But how long would that take? Hours?

Especially without phones or a way to contact Eli. The miles-long hike to Eli's campsite from here, then the hike back here. Even if she trusted Jackson, she'd have to return to town and wait for Jackson to call in backup and roll in with the cavalry.

Every second she wasted on indecision was a second less that she had to rescue Cody. Boone could come back and squirrel Cody away to a place she would never find. Or maybe he'd just kill him.

Either way, she had to make her move. She thought of her mother. How a man like this had taken her life, had stolen her from Shiloh and Cody forever.

This monster wouldn't do the same. He wouldn't get away with it.

Adrenaline drove her more than her fear. As she straightened from her crouch, the crossbow shifted on her back. Standing, she felt exposed, vulnerable.

The scent of pine and jasmine was strong in her nostrils. Leaves crunched beneath her feet as she crept from the concealment of the underbrush out into the open yard. Her eyes darted to and fro, mindful of a trap.

A blue jay chattered angrily at her from a jack pine, as if she were invading its private space. She felt the invader in every fiber of her being.

She reached the door and twisted the door handle. Locked. Slipping her lockpick set from her pocket, she inserted the tension wrench into the bottom of the keyhole and applied a slight pressure, then inserted the rake pick at the top of the lock.

It was an old lock. An old cabin. Her hands trembled. Sweat slid down her spine. She cursed under her breath and wiped her damp palms on her pantlegs.

She torqued the wrench as she scrubbed the pick back and forth, repeating the process until the pins were set.

She could do this in her sleep. Easy as stealing candy from a baby. She'd done that, too, just to see if it was that easy.

It wasn't. Babies cried.

No babies crying now. Just her own fear thudding in her ears. *Akron, Ohio. Lansing, Michigan. Indianapolis, Indiana.*

The familiar refrain calmed her, steadied her nerves. She clenched her jaw, listened for the faintest click of the spring. The lock opened. The door creaked open.

Shiloh stepped into darkness.

54

ELI POPE

DAY SEVEN

"We're here," Eli said in a low voice. "Be quiet and do as I do."

Jackson nodded.

"I'm serious. Out here, I'm in charge, not you."

Irritation crossed Jackson's features, his mouth tight, eyes narrowed. An internal war waged in the shadows behind his eyes. Like any cop, he was used to giving the orders, civilians falling into line.

Eli was no civilian. And out here, he was the expert, not Jackson.

Jackson's shoulders remained squared, but something softened in his stance, the skin around his eyes. He knew it was true. "Fine."

As much as Eli resented him, he respected Jackson's strength. It was no easy thing for a man to put his ego aside for the sake of the mission.

His AK-47 in the ready position, Eli approached the cave from the east, not along the overgrown trail the way Shiloh did. He'd told her he wouldn't follow her, but he'd lied. He made it his business to know the details, to know who visited him and where they came from.

With Jackson trailing after him, Eli circled the perimeter twice, ears straining, senses on full alert, checking for signs that anyone had been here other than Shiloh.

They moved slowly, quietly, each footstep placed with care. As they moved, Eli looked for broken twigs, torn leaves, footprints in the dirt, disruptions in the pattern of the fallen leaves and forest floor detritus.

Every minute or so, he stopped, took a knee, and listened. He scanned not just the ground but the dense woods around them, searching for shadows, for any strange movements. Twenty yards to the east, a startled doe exploded from the underbrush. Other than that, there was nothing.

Once he'd ascertained that the area was clear, he approached the cave. He noted the trash bag that she'd tied up in a tree to keep the wild animals from reaching it.

Inside the cave, her sleeping bag was made but empty. He didn't smell any residual smoke. The coals at the bottom of her Dakota fire pit were cool to the touch.

She'd been gone for a while.

"We missed her."

Eli angled his chin at a glint of metal leaning against a nearby boulder. "My bike is here. Means she left it. Wherever she went, she's on foot."

"You gave her your bike?"

"She stole it."

Jackson snorted. "No one steals from you. You see everything coming a mile away."

Of course, he'd known. And of course, he'd let her slip away. If she needed it, he was glad to give it. "Guess I've lost my touch."

"Doubt it."

"I'll find her."

Jackson fell silent, letting Eli do what he needed to do. He stood still and didn't get in the way. It was a rare skill.

After scanning the trees again, Eli lowered his gaze to the ground and focused on the story the dirt, disturbed leaves, and matted grass told him. He detected the slight drag of her left foot; she still favored her injured ankle.

Eli followed her trail in a southwesterly line from the cave across a patch of rock-strewn dirt into the woods. The forest was dense with little underbrush. Leaves, pine needles, and fallen branches littered the ground.

He found a broken spider's web, partially rebuilt. Someone or something had passed that way within the last few hours. Twenty yards later, the slight indentation of a partial footprint.

Soon after that, the trail went cold.

He retreated to the last sign he'd spotted—the broken spiderweb and half-footprint. He made increasing circles in five-yard swaths, looking for some sign of her.

There was nothing. He'd lost it.

Thirty minutes later, he returned to the cave. "I lost the trail." Frustration laced Eli's voice. "I can keep looking, but we're losing light."

"We need Lena," Jackson said.

Eli's chest tightened. "What?"

Jackson eyed him. "You don't know, do you?"

"Eight years in prison keeps you out of the gossip loop."

Jackson ignored the sarcasm. "Lena does search and rescue with her Newfoundland, Bear. They're quite the team. She's good. If anyone can find Shiloh now, it's her."

"I thought she was in Tampa."

"She's not in Tampa. I asked her to come back before the grid went down. She got in last night. She spent the night at my parents' house, but she went home this morning. To the Easton place."

Eli went rigid. "Lena is here? Why?"

"Because her father was murdered. Because her niece and nephew have disappeared. Because the UP is safer than most places she might run to. And she's smart enough to know she needed to run, to get out of the city before it implodes on itself."

Eli said nothing. Emotions he'd thought long dead warred within him. Guilt and longing. Shame and desire.

"She didn't come back for you," Jackson said.

Eli knew that. Lena must hate him like everyone else. Though she'd stood by him the longest, more than any sane person would have.

In the end, she'd left him, like they all had. Every last one of them.

Just as he'd deserved.

He said, "Then let's get Lena."

55

SHILOH EASTON

DAY SEVEN

The cabin was heavy with shadows.

Shiloh repressed a shudder and took a step inside, then another. The darkness pressed in with a physical weight.

A chill touched the back of her neck as Shiloh conducted a quick search. The narrow living room on one end, the kitchen against the other, a tiny bedroom tacked onto the living room, with a back door next to the rickety bed.

The walls and floor were constructed of rough wood planks. The kitchen consisted of plywood countertops set over a couple of cabinets. A camp stove and tin wash basin sat in one corner, with water jugs standing next to them.

There was no bathroom, no electricity, no plumbing; the outhouse was in the backyard.

A sickly green sofa sagged in the living room. A rickety end table and a glass-topped coffee table sat on a faded oriental rug. Black curtains covered the two windows, as if Boone wanted to keep out everything, even sunlight.

A battery-operated LED lantern and a lamp with the base in the shape of a hawk stood on the end table. Puzzle pieces were laid out on the coffee table, the image about seventy-five percent finished. It was a picture of a bunch of glossy Petoskey stones, Michigan's state stone.

Every minute or so, she paused to strain her ears, listening over the rush of her pulse. Nothing under the bed or beneath the mattress or in the nightstand or dresser, which were filled with items like cold medicine and Chapstick, a couple of plaid shirts and khaki pants folded neatly in a drawer.

She needed some sign of Cody's presence. His drawing notebook. His backpack. A lock of blond hair. His black hoodie. Anything.

There was nothing here. What if she was wrong? Had she made a terrible mistake?

There was a wrongness about this place. So wrong it penetrated deep into her bones.

The white-stitched boots. The pictures beneath the bed. No, Boone was hiding something. Somewhere. She just had to find it.

Thump.

Shiloh seized her crossbow and spun around. Shouldering it, she braced the stock against her cheek and sighted the windows, the front door, the sofa. Nothing.

She moved swiftly to the closest window and nudged aside the curtain. Outside, nothing moved. She scanned the tall weeds, the rusty birdbath, the rain barrels, the trees.

The sound had come from nearby. It had sounded so close.

Like it was inside the cabin itself.

Thump.

Shiloh stiffened. Adrenaline poured through her system, lit her nerves on fire. Turning slowly, she scanned the room.

Thump.

There was no one here. She'd seen Boone leave. She'd checked the bedroom. There was nowhere to hide.

Thump.

Her gaze lowered to the floor.

The muffled sound came again. Something bumping against the underside of the floorboards? Something...or someone.

Anxiety scrabbled over her skin, the desire to flee so powerful that her legs nearly buckled. Instead of running, she approached the center of the room.

Thump.

It was coming from right beneath the rug.

Her heart hammered against her ribs as she set the crossbow on the floor beside her, using both hands to shove back the coffee table—careful not to disturb the puzzle—then the end table.

The lamp nearly toppled over. The base was heavy, made of iron. It wasn't even plugged in. Not that it mattered, with zero electricity out here—or anywhere.

The Asian rug was threadbare. Shiloh rolled it out of the way, exposing rustic pine wood floors. Big heavy iron nails. Nothing to explain the dull thumping—

Her eyes snagged on a rectangular outline. Ridges in the floor where they shouldn't be. An iron handle.

A trapdoor.

Her heart caught in her throat. She stopped breathing. Here it was. Cody had to be behind that secret door. He had to be. She'd finally found him.

Dropping to her hands and knees, she slid her fingers through the cumbersome iron hook and pulled it up. Teeth gritted, her muscles straining, she yanked with all her might. *Come on. Come on. Come on.*

The trapdoor squeaked open on rusty hinges, revealing a rectangle of pitch blackness. Shiloh grabbed the LED lantern and peered into the depths.

The fetid stink of urine and feces assaulted her senses. A glimpse of hardpacked dirt walls. Wood beams filmed with spiderwebs. A five-gallon bucket in one corner, a dirty mattress on the floor in the other.

A pair of eyes gazed up at her.

Horror seized Shiloh. With a gasp, she fell back.

The white oval of a face, the red O of an open mouth.

A girl. She wore a filthy tank top and shorts. Her pale body too skinny, ribs poking out, belly concave, dirt crusting her skin. A pair of dark eyes. Once shiny red hair tangled and matted. She gripped a knotted rope in both hands.

"Ruby," Shiloh whispered. "Ruby Carpenter."

"Don't leave me," Ruby rasped. "Please don't leave me."

She must have screamed herself hoarse. Screamed and screamed and no one came. No one to hear her but the birds, squirrels, and foxes. They weren't telling; the wild things kept the forest's secrets.

"I've got you." Shiloh stretched out her hand but couldn't reach her. Their fingertips just brushed.

There must be a ladder or something, but Shiloh hadn't found it.

"Get me out!" Her eyes wide and frantic. More wild animal than human.

Shiloh fought to control her own panic. "Use the bucket to get higher. And toss me the rope."

The girl turned away from the square of the trapdoor above her and darted from Shiloh's view. A heartbeat later, she reappeared with the five-gallon bucket and dumped it out on the dirt floor.

The rancid stench of piss, feces, and vomit rose up and struck Shiloh afresh. She gagged.

Ruby flipped the bucket and stood on it, then tossed Shiloh the rope. Her teeth were smeared red, her lips bruised and cut. Raw, oozing wounds encircled each of her wrists. Rope burns. Ropes that had shackled her hands, bound her helpless and trapped here.

Shiloh let her outrage fuel her, make her stronger. Bracing her feet, butt against the floor, Shiloh lowered the rope into the pit. "Take it and pull yourself up enough to reach the trapdoor. You can grab the handle here to pull yourself the rest of the way."

"I can't—"

"Climb! If you want to live, you gotta climb."

Ruby's gaze cleared. Some deep down glimmer of willpower flickered to the surface. Who Ruby was, who she'd been before this, and who she would discover after.

If she was strong enough. If she could survive this terrible moment, then she could survive the next. Shiloh had been doing it her entire life.

Standing on the bucket, Ruby seized the rope. She was only a foot or so below the trapdoor. What would've been easy for Shiloh took monumental effort from Ruby, who was weak and dehydrated.

With a groan, her muscles straining, Shiloh managed to pull her up enough to get her arms and torso above the hole. Shiloh dropped the rope, grabbed Ruby's skinny arms, and jerked her backward.

Grunting, Shiloh dragged the girl to her feet. She stood, swaying unsteadily, blinking in shock like she'd just landed on another planet.

Shiloh looked again at her teeth. One was chipped, and fibers were stuck between her front teeth. Fibers from a rope. This girl had chewed through her own restraints. Then she'd tied a knot on one end of the length of rope and used it to smack the underside of the trapdoor again and again and again.

For how long? Hours? Days?

Had Boone heard her? Had he listened, sitting on his moldy couch, doing his damn puzzles, knowing she was the mouse caught in his ultimate trap?

Rage and fear pulsed through her, but the rage was stronger. People like Jackson promised to keep them safe, but how could he, with these monsters lurking in the dark? A windigo with a human face.

Ruby's legs sagged, a stunned, slack expression on her face.

Pity washed through Shiloh, but so did urgency. "Ruby, where is Cody?" Shiloh seized her bony shoulders and shook her. She quivered like a rag doll. "Where is my brother? Cody Easton? Five-nine, blond hair. He's supposed to be here. He has to be here."

Recognition flickered in Ruby's eyes. She shook her head dully. "No. No one else. Just me."

"Think! Did you hear anything? See any sign of him? A second voice. Footsteps up there. A notebook filled with really good drawings of ducks and fish and stupid stuff like that."

Ruby kept shaking her head, her eyes rolling loose in their sockets like marbles. Ruby didn't know anything. She needed a hospital. She needed adults to help her.

Despair threatened to choke Shiloh. If Cody wasn't here, if he'd never been here—

There had to be a clue. An answer. Somewhere. It had to be here. This made no sense. It wasn't right. Couldn't be right.

She could feel it, could feel her brother, like he was hiding in the walls, trapped between the studs and the drywall, duct tape over his mouth, but he was calling to her, trying desperately to reach her.

She couldn't hear him. She couldn't hear anything.

Pure instinct made her look up. It was like static electricity, a cobweb brushing against her cheek. A ghost breathing down the back of her neck.

Shiloh seized Ruby by her skinny upper arm and steered her to the bedroom and the back door. "Go."

Ruby gave her a look of pure terror. "Don't leave me."

Shiloh understood then how foolish she'd been, how dangerous a game she'd played by coming here. She could not fight the windigo alone.

She needed help. She needed Eli. And she needed Jackson.

"I'm coming. But if we get separated, if something happens, you need to know where to go. There's a deer trail between the shed and the stack of firewood. Follow it half a mile east to the creek. There's an ATV trail that will take you to Snow Road—"

They both heard the engine at the same time.

Ruby's eyes went round with terror.

Fear stuck in Shiloh's throat like a hook. She made the decision in a heartbeat. If they both ran, Boone would hunt them down. But if she managed to wound or kill the monster, Ruby would have a chance.

She hadn't saved her brother yet, but she could do this.

Shiloh pushed Ruby out the back door. "Go!" she whispered. "Run!"

"I'm too scared. I can't—"

Shiloh looked her hard in the eyes. "You chewed through your own ropes, bitch. You don't need me. Go get help! Go!"

Ruby turned and staggered down the uneven back steps. From the doorway, Shiloh watched her run to the tree line, red hair a flame behind her.

Footsteps outside. Coming from the front of the cabin.

He was here.

56

LENA EASTON

DAY SEVEN

It was dusk by the time Lena arrived at the cave.

With communication down, Jackson had been forced to hike back out and drive to her father's house to collect her. She'd been unpacking, but dropped everything and left with him, grabbing the SAR backpack at the door that held everything she needed.

Bear spread himself out along the length of the backseat, panting with excitement. There was work to be done, and he was eager and up to the task.

The truck raced through town. In the passenger seat, Lena checked her pump—her numbers were high, so she hurriedly bolused herself. Minutes later, they jostled along the logging road.

As he drove, Jackson filled her in. She felt it radiating from him—his fear, dread, and desperation. His fear became her own.

Shiloh out there, alone. A monster likely hunting her.

They had to find her first.

Lena and Jackson made the hike in tense silence. At the cave, Eli was waiting. He paced like a panther at the cave's entrance. He wore a camouflaged jacket covered in leaves and twigs, a rifle slung over his shoulder, pistol in one hand, his other hand a clenched fist at his side.

As Lena and Jackson approached, Bear trotting at her side, he turned to face her. Those coal-black eyes, slanting cheekbones, the firm line of his mouth.

"Lena," he said.

Time stopped. Her heart stopped with it. An electric charge passed between them. It felt like being struck by lightning. The years didn't matter. She was twelve again, then sixteen, then twenty-five.

A girl in love with a boy with too much darkness in his heart to love her back.

She'd known it—and loved him anyway.

"Eli," she said in a strangled voice. She felt a million things when she looked at him. A thousand memories, a hundred things to say, but the words were locked down deep. Yet whatever lay between them, now was not the time.

"Sorry to interrupt the reunion, but we have work to do," Jackson said. "Lena, what do you need? Tell us how to help you."

Lena cleared her throat and focused on the task at hand. "Is this the PLS? The Point Last Seen? For Bear to find her scent, we need a starting place."

"This is it," Eli said.

She withdrew a paper bag from her pack and handed it to Eli. "I need an item of Shiloh's. Preferably something she's worn recently. Use the bag to handle it. Try not to contaminate it with your scent."

Without a word, Eli strode into the cave and returned with a heather-gray T-shirt emblazoned with Yoda on the front, "Do or Do Not" scrawled in yellow print. "She wore this yesterday."

Jackson turned to Eli. Indecision twisted his features. "I need your help out there. God help me, but I do. I know your skills, your training."

"I killed people for a living," Eli said in a low voice. "I will not hesitate to kill more. You're out here with an untrained civilian and a dog and no backup. No partner. No SWAT team. No one to have your back."

"I'm quite aware." Jackson didn't break eye contact. "Are you going to have my back, Eli? Or are you going to shoot me in the back the first chance you get?"

Lena didn't breathe, didn't move. Neither did Bear. He stood stock still, watching the two men facing off, his hackles raised.

"You'll have to trust me." Eli's lip curled in derision. "Like I once trusted you."

"That's not an answer. I need to know, Eli." Jackson's jaw bulged. He looked uncertain but resolute, determined to do whatever it took to find Shiloh. "This is bigger than you and me. I need to know you understand that."

"I do." Eli leaned in. "Make no mistake, I will do what needs to be done. Hate me all you want, but you do need me."

Jackson blew out a breath. He took a controlled step backward and relaxed his fists. He shifted his gaze to Lena. Pain in his face, doubt and fear. "Eli is right. It's dangerous."

"I know the risks."

"We should have backup. A SWAT team. A swarm of deputies combing the forest. With the rioting in Detroit and in the Soo, I don't know how long it will take for anyone to arrive, if they even will. They have bigger fish to fry."

Lena raised her chin. "You aren't responsible for me. I'm responsible for me. This is my job. This is what I do."

Jackson looked at her, searching her face, and she knew he saw the fear there. She didn't even attempt to hide it.

She was terrified not for herself, but her niece. Out there alone somewhere—or worse, with a monster who wanted to hurt her.

For so long, Lena had let fear dictate her future. Fear had made her obey her father, had made her flee the UP, leaving her loved ones behind. Fear had made her abandon Shiloh and Cody.

She wouldn't let that fear best her now.

"Lena," Jackson said again. "This perp is a predator backed into a corner. Like any wild animal, he's going to fight back, because he has no other choice. He knows we're onto him."

Eli watched her; those black eyes betraying nothing. "That's why I'm here. Any threat out there will have to go through me first."

Lena met his gaze, her stomach knotted. She knew he had been with the 75th Regiment, a skilled tier one operator. Even now, she trusted Eli. Never, not once, had she ever feared him.

She hadn't doubted him back then, not for a second; she'd doubted herself.

And when she'd failed to save him, after failing to save her sister—it had been too much to bear. That stain marked her still.

Lena patted the M&P pistol tucked against her hip. It was loaded with a round chambered. "I'm prepared."

Eli gave her a nod of approval.

"How can we help?" Jackson asked. "Tell us what to do."

"Do you have a topographical map?"

Jackson pulled one out of his windbreaker pocket and handed it to her. "Here you go."

"Bear and I have one purpose out here: find the missing, and as quickly as possible. I'm following Bear, but I'm also handling him. When I'm out on a search, I'm a detective, a tracker, a psychologist. And when I find our missing person, then I'm also a paramedic, a priest, a best friend and consoler."

"We'll be right behind you," Eli said.

Lena signaled to Bear, who'd been nosing Shiloh's sleeping bag inside the mouth of the cave. He trotted over at his handler's command, instantly alert.

They had work to do.

Find what was lost. Bring the girl home.

57

SHILOH EASTON

DAY SEVEN

The doorknob turned.

Alarm clawed at Shiloh. No time to think or plan. Nowhere to hide. Her heart threatened to pound out of her chest.

The front door swung open. The creak of a footstep.

She had a second, maybe two.

As soon as he saw the disordered living room, he'd know.

Shiloh took three quick steps and exited the bedroom. She darted into the living room, crossbow against her shoulder, stock against her cheek, finger on the trigger. Trembling, she planted her feet, disengaging the safety as she brought the bow to her line of sight.

Walter Boone stepped inside and closed the door behind him. He looked up and froze.

Time slowed.

She sighted his chest through her reticle.

A startled look crossed his face. And then he gave her a friendly smile. He was an ordinary man. A harmless man. Somebody's uncle. For half a second, it threw her off.

Which was exactly what he wanted.

He lunged at her.

She squeezed the trigger.

Panic made her fumble, the crossbow shifting as the bolt released. Instead of striking his chest, the bolt drilled into Boone's right bicep.

With a howl, he staggered back.

It wasn't enough. Her fingers trembled as she reached for a second bolt, backed up against the bookcase. Nowhere to run.

He came at her again.

She grasped the bolt, lifted the crossbow.

He reached her first. With his uninjured hand, he seized her by the face. His fingers splayed across her cheeks, gripping her chin, nails digging into her jaw. He slammed her head against the wall.

Darkness exploded across her vision. Bright stars of vertigo. Nausea churned in her stomach; she nearly vomited.

Dazed, her body refused to obey her, her muscles weak and jerky.

He ripped the crossbow from her fingers and threw it across the floor. Then he seized her by the hair and threw her to the floor.

She attempted to punch him, scratch or hit, anything—nothing happened. She tried to clamber to her hands and knees. He kicked her twice in the stomach. Pain exploded through her body. She curled into herself, hands over her head, screaming insults through stinging tears.

He stood over her, breathing hard. The bolt had punctured his right arm through his bicep. Blood dripped down his arm.

This man was no kindly uncle or polite neighbor.

He wore a mask, and underneath was the heart of a killer.

"I've been waiting to meet you. I think you know that. I thought you'd slipped through my fingers, and then what do you do? You show up at my doorstep. In my secret place. My sacred place."

Her brain wasn't working correctly. His form swam in and out of focus. Everything went dark and pulsing. Time went away for a while.

When she blinked back into consciousness, he held a rope in his good hand.

He rolled her onto her belly. Her chin bumped the floor. Growling with pain, he forced her arms behind her back and twisted the rope around her wrists. The nubby fibers scratched her skin.

She tried to fight, to resist. Her bones vibrated beneath her skin. Her heart shuddered inside her chest.

Footsteps clattered. He moved away. The bedroom door swung open, and he disappeared inside. Swearing, feet shuffling. A cabinet door opened and closed.

She tried to open her eyes and keep them open. It didn't work. Tried to get her legs to move, to get her the hell out of here. Nothing worked.

He returned to the living room. There was a scraping sound, the creak of the trapdoor opening.

Boone cursed. "You let her out."

"She's long gone," Shiloh spat through bloody teeth. "She's getting help."

He gave her a long, steady stare, as if considering her words. "I don't think so. There are miles of wilderness in every direction. Someone like you can find your way around the woods, but not that one. She won't last a mile. I'll find her."

"Screw you! Let me go or I'll kill you! I'll cut off your balls and tie them around your neck. Don't think I won't."

Boone squatted beside her, a pained smile on his lips. He knew. And he knew that she knew. He was the cat and she was the mouse. And he had her.

She froze, terror coursing through her veins.

He leaned forward, and with his good hand, he pushed a strand of hair back from her face. He stroked her cheek.

She turned her face toward him and tried to bite his fingers, but he was too quick.

He jerked his hand back, out of reach. "It's time we talked, you and I."

The cadence of his voice. That bland smile. Those eyes that didn't leave hers. Her gaze dropped to the boots. Black leather. White stitching. Red laces.

And she remembered.

58

LENA EASTON

DAY SEVEN

At the foot of the cave entrance, Lena whistled to Bear. He stood in front of her, tail wagging, ears perked, alert and ready to work.

Adrenaline shot through her veins. The stakes were high and climbing with every passing second.

Lena opened the paper bag that contained Shiloh's T-shirt and offered it to Bear. "This is Shiloh. We need to find Shiloh. She's a very special girl. I need you to find her, boy. Find Shiloh."

Bear gave the shirt several enthusiastic sniffs. He looked at Lena, his huge torso quivering with pent-up energy and excitement.

The Newfoundland was strong, smart, and tireless. He would search for hours in any conditions: sun or rain, storm or blizzard, over any terrain.

Anything that Lena asked of him, Bear would do.

Lena signaled with her hand. "Find Shiloh."

Bear lifted his snout in the air. For a minute, he scented and circled. And then he stiffened, hackles up, tail stiff straight out behind him. He'd alerted on Shiloh's scent.

Together, they moved into the woods. Eli and Jackson trotted ten yards behind them, both men armed to the teeth. Eli took one side, Jackson the other. They constantly scanned their surroundings, checking for threats.

Red-bathed moonlight filtered through the canopy above her head. She couldn't see the aurora through the leaves. A crimson cast transformed the world, everything glimmering.

Within several hundred yards, they broke from the dense trees onto a narrow trail, which Bear followed. Hopefully, Shiloh would stay on the trail. Tracking someone cross-country at night would be a challenge, even with the aurora.

Bear bounded ahead of her. Every couple of minutes, the dog glanced backward as if checking on her, making sure she was following, letting her know that he was still hard at work.

The scent was easy to lose. Depending on conditions and the terrain, wind and air currents constantly shifted; the scent could loop or pool. Too much wind or humidity altered air current patterns. A stream or drainage ditch could funnel scents. On a hot day with no air movement, the scent wouldn't disperse, limiting its range.

But Bear was good at what he did. She had absolute faith in him.

As they moved deeper into the woods, she made notes of landmarks as they passed and checked her compass to keep their bearings. It was her job to search for physical signs. Tracks, footprints, broken twigs and bushes, candy wrappers, abandoned articles of clothing, anything relevant.

Twenty minutes later, Bear alerted. His body went stiff, ruffle raised along the back of his neck.

He sniffed at the base of a stump. Small twigs were broken off at the stems, as if a girl had sat on the log to take a breather or drink some water.

"Good boy. Good job, Bear." Lena flagged the alert with a piece of blue tape she kept in her backpack.

She paused to log in the location, the time, and the status on the notes app on her phone, which was freshly charged from her solar charger. The charge should last all night. After checking her pump—her numbers were good—they kept going.

Minutes later, Bear alerted again, this time on a footprint in a soft patch of dirt. Lena flagged the alerts with blue tape and used orange tape to mark their progress.

Normally, she'd call in their status and location to base. She would coordinate and receive updates from the other searchers.

This time, there was no base, no coordinators, no team. Just them.

Eli and Jackson were behind her. They stayed close, moving quiet as ghosts.

Bear moved briskly. He checked behind to make sure Lena was within sight. He scented the air, turned in a tight circle, tail stiff.

After a moment of hesitation, he kept moving in a general southeastern direction. Following the trail away from the coast, deeper into the Hiawatha National Forest.

An hour passed. She paused for a snack and water for herself and Bear, then checked the compass and noted their location on the topographical map.

In the dark, it was easy to lose yourself. The wilderness had never felt so foreign, so hostile. The dense woods bristled with malice.

Shadows stretched and quivered like beasts crouching behind boulders and trees, prowling the rocky outcroppings, the ravines and caves. She felt eyes on her, glowing pairs peering from the darkness. Waiting, watching.

Ahead of her, Bear alerted again. He stood quivering, hackles up and tail stiff, sniffing at a shadowy patch beneath a cluster of rhododendron bushes. She shone her flashlight across the ground.

Something silvery and metallic glinted in the leaves. A candy bar wrapper. It looked fresh. She caught a whiff of chocolate and caramel.

After she tagged the evidence, she looked back at Eli and Jackson, who'd stopped a few yards away. "I have a Snickers wrapper here. It looks fresh. Any chance it could be our girl's?"

"That's her," Eli said. "She's out here."

Bolstered by the find, they kept moving. Anxiety and fear tangled in her stomach. With every step, Lena had the disconcerting feeling that she was heading closer and closer to her fate.

Her destiny lay at the end of this dark and twisting trail. Whether it would be salvation or destruction, she did not yet know.

59

SHILOH EASTON

DAY SEVEN

Time folded in on itself. Shiloh was back in the salvage yard, huddled in that crushed car, gummy glass shards stuck to her hair, her heart a jackhammer in her chest. Peering through the jagged frame of the window, just enough space to see without being seen.

"He's coming. Shiloh, hide!" Cody had turned to her with a blind panic so terrifying that she had obeyed without question.

"What's going on?" her grandfather demanded.

"I saw something," Cody gasped. "I should have said something, but I didn't think he could find me. I didn't know he saw me—"

"Go to the house," Amos said. "Call the police."

"But—"

"Go!"

Cody didn't have time to run. Boone approached. He looked benign, like every boring adult that Shiloh had ever met. Khaki pants. Plaid shirt rolled up to the elbows, the top button undone.

He could've come straight from school, except for his footwear. The black boots with the red laces. The white stitching. Mud crusted the soles, like he'd been hiking.

"Amos," Boone said, panting, out of breath from exertion. Sweat stains marred his pits. His dishwater blond hair, normally combed so neatly, was windblown.

"What the hell are you doing on my property?" her grandfather said.

Boone's gaze remained on Amos, though Cody stood frozen ten feet away. "I was just out hiking the bluffs. Took a wrong turn coming back. No harm done." Boone took a handkerchief from his pocket and mopped his brow. "They say we're gonna get quite the light show tonight."

His wide, bright smile sent a shiver down Shiloh's spine. She didn't understand what she was seeing, why he was here.

They stood fifteen feet apart in a ragged triangle, surrounded by the husks of dozens of vehicles. Tension thrummed in the air.

Cody shivered like a leaf caught in a windstorm. His face bone-white, blue eyes wide and bloodshot. She'd never seen him so scared. "Stay away from me!"

Boone raised his brows. "Cody, what's wrong?" His voice was cordial, concerned.

"Don't speak to him." Her grandfather stood next to the Volkswagen he'd been working on, engine parts splayed everywhere. His hand closed on the handle of a wrench. "Get the hell off my property before I make you."

Boone looked hurt and surprised. He took a step toward them, one hand behind his back. A rusted pickup sat behind him, the hood up, more tools scattered everywhere. "Amos. We've always been amicable, haven't we? We can talk this out—"

"I got nothin' to say to you, and neither does he. Leave or you will regret it."

"No need to call the police—"

Amos shifted, revealing the two-foot wrench in his hands. "Who said anything about calling the police?"

A flicker passed behind Boone's eyes. A shadow on dark water. He seemed to be deciding something, weighing his odds, considering his options.

"He's—he's a killer!" Cody stuttered. "I saw you—I saw what you did!"

The smile dropped from his face like a sticker. Boone seized a tire iron and ran at Cody.

Abject terror shot through Shiloh. Her mouth opened in a scream of warning, but no sound came out. She was invisible, unheard.

Her grandfather moved. He lunged into the space between Cody and Boone and raised the wrench. He had once been a big, strong man, but age had robbed him of his vitality.

Boone was younger, faster. He raised the tire iron and brought it down on her grandfather's temple. Her grandfather crumpled before he could swing the wrench. Boone knocked it from his grasp and hit him again.

Her grandfather toppled backward, making a sound like a wounded animal.

Shiloh crouched, frozen, too terrified to move. The air smelled of oil and gasoline.

"NO!" Cody screamed.

Boone raised the crowbar again. Brought it down again. Then again. It happened so fast, it was over in a matter of seconds.

Blackness fringed her vision. A rushing roar filled her ears. States and capitals tumbled through her head. Disjointed and terrible. Then she was falling, flailing, toppling into darkness.

Boone pushed himself off the still form of her grandfather. He wasn't moving. One foot twitched. The tire iron in Boone's right hand was coated in red. A fine spray of red spattered his boots.

He dropped the tire iron and turned toward Cody.

Shaken from his stupor, Cody ran.

Shiloh faded, the darkness sucking her away as Walter Boone sprinted into the woods in pursuit of her brother.

60

SHILOH EASTON

DAY SEVEN

Shiloh blinked. The cabin snapped back into focus. The stench of vomit and piss filled her nostrils. Reality rushed in with dizzying waves.

Boone knelt beside her, a gun in one hand. Blood seeped through the gauze he'd wrapped around his bicep. He'd managed to remove the bolt.

Grief threatened to swallow her. Sorrow choked her throat.

The man she'd feared and resented her whole life had stepped in front of his grandson and taken the blow. He'd used his body to block Boone's view of the wrecked Altima, of Shiloh.

If only Cody had told the truth as soon as he'd come home that night. If only he'd been raised in a household where truth-telling was a safe thing, where every word or action wasn't rife with danger.

But they hadn't lived in a house like that. They'd lived with hostile silence and bouts of pent-up violence hanging over the dinner table like an explosive storm cloud.

They'd lived with a man who grieved into a bottle, haunted by the ghost of his murdered daughter. Who couldn't bear his own guilt, let alone the burden of two grandchildren who'd needed him, depended on him, who'd reminded him of what he'd lost.

He must have loved them, somewhere down deep, for him to do what he did. For him to have tried to save them in the end.

Another memory filtered through her panicked haze. She had regained consciousness at some point, the blackness receding enough to stumble from the crushed car. She remembered kneeling over the body, hands on her grandfather's chest, weeping, screaming.

And then nothing again. A blankness that descended over everything.

Shiloh raised her bloody chin. "You killed my grandfather."

"Only because I had to," Boone said. "I'm not a murderer, Shiloh. That's what you have to understand about this whole situation. I'm not who you think I am."

She blinked, forcing her gaze to clear. She would mourn later, once she got the hell out of here. Now, she had to focus. To be smart. To figure out a way to escape. "Where is he? Where's my brother?"

Contrition flashed in his eyes. "The lake took him."

"That's not true. He's alive. He's here. You're hiding him. You're lying."

"I'm not, Shiloh. I'm not lying."

"You take girls. I've seen the pictures. I know what you do."

He clasped his hands together like he was imploring her to understand. "I don't kill them. I love them, I take care of them."

She squirmed, straining against her bonds. The planks dug into her spine. The ropes burned her wrists. "You took Ruby."

He bared his teeth. "She presented herself like a gift. Normally, I only hunt further from home. There's some quote about not hunting in your own backyard."

She stared at him blankly.

"She was just a runaway. A druggie. A slut. Working one shelter to the next from Marquette to the Soo to finance her meth fix. Everyone knew what she was. No one would look for her. No one but someone like Jackson Cross, and even he was too distracted to care."

"She wasn't yours to take. Neither was Cody."

His smile widened. He looked like the cat who'd eaten the canary. "You have no idea. I've taken lots of girls. The discarded ones, the trash that no one wants. They're a dime a dozen up here."

"Where is my brother?"

He frowned then, abruptly turning morose. "I didn't want to. He left me no choice. After what happened with your grandfather, he took off running. Back into the woods. I had to go after him."

Shiloh saw it, then. Cody's panicked eyes, the terrible realization dawning on his face: that it was too late for him, that he would not win this fight. That if he tried, Boone would catch sight of Shiloh, and then they'd both be dead.

He hadn't abandoned her. He'd drawn the predator away.

"I didn't want to do it," he repeated. "He made me do it."

"No," she whispered. It wasn't true. It couldn't be true.

"He went straight to the cliffs, fleet as a deer. It wasn't my fault. Cody did it. He just went over the edge. One second, outlined against the blue sky, the next gone. He jumped. Ran full tilt and never even hesitated."

"You're wrong. You lie."

A part of her wanted to close her eyes, to block it out, to return to the safety of her blank memories. But she couldn't. She had to hear it. Boone kept talking. He wouldn't stop. With every word, she felt herself falling.

"He landed on the rocks. The lake took his body."

She felt herself draining somehow, her insides draining out of her onto the floor.

All this time, she'd been desperately searching. She had believed that if she were strong enough, brave enough, that she would be rewarded. That she would find him in the end.

Everything she had done, risked, sacrificed—it had not been enough.

That first day, when she woke with her grandfather's blood on her hands, her brother had already been lost. Lost to the lake, to the waves. Lost with no way to be found.

Boone shook his head as if baffled. "I don't know why he would do that."

But Shiloh knew. With a terrible clarity—she knew. Cody had grown up with the memory of violence deep in his bones. Her brother had always chosen his own path. He'd chosen to jump over torture and death at the hands of a monster in a sweater vest.

"Why?" she whispered. "Why Cody?"

He leaned forward, his gun hand resting on one knee. His expression was intent, like he wanted her to understand, like he was confessing at church, but there was no remorse in his eyes. None at all. "Things went wrong. She wasn't supposed to die, the other girl. It just happened. An accident. He wasn't here to help me like usual. I had to do it on my own. I tried something new. That's all. Something different. I wanted to know what it was like.

"They say the lake never gives up her dead. I took her out there, wrapped up in a tarp with chains, so she'd sink and stay down there. It was a quiet night. Still cold, so no one was out. Should've been simple. Should've been easy.

"I didn't see him in that damn boat with no lights. He saw me, though. I wouldn't have known, but he dropped something in the water—maybe he shifted and bumped one of his paddles. Once I heard the noise, I knew he was out there.

"I knew I had to shut him up. He was a witness. I didn't know how much he knew, or if he recognized me. I had no idea what he'd seen, but I had to take care of it.

"I chased him back to shore. Turned my lights on him, but I couldn't make out any details. Just a black hoodie and blond hair, scared eyes. He beached his little fishing boat and took off running.

The *Little Neptune*. I didn't know it was him, but I knew the boat, who it belonged to. All I had to do was ask one of Sawyer's men. They were glad to help, to give me his name. And of course I knew who Cody Easton was. I taught him after school."

She remembered it, then. How Cody had acted strange that day. He'd been terrified, confused, not sure where to turn. Afraid to tell their grandfather, terrified to go to the cops.

They had been raised believing that adults were dangerous, not to be trusted. Even your own flesh and blood would turn on you.

Boone scratched his head with the butt of the gun. "I didn't want to. I had no choice. He left me no choice. Your grandfather—he got in the way. And then you. I didn't know you were there until the police put out the BOLO for you. Even then, I wasn't sure until you broke into my cousin's trailer."

He shrugged. "I thought it was over. I really did. Turns out, this solar flare thing was a gift. The police and sheriff's department caught up in maintaining order."

She forced herself to think, to push away the grief. The terror and desperation. "Until me."

He tilted his head, his expression impassive. He gazed down at her like she was some bizarre creature he'd never seen before. "You went through my things. You stole from me."

"Maybe you aren't as smart as you think you are."

His eyes narrowed to slits. "I should have ended this that night, and I would have if those tourists hadn't shown up. You were damn lucky. I thought you'd go to the police, I really did. Truthfully, I hoped you'd crawled into a hole somewhere and died. When the police didn't come for Fitch, I thought maybe you had. It's a shame. The cops have him now. I'll have to figure something else out. It probably means I have to leave this place, start somewhere else fresh, but I've got a plan for that, too. You, though—this is the end of the road for you."

He glanced up at the windows, then rocked back on his heels. "I've wasted enough time. I'm going to deal with you, then I'm going after Ruby."

"You said you don't like killing. That you aren't a murderer."

He shook his head, gave her a sad smile. It wasn't reflected in his eyes. "He'll do it for me. All I have to do is throw you in that hole and wait. He'll come."

Shiloh didn't know who he was talking about, but she had zero desire to meet him. She jerked on the ropes. Her wrists were rubbed raw. "Let me go! People are coming for me. Jackson is coming."

"No one knows you're here. No one will ever know you were here. You'll disappear, just like your brother, like all the other lost girls." He hesitated and touched his bandaged arm. He grimaced from the pain. "It's easier than most people think, killing someone. It's this big taboo and then you do it and you realize you had it in you the whole the time. We all have killers inside us, waiting to come out."

She bared her teeth at him. "Untie me and I'll kill you. No problem. I'll pull your brains out through your nose."

He barked out a laugh. "You're his type. Mine, too. A little young, but what do they say? Beggars can't be choosers."

He stared at her. Something dark and ugly shone in his gaze. His eyes crinkled as he leaned in. "On second thought, maybe I will do it myself."

61

LENA EASTON

DAY SEVEN

Bear lost the scent.

They'd left the trail several minutes ago and moved through the trees, then entered a small clearing at the edge of a ravine.

A ragged oval of sky opened overhead. The blood-red sky shone above them. The aurora was weakening; threads of green and lavender wove through the undulating ribbons of crimson.

Bear began to circle, snout in the air. Maybe he'd lost the scent or picked up a cross-scent and was trying to get a new gauge on it, to figure it out.

Lena watched Bear's tail, his hackles. Every reaction meant something. Minutes passed. He kept circling, trotting here and there, trying to find it.

Trepidation snarled in her gut. If they didn't find the scent...There was no time to head back to base and pick it up tomorrow.

They found Shiloh tonight, or they didn't find her at all.

Or they found her—but not alive.

The memory of the old man she'd lost a week ago flashed through her mind. That was not an acceptable option. She couldn't allow it to happen.

Kneeling, she rubbed the soft ruff of Bear's neck. Tears sparked the backs of her eyelids. "This one's different. You feel that, right? I left her once when she was little. I was scared and selfish and broken-hearted, and I left two little kids behind who needed me. I've spent the last eight years trying to make it up to everyone but them." She shook her head. "Stupid, huh?"

Bear sensed her apprehension and whined in her ear, his doggy breath warm on her face. Pure devotion, pure love. No judgment. He offered comfort as only a dog like Bear could.

"We have to do this, okay?" She pulled the dog's head close to hers and tilted her forehead so they were eye-to-eye. She stared into the chocolate brown eyes of her most faithful friend. "You and me. We can do this. Tell me we can do this."

Bear pushed his big head against Lena's. The human knelt on the leaf-strewn ground, drained and spent, scared but resolved. The dog patient and loyal, tail thumping, tired but willing to push past every endurance for his mistress.

Bear gave a soft whuff of encouragement.

"That's my boy."

Jackson and Eli broke into the clearing behind her. Eli wore his ghillie suit. He held the AK-47 in the low ready position. Jackson gripped his shotgun. They looked like they were ready to go to war.

"What's wrong?" Jackson asked.

"We lost the scent, but we can find it again."

Lena sucked in a breath and steeled herself. Her energy flagging, she checked her pump. Her numbers were low and falling. She ate two packages of fruit snacks and gulped down apple juice.

She shared some water with Jackson and Eli, then pulled out Bear's water bowl, poured him water, and gave him kibble from a Ziplock bag. Bear worked hard; he needed a rest too, even though everything in Lena pushed her to keep moving, to press on.

"Drink up, boy. Otherwise, they'll be sending a search party out for us."

The irony wasn't lost on Lena. In this moment, *they* were the only search party. Everything had seemed to fall apart slowly, and then all at once.

Once more, Lena shrugged off her backpack and removed the brown paper bag. She opened it and pulled out Shiloh's shirt. Refresh, reward, reestablish.

"This is Shiloh. We're going to find Shiloh."

Bear's tail wagged so hard it shook his hindquarters. He barked and dashed for the edge of the clearing. She followed Bear down a ravine and up the other side, her thighs burning.

"Did he find it?" Eli asked.

Her heart surged. "He found it."

"Don't get too far ahead," Jackson said. "Wait for us—"

Lena was already scrambling after the dog. "Good job! Keep going!"

Bear moved swiftly, with purpose. The scent grew stronger. He was zeroing in, getting close. The cross currents in the ravine must have snarled up the scent cone.

Lena broke into a jog, Jackson and Eli right behind her. The world was all shadows: tree trunks and ragged branches, felled logs and rocky ledges. Shadows pooled, receding, forming shapes of demons and wraiths.

She pushed through the shadows, then broke out of the underbrush.

There, in the scarlet moonlight, not marked on any map, not registered with official documentation or county permits, stood a cabin.

62

ELI POPE

DAY EIGHT

"He's in there," Jackson said to Eli. "And Shiloh's in there with him. We need to go in now."

Eli shook his head, never taking his eyes off the cabin with his night vision field glasses. "We don't have enough intel. We could be walking into a death trap."

They lay belly-down in a nest of pine needles just inside the perimeter of the tree line, thirty yards from the front of the cabin. A fallen log offered cover and concealment. His ghillie suit provided additional camouflage, blurring his human form to anyone watching.

They spoke in low whispers, maintaining as much noise and light discipline as possible. Eli would rather they didn't speak at all, but they had not trained together. They needed to communicate to execute this mission, however ad hoc it would be.

They had sent Lena and Bear hiking back toward the closest main road, County Road 587, based on the map. Lena had her compass and heavy hiking boots. She would flag down a car and head to the sheriff's office back in Munising.

Neither of them wanted Lena anywhere near the impending

firestorm. He pushed thoughts of her out of his head; he needed total focus.

Eli glanced at his watch. It was midnight. Staying low, he had circled the perimeter twice, examining the shed, the outhouse, gleaning what intel he could. He'd searched for IED booby traps, scanned for trip wires, anything out of place.

He hadn't seen anything. It didn't mean the door wasn't boot-strapped with explosives to kill an entry team. It was impossible to discern what was inside.

Tension wound tight in his gut. How close was the target to his weapon? Where was the hostage, how was she restrained? Was there more than one hostile? He needed answers to every question, but he wasn't going to get them.

He was used to coordinated hostage rescues with the Rangers and other government agencies. They had massive resources and intel at their disposal, including drones, tactical thermal imaging cameras, and listening devices.

Eli and Jackson had none of those things.

"What toys do we have?" Eli asked.

"I have breaching rounds in my shotgun. Several flashbangs. A thermal imaging scope—but it won't help us see inside."

Jackson reached into his jacket pocket and pulled out two sets of sound protection ear plugs, handing one set to Eli. They would protect the ears from gunshots but allowed for conversation.

If they waited for the sheriff's department or the state police to arrive, or the FBI SWAT team from the Detroit field office, Shiloh may not make it that long.

Moments ago, Jackson had deputized him within his powers as undersheriff. Now, he eyed Eli's AK-47. He exhaled. "I don't know if this is the right thing."

"I am the monster you send in to take out a worse monster."

Jackson nodded, unconvinced. He rubbed his jaw—nervous, on edge. Good. He should be. This was a cluster of epic proportions.

Eli had already gone through his gear methodically, checking weapons, counting ammo, extra magazines, mentally preparing for the assault to come. It didn't matter how many times you ran through the drills, how many times you'd done this, in training or in real life, with bullets flying and enemies closing in.

It could all go sideways in a heartbeat. He'd lost too many good team members, too many brothers and sisters in combat, had seen bad luck put a bullet in a man's brain a hundred times.

"I am going to arrest him," Jackson said. "I'm going to bring him in, and he's going to stand trial for what he's done."

"You're out of your mind."

"Do not use lethal force unless you have to."

"I have to."

"He will answer to the law, not to a vigilante with a gun."

"Then I won't use a gun."

"The law matters, Eli."

"The law is broken."

Jackson sucked in a sharp breath. "We save Shiloh. What you do after that is your choice, but the consequences will be yours, too."

Eli didn't take his eyes off the cabin. The curtains were closed. Nothing moved. The forest seemed to hold its breath. "Understood."

Maybe Eli should have eliminated Jackson back there in the woods. Shot him in the spine and left him to bleed out. He'd been sorely tempted.

The truth was, they needed each other. A partner could mean the difference between an operation's success or failure. Eli would rather have a spec ops hostage rescue team at his back, but beggars couldn't be choosers.

The curtains in the left window moved slightly. A flutter as a figure moved past it. The curtains were too opaque to make out details. Someone was in there with Shiloh. Were there two hostiles inside? Three? Or just the one?

"You see that?" Jackson asked.

"I do."

"We need to go in now! He could be hurting her. Killing her." Jackson's mouth thinned, like he couldn't bear to imagine what that monster might be doing to Shiloh.

Neither could Eli, but he couldn't let hotheads compromise the mission, either.

"This will be a crap shoot. You might get him and save her or he might shoot her, shoot one or both of us. Without intel, flip a coin. He dies. Flip it again. We die. One more time. She dies."

In a go-now situation with so little intel, the possibility of losing part of the team or the hostage herself was high. Even using flash bangs could injure Shiloh, depending on where she was inside the cabin. Permanent blindness, deafness, or serious burns were possible.

He didn't like the odds.

"I don't care what happens to me," Eli said. "She does not die. That is not how this is going to end."

Jackson glanced at him. "We're on the same page there."

The unspoken agreement passed between them. Whatever reckoning was between them, it came after they saved the girl.

Eli's radio crackled. "This is Lena. Come in."

He kept the binoculars zeroed in on the cabin as he brought the radio to his mouth. "You're a go, Lena."

"There's someone out here."

"Don't engage," Jackson said. "Lena, don't you do it—"

"Too late," Lena said. "It's—it's not a threat. Call you in a minute."

"Lena—"

The radio clicked off.

63

LENA EASTON

DAY EIGHT

Less than a mile from the cabin, a figure crashed through the underbrush off to the southwest, maybe fifty yards up the ridge line of a ravine. Through the trees, Lena glimpsed a ribbon of red hair.

The sound of sobbing reached her. A girl. Female. *Shiloh.*

But no, the red hair didn't fit. This wasn't Shiloh. Then who?

Ahead of her, Bear went rigid, nose high in the air, ears pricked. He glanced back at Lena with an imploring expression.

"Go find her," Lena instructed. She drew her M&P 9, chambered a round, and held it low at her side. "But be careful."

Bear dashed ahead, shadows from the tree canopy overhead dappling his brown fur. Lena followed at a jog, leaping over fallen logs, sidestepping boulders, climbing the ravine with sure steps.

At the top of the ridge, Bear let out a soft bark. Lena broke through a cluster of trees into a clearing. A figure faced away from her. A girl, half clothed in filthy shorts and a black tattered tank top. Red hair dirty and tangled.

The girl turned at the sound of Bear's bark. Terror in her glassy blue eyes. She was trembling like a leaf.

Lena didn't holster her weapon but kept it low. Pity washed

through her. This girl looked like she'd been through hell and back. "I'm a friend. I won't hurt you." Lena looked around, tense and wary. "Is there anyone else here? Are you in imminent danger?"

The girl opened her mouth, closed it, opened it again. She gave the tiniest shake of her head. "Help."

"Yes. Yes, I am here to help you." Lena holstered her gun, shrugged off her pack, and pulled out a water bottle, which she handed to the girl. She took out an emergency blanket and unwrapped it. "What's your name, honey?"

"R-Ruby Carpenter."

Ruby shivered as Lena wrapped the emergency blanket around her shoulders and placed the water bottle in her hands. Shakily, Ruby took a sip of water.

"I'm going to check you over, okay. Does it hurt anywhere?" Lena knelt next to her and quickly assessed her vital signs, asking her questions to evaluate her physical and mental state.

The girl was conscious, alert, breathing normally, with cuts and bruising. She checked her pupils, her pulse—ninety-three beats per minute. No evidence of head injury. Lena reached into her pack again and pulled out a tube of glucose gel to get her blood sugar levels up quickly.

Ruby trembled, teeth chattering. It was clear she had experienced trauma, the kind that wouldn't always show on a cursory evaluation. This girl needed medical care, a hospital, a warm bed, people that loved her.

But Shiloh was still out there. Lena hated to do it, but for the other girl's sake, she had to press Ruby, had to ask her the critical questions.

"What happened, honey? Did you come from the cabin?"

Something flickered behind her eyes. Fear. Haltingly, she nodded. "I—I ran..."

Urgency needled Lena. "Did you see Shiloh Easton? Small, black hair, dark eyes."

"She—she got me out. But...she stayed. She stayed back there, to find her brother." The girl shook her head. "It's a bad place. A terrible place. If he comes back—if he finds her—"

The girl shook her head, mute with terror. Fear slithered up Lena's spine. She wanted to run into that dilapidated cabin herself. She was a rescuer—every fiber of her body longed to save Shiloh.

"Ruby, this is very important. The man who took you, is he alone?"

The girl stared at her blankly. Lena was losing her, she was retreating into her mind, into her terror. Gently, Lena gripped her shoulders and squeezed. "Honey, you can help Shiloh, okay? This is how you help her. Is he the only one?"

"The only one I've seen," the girl rasped. "Yes."

Lena reached for the radio.

64

SHILOH EASTON

DAY EIGHT

"When I am through with you, you'll wish you were in that hole," Boone said.

Shiloh thought of Ruby, locked down in that fetid hole in the ground. How the girl had chewed through her own ropes to free herself. She thought of Cody, how he'd chosen to leap off a cliff to give her a chance to escape. And she thought of her mother.

All the survivors who had come before her.

Some had won. Some had lost. All had fought to the bitter end.

Their blood ran through her veins, through the veins of every girl who'd ever been hurt, every woman who'd been hit, every boy who'd been damaged.

She knew their terror and their strength. Shiloh Easton would not let them down. This would not be her end.

He was the worst kind of windigo: an evil spirit who consumed beauty, who saw innocence and wanted to crush it, who ravaged and defaced and destroyed every good thing.

Like Cody, she would not let him have her.

"I'm going to kill you," she said, and spat on him. Traitorous tears leaked from the corners of her eyes.

Boone leaned over her and grasped her armpits. Shiloh writhed like a fish caught in a net, struggling to twist around and land a kick. Her ribs throbbed. She fought anyway. Surging upward, she sank her bared teeth into his right earlobe.

The man screamed and wrenched back. She did not let go. Warm blood gushed between her lips. Flesh tore. She bit down and tore out a chunk of cartilage.

He howled. "You filthy little—"

She spat the wad of flesh from her mouth and snarled. Gasping, chest heaving, hands still bound behind her, blood dribbled down her chin.

On her back, she kicked out, desperate and furious. Her heel smashed his face. A crunch of cartilage and bone. Her heart a frantic thing in her chest, terror locked in her throat.

Boone gave a wet howl. Blood streamed from his nose. Maybe it was broken. She sure as hell hoped so.

He rose over her. Eyes like dead beetles. Blood ringed his mouth like a depraved clown. He gripped the iron hawk lamp base in both hands. He raised the base over his head.

Shiloh screamed.

65

ELI POPE

DAY EIGHT

Eli crouched at the edge of the clearing, preparing himself for the assault. He pushed out the fear, his misgivings, and ticked through tactical options in his head. Weaknesses and stress points.

Jackson had already moved to the other side of the cabin, ready to breach the back door.

The existence of Ruby Carpenter changed everything. With Lena's help, they'd swiftly extracted critical information. The layout of the cabin, the furniture, the rooms, how the hostile likely had Shiloh restrained—with ropes. The trapdoor with the pit dug underneath the floorboards.

As he'd suspected, the cabin wasn't boobytrapped. Boone came and went using the front door. He had a handgun and a shotgun, plenty of ammo. And he was currently alone.

They would make a dynamic entry and go in gangbusters. Creating an environment of chaos gave them the advantage of clarity and dominance.

If they went in fast and explosive, clearing room by room, Eli hoped to take the hostile by surprise and eliminate him before he could kill Shiloh.

The element of surprise was good; the element of sheer terror was better.

With Ruby's help, the odds were no longer fifty-fifty. They had a chance.

A scream filtered through the trees. It came from inside the cabin.

Adrenaline shot through Eli's veins. He sprinted toward the cabin, weapon drawn. "We're going in hot! Go, go, go!"

66

ELI POPE

DAY EIGHT

Eli lowered into a half crouch and crossed the fifty-yard clearing, approaching the cabin from the east, windowless side. His AK-47 at his shoulder, he continually scanned for threats.

His breathing steadied, a cold calm descending over him. It was go-time.

There was little concealment between the tree line and the cabin. He moved fast and low, weeds swishing against his shins. The ghillie suit blurred his outline, but he was far from hidden.

The aurora rippled in crimson ribbons overhead, the night brighter than a full moon. Crickets whirred in the grass. An owl hooted.

He reached the edge of the cabin, ducked behind a large rain barrel, and bladed his body against the wall. Every sense on high alert, nerves raw.

A male voice came from inside the cabin, vicious and threatening.

Silently, he cut the corner, leading with his weapon, and made his way along the front of the building toward the door. At the first window, he rose, keeping his profile low, and peered inside. The black curtains blocked his sight line.

Boom! Boom! Several thunderous cracks sounded. Jackson had fired the 12-Gauge TKO breaching rounds at the hinges of the back door, blowing it open.

Urgency crackled through him. Eli sprinted for the front door. With great force, he kicked the door in, his boot striking above the door handle. The cabin was old. The half-rotted frame crumbled inward. The door crashed open.

He breeched the entry point and rushed inside, the cabin's layout sharp in his mind. He ducked to one knee, slicing the pie with the AK-47 pressed to his shoulder.

He glimpsed a living room, a sofa, a coffee table. Hostile at the twelve o'clock position. Ten feet away.

Boone had dropped a large object he held in both hands and lunged for a pistol laying on the coffee table. He seized it and twisted toward Eli.

Before Boone could squeeze the trigger, Eli fired three times in rapid succession.

The rounds stitched across Boone's chest. The force of the impacts knocked him backward into the coffee table. His arms flailed. Spent brass clattered to the plank floor.

Eli fired again. The last round drilled into the center of his face. The 7.62x39mm projectile tore through flesh and bone at 700-meters per second. As it exited, it ripped a crater in the back of the man's skull.

Boone collapsed onto the coffee table. Glass shattered. The body flopped backward onto the floor, unmoving.

Weapon still up, Eli eased around the sofa and looked down. The hostile was dead. Blood as black as oil pooled around his head.

Between the sofa and the coffee table, Shiloh cowered. Her legs were drawn up to her chest, hands bound with rope behind her back. Scared out of her mind, but alive.

He dropped to one knee, said her name. Once, twice. Blood from her split lip smeared her chin. Bruises in the shape of fingers formed over the white column of her throat.

Anger slashed through him. If Boone wasn't already dead, Eli would've killed him again. Peeled off his fingernails. Sliced off his balls and stuffed them down his throat.

Shiloh stared up at him dully, her eyes glazed and unseeing. Fear shimmered behind her eyes. "Don't touch me! I'll cut you." Her voice dissolved into a ragged sob. "Don't touch me."

She looked so young, small and vulnerable. How had this girl tracked down a child murderer and dared to face him? Reckless and stupid, but brave as hell.

"Would you like me to cut the rope tying your wrists?"

Something in her eyes flickered to the surface. She managed to nod, then twisted sideways and showed him her bound hands. He leaned the AK-47 against the sofa, drew his knife from his belt, and sawed through the ropes, releasing her.

Shiloh flinched from his touch, then scrambled to her hands and knees and scurried away from him. She backed herself into a corner next to the bookshelf. Her knees pulled up, her arms wrapped around her legs, she rocked back and forth. The crossbow lay next to her.

He moved toward her, slow and cautious, like she was a wild animal. "Hey, hey, it's okay."

He needed to make sure she was all right. Needed to ensure she wasn't going to stab or shoot anyone from shock. She was terrified; everyone and everything was a threat.

As he spoke, he checked her over visually, making sure she hadn't been hit by a round or ricochet or flying debris. Shallow cuts and bruises marred her arms and face, her lip bloody. He didn't detect broken bones or contusions. Luckily, they hadn't needed to use the flash bangs.

"You're okay, Shiloh. It's me, Eli. You know me. I'm not going to hurt you."

The girl didn't even look at him. Just kept rocking, back and forth. She needed Lena, not him. She needed warmth and softness and comfort: all the things he didn't know how to give her.

Rocking back on his heels, he picked up the rifle. He couldn't relax, couldn't drop his guard for a second. He half-turned and froze.

Jackson stood in the doorway of the cabin's single bedroom, watching him.

The body lay sprawled on the wooden floor between them.

Jackson shouldered his shotgun. He pointed the barrel at Eli.

67

JACKSON CROSS

DAY EIGHT

Jackson's gaze shifted from Eli to the body on the floor to Shiloh. His heart contracted. He hadn't seen her in days. She was filthy, half-wild, eyes crazed with panic and fear.

Alarm filled him. "Is she okay?"

"I think she will be."

She was alive. Gloriously alive.

And Walter Boone was dead.

Jackson felt dizzy, disoriented. He hated that the perp was dead and would never stand trial for his crimes, would never see justice done. And yet, a small part of him felt a flare of abject relief.

Jackson aimed the shotgun at Eli. "Put that gun down."

On one knee, crouched a few feet from Shiloh, Eli watched him, utterly still. "You know it was a good shot."

"Put it down."

Eli lowered the AK-47 to the floor.

"Your pistol, too. Kick it away."

Eli obeyed. The pistol skittered several feet across the floor. "It was a good shot. Shiloh is alive. You're still alive. So am I."

Eli was right. It was over. And yet, it wasn't.

He stood facing a killer. A killer he'd been forced to rely on to eliminate a worse killer.

The deed was done. He didn't need Eli anymore; Eli didn't need him.

As long as Eli was out and free, he presented a clear and present danger to the community. To Jackson himself.

Eli gazed at him steadily, as if daring him to go through with it.

"If it matters so much, do it," Eli said. "When you look in the mirror, what will you see? A cop or a killer? You think you can live with that?"

Jackson couldn't live with that, and they both knew it. He couldn't shoot an unarmed man, not even Eli Pope. This was not who he was, not who he wanted to be. Besides, they still had Shiloh to worry about.

Resigned, he willed himself to lower the shotgun. "This isn't over."

"I wouldn't expect it to be," Eli said. "I'm getting my weapons."

Reluctantly, Jackson nodded.

Eli retrieved his guns, holstered his H&K VP 9, and shouldered the rifle with careful movements, never taking his eyes off Jackson.

In the corner, Shiloh let out a whimper.

Compassion and concern welled inside him. They were here for Shiloh. She deserved every ounce of their attention. "How can I help?"

"She won't respond to me," Eli said. "Get Lena."

"She doesn't know Lena," Jackson said, doubtful.

"Lena can help. She'll know what to do." Eli unhooked his radio and brought it to his mouth. "Lena, come in."

The radio crackled. Lena's voice broke through, filled with static, barely audible. "I heard...gunshots. Is he...dead? Shiloh...safe?"

"Shiloh is here. She needs you."

A minute later, Lena entered the cabin. She paused in the shattered doorway, taking in the scene. "Is everyone okay? Eli? Jackson?"

Eli watched Shiloh. "I'm fine."

Jackson's legs felt rubbery. The adrenaline dump hit him hard, his whole body going weak and shaky. He needed to lie down, to sleep for a week. "I'm good. It's Shiloh we need to worry about."

Lena turned toward the girl. "Shiloh—"

Without a word, Shiloh bolted to her feet. She seized the crossbow and streaked between them in a blur, nearly knocking Lena over in the doorway. She disappeared into the night.

Eli stared after her, dumbfounded.

"What is she doing?" Jackson asked.

"What I would do in her shoes," Lena said in a stricken voice. "She's going to run."

68

ELI POPE

DAY EIGHT

"Shiloh, let us help you," Eli said. "Don't run."

Shiloh hovered at the edge of the clearing, skittish as a deer. She held the crossbow pointed at the ground. It was loaded. "I don't have anybody."

The aurora undulated overhead, weaker but still bright. Transparent waves of crimson, tangerine, and shades of coral and wine cast the clearing in a reddish glow, the edge of things glimmering like burnished copper.

"You do. You do have someone." Lena stepped forward. She looked astonished at the sight of her niece, enraptured, smitten. Hope shone from her eyes but so did fear.

Shiloh looked from Jackson to Eli to Lena. Confused, bewildered. Edgy and scared. In a minute, maybe less, they'd lose her.

"This is your mother's sister," Eli said. "Your Aunt Lena."

"Hey," Lena said softly.

Shiloh retreated a step. Toward the woods. Toward the safety of trees and space and sky, independence and freedom, cold nights and an empty belly. Toward loneliness.

Eli knew that loneliness as intimately as his own scarred soul. He recognized that terror in her eyes, because it was his own.

"You can trust her," Eli said.

Shiloh shook her head. Her eyes glittered. "I don't have an aunt. My grandfather said she was dead to us. She didn't want anything to do with us, and so we shouldn't have anything to do with her. She left when my mom was killed because she was too selfish to take care of her own flesh and blood."

Lena flinched like she'd been punched in the stomach. Eli could see it etched on her face—pain, guilt, regret. She opened her mouth, closed it. Her shoulders hunched like she was warding off a blow.

"I don't want anything to do with family like that. I can take care of myself. Eli knows that. I don't need you. I don't need anybody."

Jackson took a step toward her. "Shiloh."

Shiloh leapt back like he'd tried to bite her. "Stay away from me! I'm warning you!" Her voice was high and raw, her arms shaking. Her eyes darted from one person to the next, unable to settle.

Eli knew that they needed to be very, very careful. She was a grenade about to go off. She wasn't herself, teetering on the brink of a psychological break. She could easily slip into a fugue state.

This was a girl who'd endured severe emotional trauma. She'd witnessed her grandfather's murder. Then she'd been trapped in a cabin with a psychopath, a man who'd tied her up, beaten her, and had nearly buried her in that pit beneath his cabin.

Eli took small, gradual steps toward her without drawing her attention. He was close enough to tackle her if that crossbow rose, if she pointed it at Lena. He couldn't risk Lena's life. He wouldn't.

If they dared take her by force, she would hate them forever. He knew that about her like he knew it about himself. Force was a last resort; he would do it if he had to.

"You're right," Lena said softly.

Shiloh's head jerked up, dark eyes narrowed in suspicion.

"You're right," Lena said, louder this time. "I should have been here. I never should have left you. I left this town, I left my father—your grandfather. That's what I left. That's what I was running from. My own fear and my own shame—"

Lena's gaze shifted to Eli before returning to Shiloh. "Not you, Shiloh. Not you and not Cody. I loved you. I love you. I know you can't believe that right now, and that's okay, I understand. I hope someday that you will believe that it's true."

Shiloh listened, trembling but rapt.

"I know what it's like to feel like you're running from something bigger and scarier than you are. I know what it's like to feel alone and like you can't trust anyone. If I had been here—" Lena's voice caught. "This wouldn't have happened to you, precious girl. None of this would have happened."

"Lena—" Jackson started.

Lena waved him off. She held her hands out to Shiloh, palms spread, placating, begging. Guilt and hope warred across her face. "I'm not leaving this time. I'm not going anywhere."

Eli felt their pain. He felt the years of bitterness, resentment, and betrayal. This moment was theirs. He couldn't step in. Jackson couldn't step in.

Lena would win Shiloh in this moment, or not at all.

Shiloh's crossbow wavered.

Eli tensed, ready to intervene.

"I'm going to walk toward you. Tell me to stop if you want me to, and I will. I won't do anything you don't want me to, okay? We're a team. That's how I work." Lena didn't point, didn't gesture, her hands didn't move at all. Her voice was calm and steady. "Do you see that dog over there? That's Bear."

Shiloh's gaze flicked to Bear, who'd sat up at the sound of his name, ears pricked and tail wagging. He'd been sitting with Ruby, who huddled against a tree trunk across the clearing, wrapped in an emergency blanket.

Shiloh nodded.

"Together, we find people who are missing. We bring them back home. We save them. I can't do it without Bear, and he can't do it without me. We need each other."

Lena took another step. "I think that you and I could be the same way. We can be a team. We can help each other, watch out for each other."

Bear rose to his feet and trotted to Lena's side. He pressed his furry torso against Lena's thigh and looked at Shiloh with interest.

Lena took another step. Five feet between them now. Eli didn't take his eyes off them, off that crossbow.

"Bear would like to meet you. Would you like to meet him?"

"I don't know."

"It's okay. Take your time. No one is going to force anything on you, okay? It's your choice."

Shiloh stared at the dog.

Lena took another step, and another. Bear moved with her, right at her side. A foot between them. Shiloh stared up at her, scared and angry and uncertain. Her hands trembled on the crossbow.

"Shiloh," Lena said. "Could you please put the crossbow down? You don't need it right now."

The girl's lower lip quivered. Her skin was bone pale. She was going to collapse or try to kill someone. Eli would be ready, either way.

"You're safe, Shiloh." Lena did not reach for the crossbow. She kept her hands open, palms out, showing Shiloh her vulnerability. That Shiloh had the choice, every step of the way.

It worked.

Shiloh set the crossbow on the ground, still loaded but facing away from Lena and the others. Eli stepped in quickly and took it.

"Cody," Shiloh whispered. "Cody is dead."

Lena said, "Oh, honey. I'm so sorry."

Out of the corner of his eye, Eli saw Jackson go rigid, a stricken expression on his face. They had all held out hope, even against the odds.

Lena motioned with her hand, signaling to Bear, who bounded to Shiloh. The dog could have bowled the girl over, but he stopped short, sniffing her hair, tail wagging. Startled, Shiloh froze.

Bear licked her face. She melted, her arms slipping around the dog, the dog pressing against her.

Lena sank to her knees beside the girl and the dog. Gently, she placed one hand on Bear's back, one hand on Shiloh's. She spoke low, soothing words Eli couldn't discern, but he didn't need to.

He'd seen it in Shiloh's eyes. Lena had captured Shiloh's heart as fully as she'd captured his own. They had a lot to figure out, a long road to healing, but they would be okay.

Over their heads, Eli and Jackson locked eyes. Mortal enemies they might be, but they shared this connection, whether they liked it or not.

For Shiloh, he held in his animosity. And for Lena.

The memories rushed back in—the familiar feelings, that pull. Not even prison could kill that part of him, much as he'd tried. Tried to forget how she smiled, the tiny dimple in the center of her chin, her husky laugh.

He'd lost her when he'd cheated, but he'd never stopped loving her. Her heart was stronger, fiercer, more compassionate than anyone he'd ever met. He remembered how she used to look at him. Like he could be the good man reflected in her eyes.

That was an eternity ago. A century. Another man had lived that life. Another man had been given that chance at a different future, and he'd squandered it.

Second chances didn't exist for him. Not in this harsh world. And yet. His heart constricted when he looked at her. He watched them, kneeling, clutching each other, a moment of grace that stole his breath away.

The wind picked up. A cool breeze rushed through the hushed clearing, rustling the leaves. The shadows wavered and stretched across the ground.

Bear wriggled from Shiloh's arms. He trotted several yards away, then turned in a tight circle, hackles raised, nose high in the air. He whined deep in his throat, low and mournful.

Lena raised her head, alert to her dog's body language. She smoothed Shiloh's ragged hair from her face and rocked back on her heels, her attention on Bear. "What is it, boy?"

The dog trotted to the edge of the clearing before glancing back at Lena, ears pricked but tail down, tucked between his legs.

Lena rose to her feet. Shiloh stood with her.

"What is it?" Jackson asked.

"Bear just alerted."

"What does that mean?" Eli asked.

Lena kept her arm around Shiloh's shoulders as she turned to face Jackson, her expression grim. Sorrow evident in her blue eyes. "That's his sign for cadavers."

Eli's body went taut. Adrenaline coursed through his veins. His hand moved to his VP9. "You mean Boone's corpse?"

Lena met his gaze and shook her head. "Not him. There's another dead body here."

69

JACKSON CROSS

DAY EIGHT

Behind the cabin, they found the graves.

Bear had looked like a dog who'd been whipped. Whimpering, head down, tail tucked, the Newfoundland slunk among the trees, stopping and alerting three times. Then four. Then five.

Jackson placed a small flag at each spot. His guts turned to water with each new marker.

Seven grave sites. Seven dead bodies.

Crime scene tape fluttered in the sweeping flashlight beams. Gas-operated spotlights had been set up around the perimeter. The hushed voices of law enforcement officers murmured as they moved around the mounds of dirt and body bags, snapping photos and collecting evidence. A low hum of dread vibrated through the clearing.

Jackson hadn't wanted to leave the crime scene, but he'd used the Jeep Wrangler that Boone had hidden less than a quarter mile away. They'd found the missing Ford F150 with it. On a wider sweep of the property, Eli had discovered both vehicles camouflaged beneath pine boughs along an overgrown, abandoned forest road.

Jackson drove the rutted forest road that came out onto a paved road several miles west back into town. Lena, Shiloh, and Ruby rode with him.

With satellites and ground stations damaged, even satellite phones were inoperable. And with the repeater network offline, their two-way radios were reduced to a shortened range of only a few miles.

Once he was within radio range, he'd flagged down Devon. Devon had taken Lena and the girls to the hospital. She promised to contact Michelle Carpenter as well. Ruby was traumatized, but she was alive.

Both girls were alive. By any measure, it was a win.

Devon had located the sheriff and several deputies, plus the Munising Police Chief and three police officers. Jackson and the other law enforcement officers had traveled back to the cabin in trucks and ATVs.

The indigo sky lightened to shades of gray. Dawn hid behind the trees.

Eli had been sequestered on scene by two deputies. Though he'd been deputized, he'd shot and killed a suspect. It was a homicide. It would be up to the D.A. to determine if it was a justifiable homicide. Such investigations could last a long time, up to a year. He wasn't sure what would happen.

In the morning, reporters would descend upon them in a frenzy. The state police would come up from Detroit, probably the FBI. They needed forensic anthropologists and pathologists. The case would be taken from them; they'd be treated like country-bumpkin cops who spent more time eating donuts than solving cases.

Or maybe not. That was the way things used to be.

The world was changing so rapidly, it made him dizzy.

Behind the cabin, the medical examiner crouched over a mound of freshly upturned dirt. A black body bag lay unzipped on the ground beside her. Moreno and Hasting stood nearby, watching.

She looked up as Jackson approached. "The six remains that we've uncovered so far have been here for several months to several years. Their clothes are disintegrated from the acidic body fluids, but for the nylon in seams and waistbands. Due to the shorter sacrum and wider pelvic bones, I can tell you that the skeletal remains are female. Since bones continue to grow and fuse until the age of twenty-five, I can also estimate that the victims are between their late teens and early twenties. I'll be able to compare the bone growth charts and narrow it down in the morgue."

Jackson wanted to curse, to scream at the sky. How could they have missed this? These poor lost girls, buried beneath the earth for so long. They had called out, and no one had heard them. No one had saved them.

Moreno covered his mouth and nose with one gloved hand. The stench of human decomposition was distinct, like nothing else Jackson had ever smelled. "What about this one?"

The ME bent closer to the grave site and pointed. "This corpse is fresh, comparatively speaking. Judging by the maggots and insects' stages of development and the level of soft-tissue breakdown, it's in advanced decay. I roughly estimate a month."

Moreno and Jackson exchanged tense glances. This got worse and worse.

Dr. Virtanen pointed to an object in the dirt that she had brushed away from the corpse. "You should see this."

Hasting squatted and picked it up with a pair of tweezers, his hands gloved. The dirt-clotted object glinted beneath the spotlight. Jackson could make out the gold chain, the half-heart locket.

A locket just like the one that had been found on Lily Easton's body.

A hole opened in Jackson's chest. It was hard to breathe. The whir of insects filled his ears. The cool morning air kissed the back of his neck like the breath of a ghost.

His words felt like glass in his throat. "Check the victim's hair."

Dr. Virtanen showed them a section of hacked off black hair. "Is this what you were looking for?"

"And the locket? What's inside?"

With great care, Hasting opened the locket and revealed a matching swatch of hair curled inside. The exact appearance of the locket had never been released. Neither had the detail of the victim's hair inside the locket.

"The signature of the Broken Heart Killer," Moreno said, shocked.

"Were these victims strangled?" Hasting asked.

"Preliminary findings? Yes. You can see the hyoid bone is broken here."

"Were they beaten as well?"

"Too early to tell. I need to conduct the autopsies."

For at least several of these homicides, Eli Pope had been locked away in prison. It didn't make sense.

"A copycat?" Moreno asked.

Jackson shook his head. A copycat wouldn't know such intimate details. "What about the other victims?"

The ME nodded. "We haven't found the locket on every corpse, but we've just started. But yes. Three so far."

Hasting slipped the locket into an evidence envelope. He stood and brushed off his pants. "You think Boone did this? That he was the Broken Heart Killer all along?"

Jackson didn't answer. Neither did Moreno. Jackson fisted his hands on his hips and half-turned, gazing at the bleak clearing, the sad mounded graves, the flags a snap of color in the gray light.

A tsunami of doubt washed over Jackson. All these years, he'd been so certain. That certainty had defined him, had driven him, justified him. In doing one thing wrong, he'd righted the world.

That foundation moved beneath his feet, no longer solid but cracked and crumbling. Things shifting, altering, pieces falling into place.

Though he was standing upright, he had the disorienting sensation of falling.

He'd been wrong. So terribly wrong.

70

JACKSON CROSS

DAY EIGHT

Hours later, Jackson and Devon visited the Munising hospital. He hadn't slept. He was weary to the bone, his eyes gritty. Adrenaline and sheer willpower drove him on, kept him upright.

The hospital's generator was still running, but medical supplies were running critically low. Wait times in the ER were over twenty-four hours. The doctors and nurses looked as exhausted as he did.

Shiloh sat up in the hospital bed, a crisp white sheet spread across her legs, machines monitoring her vitals beeping softly. An IV was hooked to her arm. The air smelled sterile.

Eli was present. He paced like a caged panther in the narrow confines of the hospital room. Though the shooting investigation was ongoing, Eli had been released on his own recognizance.

Lena sat next to the bed in a plastic chair, holding Shiloh's hand. Bear lay on the floor at her feet. His tail thumped as Jackson and Devon entered.

"Hey you," Lena said tiredly.

Eli said nothing at all. Jackson could barely look at him. He could feel Eli's dark eyes burning holes in his soul. He knew he would have to face Eli, that a reckoning was coming, but that time was not now.

Jackson managed a smile for Shiloh and pulled a plastic chair next to Lena. Devon stood behind him with her notebook and pen. "Can we talk about what happened? It's better when it's fresh, but only if you're okay with it."

Dressed in a hospital gown, Shiloh leaned forward, eyes alert and burning like two black coals. Her cuts had been bandaged. She was clean, her black hair washed and glossy.

Still, she looked like a girl who'd fought her way through the Underworld, dragged into hell like Persephone. But she hadn't demurely accepted her fate—she'd clawed and bit and scratched her way to freedom.

"Ask," she said. "Ask the questions you need to ask."

Seeming to sense Shiloh's stress, Bear rose, sniffed the girl's hand, then leapt on the hospital bed. The frame shuddered beneath his weight.

Chuffing in pleasure, Bear flopped onto Shiloh's thighs like a giant overstuffed teddy bear. Shiloh hesitated for a moment, then buried her hands into the ruff of the big dog's fur, letting him give her strength and comfort.

Lena leaned forward and rubbed Shiloh's back. "We can do this later. You don't have to—"

Shiloh looked at Eli. Eli stilled. They exchanged a wordless glance heavy with things Jackson didn't understand and wasn't privy to. After a moment, Eli nodded at her.

Her narrow shoulders straightened. She lifted her chin. Her cheekbones were sharp as knife blades, her eyes dark wells. "I'm ready."

Her words came stilted and jerky, but they came. What had happened that day at the salvage yard. How Cody had told her to hide, how he'd sacrificed himself to save her. And how Easton had fought for his grandchildren in the end.

In his last moments on this bleak earth, he'd chosen to be a hero. Jackson heard it in Shiloh's voice—she knew it. A small gift. A spark of hope in the darkness.

"Can you tell us about last night?" Devon asked. "Start from the beginning. Take your time. What happened?"

In a halting voice, Shiloh told them how she'd seen the man in the black boots in town. How she'd figured out how to find the cabin. How she'd discovered Ruby Carpenter, freed her, and then found herself trapped with a predator.

Her gaze flicked to her backpack at Lena's feet. "I have a picture that you need. It's in there. I found it in Calvin Fitch's trailer under his bed. It wasn't his."

"We know," Jackson said gently. "We found the box."

"Look," she insisted.

Even though the chain of custody had been broken, Jackson donned a pair of latex gloves, opened her backpack, and retrieved the manilla envelope with the note she'd written, the words cut from magazines.

He withdrew the photo. The face of an Ojibwe teenage girl stared at him, both hostile and vulnerable. A face he recognized.

Heart in his throat, he slid the photo back into the envelope and handed it to Devon. They hadn't yet identified the remains of the corpses, including the freshest one. He feared they had just found her. "This is Summer Tabasaw. She's from Marquette."

Jackson turned back to Shiloh. "Boone is dead now. He's never going to hurt you or anyone else again. It's over, honey. It's over."

Shiloh's hand shot out and seized his. Her skin was cold as ice, but her fingers were strong, firm. Her eyes burned with dark fire. "There's another one. Walter Boone was not alone."

71

JACKSON CROSS

DAY NINE

Jackson stared at the crime scene photos tacked to the bulletin board against the wall. The power was off in the building. No generator hummed. Battery-operated lanterns provided light.

"Hell of a thing." Sheriff Underwood came to stand beside him. He clasped his hands behind his back.

"That girl is lucky as hell you and Pope found her." His granite face hardened. "What the hell were you doing with him at that cabin?"

"It's a long story. I've written up the report."

"It's a cluster of epic proportions. You realize that, right? You deputize a convicted felon, who then shoots our perp. What the living hell happened?"

"The investigation will clear him. He's a better shot than I am, and he was special forces. It was the right play. We only had one chance to save the hostage."

Sheriff Underwood shook his head. "I don't even know where to start. It's not even the most bizarre part of the case. We're riding the crazy train, and no one will let us off."

"Eli Pope is innocent." The words were glass in his throat. "He didn't kill Lily Easton."

Guilt ate at Jackson. A darkness he could not yet face, but he knew he would have to. The reckoning that Eli Pope had promised him was coming—and he would deserve it.

Sheriff Underwood ran a hand over his bald head and frowned. "Even if Pope is innocent, the town won't like it. They won't accept it. They've hated him for too long."

"Maybe," Jackson said. "They'll have to. They won't have a choice."

"Another problem for tomorrow. We ready to close this case?"

"Shiloh said Walter Boone had an accomplice," Jackson said.

"Did she see someone else? Does she have a name? An ID?"

"No."

"He could have been lying to her. It wouldn't be the first time a perp minimized his crimes to his victims. Or she was mistaken in her fear and panic."

"It's possible," Jackson allowed.

"Stop chasing ghosts, son. We got him." The sheriff's gaze went distant. Jackson didn't like the look in his eyes. There was fear there, and weakness.

Sheriff Underwood wanted to believe that Boone had killed Lily, that he was the same monster who'd killed and buried seven girls in the deep woods of the Hiawatha National Forest.

He wanted to believe because it was the easy choice, and Sheriff Underwood always took the easy way.

Jackson was not convinced. He had no evidence to go on other than Shiloh's testimony. And it was true, Boone could have lied to her, but he didn't think so.

Lily's ghost had never let him go because he hadn't caught the right killer. It had not been Eli. And it wasn't Boone. Jackson felt that truth deep in his bones, though he couldn't prove it. Not yet.

Boone had chased Cody over the cliff. He'd dumped a body somewhere in Lake Superior. He'd kidnapped Ruby Carpenter and locked her in an abandoned, derelict cabin, as he'd done to a numberless group of vulnerable girls before her. For years, maybe for decades.

And then, when he'd tired of them, he had offered them to someone else.

An unsub who remained at large, hunting the shores of Lake Superior, who prowled the rural towns of the Upper Peninsula, whose playground was the isolated wilderness that Jackson called home.

Were there more girls? More secret gravesites? Were they all dead, or were some of them trafficked somewhere else in the UP? There was so much more that he needed to uncover.

Jackson said, "If there's a second unsub, I'm going to find him."

The sheriff rubbed his eyes and turned away from the crime scene photos. "Get some shut-eye, son. I haven't slept in a week, you know that?"

Jackson didn't doubt it. Deep shadows ringed his eyes. His brown skin was ashen. Deep brackets lined his mouth.

"None of us have, sir."

The sheriff stared at nothing, impotent and overwhelmed.

"I need a team," Jackson said. "We bring in the FBI. They'll trample all over this case, but they have resources we don't, especially now."

"The feds have their hands full. Hell, so do we."

"We'll get it done. We have to."

"You know there's rioting in Marquette and the Soo?"

"I heard."

"It's spreading. The grocery stores in every city in the entire state are empty. Empty. You expect this in Detroit, Grand Rapids, Kalamazoo. But here? The governor declared a state of emergency. The National Guard has been called in. The Coast Guard and Army Corp of Engineers are trying to maintain order at the Locks. We're hearing reports of whole hordes of people trying to cross the Big Mac," he said, referring to the Mackinac Bridge. "In cars, on bikes. A few ran out of gas, and they're pushing damn shopping carts. Can you imagine? They think they'll be safer up here. Ten days into this thing, Cross. It's like everyone lost their minds when those transformers blew. What the hell is happening?"

Jackson recalled Lena's words, the chill that had crawled up his spine at his first glimpse of the aurora. The millions of lights blinking out, one by one. "The beginning of the end."

"That's the same thing all those conspiracy videos on YouTube said. You scare the hell out of me when you talk like that."

"I only say what I see right in front of me."

Sheriff Underwood rubbed his grizzled face. "Well, stop it."

"I need a team," Jackson said, quieter, firmer.

"You never listen, you know that?"

"There's a killer out there, and I'm going to find him."

"We have to protect this town!"

"That's what I'm doing."

For a long moment, Sheriff Underwood didn't speak. "I don't have the manpower, Jackson. You understand? I need you. If you're right..." He shook his head again. "Damn it! I need every hand I have available. We need supplies. We need to maintain order. Put up roadblocks. Figure out how we make this work going forward, and make damn sure the masses downstate don't reach us and wreck what we have."

"I know." He'd said this before and had been ignored. At least the sheriff was listening now. It wasn't too late. He hoped it wasn't. "I know."

The sheriff heard him, but he couldn't help. He was drowning, and he knew it. The man headed for the door, leaving Jackson alone with the case, with his ghosts.

Sheriff Underwood hesitated in the doorway. "Don't let this case eat you up, Jackson."

Jackson didn't speak. He couldn't. His mind whirred, sifting through facts and clues and possibilities. He could feel the killer out there, slinking through the shadows, just out of his reach. One who would see the coming chaos as an opportunity.

Shiloh's words echoed in his mind. *There's another one.*

And as the world lost its light, Jackson didn't know if he had what it took to bring him down.

72

JACKSON CROSS

DAY TEN

The aurora was gone.

Not that it mattered. The sun had already done its damage.

In the blink of an eye, half of the planet had been thrust one hundred and fifty years into the past. Hundreds of millions of people in shock, with no idea how bad things would get, or how quickly.

The world was reeling; the aftershocks were just beginning.

Jackson moved through the darkened house, past the candles on the mantle with the photos of his missing brother like a shrine, past the shadowed dining room with the empty chairs and the dust gathering on the buffet to the French doors leading to the expansive deck.

He could feel his father's eyes on him. His sister and his mother. All watching him, studying him, analyzing him, finding him wanting.

He fumbled at the latch, swung the doors open, and stepped onto the deck.

The setting sun dipped low on the horizon. Vibrant yellows, oranges, and crimsons streaked the clouds. Lake Superior reflected the jagged shoreline, the limestone cliffs, the lush trees. Sunlight like burnished gold painted the waves.

It was a sight he'd seen a thousand times. Familiar, yet no longer comforting. Instead of the tranquil beauty of the great lake, he felt the coldness in his bones. The great sunken ships rested in the dark, symbols of man's hubris, their weakness against nature's wrath.

The placid surface hid the bodies of the dead. Cody Easton was among them. They might never find his corpse. But he was out there. He was a part of it now—the icy lake, the harsh wild, the ghosts of the deep.

A great grief rolled through him, the crumbling of things he didn't yet fully understand as the foundation of the everything he knew gave way.

The world was disintegrating. It was slower here, but it was happening. He could feel it, could see people fraying at the edges. Things were bad and about to get much worse.

He had relied upon the laws and the rules to protect him, to protect them all. And what now? How would those laws change? Who would enforce them, protect the people?

As the sun sank, a seed of resolve grew within him. He could not fix the breaking world, but whatever was in his power to fix, he would do it.

For Lena, his best friend, returned home at last. For Shiloh, the fierce orphan he adored. For Lily and Cody, those who he had failed.

And for Eli, the boy he'd loved like a brother and then betrayed.

For all of them, for the innocent children they once were and the broken men and women they had become.

There had to be redemption.

It existed. He believed.

ACKNOWLEDGMENTS

As I embark on a brand new post-apocalyptic series, I want to thank all my readers for coming along for the ride. I hope you enjoyed it! There is more to come from Jackson, Eli, Lena, and Shiloh. And of course, Bear.

First, I want to give heartfelt thanks to the behind-the-scenes readers who give early feedback on the raw manuscript. They are invaluable as I shape the final story that you hold in your hands.

To my fabulous BETA readers: Ana Shaeffer, Fred Oelrich, Melva Metivier, Jim Strawn, Sally Shupe, George Hall, Jose Jaime Reynoso, Randy Hasting, Annette King, Rick Phipps, Kathy Schmitt, and Courtnee McGrew. Your thoughtful critiques and enthusiasm are invaluable.

To Michelle Browne for her line editing skills. Thank you to Joanna Niederer, Cheree Castellanos, and Jenny Avery for detailed feedback and proofreading.

Much appreciation to detective Adam Richardson for checking the law enforcement scenes.

A very special thank you goes to David Kepford for his tactical expertise and excellent advice.

And to Karen Colley Cleaver for sharing what it's like to live with type 1 diabetes. Your experience has helped to shape the character of Lena Easton.

Any errors are my own.

Thank you to our armed forces who put their lives on the line to keep us safe and protect freedom around the world.

To my husband, who takes care of the house, the kids, and the cooking when I'm under the gun with a writing deadline. To my kids, who show me the true meaning of love every day and continually inspire me.

Thanks to God for His many blessings. He is with us even in the darkest times.

Thank you.

ALSO BY KYLA STONE

The *Edge of Collapse* Post-Apocalyptic Series (EMP):

Chaos Rising: The Prequel

Edge of Collapse

Edge of Madness

Edge of Darkness

Edge of Anarchy

Edge of Defiance

Edge of Survival

Edge of Valor

The *Nuclear Dawn* Post-Apocalyptic Series (Nuclear Terrorism):

Point of Impact

Fear the Fallout

From the Ashes

Into the Fire

Darkest Night

Nuclear Dawn: The Complete Series Box Set

The *Last Sanctuary* Post-Apocalyptic Series (Pandemic):

Rising Storm

Falling Stars

Burning Skies

Breaking World

Raging Light

Last Sanctuary: The Complete Series Box Set

No Safe Haven (A post-apocalyptic stand-alone novel):

No Safe Haven

Historical Fantasy:

Labyrinth of Shadows

Contemporary YA:

Beneath the Skin

Before You Break

ABOUT THE AUTHOR

I spend my days writing apocalyptic and dystopian fiction novels, exploring all the different ways the world might end.

I love writing stories that explore how ordinary people cope with extraordinary circumstances, especially situations where the normal comforts, conveniences, and rules are stripped away.

My favorite stories to read and write deal with characters struggling with inner demons who learn to face and overcome their fears, launching their transformation into the strong, brave warrior they were meant to become.

Some of my favorite books include *The Road*, *The Passage*, *Hunger Games*, and *Ready Player One*. My favorite movies are *The Lord of the Rings* and *Gladiator*.

Give me a good story in any form and I'm happy.

Add a cool fall evening in front of a crackling fire, nestled on the couch with a fuzzy blanket, a book in one hand and a hot mocha latte in the other (or dark chocolate!): that's my heaven.

I love to hear from my readers! Find my books and chat with me via any of the channels below:

www.KylaStone.com

www.Facebook.com/KylaStoneAuthor

www.Amazon.com/author/KylaStone

Email me at KylaStone@yahoo.com

Made in the USA
Monee, IL
13 November 2022

17655810R00229